GHOST WRITER

WRITER

ALISON BRUCE

GHOST WRITER

http://www.alisonbruce.ca

SECOND EDITION Trade Paperback

March 15, 2019

Deadly Press: http://www.deadlypress.com

ISBN: 978-1-9994277-1-9

Cover designed by Ryan Doan: http://www.ryandoan.com

Praise for GHOST WRITER

"A compelling mystery with a unique setting and skillfully handled supernatural twist." —Kelley Armstrong, *#1 New York Times* bestselling author

"A maritime mystery full of twists and turns, heart-pounding suspense, and ghosts! *Ghost Writer* plunges you into the icy depths of the Arctic Ocean with breath-stealing twists and turns, maritime adventures, page-turning suspense ... and ghosts. A great read!" —Ann Charles, *USA Today* bestselling author of the Deadwood Mystery Series

"Alison Bruce weaves a masterful mystery set in the Arctic that will have you reaching for a hot cup of coffee and a blanket as you feel the cold water splash up off the pages and into your face. With equal parts of paranormal and practicality, *Ghost Writer* will keep you up all night as you work your way through this addictive page-turner." —Sheryl Nantus, award-winning author of *Hard Run*

"*Ghost Writer* is a must-read for fans of Barbara Michaels, AKA Elizabeth Peters. In *Ghost Writer*, Alison Bruce provides it all—sly humour, a feisty yet vulnerable heroine, hunky romantic interests, believable characters, a carefully researched and unusual setting, and page-turning suspense." —Janet Bolin, author of the Threadville Mysteries

Dedicated to my ghosts, seen and unseen, for their inspiration; and, to my children, Kit and Sam, for cheering me on.

Acknowledgements

I'd like to thank the Deadly Dames: Catherine Astolfo, Janet Bolin, Melodie Campbell, Joan O'Callaghan and Nancy O'Neill for their support, constructive criticism and occasional kick in the butt.

Thanks must also go to my father, A. Nelson "Spud" Bruce (Royal Canadian Navy) for the snippets of navy life that he shared and the interest it sparked in me.

Chapter One ~ *Ghosts of the Past*

When I was six years old, I woke to find my grandmother standing at the foot of my bed. She wore her habitual expression of worry blended with faint disapproval. Her eyes narrowed, and I waited to find out what I had done this time to annoy her. Then she nodded and disappeared.

In the morning, my mother came to tell me that Grandma Allard had died. She had a heart attack in the evening, and my father had been called to the hospital shortly after my bedtime. I could stay home from school if I wanted, which of course I did. It wasn't that I was shocked or particularly grieved to learn my grandmother was dead, but a day off school was not something you turned down. I wasn't even worried that I had apparently seen a ghost.

When my mother left me, I tucked up in bed and went back to sleep. I dreamed of Grandma Allard. I saw her in bed asleep. Then she stood and looked down at her dead body. What followed was a montage of her life, peeled back like an onion: Grandma Allard, the stern Catholic widow, insisting on order and piety in her world; Madame Allard, the widow with three daughters and a son to care for, hiding her mixed emotions under funereal black; Elise Allard with three young children and one on the way and an abusive husband—brave one moment, cowering the next; Elise Goderich finding out she was pregnant at age fifteen, in succession devastated, excited, anxious, and determined.

My six-year-old self was interested, but couldn't appreciate the scope of my grandmother's life. I could understand a day off school. So could the young girl in pigtails, dressed in a faded blue dress and a crisp white pinafore. She smiled and waved to me before skipping off.

That was my first ghost.

My last ghost was Uncle Allen, my mother's younger brother. My father's side of the family had issues with him, but I loved him so much that when I was too young to know better, I declared that when I grew up I would be gay too. My ignorance of sexuality was a source of great amusement in the family for years after.

Like my grandmother, Allen appeared at the foot of my bed one night. I could barely see him, but I knew what it meant. I rushed out to find my mother. I couldn't explain what I saw. I couldn't get the words out. She found out soon enough. Her brother had been beaten to death outside a gay bar.

For weeks after I was afraid to go to sleep in case I saw how it happened. I never wanted to see a ghost again.

Chapter Two ~ *Dora the Explorer*

My name is Jen Kirby. I have several things going for me including great hair, nice eyes, and an ability to turn experts' research into readable prose.

I have a few weaknesses. I enjoy chocolate too much. I hate enclosed spaces. And I prefer to experience open bodies of water from a distance. One sailing trip with my cousins made me swear off boats for life. So, you'll understand how much I wanted the job when I said I'd go to the Arctic Ocean to look for a sunken underwater base.

The offer came from Dr. Dora Leland, a forensic psychiatrist and my good friend. Dora is a professor at the University of Toronto, a consultant to various law enforcement agencies, and author of seven books which I have ghostwritten with her. Her idea of a vacation is volunteering her skills to researchers who would never have thought they needed a forensic psychiatrist on their team, let alone afforded one.

Her latest project was helping out a team who were bent on raising US Navy's Arctic Station Alpha and finding out what happened to its crew. AFFA, which stood for "Answers For Families of Alpha"—not the Hell's Angels motto "Angels Forever, Forever Angels,"—included now grown children of the crew. Other family members contributed funds or in kind services. But it was Dora and her agents that made the expedition possible.

As the only team member who wasn't paired off, Dora anticipated needing a buddy to play cards with in the evening. She sold the deal by offering me co-author credit on the book we were going to write.

It was an offer I couldn't refuse.

So, after leaving my son with my ex, I started a journey that involved a series of aircraft, each one smaller than the last, to the dock where the *Émil Gagnan* was berthed. Compared to the fishing boats, it was a fair size, but it still took a lot of will power and a not-so-gentle push from Dora to climb the gang plank.

"*Bienvenue à bord*. Welcome aboard. I am your captain, Guy Franchot, fondly known as the Skipper. You will be happy to know there is no Gilligan aboard to strand us on a desert island. You must be the illustrious Theodora Leland, MD, PhD, award winning author, a veritable star of screen and page." He punctuated his welcome with a flourishing bow.

As well as being charming, Franchot was rakishly handsome in a Douglas Fairbanks style. He pronounced his name in the French way, but his English was unaccented, unless you counted the stagey, gentleman pirate lilt. I could easily imagine him swashing a buckle or swinging down from the yardarm, if we had one. I wasn't sure. There was something like one up there, but I was pretty sure it was some kind of an antenna.

Franchot pulled my attention back. Now that he put the image of Gilligan's Island in my head, I knew I'd have a hard time calling him Skipper. "And you are Dr. Leland's assistant, Jen Kirby."

That's when Dora dropped the bomb. "No, Skipper. Jen is the documentary's onsite writer and interviewer. She has helped me on other projects before, but in this enterprise, she only answers to the documentary's executive producer."

"And to me, ladies. At sea, the captain is the final word."

"You could have warned me."

We were sharing a compact cabin. I had been in larger closets. Shoe-horned into the space were two bunks, two desks, two narrow chests of drawers and a shared wardrobe, all built in, plus two stools that fit under the desks. It was clean, cleverly organized, and intensely claustrophobic. I tried not to think about that.

"I won't be expected to go in front of the camera, will I?"

She shrugged. "Maybe, who knows what the executive producers might require of you."

Dora was one of the executive producers, the only one onboard.

"I packed for a field trip, not a video appearance."

She rifled through my khaki cargo pants, black yoga pants, and earth-tone t-shirts and sweaters. "Works for Michael Palin."

"I'm not Michael Palin. No disrespect to your friend, but I don't want to look like him on camera."

"I don't think anyone would confuse you."

I'd never met the man. My image of him was at least a decade out of date and conflated with his Monty Python days. So, my immediate thought was, true, I've never dressed like a middle-aged housewife. Also, he was lanky. I was curvy. He had a tanned and weathered face, and I had the paleness natural to people who spend most of their time in front of a computer.

On the other hand, if John Cleese had a sex change, he'd look just like Dora Leland. She was long and gangly, with salt and pepper gray hair which she wore short enough that, after a shower, her hair was dry before she was fully dressed. Her eyes were equally good at twinkling and glaring. When she laughed, it was a whole-body exercise. And she never minded being in front of a camera.

"So?" Dora prompted after my long silence.

"Fine."

Dora rewarded me with a hearty slap on the shoulders. "Excellent!"

We set sail at 0500 hours. Barely able to stay awake, I lay down for a nap before dinner and didn't wake up until Dora shook me awake at half past four. So I met the team for first time on deck.

Dora introduced me. I received a chorus of "Hi, Jen," "Hello," and "Yo." I wasn't totally unknown to them, as we had communicated via email, so I didn't take offence when they immediately went back to watching our progress leaving dock. Only Dora's research assistants, a pair of grad students in search of career direction, stayed close. Since she had chosen them because they were already a couple, they were more interested in each other than in me. And that was fine. Being the centre of attention wasn't my thing.

I soon discovered how different sailing on a ship crewed by professionals was from being capsized multiple times in the kind of boat you'd let preteens sail on their own. The others gradually left to have breakfast, leaving me to watch the harbour shrink into the seascape. Finally the need for coffee overcame my mesmerisation. I tore myself away and got as far as the door to the wardroom when the smells drove me back to the deck.

Great, I told myself. *You are about to spend the entire summer at sea and now you discover you get seasick.*

White knuckled, I gripped the rail and tried to force my stomach to behave. We reached an accord. As long as I was willing to stand still and stare out over the waves, my tummy was willing to stop torturing me.

Chapter Three ~ *Sea Legs*

"Penny for your thoughts."

Startled, I turned and nearly bumped into a big man I could have sworn wasn't there a moment ago. Then I bumped into the rail as I tried to back up. Obviously part of the crew, the guy wore a black watch cap, black turtleneck, and a black windbreaker with the ship's logo on one side and an embroidered name badge on the other. According to the tag, he was JL GRAVELL FM.

He handed me an embroidered name badge: G JEN KIRBY. It had a Velcro back that mated with the strip on the bright orange windbreakers provided to the team. I attached it, a bit askew.

Gravell stripped it off and put it back straight. "Wear it anytime you're on deck, okay?"

"Okay," I agreed, backing up a step to recover my personal space. He reminded me of my mother's expression 'built like a brick outhouse.' I'm not sure what she meant, but for me it conjured up the image of someone thick and immovable. In contrast his voice made me think of dark, Swiss chocolate—Swiss because of the slight, hard to place accent.

"What does the 'G' stand for?"

"Genevieve. What does the J.L. stand for?"

"Jean Luc Please-don't-call-me-Picard. You can call me Chief or Chief Gravell. That's how the crew addresses me."

I would never use the Picard joke. Too obvious. I might indulge in 'Sorry about that, Chief' if given the opportunity. "What are you chief of?" I asked.

"The crew, cargo, and passengers. If the captain of a ship is god, I'm his archangel."

"Is there a doctor on the ship?"

"We have a couple of paramedics. But if you're seasick, that's in my bailiwick."

He pulled a small container out of his windbreaker pocket and handed it to me. I peered at the label: Quick dissolve anti-nausea pills. Then he held up a water bottle I hadn't noticed he was carrying. It was steel, with a bright orange foam ring around the lower half and the ship's logo printed on the top half.

"You are an angel," I sighed after popping a pill.

He chuckled. "That's my job. Your name is etched on the bottom of the bottle. We have cooks, but you're on the economy plan so there's a duty roster for galley help, before and after meals. Your team and the divers are on the rota until we reach the diving site, then operational crew will pick up the slack. Everyone's responsible for their own bottle. They'll remind you to keep hydrated and make dandy souvenirs of your voyage."

I smiled.

He continued, "Coffee, tea, and juice are available twenty-four seven and there are always fixings for sandwiches. You met the Skipper when you boarded?"

"Captain Franchot? Yes, briefly."

"Good. You know where he and I stand in the hierarchy. In an emergency, any member of the ship's crew can tell you what to do. Otherwise, they should respectfully accommodate your needs."

His eyes rolled upward as though checking an invisible prompter. "After lunch, there will be a lifeboat drill. It shouldn't take long. I think that's all you missed besides breakfast. When you're ready, go to the galley. Cookie will find you something to eat. You can keep the pills. I have a case."

I gave him a heartfelt, "Thank you," then swallowed a couple of times as the water and medication threatened to come back up on me.

He rubbed my back. "You'll feel better soon."

I was already well enough to feel a pang of disappointment when I spotted a wedding ring on his finger. *Ça va comme ça va*, as my father would say. It goes as it goes.

The drill was a little scary and a lot boring. Between listening to instructions and waiting to be released, I planned the work ahead. We had three days at sea before we reached our destination. In that time I wanted to interview the members of Dora's team and the crew of the *Émil Gagnan*. The question was, where? If I had my choice, it would have been on deck. Even with the anti-nausea medication, I felt better outside. It wasn't a practical choice.

After I stowed my life jacket or Personal Flotation Device as I was informed it was properly called, I went in search of Gravell.

"Still feeling sick?"

"So-so. I have a logistical problem this time." I outlined my needs: an area large enough to set up a camera, reasonably undisturbed, and not too far below decks for the sake of my stomach.

"The ops room won't be needed until we arrive at the site. I'll get it cleared for your use. There's a chart table and a couple of user-defined work areas that you can use."

I gave him a grateful smile. "That would be terrific. There is one other little thing."

"Name it."

"Time permitting, I'd like to interview members of the crew. I don't know how much of it may get used in the documentary. It will definitely help me with the book. You, the captain, and the lead divers are a must. If I have time, I'll do a brief interview of everyone on board."

"Thorough."

"It's all grist for the mill. Besides the more people in the book, the more copies sold."

He chuckled. "Tell me when you're down to your last couple of team interviews. I'll work out a roster then. Meanwhile, fill your film crew in and schedule your interviews. You can start tomorrow. I'll meet you in ops at thirteen hundred hours. You know that's…"

"One p.m. I know. My son is in cadets."

"Sea Cadets?"

"Navy League Cadets. He's only eleven."

"I was a Sea Cadet."

"He wants to go into Air Cadets eventually. He gets sick on boats."

He gave a Gallic shrug. "Like you, he just needs to find his sea legs."

I pushed through the drowsiness long enough to meet with the team and plan the first round of interviews. The ship was severely lacking in deck chairs, but there was a designated passenger area astern, above the diving deck. It was equipped with fixed tables and benches. After the meeting, I stayed until Dora dragged me, half-asleep, to our cabin and made me nap in bed. She also got me up in time to shower and dress for dinner.

I tried, but one step into the wardroom and I knew I couldn't stay. Once again, Gravell found me at the rail.

"Nice night," I commented.

"You've got to eat. It'll help settle your stomach."

"I know. I just couldn't handle all the food smells. I'll go later and fix myself a sandwich."

He handed me a sandwich.

"Thanks. You don't have to keep coming to my rescue...but I appreciate it." I aimed for a winsome smile. Judging by the concerned look on his face, it was probably more like a wan grimace.

In any case, he rubbed my back again, which might have seemed like a romantic overture if his tone of voice was less like a hospice nurse. "Before you know it, you'll be so used to the motion that you'll get land-sickness on shore."

"In the meantime, I'll just stand here."

"No. You're going to eat your sandwich and then hit your bunk. Against all expectations, you are going to sleep like a baby tonight and then get up early and do your turn in the galley. I've arranged the roster so you only get breakfast prep. Less food to smell."

"I see."

"Still your hero?" he asked, moving his hand to my shoulder.

"Maybe. Depends what kind of sandwich you brought."

It was roast beef with tomato slices and a little Dijon mustard. Fresh salty air was the final condiment. While I ate, Gravell kept me company. We talked about his family and my kid. He didn't mention a wife, but had lots to say about his extended family of brothers, sisters, cousins, grandmothers, and a widowed Aunt Therese. By the time he escorted me to my cabin, I pegged him as one of those guys who seems like he's interested in you, but is just universally nice.

Chapter Four ~ *Wind and Waves*

Chief Gravell was right about me sleeping like a baby. I woke every two hours.

The *Émil Gagnan* was not a cruise ship. Most of the openings that looked like windows were part of the sheltered deck. There were no portholes in our cabin. No natural light. When the medication induced drowsiness wore off, I couldn't get into a deep sleep. I never thought of myself as afraid of the dark, but I'd never stayed in a room so black. I longed for an LED display clock, even though I usually hated them. At home, I even covered my phone when it was charging so the little green light wouldn't bother me. In the end, I plugged in my phone and used the green glow as a night light.

Of course, as soon as I dropped into a deep sleep, it was time to get up.

Dora shook my leg and had to dodge my reflexive kick.

"Shit, Jen! Don't kill the messenger. You're going to be late for galley duty. Oh. My. God."

"What?"

I had pushed back the covers and forced myself to sit up. Dora was staring at me, eyes wide, biting her lip. "Look in the mirror, sweetie."

This might not have been a cruise ship, but it did have some of the amenities you would expect in a passenger vessel. Our bathroom crammed a shower, toilet and sink into the smallest possible space, but it was our own. I opened the pocket door and was shocked at the reflection.

My thick wavy hair was now a storm of frizzy curls.

"Yikes! Maybe a shower will help."
"You don't have time."

Health and safety protocol demanded that I wear a hairnet while I worked. It barely fit and felt like it might pop off any minute. I had to wear it even though I was washing dishes not prepping food. This mostly involved rinsing plates in warm salty water, and loading and unloading a steamy industrial dishwasher. I could almost feel my curls coil and was afraid of what would happen when I removed the net.

The worst part was that I also had to carry the tubs of dirty dishes from the wardroom to the galley, which I mistakenly referred to as the kitchen, and make sure the self-serve buffet was well-stocked. That gave the team and crew plenty of opportunity to remark on what looked like a squishy white ball encompassing my head.

Most of them were nice enough to stifle their grins, but Dora had to poke it. "Amazing! It bounces right back again."

I would have poked her back, but my hands were full. Instead I stuck my tongue out. She responded in kind. That was good for a few laughs. Not long after that I realized I no longer felt queasy. I even felt I could sit in the wardroom and do a little work after Cookie's deputy released me from duty. As much as I wanted a shower, I wanted coffee and some breakfast first. No eggs though. I wasn't feeling that brave.

With coffee in one hand and a breakfast plate of bagel, cream cheese, and smoked salmon in the other, I found an unoccupied table and pulled out my smart phone. The device doubled as a tablet. It wasn't easy to write on, but I could read over my research notes in preparation for the interviews.

Forty years ago, when I wasn't even a gleam in my father's eye, eight men disappeared in the depths of the Arctic Ocean. There was no investigation. An investigation might have exposed that, during a politically delicate time, what was supposed to be an experimental undersea research station was, in fact, a US subaquatic military base.

The world changed. The Arctic changed. Commonly available, detailed, satellite images of the planet, coupled with the receding icecap, made it difficult to hide evidence of a vintage, nuclear-powered, underwater station the size of the Goodyear blimp.

It was about a thousand kilometers from where it was supposed to be and in Canadian territorial waters. It was possible that it got there because of the current or storms, or it might have been in Canadian waters all along.

Once again, it was a politically sensitive time, but environmental groups demanded its removal and the Canadian Government wanted to assert its sovereignty in the Arctic. Suddenly, Dora and her group had the leverage they needed to lead an expedition.

Expenses were not a big problem. With three family members of the lost crew on the team and the fact that the U.S. Military establishment was trying to block us, we had a hefty advance on the book and documentary. I just hoped it turned out to be a Titanic, not a Capone's Vault, or the profits (that is, my income for the next year) would be pretty dismal.

Chapter Five ~ *Reuben and Lil*

The documentary crew were early for our one o'clock appointment in ops. Location director, Tim Neville, was nothing if not gung-ho. Twenty-something, a product of the digital age, he used the lingo of celluloid and would probably invite us to view the rushes or dailies at some point. If there was a national average, Tim was it. His one distinctive feature was his eyes; they protruded slightly and gave him a default expression of rapt attention. Maybe that helped him get the job.

Gravell helped set up. Then he introduced us to our crewman of the day who would make sure we were taken care of and stayed out of trouble. Meanwhile, I called up my electronic notes and arranged my hard copies while lighting levels and camera angles were adjusted, then readjusted when Tim decided he wanted me to be in the long shots.

I was sent to join Reuben and Lily in the user-designated area that Production Assistant Yvonne was using as a makeup station. Yvonne was the younger sister of the senior cameraman, Zoe. Zoe was on Camera One, focussed on the interviewees. Camera Two, operated by Bruno, was used for the long shots where I would be seen. Add a gaffer named Chuck and you had the entire documentary crew.

Finally Tim was satisfied with the set up. Chuck stepped between us and the cameras and snapped the clapperboard. We were rolling.

"My name is Reuben Dawes. My father was Lieutenant Aaron Dawes, the station's medical officer and marine biologist."

I looked between the photo on my screen and the man sitting kitty corner to me. There was a strong family resemblance between father and son. Both had angular, Semitic features, dark curly hair, and near-black eyes. Reuben was about the same age as his father had been at the time of the photo, with about the same number of laugh and worry lines around his eyes and mouth.

"I was thirteen years old when my father was reported missing. For years I've been making a pest of myself asking questions about him. Who was Aaron Dawes? What happened to him? Where is he now? Finally, I hope to get some answers. Maybe I should be solemn. Right now I feel stoked!"

I grinned. Reuben had a successful law practice, and I suspected he won clients, if not cases, on the basis of his smile and infectious optimism.

"Tell me what you remember about your father."

His smile turned wistful. "He laughed a lot. He made silly jokes and liked to play. When he was home, he'd read me stories at night, putting on funny voices. He would take Mom out dancing."

In a phone interview, I talked to Reuben's mother, Lorraine. When Dawes was declared dead, she married a dentist. I don't know if he danced, but he came home every night.

"When did you decide to investigate your father's disappearance?"

"For a long time I hoped he'd just show up. When my mother told me that she was going to remarry, I told her she couldn't. I was angry. I eventually saw that my stepfather was a good guy and that he was good for my mother. I figured my dad would understand as long as I didn't give up on him. I studied law just so I could learn how to untangle the government red tape and get answers. The first thing I did was find out who else was missing, who they were survived by, and what they were doing. That's where Lil came in." Reuben gave his wife's hand a squeeze. It was both affectionate and a cue for her to take over.

"Fifteen years ago Reuben hired me to do some work for him in my capacity as a private investigator. His mother gave us our first lead. Norma Shore was one of the few Navy wives that Lorraine stayed in contact with after remarrying. Norma died years ago. She never remarried. I managed to track down the daughters, but only one of them would speak to us."

Lily paused to give a small sigh. "We talked to Shore's youngest daughter, Misty. My first thought was, what were her parents thinking? It turned out her given name was Michelle, for her father. Though she didn't hold out much hope, she agreed to join the survivor support group Reuben was starting. She gave us her mother's address book."

Reuben put up a hand and cut in. "Unlike my mother, Mrs. Shore tried to stay in contact with the families."

"It was quite an investment, hiring a private detective. What made you choose Lily?"

Reuben affected a film noir detective voice. "She was cheap, and I didn't have much money. She also had legs up to here and every inch was tanned and smoothly muscled. I was at that stage in a young man's life when, next to finding my father, I was obsessed with sex."

Lil laughed then quickly returned to point, outlining how she found the other family members of the lost men. I knew most of it. This was strictly for the audience. "The really tough ones were Lieutenant William Minton and Chief John Margolo. Both were bachelors, good friends of Shore and Dawes, and often invited to joint family social gatherings. Margolo always came with the date de jour. Minton often got fixed up with someone's friend. Reuben contacted Margolo's sister, Rose, before we met. She contributed money to the project in memory of her brother."

"Money that mostly went to you, Lil," said Reuben

"A gal's gotta make a living. Anyway, when I contacted her, she was a little more forthcoming. Her brother was an engineer by profession and an adventurer at heart. Ashore, he was a trouble magnet."

"He was always good to us. He never showed up without some kind of gift for us kids and he told great stories. He was like an uncle." Reuben patted his wife's hand. "Even Lil wasn't able to find any family for Will Minton. His parents passed away when he was in his teens. He left no wife or girlfriend behind and his best friends disappeared with him. The Navy was his only home. He had risen up through the ranks to become Shore's second in command. He was a nice guy—a bit of a plodder."

Lily grimaced. "You just say that because he was the responsible one. Your mother remembered him fondly."

The rest of the questions were about AFFA and getting the current expedition together. Reuben did most of the talking with Lily contributing when her husband forgot to give himself credit for all the work he put in.

When the answers started to get too involved, Tim called "Cut. Wonderful! Very thorough. We should have just enough time to do the interns."

After thanking Lil and Reuben, I started making notes while my thoughts were fresh.

"What do you think so far?" asked Tim.

"It wasn't as weird as I thought it would be. I almost forgot that I was on camera."

"I meant the Dawes. Great human interest, huh? Maybe we don't need so much detail with the others. We want to keep things moving."

I shrugged and went back to typing my notes. I didn't care if he wanted to film it all. I had a book to write and my interviews were going to be thorough.

Chapter Six ~ *Conspiracy Theories*

Bruno ushered Dora's grad students, Jamal Martouk and Tracy Dern, into place. At their request, I interviewed them together. After some warm-up questions, the students unfurled before the cameras.

"It is clearly a conspiracy," Jamal announced. "We have uncovered only the tip of the iceberg. There are layers to this that we cannot yet fathom."

Tracy rolled her eyes. "The only conspiracy is that the military wants to cover its ass. Everybody knows that they spy on everybody and everybody spies on them. No one wants to be caught with their pants down, that's all."

This degenerated into an argument that Tim allowed to continue for about five minutes, signalling me not to interrupt. Then he cut and we wrapped for dinner.

"Guys," I said, coming up behind Jamal and Tracy, "if I wanted audition pieces for the next reality show, I would have said so."

Tracy blushed.

Jamal looked defiant. "The director liked us."

I shook my head. I thought that maybe Tim wasn't the best choice of directors for a documentary, but I wasn't about to undermine him. "Even documentaries need comic relief."

I thought we were done for the evening. I was wrong.

For the first time in days I was enjoying a cooked meal. I wasn't gobbling it up with the gusto of Dora, but I was eating hot food in the wardroom instead of a cold sandwich on the deck. Tim was sitting with us, briefing the Dora on the day's work and explaining why he didn't have the daily rushes ready for her to review. When I saw Gravell approach, I was grateful for the interruption. I was especially pleased that he seemed to be focussed on me, not Dora or Tim.

I should have known it was too good to be true.

"Madame Kirby, the Skipper wants you to know that this evening would be a convenient time for his interview. Can you be ready for him in twenty minutes?"

"I gave my crew the night off," said Tim.

"You left everything set up. I thought you'd be continuing to work after supper."

"That's for tomorrow morning."

Gravell shook his head. "You can't do that at sea. Equipment has to be secured when not in use. Since you'll have to do that, you might as well do the interview first."

Tim looked like he might argue the point so I stood up and stepped in.

"Gather the troops. I'll go freshen up."

He heaved a sigh and got up. "Fine. Just wear something other than khaki. You looked like a beige blob on camera." With that uplifting comment, Tim walked out, followed by Zoe and Bruno, who were close enough to hear the discussion.

Dora looked at the exiting director and then at me. "You didn't bring anything that's not some shade of brown, did you?

"I told you I didn't pack for the camera. I told you." I was embarrassed and a bit hurt by Tim's wardrobe critique. I was pissed off too. I hadn't wanted to go in front of the camera in the first place, and I didn't see the point. It wasn't like I was a celebrity or anything, so why were they picking on me?

Gravell cut in on my internal pity party. "Come with me. I have something not beige for you."

Thirty minutes later, I took my place wearing a form fitting black turtleneck with the ship's logo over the right breast. Tim gave me an odd look, but he was satisfied with my choice. Franchot was tickled pink.

I mentioned that Guy Franchot was handsome and charming. He was also highly entertaining. He managed to make the technical details of the upcoming dive sound exciting. The only drawback was that he kept going off topic, weaving stories of other wrecks, in other seas. I eventually curbed his tales because the video crew was starting to wilt, I was starting to feel nauseous and it didn't seem as though Tim was ever going to say "Cut!"

Franchot took my subtle hint. "You look like you need air, Ms. Kirby. Shall we call that a wrap?"

Tim took Franchot's heavier hint. "Yes. Let's pack up guys. Skipper, I'd like to talk to you later about getting access to the crew areas for establishing shots."

"Work it out with Gravell. Ms. Kirby, if I might have a moment of your time."

I gathered up my stuff and followed Franchot. He led me to the forward deck. Above, the windows of the bridge bowed outward. Below I could see the anchors and rigging. Beyond that, light from the setting sun played on an inky black sea. Above, stars could be seen in the twilight that passed for night in the arctic summer. Cold mist soaked my face and hair. It was glorious. He made a sweeping gesture, indicating I was welcome to enjoy the view.

"Let me take your things. You take your time."

I don't know how long I stood there. Eventually a warm hand fell on my shoulder, making me realize I was getting chilled. I turned to see Gravell.

"Come on," he said, raising his voice to be heard above the wind.

Our destination was the Captain's Cabin, which combined office, sitting room, and bedroom. Franchot was waiting for us at his desk with three cups of steaming hot chocolate. I was ushered to the seat opposite my host and happily wrapped my hands around the warm mug.

"Coffee in the morning, tea in the afternoon, cocoa at night, and since none of us has the night watch, a little nip of rum in the cocoa will not be remiss."

I tasted the cocoa and figured there was a large nip in the mug. Lubricating my vocal chords, I wondered? It didn't take long to figure out that it was my turn to be interviewed.

I sipped on my cocoa and answered most of the captain's questions. There were some questions about AFFA that I couldn't answer and a couple about myself that were none of his business. While Franchot interrogated me, Gravell sat back and watched. I was reminded of my early teens, being grilled by my father the cop and my mother the school principal. I never lied because they would always know. I didn't lie now, but I was getting tired of the questions.

"You've got everything I can give you, so, do I pass? And what was I being tested on anyway?" I looked from Franchot to Gravell and back again.

Gravell's expression said nothing.

Franchot leaned forward and tapped the desk in front of me. "With all due respect, you are a late addition to the manifest. I wanted to make sure you weren't a ringer."

I turned to Gravell. I didn't know what I was supposed to be a ringer for, but I had to ask. "Is that why you gave me so much of your time?"

"No."

"I didn't share my suspicions until this evening, after I suggested you interview me. Gravell bet me a bottle of rum I was wrong."

"Wrong about what?"

"Arctic Station Alpha was a secret military station. Even after all these years, it may disclose secrets that certain three-lettered agencies might want to keep undisclosed."

I rolled my eyes. "Yes, I know that. But I can't believe you think I'm a spy. Who am I supposed to be spying for? The Canadian government? Or maybe the World Wildlife Association. I'm a card carrying member, you know."

"I'm not worried about Canadian spies."

I couldn't keep a straight face. "You think I'm CIA spook? I can't wait to tell my son—and my father. Holy shit! He's going to laugh himself silly. So, did I pass the test? Or will I be sleeping with the fish tonight?"

Gravell was surprised into laughing.

Franchot gave an eloquent shrug. "You joke, but I'm beginning to have second thoughts about this job. Last minute changes to the plans, governments breathing down my neck."

His eyes darted to Gravell who gave the tiniest of shrugs in response.

"This wreck had better be worth it. I don't know if Dawes mentioned anything to you. We're silent partners in this venture. His team couldn't have afforded us otherwise."

Reuben hadn't mentioned it, but it made sense. He and Dora had a similar arrangement with me, in that I was trading sure money as a ghostwriter for named credit for my work.

That wasn't what caught my attention. "When you say last minute changes to the plans, do you mean me?"

"Not entirely. There's a Canadian frigate joining us. Not only are they going to be looking over our shoulders all the time, they are escorting a party of US Naval personnel, which will certainly include a spook, who will be there as watchdogs."

"Does Dora know about this? Or Reuben?"

Franchot shook his head.

"I'll make an announcement tomorrow."

"And Gravell gets his bottle of rum?"

The Skipper gave me a speculative look.

"At the end of the voyage. Just in case."

Chapter Seven ~ *Mary Lou and Mike*

I volunteered for extra galley duty to stay out of Dora's line of fire when Franchot made his announcement. I gave up my relaxed breakfast for nothing. Franchot didn't show. Instead, I took coffee and a bagel to go so that I could prep for the next team interview.

I was going to interview Mary Lou and Mike Naire individually, since they were related to different crewmen, but Mike wasn't having any of it. He stuck to Mary Lou like a guard dog.

Mary Lou looked exactly how you'd expect a Mary Lou at forty to look. She had wide blue eyes, a pretty face and wore her hair in a ponytail.

Mike looked like a guy who would be equally at home in the 'hood' or a Kung Fu movie—mature heavy number five. Right now he sat next to his wife, his hand on her back, a gesture that probably was meant to be supportive, but suggested territorial possession.

"Would you like to start, Mary Lou?"

She had a sweet voice without coming across as girlish. Dulcet came to mind. "My father was Lou Boreman. He was an engineer and he used to race stock cars."

Judging by the photos I'd been given, Lou Boreman was a good ol' boy from North Carolina and had high-test, not blood, in his veins.

"You're a forensic technologist, Mary Lou. Tell me about that."

"I work in a crime lab in Raleigh."

"What do you do?"

"I do all kinds of things, but most things to do with cars and trucks."

It was a good job I'd done my homework, or I might have given up about then.

"Is that what you've always done?"

She shook her head. "When I first met Reuben, I was a mechanic in my grandpa's garage and taking night courses at college. I'm good at diagnostics. Y' know, figuring out what's wrong with an engine? It occurred to me that if I learned a bit more, I might be able to figure out what went wrong—what killed Papa. So I started takin' classes in forensic investigation. I eventually joined the Raleigh Police Crime Scene Unit. Now I investigate vehicular homicides, mechanical sabotage, car bombings. I've been researching nautical engines and did a job trade with one of my counterparts working for the Coast Guard."

Talking about her work, she seemed less vulnerable. She sat up straighter, her language was more formal. I noticed a smile play at the corner of Mike's lips. He kept a possessive hand on her, but he was clearly proud of her. I started to rethink my assumptions about their relationship.

Now that she was warmed up, I asked her about her father.

"I suppose I didn't really know him well except through Grandpa. I was only four when he disappeared. I wish I could have known him better. I was named for him and his mama. Grandpa says I remind him of his son when I'm around cars, and my grandma the rest of the time. I've got a couple of photos of him winning stock car races and lots of photos of him wrecking cars in races. Mama says he was a player before they married, but she never worried about him after. He joined the Navy when my brother was born to give Mama more security. Ironic, ain't it?"

I thought about the pension her mother must have received and figured Boreman succeeded in his goal.

"Still, he loved the Navy almost as much as he loved cars. The Navy gave him an education and when I was born, he got a posting on a submarine. Mama says he was almost as excited by that as he was in having a little girl."

According to Mrs. Boreman, her husband was equally excited. He would have longer deployments serving on a sub, but also longer periods at home. Life was good. Lou's father painted a similar picture. He was proud of his son and sure that as long as Lou was fixing the engines, not driving them, any mishap would not be his fault.

"What about your brother?"

Mary Lou frowned. "Ray never really knew Papa. Dwayne, Mama's second husband, was the father he knew. Ray's a Phys Ed teacher. He's got a nice wife and three beautiful kids. He doesn't feel the need to dredge up the past."

That matched with my assessment. I had a short telephone interview with Ray. He was a nice guy, very polite, but he accepted his father's death and didn't see the point of 'picking old scabs,' as he put it.

"How did you meet Mike?"

Mary Lou blushed like a teenager.

"I seduced her," said Mike, grinning. "Reuben got us all together about seven years ago. We all met in a hotel in San Francisco. Before that, we stayed in contact through a newsletter he produced. Mary Lou had been sending us all Christmas cards for a couple of years, and I had this image of her as this mousy thing. I started chatting her up before I made the connection. I went too far and she decked me. It was a sucker punch—embarrassing, since I was still in the Navy, and I was in uniform at the time."

Mary Lou laughed at the memory. "The hotel manager offered to report him, but Reuben showed up and smoothed things over. That might have been the end of it, but we were thrown together for the weekend and…"

"And I don't give up easily," Mike said, voice throaty and warm.

"Mama says Papa was the same way with her."

I looked at the rakishly handsome man in the photo in front of me and up at the exotically good looking man sitting beside Mary Lou and it fit. Though very different in appearance, Lou Boreman and Mike Naire were barely reformed bad boys. Even when they don't know them, girls often marry their fathers.

Not me, of course. But I'm divorced.

Chapter Eight ~ *Rough Weather*

Franchot broke the news when we gathered for lunch.

It turned out Reuben knew all about the Navy involvement. As AFFA's legal counsel, it was one of the compromises he had to make to be permitted to explore a military site. Franchot commanded the *Émil Gagnan*. Reuben and Dora were supposed to be leading the expedition. Tim was in charge of the documentary crew. But none of them really ran the show.

Our lunchtime had become an impromptu summit meeting. The only one missing was Gravell, but I suppose someone had to run the ship. Otherwise, all the key players were there—plus me. I suggested we move to a more private place. Franchot invited us to his cabin.

If the peacemakers are blessed, I was blessed then. In fact, I might have saved Reuben from bodily harm. I don't think he realized how betrayed Dora felt. The short walk gave her a chance to cool down so, when Reuben started making excuses, she used her words, not her fists.

"I thought you knew," he said, shrugging.

"You fucking bastard! You bloody well knew that I didn't know." This was followed by a string of expletives and a few suggestions on what Reuben could do with himself that would have bent a Cirque du Soleil performer out of shape.

Reuben took it well. Tim was shocked. I think Franchot was impressed.

Then she turned her attention to him. "How long have you known?"

"Madam…"

"Don't 'madam' me, you horny sea pirate. I'm a doctor and don't you forget it."

That was disappointingly mild for Dora. Then she launched into German, and I was happy to see that it was not a language Franchot was fluent in. When she switched to French, I decided to intervene.

"Enough. It's not like either of them was given a choice. Maybe Reuben should have told you sooner. He was probably was afraid you'd raise a fuss, like this one, that might cost the team its permits. As for the Skipper, he is probably as put out as you are."

Both men made affirmative noises.

Dora heaved a sigh and slumped back in her chair. "I need a drink."

Franchot poured her large rum. It only took one sip to revive Dora.

"Thank you, Skipper. I hope you know I would never have vented my anger on you in a more public place. Reuben is another matter. He's an old friend who should have known better."

"I understand, Dr. Leland."

"Dora is fine. Just don't call me madam."

I scheduled Dora's interview for after lunch, but she begged off. She decided she'd rather go last so she could fill in the gaps. Instead, Franchot rounded up his diving team, and I did a group interview. This was a bit challenging. English didn't seem to be the first language of any of the crew. They all spoke French, but not the dialect of French Canadian I learned from my father. For a few, French was their second language. Judging by their accents, and a few odd words thrown in, I picked out an Italian and a Greek among the divers. Cookie spoke French and English perfectly, but Spanish was his first language. I could have used him as translator if he wasn't busy in the galley. Gravell could have helped, but I hadn't seen him since breakfast.

The camera crew weren't entirely happy with the set up either. Light and sound levels had to be adjusted repeatedly. Tim's directions had to be translated and, since I was doing the translating, misunderstandings arose. We were running into dinner time when we finally wrapped up. I offered to help with the packing of the equipment. It was appreciated, but refused. I can't say I was sorry.

Dora greeted me almost as soon as I entered the wardroom. "Where the hell have you been?"

"I was working. Interviews. I'll need to do yours tomorrow."

"No problem. Now, go get your supper. We've started a euchre tournament, and I expect you to be my partner.

I agreed, even though I really wanted to go back on deck until I was too tired not to fall asleep. My stomach still felt delicate. After a while, with my attention focussed on the cards, I forgot about it. I never did work out how the overall scoring worked. I won more games than I lost and it was all good fun.

Once upon a time, when the Arctic Ocean was a few patches of open water between ice flows, the sea was calm most of the time. With the ice receding more and more each summer, the Arctic started to see big waves, but it was still pretty calm compared to, say, the North Atlantic.

This was a bit of not so trivial information I picked up preparing for the voyage. It did not prepare me for our first patch of rough weather.

Gravell warned us that it might get choppy overnight and that he had Gravol for anyone who needed it. He repeated the warning to me personally, telling me to be proactive and pop a couple of pills after supper. Because of the euchre game, I forgot. I remembered after I threw up dinner.

Impervious to seasickness, Dora slept through it all, including me getting up. Once the nausea passed, I discovered that if I kept absolutely still in my bunk, I could pretend I was being rocked in a cradle. When my alarm sounded, I managed to drag myself out of bed and dress with minimum fuss. I wasn't seasick, but the drugs in my system made me a bit dopey.

It was raining and the ship seemed to be rocking and rolling to the beat of its own drum. Leastwise, my legs were having trouble with the cadence. Fortunately, Cookie decided this would be a cold breakfast day. The smell of cooked meat or eggs would have probably sent me over the edge. The aroma of the coffee brewing almost did it and I love coffee. No interviews today. The cameras wouldn't be stable. Instead, I took coffee, a towel and my shoulder bag, and found a sheltered spot on deck to go over what I had so far.

Sheltered was a relative state. I had a deck above me that kept most of the rain off, but gusts cold rainwater and icy sea spray reached me even though I was as far back from the side as you could get. Fortunately, I had the foresight to upgrade my smartphone case to the kind that withstands anything short of a sledgehammer blow. It also had enough aps on it to let me do almost as much work as I could do on my laptop. It even supported a portable keyboard, but that wasn't protected against the weather. Instead I read over my notes on the other crew members.

Petty Officers Lawrence Kant and Niles Golanger had no representatives amongst AFFA, either here, or on the support team. Lil had tracked down the families, but there was no interest among them to pursue the mystery.

Kant was survived by an older brother and younger sister, Ira and

Sarah. Ira had opposed his younger brother joining the Navy. He was sorry that Larry was dead, but said he had brought it upon himself. A little chilling, I thought at the time.

Sarah understood why Larry joined up. He wanted to break free of his family. He wanted adventure. He looked the part. His swarthy complexion, dark eyes, and half-smile was worthy of a supporting role in a pirate movie. She didn't want to spoil the fantasy she had built around her brother's disappearance.

"I like to think he got his adventure. I hope it was worthwhile. I don't want to find out something mundane and stupid killed him."

Niles Golanger was the only child of Betty and Bert. When first contacted by Reuben and Lil, they were convinced that their son was still alive. Both had since passed away.

Golanger's photo showed a man, evidently in his mid-twenties, who could have passed for a recruit. His boyish face was smooth, his eyes wide and curious, his mouth curled in a smile of mischievous good humour. He brought to mind what my son might look like in a decade.

I shivered and closed my eyes.

Seamus was eleven years old. Next year he planned to join Air Cadets. In six years, if he so chose and I gave permission, he could join the Reserves. In seven he could join the Canadian Armed Forces. We had talked about it. He didn't like the idea of going to war, but he did want to help people in emergency or disaster situations. Since he also liked aircraft, he thought he'd like to pilot a search and rescue helicopter. Air Force training was one path to that goal. I respected his ambitions but, as a mother, I hoped this was just a phase and he'd settle on a safer career.

A warm blanket was dropped around my shoulders. I looked for the source and found Gravell.

He wasn't smiling. "You're going to catch pneumonia. You're probably soaked to the bone now."

I supposed I was. I hadn't noticed. As my son would be the first to point out, when I get caught up in a project, or even my own thoughts, I am oblivious.

"You can't catch pneumonia in the rain, it takes a virus or bacteria," I pointed out, pulling the blanket around me regardless because I was feeling chilled.

"How much Gravol are you taking?"

I told him.

"Double it."

"I'll fall asleep."

"Then sleep. You won't be the only one in your party who's taking this squall lying down."

"But I like it up here. It's cold and wet, but with the air moving I feel okay. Down below, I feel dizzy and nauseous, and I feel like I can't breathe properly." I was whining so I suppose I deserved his impatience.

"I can't babysit you right now."

I flushed with embarrassment and anger. I wanted to argue. Then I remembered. He wasn't just a nice man who had been looking out for me, he was the First Mate.

Suck it up, Kirby, I told myself. "Aye-aye, Chief. I will do my best to cope with my deficiencies without endangering my health or disrupting your duties."

Okay, there was a slight edge to my voice. No one likes to find out they are being too much trouble.

"My other duties," he said, correcting me.

Once he ushered me inside, he stopped, took me by the shoulders and turned me to face him.

"One of my duties is to make sure our passengers are taken care of. In your case, it isn't an onerous duty. It just can't be my priority right now."

I sighed. "Understood."

He gave my shoulders a squeeze, turned me around again and nudged me off towards my cabin. I was cold and wet and suddenly very tired. Maybe a hot shower and a day in bed might just be the sensible choice. I even popped another anti-nausea pill. Soon I was warm, reasonably comfortable, and asleep.

I am on a bunk, but it isn't the cabin I share with Dora. This is a larger room with four sets of bunks and lockers.

I get up and look around. There are family photos and cheesy pinups on the walls. One bunk has a tea cloth-sized crazy-quilt on it. Another has a tiny teddy bear on the pillow. I try to look at the photos, but I can't quite focus. That's when I realize I am dreaming.

This is the common sleeping area for the station. I know it from the plans. Arctic Station Alpha was the core of what was supposed to become a large underwater base. Like the astronauts that were making history at the time, the submariners shared common living quarters, regardless of rank or position. Eventually there would be cabins and maybe laboratories for visiting scientists, but for now it is a bare-bones military outpost.

One bunk seems devoid of human touches. The bed is made with military precision. I bet I could bounce a quarter on it. But there are no pictures on the adjoining wall. No personal touch on the bed.

Whose bunk is it? Perhaps I could work it out by process of elimination. I started to look around again. There is blood everywhere. Someone is retching.

I woke.

Dora was throwing up in the waste basket. Thank heaven it was lined.

"Sorry," she mumbled. "I shouldn't have had that *verdammt* dessert."

"Don't tell me about it! My stomach is having enough problems as it is."

It was seven o'clock. I had slept through lunch and dinner. Now I dosed Dora up with Gravol and tucked her into bed. I tied up the bag and left her with a fresh-lined can, just in case. As quietly as I could, I brushed my teeth, dressed, and gathered up my tablet and shoulder bag. The garbage had to go, and I didn't want to return until the fan had cycled the last of the acrid smell.

The sea was much calmer and it had stopped raining. After taking care of my disposal problem, I decided I was hungry and went to try my luck in the galley. Some of the crew were still dining and made me welcome. I got to practice my French while enjoying the meal despite myself.

Later, I stood at the rail looking out to sea for the pleasure of it. We were far enough north now that night was just a short period of twilight between sunset and sunrise. After the storm, the sky seemed to hang like a sheer drapes across an evening window. Through the mist I saw the ghostly shape of a ship.

Chapter Nine ~ *Calm Before the Storm*

"It's the HMCS *Nottawasaga*," said Gravell appearing suddenly beside me.

I nearly jumped out of my skin. "Shit!"

He laughed. "Sorry. I didn't mean to startle you. Still feeling sick?"

"Much better, actually."

"Still mad at me?"

"No. I realized that you were just putting on a show because I was at risk of falling in love with you and that would have been hard to have explained to the wife."

He squinted at me, trying to determine if I was serious. "You're teasing me."

"A bit," I said. *Not entirely*, I thought.

Remember this, gentlemen, there is something very sexy about a man who wraps a woman in a warm blanket when it's needed, and holds the bucket if that's what's required.

The *Nottawasaga* followed us, gradually closing the gap. According to Gravell, we were about eighteen hours from our destination. That meant that I had to finish my last two pre-dive interviews *tout de suite*.

Dora was ready for the cameras and went first. I asked the usual establishing questions then gave her the question she needed to steal the show. "You have no family involved. You're not even a United State citizen, so what drew you to this mystery?"

"That's a good question." Well, of course it was, she came up with it. "I feel that my formative years were shaped by the Space Race and the Cold War. As a Canadian, it confused me that one country, the United States, could be reaching for the stars with one hand, and reaching for the Armageddon with the other. It was my first indication that we all have a sinner and a saint within us, whether we are a person, a business, or a country."

She leaned forward and spoke to the camera as if she could see her audience beyond the lens. "I thoroughly believe that everyone is capable of committing theft and murder under the right circumstances. They might choose not to. They might resist their behavioural imperative, but it is there nonetheless."

"So you think a crime has been committed?"

She sat back. "Absolutely! If nothing else, there are members of our governments who have hidden the truth. The families of the lost crewmen deserve answers."

"What about the argument that national security is involved?"

Dora dismissed the suggestion with a wave. "All the more reason to investigate. As I have often argued, transparency of process does not need to include the revelation of all secrets whether they are personal or national."

She was on her soap box now.

"An investigation could have been made and the public could have seen the process, if not all the particulars. Yet, as we now know, there was no real examination of the incident." Dora lowered her voice dramatically. "Consider, if we find out that those men died over the period of weeks, long after they were reported missing, the absence of an investigation could amount to negligent manslaughter."

Gravell hung around for Dora's interview, but was strangely absent when it came time for his. I had to get help from Franchot to make him sit in front of the camera.

"Don't worry, I'll be gentle," I said.

Franchot chuckled.

Gravell gave him what Grandma Allard called the evil eye. It was gone when he turned back to me. "Whenever you're ready, Madame Kirby."

I eased him into the interview by asking him about Sea Cadets and how that influenced his career choice. It worked like a charm. I thought my next question would be equally relaxed. "How long have you sailed with the *Émil Gagnan* ?"

There was a slight hesitation. "Not long. I'm filling in for the Skipper's regular first mate."

That was a surprise. There were photos of the crew working on other jobs in the wardroom. I hadn't seen Gravell in any of them, but I assumed that was because he was taking the photos. My family photos have a similar absence of me since I was old enough to own a camera.

That pretty much ended the interview. I asked more questions, but Gravell didn't have an opinion about the wreck. He had no vested interest. This was just a job for him. When I remarked that he seemed to have developed a good working relationship with the Skipper, he said was that he was good at getting along with people.

I tried a different tactic. "What kind of work do you usually do?"

"Whatever is needed—and I am needed elsewhere."

That night, I dreamed of the station again. This didn't surprise me. All my life, whenever something big was looming on my horizon, I would dream about it the night before. I rehearsed exams, job interviews, even giving birth although the last one had little bearing on reality.

I knew my husband was going to leave me three nights before he took me out to an expensive dinner and had the talk. Of course, in that instance, there had been signs, not ones I wanted to acknowledge, but signs nonetheless. In my dreams, my mother, who had died a few years before, told me Will was seeing someone else and hadn't she warned me about him in the first place?

The station dreams felt more like my pre-birth dreams, filled with anticipatory anxiety. There was a lot of blood in those dreams too.

I had a repeat of the first dream, woke up, walked around a bit, and went back to sleep only to have it repeat again. When I saw which way the dream was going, I decided I needed to wake up. Usually I can do this when I know I'm dreaming. This time, it was like waking up and discovering that reality was scarier than the dream.

The room is sterile. All I can see is mirror-bright stainless steel kitchen equipment. Then I hear voices. I can't make out words, but there are several people talking and laughing. I hear the slap of cards and rattle of chips. I look around.

Six men sit around the table playing poker. They are drinking coffee, though as I watched, one man pulls a flask out of his pocket and hands it around. A few are smoking. Contrails of cigarette smoke drift towards the exhaust fans.

A seventh man enters. The flask disappears and two of the smokers stub out their butts. The game continues, but there's no laughter. Then comes the blood and the screams. There is a murderer aboard the station. He has killed all the others and is now coming for me.

I woke in a sweat, feeling dizzy and nauseous. A shower and clean teeth helped. I quietly dressed, grabbed my water bottle, and went up on deck. It wasn't until I was outside that I realized we were no longer moving. Up and down, yes, a little side to side, but no longer forward. We had weighed anchor overnight.

It was only five o'clock. I had an hour before I was expected in the galley to help with breakfast. Meanwhile, I could get coffee. There was always fresh coffee. They had a machine that made it fresh, in your choice of city roast, dark roast, or decaf. They used something like a K-cup except that it was loaded internally and made entirely of compostable materials. I knew this because I cleaned out and reloaded the machine every morning I had galley duty.

In a couple of minutes I had a cup of dark roast and was scooting up to the observation deck. I felt like a kid on the first day of school, full of excitement and dread. I wasn't the first to the party. Reuben and Lil were there, as was Jamal. They were clustered together, pointing and staring. I couldn't blame them. Up close, the *Nottawasaga* was massive compared to the *Émil Gagnan*. Yet, that wasn't what they were pointing at. As soon as I reached the rail, I knew the object of their attention. It wasn't as big as the Canadian warship, but it was twice as scary. Our American observers had arrived in a submarine.

Chapter Ten ~ *Storm Warnings*

It was like Empire Strikes Back, when Lando Calrissian made a deal with Darth Vader and the deal got progressively worse. First we got permission to dive. Then we found out that we'd have a Canadian warship looking over our shoulders. Now we had the USS *Scranton*, a tactical sub, for added intimidation value.

Franchot made the official announcement at breakfast. There was a lot of grumbling speculation, but only one real eruption.

"Fucking bloody merde, schietz, excusado…" Dora maintained a string of multilingual swear words as she violently skewered sausages and home fries on her fork. "Son of a dog's excrement!"

When she was really pissed off, she made up her own epithets. It's a testament to her expertise that this behaviour never got her into trouble. I couldn't get away with it. I had to be the calm and courteous one.

"I know this is aggravating, but we always knew we were here on sufferance."

She gave me the icy glare you might expect from a lecturing professor being interrupted a smart-ass student. "It would be naive to think that anything could be done without the permission and blessing of the military, and I am not naive. Now we must ask ourselves, which country's military will mete out permission and which will add their blessing?"

Shrugging, I concentrated my attention on buttering my toast. I neither had an answer, nor did I want to dig myself into deeper shit. On the other hand, Dora's silence gave me a chance to think of a way of fighting back, in a manner of speaking. I would ask for interviews. The US and Canadian commanders didn't have to know that I was a ghostwriter, not an investigative reporter. As my mother used to say, "Fake it 'til you make it."

Captain Tinsdale of the *Scranton* made no bones about it. He wasn't allowing any civilians aboard and he wasn't leaving his boat. His spokesperson, Lieutenant Redding, sounded friendly, if a bit patronizing. He granted me a few words via radio and was apologetic about not being able to meet with me aboard the *Émil Gagnan*. His hands were tied. The captain had decreed that no interviews were to be given at this time.

Captain Campbell of the *Nottawasaga* agreed to a video call. The first thing I noticed was his looks. Without being quite as handsome, he brought to mind Cary Grant in *Charade*. Mature. Smooth. Charming. While Tim got organized, we chatted.

"Have you enjoyed your voyage so far?" he asked.

"It's had its ups and downs."

"That's life at sea." He said that so blandly, I wondered if the joke was unintentional.

Tim indicated he was ready, and I took a couple of deep breaths in preparation.

"Are you all right, Ms. Kirby?" asked Captain Campbell.

"I'm fine. We're ready to start."

I put on my front-of-camera smile—friendly, but serious. After getting the introductory questions out of the way, I got to the meat of the interview. "Tell me about your mandate for this mission."

"Mission...That sounds so intriguing. The *Nottawasaga* is simply here to ensure the safety and security of the Canadian people...and visitors of course."

"What about the issue of Canadian sovereignty? Arctic Station Alpha is a US military installation in Canadian territorial waters."

"Station is a bit of a misnomer. I understand it was intended to be a slow, but mobile, research and observation platform."

"Observation, as in spying?"

He spread his hands in and expansive gesture as if allowing that it might be possible, but he wasn't going to say so. "It was the Cold War. However, unlike the US and Russian submarines that plied the same waters, the station was also intended for scientific research."

He was pleasant. He managed to answer all my questions without telling me a single thing I didn't already know. When he had enough, he closed the interview, not Tim and certainly not me. "It has been a great pleasure to meet you, Ms. Kirby. I am looking forward our future meetings."

Charming, or perhaps just polite?

Typically Canadian.

In the shadow of the warships, the recovery crew worked. Aquatic robots filmed and scanned the sunken base. Measurements were collated, equated, and processed to determine the best places for the bots to attach the freshwater salvage balloons that would raise their prize.

While Franchot directed the salvage operation, Gravell fed us information. At every meal, he'd give a progress report and answer questions. I was glad I'd done my homework, otherwise it might have been me, not Lil that asked, "Why freshwater balloons? Why not saltwater? Or air?"

"Freshwater is more buoyant than saltwater and it's easier to manipulate than air."

"Okay, but we're in awfully cold water here. Wouldn't the freshwater freeze? And a solid is heavier…"

Before Gravell framed an answer, I pushed an ice cube down in my glass of water with a spoon and let it bob to the surface again. Lil, who was across the table from me, noted the demonstration.

She laughed. "Of course!"

It was more complicated than that, and Gravell explained in detail, but my demo made the point. He acknowledged that later.

"I'm going to remember that next time I have to explain buoyancy. You've got a knack for simplifying things."

"It's a big part of what I do."

I had stayed at the table to work. The cabin felt claustrophobic for anything besides showering and sleeping. Besides, working in the wardroom gave me easy access to the coffee.

"What are you doing now?" he asked.

I called up photos taken by the *Émil Gagnan* bots on my laptop. Then I tiled the photos with a schematics of the station gathered from…well, I never asked. Another touch and the windows moved over to make room for a cross-referenced and indexed catalogue of photos, drawings, and notes.

"Every scrap of information gathered is documented by me for when Dora and I start writing the book. Plus, I'm keeping a running journal of what I experience and observe like the undercurrent of excitement, the difference between the American and Canadian navies, and how many times the Skipper says 'Feh!'"

He laughed. Then we both reached for my coffee mug at the same time. Our hands met and there was a moment. His hand overlapped mine, our eyes met, and I knew the attraction was mutual.

Cool.

Damn.

I'd have to be more careful.

With mixed emotions, I shifted my hand. He kept hold of the mug.

"Another cup?"

I nodded and let him fetch my third cup of the morning.

I didn't record my feelings about Gravell in my journal. Instead I waxed poetic on the events of the afternoon. Arctic Station Alpha breached the surface like a shy Beluga and was greeted by a rousing chorus of cheers and applause.

Then the boom dropped again.

Chapter Eleven ~ *Obstacles*

"Schweinhund!" Dora slammed the door to our cabin. "Mascalazone! Asshole!"

"Mas-ca-la-zo-nay?"

This one was new to me.

"Scoundrel. Italian." Dora couldn't speak Italian, but she could swear in it.

"Who is the scoundrel?"

"Who else? Tinsdale! He's told us all to put away our cameras and equipment, on threat of confiscation. We have to sit back and twiddle our thumbs while he decides if we will be allowed on board. Tinsdale's knickers are in a twist because a couple of our divers went on board to check on the structural integrity."

"Why would that bother him?"

"They let Tim Neville go with them. Evidently he's a recreational diver when he isn't making low budget documentaries. He took video."

"Oh. What about Captain Campbell? Isn't he intervening on our behalf?"

"Right." The word was supersaturated with disdain. "As if he could do anything."

I decided it was best not to argue.

A day went by while the *Scranton* crew made their own check of the integrity of the vessel or so they said.

Franchot took the high road. In front of the camera he allowed that it was understandable that the US Navy would think they were better equipped to evaluate one of their own vessels. It wasn't necessarily so.

Off camera he said it was bullshit.

A second day passed.

I decided to try interviewing the commanders again more because I needed a break from Dora than any expectation of success. Tinsdale was unavailable for comment. Lieutenant Redding gave me a few minutes via radio, but no information.

It was late afternoon before I got a response from the *Nottawasaga*. This time I was invited aboard, though politely told that the invitation was not extended to the video crew. That was fine with me. It was more likely I'd get information without a camera present.

Gravell accompanied me. There was no posse to greet us, just one man with a sidearm who escorted us to Captain Campbell's office and stayed to serve tea. Tall, broad shouldered, and square jawed, he made an odd choice for butler, but a great choice for a bodyguard. He looked more like a soldier than a seaman (or a butler) and more like a football player than anything else.

Looks notwithstanding, he did a decent job. "Would you like Earl Grey or Orange Pekoe tea? Or we have coffee"

"Coffee, please."

He had an east coast accent that came out in his cadence. According to the patch on his uniform, his name was Rankin. If I had to guess, I'd place him in Nova Scotia. "Milk? Cream? Sugar?"

"Black. No sugar."

He gave me my coffee. It was in a proper cup and saucer, white with a gold rim and the emblem of the *Nottawasaga*. Very classy.

He turned to Gravell who responded before he was asked. "Tea, Earl Grey."

If he had added "hot" I would have laughed. As it was, I had to bite the inside of my cheeks to keep from grinning. Jean Luc 'Don't-call-me-Picard' indeed.

Rankin managed to keep a straight face, but he obviously got the *Star Trek* reference. He poured the tea and added a lump of sugar and a lemon slice before passing it to Gravell. Without asking, he poured the Orange Pekoe, milk, no sugar, for Captain Campbell.

Except for the absence of a desk, we were in almost the exact same seating arrangement as I had been when being interrogated by Captain Franchot.

The captain sat opposite me, in his perfectly pressed uniform, looking like the gentleman he legally was, and told me that there wasn't much he could do to help me, but he was pleased to enjoy my company.

Gravell sat kitty-corner to me, dressed in the usual black turtleneck, black jeans and *Émil Gagnan* windbreaker, currently worn open. He was casually watchful, though I could see that he was mostly watching me.

On the other side of the captain, Rankin stood at ease, ready to refill cups or put me in irons as the situation demanded.

At least, that's how it felt.

I sat there, in a t-shirt, denim jacket, and jeans, none of which were as fresh as they should be, trying to be the hard-boiled investigative reporter I was not.

I had already covered my usual warm-up questions like what kind of ship was the *Nottawasaga* (a Halifax Class, multi-role patrol frigate), how long he'd been in the navy (twenty-three years) and how long had he been captain of the *Nottawasaga* (four years). Now I had to get creative. "You said last time that you had worked with Captain Tinsdale before. Do you know him well?"

That surprised him and he answered cautiously. "Well enough to work smoothly together. The Arctic is not a good place to get contentious."

"But things do get tense, don't they? I mean, you're here to ensure Canadian sovereignty in the north, right?"

"More or less."

I nodded and took a moment to sip my coffee. I did my best to look and sound as relaxed as Campbell and Gravell. "Perhaps you can help me understand something."

He gave me a cautious nod.

"These are Canadian waters, correct? Then why is Captain Tinsdale calling the shots?"

There a moment of anger apparent in the tightening of his mouth and the narrowing of his eyes. Then it was gone and he was the urbane and unflappable captain again. "I'm afraid I can't help you, Ms. Kirby."

"If you can't, who can?"

"Possibly the Minister for Defence, or you could take your case to the Prime Minister."

He gave me a patronizing smile. Gravell's eyebrows were raised in mild surprise, or perhaps amusement. It was hard to tell. What wasn't hard to spot was the moment that Rankin looked over at Gravell when I asked who could help. He had also known how Gravell took his tea.

Yes, the men were positioned so they could watch me, but I could watch them too.

When I didn't respond to his quip, Captain Campbell continued, "Captain Tinsdale and I are working within agreed protocols. You just need to be patient."

I wondered if that was how I sounded to my son when he asked, "Are we there yet?"

"Okay. While I'm being patient, let me see if I understand the circumstances. The Canadian and US governments were pressured to agree to this project. It was politically expedient, but not militarily advisable. So you're here to keep a lid on things. What I'd like to know is, if there are still secrets down there, why not go after them? Why wait for civilians to do the job for you?"

Campbell said nothing and his smile didn't falter. I looked at Rankin who was staring at me, as unwavering as a cat. Then he noticed that my cup was empty and refilled it.

Oh so polite. Oh so bloody useless. I was only here to be humoured. Was that the only reason the team was there? Were we allowed to join the expedition only to show the world how open the military was willing to be?

Then I had a flash of insight. "Unless we're the only ones who can get away with it. You can't dive for it without offending the Americans and they can't dive for it without permission from the Canadian government, which, given the controversy over Arctic territory isn't likely to be forthcoming."

Campbell betrayed a moment of surprise. Rankin was impassive, but Gravell's eyebrows raised a notch.

My frustration melted away, knowing that I was on the right track. "We're perfect, a joint American-Canadian research team aboard a Canadian registered ship with an international crew."

Campbell retreated behind an expression of bored courtesy. "I cannot confirm or deny your statements."

I sat back, trying for a Mona Lisa smile. "I'll quote you on that."

Chapter Twelve ~ *Arctic Station Alpha*

At breakfast the next day, Franchot announced that we would be going aboard the station after lunch. He gave us the news with his usual flare for the dramatic.

"My friends, I've got good news and bad news. Good news is that the interior is intact and dry. They don't want to engage the old nuclear power generators, so the *Scranton* has attached an umbilical, providing power for lights and air recycling." He sighed wistfully. "It will be like stepping back in time. Wish I could be there. Bad news is, only the members of AFFA will be allowed to go this time. Our divers are excluded and so is the documentary crew."

Tracy asked the question we were all wondering about. "Is this because of the bodies?"

"No. That is another case of good news and bad news. The good news is there are no bodies in the areas you will be allowed access to. The bad news or weird news is, they haven't evidence of bodies anywhere else either."

"So this is just military officiousness," said Jamal.

Franchot shrugged. "Gravell is going to review our protocols. Later, someone from the *Scranton* will do the same. Use your common sense when deciding which protocols to follow."

Lieutenant Redding briefed us via video conference a couple of hours later. The moment we stepped aboard the station, he told us, we were under the jurisdiction of the United States Navy. Navy personnel from the *Scranton* would be aboard checking out the operational areas.

We would be allowed into the living quarters only, under Marine guard.

As soon as he signed off, Dora stood up and gave her own manifesto. "We'll do what we have to do to get along with these bozos, but anyone not following Mary Lou's protocols for evidence collection will have me cutting them a new one. Understood?"

We all nodded. I, for one, was less afraid of military reprisal than the wrath of Dora.

Our videographer, USN Petty Officer Matt Parker, was introduced to us at lunch. He must have had ambitions to go to Hollywood after his tour of duty, because he made nice with the professionals, asking Tim what he wanted and conferring with Zoe and Toby. He took one of their hand-held cameras in addition to the shoulder mounted tactical camera that would transmit information to the *Scranton*.

"I know this isn't what you wanted. Rest assured, I'll do my best to satisfy your needs as well as the needs of the captain."

He then spent a half hour deftly answering and not answering questions. By the end of the meal, he was on a first name basis with everyone. Dora, the hardest sell of all, agreed that he was better than they might have expected.

Despite the fact that there was no beach in sight and the water was freezing, most of us stood around in bathing suits. Personally, I opted for cotton boxer-briefs and sports bra. I bought two new sets for the occasion, one in black and the other in athletic grey. I wore the black in deference to the dead.

Dora, in contrast, wore a bright floral one piece bathing suit. Tracy wore a bikini and was drawing a lot of attention, mostly appreciative. Lil's modest one piece drew even more attention because of the body inside. Jamal was wearing a Speedo so revealing I didn't get any further in my observations.

Under the direction of our divers we pulled on thermal gear and bright orange, waterproof coveralls. This outfit was topped with flotation jackets. Although the station was dry, the ride over on the rigid-hull inflatable boat wouldn't be. If something happened and we went in the water, we'd need to stay warm and afloat long enough to be fished out. Once we were at the station, we'd still need the protection. There was light, but little heat.

Excitement mounted with every layer of clothing.

When we boarded the boat, we were buoyed by more than air. Mary Lou and Reuben couldn't get their eyes off the station or that part visible above the waterline. Mike was totally focussed on the station. Lil's eyes darted from the station to the *Scranton* to the *Nottawasaga* and back again, as if one ship or the other might open fire on us any time now. We certainly had an audience. The decks of the *Émil Gagnan* and *Nottawasaga* were lined with observers from their respective crews. Even the *Scranton* had watchers on their tower.

From a distance it looked like an oversized cartoon submarine. Close up, you could see that it was more bulbous, especially compared to the *Scranton*. It was also taller and more menacing at sea level than it had appeared looking down on it. I wasn't sure I wanted to go inside after all.

When we finally transferred from the RHIB to the station, Parker was first onboard. He scurried expertly up the ladders and disappeared. A second seaman climbed up and waited to help us as we ascended. I would have rather had someone helping me descend into the dark. Looking down, the tower ominously brought to mind the dark tunnel of death with the bright light at the end.

Mike took the lead. I hung back, wanting to keep open sky above me as long as possible. The seaman on deck had to chivy me along. He followed me, dogging the hatches behind him. For an awful moment I thought my chest was imploding.

"Slow deep breaths," he advised. He took my arm and we followed the others.

I nodded. Chances were he wouldn't see that, but I couldn't speak yet. Sooner than I expected, the tunnel gave way to open space, then a landing. I paused to take a couple more deep breaths and look around. Because of the lights shining up the tower, I couldn't see anything but shadows.

"This is my stop," said the seaman, patting my gloved hand with his. "You keep going down. And keep breathing."

I forced a smile. "Always a good idea."

I was used to using the steeply inclined steps that passed for stairs on the *Émil Gagnan*. This flight wouldn't be much worse if I could have seen my feet past the bulk of thermal and safety gear. I descended backwards, holding the rails until Mike and Reuben guided me to the deck.

Two Marines had joined us. They weren't introduced. According to their headgear, they were Madison and Dippel. As soon as I had my feet, Dippel took the lead as guide. Madison brought up the rear, making sure no one lingered too long as we passed through the operations room on the way amidships to the living quarters. Abaft was engineering. Forward were weapons' control, sick bay, and the labs. We might, eventually, get to see those areas once they were cleared. For the time being, I was only really interested in where the crew lived.

What we saw of the station's interior brought to mind old episodes of *Star Trek*. The bulkheads were near-white and seemed to glow with reflected light from the covered panels. Yellow and black stripes marked the coamings, those ridges at hatches and other entries that kept water from slopping and tripped me up about twice a day on average. Red signs outlined rules and prohibitions. Blue signs marked location and directions. The overall effect was much more cheerful and less military than I expected. Perhaps it really had been intended to be a research station.

Dippel stopped at a hatch and ushered us through.

We flowed in silently. I was last in, besides the Marines, and Dippel had to ask me to move. I was frozen in the hatchway.

The room was exactly as I had dreamed.

This was too weird. My mind had to be playing tricks with me. There was the crazy quilt, neatly laid out on one bunk. There was the tiny teddy bear. The photos I could see looked roughly correct. I had never been able to see much detail in my dreams, only positions on the wall and basic composition.

I continued scanning.

There was the gas station pinup calendar. Next to it should be the photo with the woman and baby. I didn't see it. I climbed up. The photo had fallen onto the pillow.

Dora yelled, "Jen! What are you doing? Don't touch anything until everything has been recorded."

I blushed and stuttered an apology. Who'd have thought I would be the one to get caught up in the moment?

Calmer, Dora spoke to the team. "We've been over this before. We're treating this like a crime scene. Everything gets photographed and itemized before it is bagged and tagged. Enough sightseeing. Let's get to work."

Although Petty Officer Parker was the only one with video equipment, the team was equipped with digital SLR cameras. Lil and Reuben placed reference markers and took photos while Dora described what she saw, and her initial deductions, speaking into a digital recorder. Mary Lou followed, looking for trace evidence, hairs, blood, that sort of thing. Mike acted as her assistant, diligently handing her equipment. Jamal, Tracy, and I brought up the rear, bagging and tagging artifacts. I collected the paper letters, diaries, photos, even the pinups filing them in a water-proof satchel I carried over my shoulder. They took everything else, packing the bagged items in a soft-sided chest that they carried between them.

While we worked, Parker watched and filmed. Through his shoulder mounted tactical camera, the *Scranton* and possibly the *Nottawasaga* also watched. Periodically, I heard Parker responding to something over his headset, but he didn't interfere with our labours.

Processing the room took longer than expected. Parker suggested that we return the next day to do the wardroom and galley. Although I wouldn't have minded a coffee break, none of us were ready to quit for the day. Who knew if or when we might be let back onboard?

Dora and Reuben vetoed Parker's suggestion with a unified, "No way!"

"At the very least, I'd like to do the overview of the wardroom," said Dora.

Parker gave the Marines a shrug and consulted the *Scranton* via his headset. After a short exchange, he nodded and led the way onward. Hitching the satchel up on my shoulder, I brought up the rear. Looking back, past Madison who was chivying me forward, I thought I saw a man on one of the bunks. I blinked and he was gone.

The wardroom and galley were combined in one room accessible directly from the living area via a hatch which, Dora posited, was probably left open most of the time. The hatch led to a landing, and a couple of steps down to the deck. According the plans we had, the galley had higher ceilings to allow for fire control systems and was against an outside bulkhead at one of the points designated for future expansion. In one of the more ambitious conceptual drawings Reuben had acquired, what was now a bare-bones facility would become the master galley, provisioning several wardrooms throughout the expanded station.

Right now it sent a chill down my spine. Everything was stainless steel and the metal radiated cold. There were no personal touches. No photos. No cheesecake calendar.

"This won't take long," Reuben remarked.

Dora shook her head. "Maybe. Maybe not. We need to keep our eyes open. This place strikes me as too antiseptic. Perhaps something was missed."

With those cryptic words, she set us to work.

Dora started with the food storage area, which consisted of two rows of food lockers full of sacks, cases, and industrial sized-cans, all long past their due dates. She and Reuben catalogued the remaining supplies to compare with the original manifest. Lil followed, taking photos.

Mary Lou and Mike looked for traces on the apparently bare surfaces of the table and benches that served as the dining area. I watched as she solemnly touched the bench where her father might have sat. Mike laid a hand on her lower back and she leaned against it. Turning away from the intimate moment, I saw that Parker was recording the scene. No doubt it would be a prized moment in the documentary. He caught my eye and gave me an oddly sentimental smile.

I looked back towards the table. This time I didn't see Mary Lou and

Mike. I saw six men sitting around, playing poker. I couldn't hear them, but they seemed to be laughing at a shared joke while placing their bets. I blinked and saw Mary Lou sticking a swab in the crevice between the fixed bench and the wall.

This shook me up. It had been a long time since I'd seen ghosts, but not so long that I had forgotten what they looked like.

Not sure what else to do, I busied myself looking around the food prep areas. I found a duty rota for the galley. It was a neatly printed chart, using three coloured pens. The paper had yellowed; otherwise it was pristine, like the rest of the galley. I wondered what Dora would deduce from it and was about to draw her attention to it when our world was rocked and we were drenched in darkness and icy seawater.

Chapter Thirteen ~ *Twist and Shout*

The explosion knocked me off my feet. I knew people were yelling. They seemed muffled and far away. I felt, rather than heard, the metal squeal as it twisted and sheared. Yet, I could hear water rushing in. It was the most terrifying sound I ever experienced.

The lights flickered back on; a dull light, but better than nothing.

I rolled over to a sitting position and assessed. Despite the pain where I slammed down on one knee, my legs worked. My hearing loss was probably temporary.

Our Marine escort was hustling everyone out the door. Jamal and Tracey seemed to argue briefly about bringing the artifact chest. It was quickly settled when Madison scooped it up in one arm and pushed them out the hatch with the other. Mary Lou and Mike exited with no fuss. Reuben and Lil, were next. Dora must have hurt something, because Dippel was helping her up to the hatch.

I looked around. Parker, like me, was on the deck. I saw him. No one else would be able to, the food lockers blocked their view. He was on his hands and knees in the water. Something was sticking out of the back of his neck. For a moment our eyes met.

Scrabbling to my feet, I sloshed towards him, against the flow of incoming water. Grabbing him under the armpits, I tried to drag him towards the hatch. He slumped, pulling me down with him. I yelled for help. I couldn't tell if they responded. My own voice seemed distant to my ears.

Icy water flowed around me. Warm blood flowed over my hand,

despite my efforts to staunch the wound. Then, suddenly, there was a clang.

Through the steady rush of water, and the dullness of my hearing, I heard the dogging of the hatch. The sound resonated. It was like a guillotine blade falling, or so it seemed to me at the time. Perhaps my memory is coloured by the fact that, at that same instant, I could feel Petty Officer Parker die in my arms, as though the sound cut the last thread of his life.

My first reaction was anger. How dare he die when I got trapped trying to save him? This was immediately followed by a sinking feeling.

The room was slowly filling up with water. That had to stop.

I had an idea and prayed it would work. Pulling myself free of Parker, I found a utility knife in the galley, opened up the storage compartments, and grabbed sacks. In a one-woman relay, I gathered and stuffed mouldy bags of flour and oatmeal into the hole in the inner hull, which spouted a steady stream of seawater. Any bag that didn't split on its own, I stabbed with the knife.

Add water, grains expand. The rush slowed to a trickle.

I had no idea how long my doughy patch would last, but I'd bought myself some time.

Next, I checked the hatch. Maybe it was imagination when I heard it lock. Maybe I could open it and get out. No such luck. It was locked down from the outside. If there was a way of opening the hatch, I couldn't find it.

I felt a rumble like distant thunder.

The deck listed to one side with a jolt that knocked me off my feet, down the steps, and sent me skidding across the wet deck. I smashed my knee again. In agony, I screamed a long string of obscenities. Dora would have been proud. The thought pushed me through the pain.

Overhead lights flickered and went out. Red emergency lights cast an eerie glow over the galley. I rolled over and sat up, blinking back tears. Too much. Way too much to deal with.

A phone rang.

It was a high-pitched, penetrating sound that cut through the cotton wool that seemed to be stuffed into my ears. It took me a minute to realize the sound was coming from the body of Petty Officer Parker. Afraid of falling again, I crawled over to him, favouring my bad knee. On the way, the sloshing water found places to creep under my protective garments. Unable to see what I was looking for, I found the oversized cellphone-like unit by touch. I unclipped it from his belt, and answered with a breathless, hope-filled, "Hello?"

"Parker?"

I rolled to a sitting position and took a couple of deep breaths, fighting down the sobs that were working their way up my throat.

"Petty Officer Parker is dead. This is Jen Kirby. What happened?"

There was a long pause then another voice. Captain Tinsdale maybe?

"What happened?"

I had just asked that question. If I knew the answer, I wouldn't have asked. I waved my hand in front of the tactical recorder, still secured to Parker's shoulder.

"I thought this thing would tell you, maybe even let you know you were leaving a crewman behind, not to mention me."

There might have been a hint of hysteria to my voice.

"We lost the feed from Petty Officer Parker right after the explosion. His tactical camera must be damaged, so, I ask again, what the hell happened to my man."

It irked me that I was the one trapped and he was badgering me. For Matt Parker's sake, I tried to play nice.

"Something hit Parker in the back of the neck. No one else seemed to see him, so I went to him. I tried to stop the bleeding. I called for help. No one heard." I gulped air in an effort to push down my need to sob or retch, or both. "He just died in my arms."

"Damn."

"So, I ask again, what happened?"

Tinsdale skipped the question and went back to badgering me. "You should have followed the orders of the Marines assigned to you. It was foolish to stay."

"I was trying to save your bloody petty officer, remember? Why were we left? Don't Marines learn how to count?"

There was a pause. Maybe a five count.

"Panic won't help."

"I haven't panicked yet. I might if someone doesn't tell me what the hell is going on and what you are doing about it."

There was longer pause. I half expected hold music to start playing. While waiting, I climbed onto a counter to get out of the water. After a bit, I tried shouting "hello" into the receiver. It seemed dead and I was wondering what to do about that when a different, more familiar voice spoke.

Chapter Fourteen ~ *Captain Campbell*

"Ms. Kirby, this is Captain Campbell. The *Scranton* has routed you to me."

I could just imagine Tinsdale saying something like, "She's a Canadian. You deal with her."

"Are you going to tell me what's going on?" I asked.

"I know this is very distressing. I'm sure, if we cooperate, we can sort this out."

The impenetrable calm of his voice was less irritating in these circumstances. Better than being badgered. I still wasn't getting answers, and I was ready to channel Dora at any moment now.

"Please, Captain, tell me what is going on."

There was a short pause, as long as a deep breath. "Although we aided in the evacuation, we have not yet been granted access to the station. Nor have the Americans been forthcoming. We think there might have been charges rigged to prevent the base from being captured. I understand that there were some injuries amongst the Americans examining Command and Control and there was an explosion in engineering. Your fellow researchers were recovered safely with only scratches and bruises. They are here, aboard the *Nottawasaga*."

"I noticed that Dora...Dr. Leland had to be helped out."

There was a pause, long enough for a consultation. "She twisted her ankle. Otherwise she is safe and sound. I am being honest with you, Ms. Kirby."

I felt chastised, but shook it off. I had every right to be concerned. "I just wanted to be sure."

I was feeling sorry for myself, and I was dreadfully afraid, but I was polite and trying to at least sound calm. "Is anyone trying to get me out?"

No hesitation this time. "I am."

Okay, I thought. *He's calm and assured. That helps even if I'm not sure whether to believe him.*

"Can you tell me what's happening?"

There was another one of those consultation length pauses. "The *Nottawasaga* will be overseeing a combined rescue operation. We will have you out as soon as possible"

"Is the station sinking?"

Silence.

"Am I sinking?"

"Not for now. The tower is about two metres under the surface and holding. The situation is currently stable."

I nodded in the dark. "Okay. Tell me what's happening. Please."

Another pause. When he spoke, Captain Campbell's voice was cool and professional. "Captain Franchot of the *Émil Gagnan* has directed his mini-subs to assess the damage. Captain Tinsdale's crew is analyzing the station logs and schematics. I will send divers to extricate you when we have a better idea what is going on. We have to go carefully, so we don't make the situation worse. Can you tell me what's happening where you are? As you know, we lost tactical feed. You are now our eyes and ears."

I told him where the breach was, relative to the entry hatch. He asked me to estimate the measurements of both the breach and its location. Warning him that spatial acuity was not my forte, I guessed.

"How much water is on the deck?"

"Where I am, no more than a few centimetres. The deck isn't even and there's more water at the low end."

"Is it still flowing?"

I told him about the flour patch. That made him pause. I might have impressed him. I impressed me. I then told him about trying to open the hatch and being thrown off my feet.

"By the way, what was that about?"

"There were two hull breaches. You slowed the inflow in the galley. The affected compartment in engineering continued to fill. Eventually, it upset the balance of the station. The salvage balloons compensated for a while, then one gave way and the station tipped."

I nodded in the twilight of the emergency lights.

"The power is off," I said. I had forgotten to report that earlier.

"The umbilicals had to be released. Do you have emergency lighting?"

"A dim red light? Yes."

"The batteries were hooked up to the *Scranton* long enough to recharge. You should have at least twelve hours before they run down. We'll have you out long before that.

"And air?"

"Given the size of the room and allowing for moderate activity, you should have enough air. Would you like an exact calculation?"

"Not really."

"So, how are you?"

Stupid question. How the hell was I supposed to be? "Scared shitless. My knee is throbbing, and I'm cold and wet." *Not as cold or wet as I could be*, I thought. The highly unflattering orange-wear had kept out most of the water and a lot of the cold. I revised my statement. "I'm okay. Other than bruises, I'm intact."

"Good. We have some time, what shall we chat about while we wait?"

"Aren't you too busy running things to chat?"

I heard a soft chuckle. "I'm the captain, Ms. Kirby. I make other people busy."

It was a strange conversation. I knew he was only encouraging me to talk to keep my mind off things. Since it seemed to work, I didn't object. I wasn't surprised that I was expected to carry the conversation. I was astonished that he was actually paying attention to my rambling.

He asked me how I started writing. I told him telling stories as a kid and writing one act plays in high school. Then I took journalism at college, worked as a community reporter for the neighbourhood advertiser for next to nothing before getting a regular paying job as a copyeditor with a magazine.

"And then you left it all to work from home."

"My son had some health issues when he was a baby. I wanted to stay home to take care of him. So I started working freelance. Fortunately, by the time my husband left me, I'd met Dora and was getting better contracts."

"And your son?"

"Fit as a fiddle now."

"And a Navy League Cadet, I hear."

It would seem that Gravell had been talking to Captain Campbell about me. Either that, or they had a detailed dossier on me. I wasn't sure I was comfortable with either possibility.

"Still there Ms. Kirby?"

"Nowhere else to go, Captain Campbell."

"Let's keep talking then. Was this the kind of writing you imagined you'd be doing when you were writing school plays?"

I gave a short laugh. "Back then, if you asked me if I wanted to be a ghostwriter, I would have probably thought that meant writing about ghosts and said yes."

I told him about my love of campfire stories. It was one of the few things I really enjoyed about Girl Guide camp. The stories, the campfire, and stars you couldn't see in the city.

"I was a good storyteller. I especially liked telling ghost stories. I could be really scary. Too scary."

"Why too scary?"

I sighed. As a child I used to see ghosts all the time. The scariest part of my ghost stories was that they seemed so real, because they were.

"It was late fall. We were in a huge, two-storey log cabin with six bedrooms. Each room had two double bunk beds, so up to eight girls could sleep there. I was the patrol leader, responsible for them. That time of year, we had to stay in after dinner. Forty pre-teen girls can make even a huge cabin seem small if they aren't quietly occupied. So, I held court and told my patrol, and whoever else wanted to come in and listen, a ghost story about the Black Chicken of Death."

I heard a soft sputtering.

"You can laugh. To be honest, most of the girls laughed. Two of the younger girls were scared shitless. Half an hour later I was told that they were in tears and wanted to go home."

I didn't tell him that the cabin was built on the site of a farmhouse. The area came with a veritable Old Macdonald's Farm of ghosts, including a nearly headless chicken that seemed to have no clue it was dead. The trouble was, now they knew about the chicken, some of the girls could see its ghost, scratching in the snow outside.

"After sharing this information with me, our Guide Captain said she'd rather send me home...which was kinda cold since she was also my mother. So, I had to make good."

"You recanted?"

"No. That's what my mother suggested. She gathered the girls together in the main room. This was where we ate, did crafts, and other activities. It was the one place everyone could congregate. I was supposed to give a public apology and retraction. Instead, I retold and finished the story."

My leg was cramping so I shifted to a more comfortable position.

"Go on, Ms. Kirby."

"Huh? Oh. I told them about the ghostly farm dog that guarded the cabin from all harm."

This part was roughly true. Obviously, the dog took his role very seriously, because he had to have been hanging around for fifty or more years, since the original farmhouse burned down.

"The dog fetched a guardian spirit from the woods, a beautiful young woman with flowing hair."

Okay, she was pretty in an ordinary way, and just another resident ghost. She had always struck me as a benign spirit, so I didn't think she'd mind cast in a semi-angelic role.

"The guardian spirit was able to speak through me, and I spoke in what I imagined was an ethereal tone: 'Fear not, dear girls. The Black Chicken, Harbinger of Death, only foretells the death of chickens. She has shown herself to remind you to be thankful for the chicken fingers you ate for dinner.'"

There was a deep chuckle that faded into a dead silence.

"Sorry," he said, returning, "the com officer was wondering why I was laughing."

So, I wasn't on a speaker. Interesting.

"I have to leave you for a bit. Your intrepid Mr. Neville has come over from the *Émil Gagnan*. I believe he wants to interview you for the documentary. Since we want to keep this line open and you awake, I'm allowing him to talk to you. Stand by."

While I waited for Tim, I decided to risk moving. All the time I was talking to Captain Campbell, I had stayed beside Parker, irrationally afraid that I might lose the signal if I moved. Now I sought out the high ground of the dining table.

Water had seeped in at my collar and cuffs when I was stuffing bags into the hole and crawling about the deck. It wicked the cold past the thermal protection of my orange costume. My hands, feet, and face were frigid. To fight the chill, I stomped and swung my arms until a distorted voice called my name.

"Hey, Jen!"

"Hey, Tim. How is everyone?"

"Everyone is good. Bad luck you got caught in the explosion."

That struck me as a singularly stupid remark. "Yeah, bad luck. Parker had worse. He's dead."

"I'm so sorry."

There was an awkward silence.

"I'm sorry, Tim. None of this is your fault."

"It's okay."

Judging by his tone, he quickly recovered his spirits. "Have you heard? You practically caused an international incident. Rumour has it a couple of Marines are facing a Captain's Mast. That would be something for the documentary, wouldn't it? Not that Tinsdale is going to let us on his boat. Maybe I could get a transcript and we could do a re-enactment. We could do that for the explosion too. Details! I need you to give me details."

I did my best to oblige. He asked me about Parker's death. Where had he been standing? What hit him in the neck? Had he been thrown forward in the explosion? How far away was he from the damaged bulkhead?

I sort of knew where he had been when the lights went out. What happened between then and when I could see him on his knees, I couldn't say. On the other hand, by examining the body, I could tell him that a shard of metal had imbedded itself in his neck.

"What was it like?"

I hesitated, sincerely hoping that he wasn't asking how it felt to have Parker die in my arms.

"The explosion?" I asked.

"That too, but I meant the place. It doesn't look like I'll get a chance to go and look for myself."

"Guess not."

"Was it spooky?"

"Actually, it was eerie how normal it looked. There was no sign of violence or emergency. It looked like everyone just tidied up, went to work and never came back except…"

I stopped.

"What?"

"You'll think I'm nuts."

"Who, me?"

Yes, you, I thought, *and whoever else is listening to this conversation.* If they're recording communications, which was practically given, they would have evidence that I'm looney-toons.

"It felt it feels like not everyone left. It's too tidy. It's as if someone stayed behind to tidy up.

There was a long silence.

I tried to break it, asking, "Did I freak you out?"

Nothing.

"Hello?"

I looked at the phone which was obviously not your average consumer device and wondered if I hit the disconnect button by accident. If I understood the icons correctly, it was still on and almost fully charged. So, why the hell wasn't it working?

"Hello. Is anybody there?" Should I hang up and let them call again? "Hello!"

Reluctantly, I disconnected. When the phone didn't immediately ring, I had to fight down a moment of panic. I looked for a call-back button or something that would give me a menu, afraid to experiment in case I messed something up.

Without the steady flow of conversation, I noticed how cold it was and heard faint, ominous creaking and metallic moans. Nothing wrong with my hearing now. My eyesight was another matter. With the weird shadows created by the emergency lighting, it would be easy to convince myself that I was surrounded by the ghosts of the missing crew.

I used to look for ghosts when I was younger. To this day, I don't know how many were real and how many were the product of my overactive imagination.

Now, not only did I know they were hovering at the edge of my consciousness, I knew I might be joining them soon. I tried to push that possibility aside because that meant leaving my son, and I couldn't bear that thought.

To distract myself, I did a little work.

The deck listed away from the leak, making the damaged bulkhead the driest area in the room. I dragged Parker's body to the higher ground. First, I used the hand-held camera to record his position and took a close up of his wound. Once I had him out of the water, I retrieved his gear, including an almost full water bottle. That lifted my spirits a bit. My bottle was almost empty. I only wish one of us had packed food. I also found a spare headset, which I put on. I was picking his pockets for items to return to his family when the phone rang.

It was on ring number six before my numb fingers found the phone in the pocket where I had tucked it while I worked; ring eight before I connected the headset and was able to answer.

"Are you okay?" Captain Campbell's voice was sharp, worried.

"I'm okay. Where were you?" I checked myself. That had sounded accusatory. "Sorry. The line went dead, so I hung up. I pocketed the phone when you didn't call back immediately. It took me a while to remember what pocket I put it in."

There was a huff of air. Was it a sigh? Or a snort of laughter? Maybe both.

"We were suffering technical difficulties, a few personality difficulties too."

"Oh?"

"Later, Ms. Kirby. In the meantime, my chief medical officer wants to ask you how you are."

"A little colder. A little wetter. I'm still not injured. I don't seem to have a fever. I wish I had a warm blanket and a hot cup of coffee."

"I'll make sure they're waiting for you. Doc insists on grilling you personally, but I'll be back soon."

"You said that last time."

Pause. "This time I promise."

Dr. James Stern introduced himself, and then dove straight into the usual questions. On a scale of one to ten, one being uncomfortably warm and ten being a popsicle, how cold was I? Did I feel any pain? Any numbness? Any dizziness? How about nausea?

I gave him an eight on the cold scale. On the upside, the cold reduced the pain in my knee to a five. I wasn't numb or dizzy, but I had some low-grade nausea, the kind that comes from going too long without food.

"When was the last time you ate?"

"Lunch. I wanted to bring a thermos of coffee and some snacks, but Mary Lou vetoed me. She said we might contaminate the scene. If I live through this, I'm not going to let her live that decision down."

"All going well, you'll soon be able to take her to task. Now tell me about your drinking water."

"I have about two thirds of a bottle."

"Did you check Parker?"

I sighed. "That is Parker's. My bottle is empty. I've been rationing myself but…"

"Don't. Don't ration yourself. I want you to drink half of the water now. You'll stay hydrated longer if you're fully hydrated. Drink the rest in sips when your throat gets dry."

He told me to move around periodically, to keep my circulation going, which I was already doing, and stay out of the water, which would transfer the cold faster than the air. Contradictory advice under the circumstances. There was nowhere to move around that wasn't wet.

"How about air?"

"Moderate activity won't significantly use up your air supply. Don't worry. Hang in there."

Hang in there? Was he serious?

"Hello, Ms. Kirby, I'm back." It was Captain Campbell.

"Any progress?"

"Plenty. We have a working plan. You and I still have a couple of hours or so to wait. Shall we continue our chat?"

"Okay, but you talk for a while. Why did you join the navy?"

"I joined the navy to see the world…mostly I saw the sea."

"You saw the Atlantic and the Pacific, but the Pacific wasn't terrific and the Atlantic isn't what it's cracked up to be," I sang.

"Ms. Kirby?"

"Not crazy. Just a Fred Astaire fan."

There was a pause. "I can't sing, but I can dance a little."

He talked. I talked. It was the kind of conversation you only have with total strangers or best friends. Movie tastes: we both liked screwball comedies. He liked art films. I preferred action flicks. Failed marriages and kids: we both had one of each. His daughter was at the Royal

Military College in Kingston. My son we had already covered. Both of us got along okay with our former spouses. Whatever rancour led to the separations was history. Favourite foods: we were all over the map on that one. We concluded there was enough overlap to be able to go out for dinner when this was all over.

While we chatted, I used the dim red light to strip the memory out of Parker's tactical camera and improvise waterproof containers for the chip and his personal effects. This wasn't as easy as it sounds. My fingers were cold to the point of numbness, and I had to pause, from time to time, to warm them up by stuffing them in my armpits. Periodically I'd jiggle my arms and legs to keep them from stiffening up. I used the pockets in my orange flotation jacket to store the items, and the hand-held. As long as I made it out, even if I didn't survive, the items would get out.

I blink. I must have dozed off. The lights are bright now and the water gone. The galley is shipshape. The bulkhead is intact. People are sitting around me; they don't notice me sitting on the table. Although I can't hear them, they appear to be having an animated discussion. I get out of their way.

I stretch. It feels so good to be able to move around without wading through icy water. I don't even feel cold anymore. The hatch to the living quarters is open. Great! I can leave.

There is someone on one of the bunks, writing in a journal. He doesn't pay any attention to me, he's too intent on what he is writing. What is really strange is that I recognize the journal. I bagged it earlier. The photos and letters posted on the bulkheads are back in place. Plus, there is a photo that I don't remember seeing. It looks like three generations of Navy officers, cut-and-pasted to make a collage. I reach out for it.

"Ms. Kirby!"

"What?"

I had fallen off the table and was half-lying in a foot of blood-freezing seawater. I pulled myself up onto the bench seat.

"Ms. Kirby!"

"I'm here. I guess I fell asleep. And then I just fell."

"Are you okay?"

"I'm okay."

I was lying. I was cold and tired and my throat was feeling raw. I took a sip of water, but it didn't help much. It was so cold it burned.

"I'm sorry I dozed off on you."

"Just don't do it again."

"Aye-aye, Captain."

That came out grumpier sounding than I intended. I adjusted my tone to sound more calm and collected. "How's that working plan going?"

"The plan is fine. We just had a little trouble getting all parties on board. Now that's sorted out, it's just a matter of logistics. Gravell would like to talk to you. Try to stay awake."

Gravell ? What was he doing aboard the *Nottawasaga*?

"How are you doing, Madame Kirby?"

"I've been better. On the bright side, I don't feel seasick."

Instead, I was feeling a heartsick. My brain had finally collated all the clues I had been picking up since my first interview with the captain.

"So, you're the ringer."

Chapter Fifteen ~ *Spooks*

He said nothing. It didn't matter.

"You're the Canadian spook. No wonder Captain Franchot was only looking for the American one. Is your real name is Gravell. How about Jean Luc? Or are you just a *Star Trek* fan? I bet you aren't even married."

Silence. That was fine with me. I wasn't sure that I wanted to talk to him anyway.

When he finally spoke, he sounded a little different. More formal. Less friendly. "I was christened Jean Luc Gravell. Luc Gravell is the name on my driver's license. I never said I was married. You just assumed. Since I qualify for the rank of chief in the merchant marine, going by Chief is not a lie. But yes, I work for the Canadian government."

"CSIS?

"INSET."

Of course, the Integrated National Security Enforcement Team, Dora consulted for them, among other agencies.

"Does Dora know about you?"

"No one on your team knows about me except you. Since you know, I can be direct in my debriefing."

He asked me to go over the events of the afternoon from when we boarded the station to when I was cut off while speaking to Tim. He was particularly interested in my conversation with any members of the *Scranton* crew.

In return, I asked him for an update on the rescue, what the mini-subs had found and the extent of the damage. Surprisingly, he answered my questions, perhaps not fully, but at length. I think that's what lulled me off to sleep.

The man on the bunk looks up from his writing and beckons me over. He shows me the page he was writing. I can't read it. While I watch, he writes one word and underlines it several times: Danger!

"Madame Kirby!"

I started at the sharp voice. "Sorry about that, Chief."

"I understand. You are very tired, but it is not a good idea to fall asleep in the cold."

I knew that. Too bad he didn't know the *Get Smart* reference. It might have lightened the mood.

"I need to move. There's a clear stretch of counter near Parker. I'm going there."

"Is it in line-of-sight with the hatch, Madame Kirby?"

"I think so. I'll check when I get there."

Once I confirmed that I had a clear view of the hatch, I made myself as comfortable as I could. I needed to keep my mind engaged, so I turned on the hand-held camera and switched to play mode. While working my way through the songs in *The Gay Divorcee* to prove I was awake, I went over the footage from the living quarters. I couldn't find the photo I saw in my dream. I did see a gap where it might have hung.

Using the zoom, I looked closer at the photos on the wall. One seemed to be a group shot of the crew. One officer in particular stuck out. He had large, protruding eyes and a long, hook nose. If Gonzo the Muppet were human, he'd look like this. He was the one on the bunk, the one with the journal. Casting my mind back over my files, I put a name to the face, Lieutenant William Minton.

I segued from Fred Astaire and Ginger Rogers, who my mother adored, to *The Muppet Movie,* but only got as far as "The Rainbow Connection" before my voice gave out.

Meanwhile, I retrieved the shoulder bag I had been using to collect the bagged photos and letters. Thank heaven it was waterproof, and I had sealed the opening. It was on the deck beside Parker and had been standing, for who knows how long, in rising seawater. I slung it over my head and shoulder. If I made it out, it was coming with me.

"Madame Kirby?"

"Hmm?"

"You stopped singing."

"My throat's sore. Maybe you should sing to me."

Silence. For a panicked moment, I thought I'd been cut off again. I was still mad, but I didn't want him to go away. Finally he spoke, sounding like the man who brought me coffee and told me to get out of the rain. "When I was talking to you, you fell asleep. If I sing, you might fall into a coma."

I laughed. It hurt. "Good point."

"Perhaps you could hum. Or you could tell me what is engaging your attention."

I hummed the score of *Raiders of the Lost Ark* and turned my attention to the journal. I pulled it out of its plastic bag and strained to read it by the light of the hand-held's blue-screen, not wanting to waste the batteries by using the filming lights. I skipped over the first part which had been written as though ink and space were in short supply. Later, he was less stingy and more worrying.

They're playing poker again. Mitch thinks I should join in. He knows I disapprove of gambling—even if the stakes are penny-ante. No real harm, he says. Perhaps he's right about the gambling, but they smoke and drink. The smoke makes me sick and the drink makes them obnoxious.

I stared at the table. I could barely see it. That was all right. What I wanted to see was the vision from my dream.

I never heard ghosts, but I sometimes I could see their memories, some of their memories, in dreams. I was hoping for a waking dream now.

Minton, the journal writer, was spying on the group. I was seeing through his eyes.

Four men sit around the table. There is coffee, no cards, no chips, no flask being passed from man to man. The faces wear expressions ranging from worried to belligerent. Doc Dawes is tapping a finger as he listens to Boreman, who is punctuating his statements with table thumps. Kant is fiddling with a cigarette pack, turning it over and over in his hands. Golanger seems worried. He keeps looking around and gesturing Boreman to keep it down.

Commander Shore enters the room he says a few words. Boreman and Golanger leave. Then Dawes takes the Commander aside. Shore nods towards the storage area, towards me. Towards Minton.

Where is Naire? Where is Margolo?

"Madame Kirby?"

"Chief Gravell?"

"You're not sleeping are you?"

"I don't think so."

"Then what?"

I hesitated. What did I want to admit to? Who could I trust?

"You can trust me," he said, as though I had voiced the last comment aloud. Had I?

"No offense, but you'd say that if I couldn't trust you—especially if I couldn't trust you. *C'est vrai, n'est pas?*"

He made something between a huff and a guffaw. It was true. "You can trust me to act in the best interests of our country and your safety."

Fair enough, I thought. Of course there would be an agent of the Canadian government on board the *Èmil Gagnan.* The whole crew could be spies. Truth be told, my anger was fading as my pragmatic side asserted itself.

"Madame Kirby?"

"I've been reading a journal. I think that whatever happened was the result of a conflict between one or more members of the crew."

"You found proof in the journal?"

"Not proof, indication. I think the writer is..." I searched for the term, "a person of interest in the investigation."

"Perhaps this is something we should keep between us, at least for now."

I almost laughed. "Who am I going to tell? The only other person I've been talking to at length is the captain."

Pause.

"It probably won't come up, but it would be better if you don't discuss it at all. Not until you are safely out of there."

I made a mental checklist. I had talked to Captain Campbell. He was okay. Dr. Stern might think I was crazy. The com officer talked to me. I talked to Tim just before I got cut off.

I had a bad feeling. "What was the technical difficulty, Chief Gravell? Who or what disconnected me earlier. Could Tim have accidentally hit a wrong button?"

Silence, then, "We don't know yet."

If Tim touched something he shouldn't, that was accident. What if it was someone on the *Scranton* who blocked the signal?

"You don't know. Can you guess?"

There was a brief, but ominous pause. I realized, too late, that the *Scranton* was probably monitoring our communication.

"Sing, Madame Kirby, or hum. It won't be much longer now."

I strained to read a few more pages. Something disturbing had happened here. Something disturbing might be happening again.

Chapter Sixteen ~ *Voices in the Dark*

I didn't believe for a moment that I was cut off due to technical difficulties. Human agency was the cause, I was sure of it. The captain mentioned personality difficulties. Based on what I was reading in Minton's journal, I think the station crew suffered personality difficulties too.

I found myself humming the "Imperial March" from *Star Wars* in a dirge tempo. Above me, a story of power was being played out between the *Émil Gagnan* , the *Nottawasaga,* and the *Scranton*. The Empire wanted to protect its secrets. The Dominion wanted to protect its sovereignty. The feisty rebels wanted truth, justice, and a good story. Did a similar power struggle occur in the past? Had the station been infiltrated? Was it mutiny?

Okay, a little melodramatic. The place was getting to me.

I put away the journal and made sure the satchel was properly sealed. So far, that little book was my only witness to the events. I didn't want anything happening to it.

Segueing into "Luke's Theme," I pulled my legs up on the counter. I was cold and tired, and I wanted someone to talk to me. At the same time, I didn't want to interrupt the process of getting me out.

I sang, "Kind friends and companions, come join me in rhyme. Come lift up your voices in chorus with mine."

A rich baritone voice joined me.

"Come lift up your voices, all grief to refrain, for we may or might never all meet here again."

"Chief Gravell?"

"Yes, Madame Kirby."

I thought so, but it was a bit—no very— unexpected. "Chief Gravell, you haven't just undermined your credibility for my sake, have you?"

He laughed, low and throaty. "No, Madame Kirby, my credibility is still intact. It's a well-known fact that all sailors sing. Besides, that's a sea shanty. I'm curious how you know it."

"I learned the song listening to one of my son's video games."

The emergency light was a faint red glow. Otherwise, the room was black. However, it no longer felt like the dark and cold was closing in on me. I no longer saw nor sought the ghosts of the past. Maybe they were waiting for me but, for now, I was doing my best to stay connected to the living.

I worked my way through my repertoire which ran the gamut from the old jazz standards my mother loved, through the classic rock and roll my father enjoyed, to the more singable pop songs my son listened to repeatedly. Gravell sang along to the jazz and rock standards. I also wracked my brain for sea shanties and French folk songs he might know. I had no idea how much time had passed since the explosion. Judging by my voice, I had been down there a hundred years.

"What other songs do you know?" I croaked.

There was a pause. For a moment I feared that I had been cut off again.

"I regret, Madame Kirby, that is a question I will have to answer another time. The doctor wants to talk to you again."

Dr. Stern asked me the familiar questions, making sure I still knew who and where I was. When he was done, I countered with my own question.

"So, do I still have all my marbles?"

"You seem to have a full set. Just remember, there's plenty of air trapped in there with you. Cold is your worst enemy. Try not to fall asleep. Keep moving."

Yeah right, I thought. As I discovered the hard way, the water was deeper. It came half way up to my knees. Even so, I got up and sloshed around. It did help. Maybe Doc did know best.

Then I heard the captain's voice again. "I'm sorry to have left you so long. You'll be happy to know my time was well spent."

There was a moment of silence, perhaps another consultation. Then the captain continued. "Normally we would either send a diving bell down to extract you or try to raise the station using the salvage balloons still attached. I won't go into technical details. Neither option is feasible at the moment. So, we've sent divers down with rescue gear to get you. They're on their way now and will enter via the breach in engineering."

"Okay," I said, although I suspected that the situation was anything but.

"Brace yourself. There might be a shudder when they blow the hatch in engineering. and another when they enter the galley. I'll let you know when they get close. Meanwhile, stay clear of the hatch and be prepared to move quickly when they reach you."

There was a slight pause. "It's unlikely that we will be able to retrieve Petty Officer Parker's body, so, Captain Tinsdale asks if you would bring his camera with you."

"The whole camera or just the memory-card?"

There was a short pause. "The card will do. And his dog tags, if you can find them. They'll probably be in a pocket."

I told him that I had both.

"There should be two tags."

"I know. One goes in his mouth. I did that too."

I am a treasure trove of trivia. Sometimes it comes in handy.

"Just leaving it on his person would have been sufficient."

And sometimes my trivia is out of date.

The captain picked up an earlier conversation about favourite authors. While we compared Zane Grey to Louis L'Amour and debated the relative merits of thrillers versus mysteries, I listened for the first explosion. When it came, I didn't hear it so much as felt it.

"Okay, Ms. Kirby. They're ready to come through. We won't be able to talk for a while. Regardless, I want you to keep the line open as long as possible so I can hear you…Good luck."

"Thank you, Captain. For everything."

Pause.

"It has been my pleasure. Stand by."

Patting my pockets and collection satchel to ensure everything was in place, I slid off the counter into icy water and braced myself. Good job I did. If I hadn't been holding onto the counter, I would have been knocked off my feet by the explosion. Instead, it was the rushing water that made me fall.

Once I got my feet under me, I had to fight the flow and the inclination of the deck to get to the hatch. No doubt it was my imagination, but I felt as though hands pushed me from behind. Then, real and solid hands grasped my outstretched arms and pulled me into the firm grasp of two divers: one tall and slender; one shorter and square. A diving mask was pushed over my face. It was linked to a spare tank on the taller one's back.

Clean air. Until then, I hadn't realized how stale the air had become in the hours since I was trapped. The compressed air was an elixir, keeping me on my feet when I felt ready to collapse.

The water stopped rushing, but it continued to rise as we proceeded through the gloom. For a moment, in the living area, I thought I saw the man on the bunk get up and walk toward me. I blinked and the vision was gone. We passed the steps that led to Command and Control and cut through the auxiliary control room to the hatch that led to engineering.

With hand signals, the divers let me know the way out was underwater. I nodded and did exactly as indicated, which included hanging up the phone and giving it to one of the divers.

That was hard. Even though I couldn't hear or speak to the captain, I felt connected. Now I wasn't.

The spare tank was transferred to my back. Until we submerged, the tank felt heavy on my tired shoulders.

It was surreal, like living through a Hollywood disaster movie. They guided me through an underwater obstacle course of machinery and debris. One or both of them kept hold of me at all times. The hull breach appeared. One edge looked raw and burnt. The rest of the opening was smooth in comparison. No doubt they had widened the hole to gain access. We sidled through, one-by-one, then my guides took a firm hold of me again.

If I had thought the water was icy in the galley, I was wrong. In the open water, I could feel the cold cut through my protective garments and burn the exposed parts of my face. It seemed to squeeze me, taking my breath away. One of the divers sensed my distress and signalled me to take deep breaths. At least, I think that was what the hand gestures were meant to convey.

They pulled me onward. A rescue basket appeared and they helped me inside. Then, very slowly, I was hauled in like the catch of the day.

Chapter Seventeen ~ *Nottawasaga*

The divers swam alongside, hanging onto the outside. Three other divers were visible on nearby cables where working lights illuminated the cockeyed base and its ring of overworked salvage balloons. The play of light and shadow made it look like a thing of flesh and blood, not metal. I watched the sea monster slowly recede and was surprised when we finally broke the surface and a crane hauled us up onto the deck of the *Nottawasaga*.

After the gloom of the galley, and the twilight shadows of the dimly illuminated water, the lights on deck blinded me. We were greeted by a cheer that was deafening.

One of the divers helped me out of the basket. People rushed forward. Strong arms supported me. My legs were so shaky. Someone gently removed my mask and lifted the tank off my shoulders.

"Thank you," I croaked, peering into the face of the diver holding me up. She had her mask off and smiled at me. I couldn't hear the words, there was too much noise, but I could read her lips.

"You're welcome."

I then turned to thank the other diver. He took my hand and squeezed it firmly. Other hands reached out to me, patting my shoulders and gently moving me along. I had no clue where. I was surrounded by well-wishers. I tried to offer my thanks for their work on my behalf. My voice seemed to have disappeared. That, and the kaleidoscope of washed-out colours that passed for my vision, made me feel like I was caught in a dream.

Someone wrapped a blanket around my shoulders and guided me away from the crowd, the bright lights, and the confusing buzz of noise. I was peeled out of my orange-wear. A fresh, heated blanket was wrapped around me. Then I was gently pushed into a wheelchair.

Someone, I assumed a paramedic, checked my pulse and oxygen saturation with one of those monitors that clip on your finger. A thermometer was aimed at my forehead and the gloriously warm blanket was shifted so a blood pressure cuff could be wrapped around my arm. The air that seemed warm after the water, felt cold now. As a reward for my suffering, he handed me a cup of juice. I wasn't sure what kind of juice it was, but the sweet-tart, syrupy liquid was like high-test to a grinding motor.

"She's cold, dehydrated, and a good candidate for pneumonia," he announced.

I recognized the voice as Dr. Stern's. He turned to me and I was surprised how young he was. His voice and country doctor' manners had led me to picture a man in his fifties, either tall and thin, or padded and short. This man was thirty-something, fit, trim, and almost handsome enough to play a surgeon on TV.

"You're mine now, Ms. Kirby," he said, giving me a twisted grin and suggestive waggle of his brows.

I shook my head.

"Not yet."

Though lubricated, my voice was still rough. Sore too. It hurt to talk.

"I have to see the captain first."

"I'm right here," said a familiar voice.

My heart jumped. I turned toward the speaker.

He was right beside me. He had been there all the time. Rumpled, unshaven, wearing a jacket and watch-cap, I hadn't recognized him for the scrupulously well-groomed commander I had interviewed twice.

"Captain Campbell?"

"In the flesh."

I jumped out of the chair and threw my arms around him. Worse, I started to cry on his shoulder. He was very gracious about it. After only a moment's hesitation, he held me tight with one arm while the other patted my shoulder soothingly.

Eventually, I brushed tears off my face and allowed the captain to ease me back into the wheelchair. The satchel was at my back. I was about to say something, but the doctor put a fresh warm blanket around me, passed me another cup of juice, and admonished his superior to bring me to sick bay ASAP or he'd exercise his CMO's prerogative. I decided the satchel could stay put.

"I need to tell you…" I started.

The captain stopped me with a shake of his head.

"Business, before pleasure, Ms. Kirby."

I was about to tell him this was business. Then I saw the reason for his interruption.

A USN officer and a Marine contingent of three, including Dippel and Madison, were waiting. Perhaps they had always been waiting, but now I could see them. The world was back in focus. That juice was marvellous stuff. I took another gulp.

The officer stepped towards me.

"Lieutenant Redding?"

"Ms. Kirby. It's good to see you."

"Good to be seen."

He smiled. "I know you want to rest, but Captain Tinsdale is anxious to get the memory chip from the tactical camera and Petty Officer Parker's dog tags."

"I totally forgot."

The look on his face was comical.

I took pity and clarified quickly. "The chip and Petty Officer's personal effects are wrapped in vintage cellophane in one of the inside pockets of my flotation jacket. I forgot to take them out before they were taken away."

I looked at Captain Campbell, who transferred the gaze to a group of armed crewmen standing nearby three Canadians to balance the three Marines. One stepped forward.

"This way, sir," the man said, his deep, smooth voice immediately identifying him to me.

I gave Rankin a smile. He responded with a slight nod of the head.

Redding nodded and signalled one of his Marines. "Take care of it, Gunny."

Dippel separated from the trio and followed his Canadian counterpart. Redding turned back to me.

"Captain Tinsdale has ordered," he hesitated and his tone inserted quotation marks around the next few words. "He ordered the temporarily confiscation of all research materials aboard the *Émil Gagnan* pending a thorough investigation." That includes the hand-held camera Parker was using."

"It's also in one of the pockets of the jacket," I told him.

"The captain is also making a formal request to debrief Ms. Kirby."

Captain Campbell's tone and posture was stiff. "Not in the foreseeable future."

I didn't heave a sigh of relief, but I wanted to.

Redding took the news stoically. "Fair enough. Maybe we can have an informal chat later, Mrs. Kirby."

He took his leave and the captain started pushing me, presumably to sick bay.

"Captain, I still have to talk to you."

"I know. Do you think you can walk? Otherwise, you're in for a bumpy ride."

I remembered all the coamings I had to step over when I was brought onboard last time, and decided that I could walk. With only a little shakiness, I stood. Automatically, I put the satchel over my shoulder.

The captain took my arm in such a way that he supported part of my weight, without making it obvious. I was grateful for the help.

We didn't go far. There was a small canteen on deck for crew to take breaks. No one was in it. He signalled one of the armed seamen to stand watch and make sure we remained undisturbed. He helped me sit so that the warm blanket stayed on my shoulders. Then he brought me coffee. I was so grateful, I started to cry again. He sat and put an arm around my shoulders until I calmed down.

It was very comfortable and comforting, but I knew I needed to pull myself together. That meant pulling myself away.

"Thank you for coming to my rescue, Captain. I suspect Captain Tinsdale would have let me go down with the ship."

He turned and looked at me sharply. "No. Not that."

I shrugged, unconvinced. "Did the Americans scuttle the base? Will they?"

"I don't honestly know. His team found something in C and C before the explosions. I don't know the particulars yet. You and your group are safe. They are all on board and Gravell has sent a few men to join the crew of the salvage ship to ensure they are secure—which raises a problematic issue."

"Am I going to blow his cover?"

He nodded.

"Probably. I won't be able to hide the truth from Dora. She knows me too well."

"Will Dr. Leland keep the information to herself?"

I thought about that. I wouldn't put it past Dora to have spotted Chief Gravell's deception by now. I worked it out and she was a helluva lot smarter than me. "She might have been keeping his secret all along. Or she might not have sussed him out, in which case she'll be too angry to keep quiet. On the whole, I think Gravell should come clean. It would be simpler."

He nodded. "That's what Captain Franchot advises too, and I concur."

I nodded, then sighed. "They took the artifacts we collected on the station, didn't they?"

He nodded. "I am going to get the material back—intact if possible. I am making the safety of the *Émil Gagnan* and your research group a sovereignty issue."

"Thank you."

He covered one of my hands with his. "Captain Tinsdale isn't a bad person. He has a job to do. That's all."

I looked down at my hand, engulfed in his. He was not an exceptionally tall man, but his hands were big and his shoulders broad, besides which, I am a rather short woman. I felt small beside him, which was odd because generally I had enough ego to overcome my deficiency in height. My ex never made me feel like this, though he towered above me physically. Maybe that's why I chose my next words carefully.

"Captain, I don't want you to take offence. Know that I would trust you with my life, and I appreciate, more than I can tell you, what you did for me, but I need to know, can I trust you with something a bit more…" I fought to find the right word. "…controversial?"

"How will you know you can trust my word?"

"If you give it, I'll trust it. I'll also understand if you feel you can't give it."

He gave my hand a squeeze. "It's given."

Reluctantly, I retrieved my hand from his grasp so could I open the satchel and pulled out the bagged journal and re-sealed it.

"These are photographs and personal letters," I said, tapping the satchel. "I have the permission of the families involved to scan the items for the purposes of the book and documentary, before they are returned to the survivors of the deceased. Can you make sure Dr. Leland gets them in the meantime?"

"Yes."

I unzipped the front of my coverall. Tucked in my bra, in the valley between my breasts was my smartphone.

"All my notes are backed up here. I'm going to be unconscious soon. I need to know they'll be safe."

I closed it, put it on top of the journal, and held them out.

He wrapped both of his hands around my hand, the journal, and the case. His clear grey eyes found mine and locked them in his gaze. "They'll be safe."

I was put to bed with an IV drip with prophylactic antibiotics. A pleasant young woman with the insignia of a medic sat with me until I fell asleep, maybe longer. She introduced herself. Her name didn't register. If I dreamed that first stretch, I don't remember. When I woke, the woman was gone. Instead, a faint, ghostly figure stood looking down at me. I knew I wasn't asleep; I did wonder if I was crazy. Now I was no longer trapped, I wondered how much of what I experienced was real.

"Lieutenant Minton?"

The ghost nodded.

"You followed me?"

He gave a half nod, half shake and held up a ghostly copy of his journal. He tapped it meaningfully.

"You come with the book?"

He nodded.

"Am I going crazy?"

He grinned and shook his head.

"Well, that's a relief."

"Ms. Kirby?"

The medic walked through Minton's shade and he disappeared.

"Do you need something?" she asked.

"Something to drink would be nice. That juice was good. It tasted like orange juice and felt like the elixir of life."

She chuckled. "The Doc's special blend," she said. "I'll go get some."

After she left, I whispered, "Will Minton?"

Nothing.

Maybe I was crazy.

The next time I woke, Dr. Stern was standing over me, removing my IV.

"Good morning, Ms. Kirby. May I call you Jen?"

I nodded.

"Call me Doc, everyone does. Of course, some call me Grumpy behind my back."

I smiled.

"That's better," he said, smiling back. "How do you feel?"

"Achy and tired, but better than last night."

"That's a good start. We need to make sure you don't succumb to pneumonia. The air quality down there wasn't as good as I hoped and you were chilled to the bone when you got to me."

"You've given me antibiotics. So, the next thing is bed rest alternating with short walks to keep my lungs clear."

"You know the protocol."

"My mother had chronic pneumonia due to emphysema. I spent a lot of time with her, in and out of the hospital."

"Smoker?"

"Yes."

"You?"

"No."

He heaved a sigh. "Good for you. Still, we'll be extra careful, won't we?"

I agreed and let myself be led around the room, though I felt as limp as a dishrag. It was a bit creepy. This is what I had done for my mother, walked her around gently, supporting her when she felt weak.

After my walk, I was allowed some food. Since I had slept through breakfast, I had lunch. A little while later, the captain stopped by for a visit.

"You look healthier. Doc said I should walk you. I pointed out that you were not the family dog. Still, I agreed to take you for a stroll if you feel up to it. I thought you might want to get some fresh air."

I was wearing scrubs as pyjamas, not the ubiquitous hospital gown. All I needed were shoes and a jacket. Petty Officer Briseau, my Florence Nightingale, provided a pair of running shoes. The captain had anticipated the need for a coat and had brought a windbreaker with him.

This was no cruise ship. There was a big gun on the forward deck and a landing pad near the aft deck. Instead of sturdy rails with gates, like the *Émil Gagnan* , there were cables rigged between posts and chains with hook and eye-like closures at egress points. It made me nervous to get so close to the side, but Captain Campbell seemed confident so I grabbed a post and looked outward.

From the frigate, the *Émil Gagnan* seemed tiny. The *Scranton* looked a bit surreal, large straight on and yet so narrow like a cardboard cut-out of a submarine. The three vessels made a lopsided triangle around the station which was visible as a dark patch in the water.

I felt a presence on the opposite side of the captain. Faintly, I could see Minton's outline. Though the light of day made him seem more transparent, he also seemed more there than when he visited me earlier.

"You have the book with you," I said, making an intuitive leap.

"Yes," Campbell replied, surprised. "And your phone. I thought you might want them now that you were awake."

He handed them over.

"Have you looked at this?" I asked, holding up Minton's journal.

He hesitated. "If I knew that this came from the station, I would be bound to turn it over to the Captain Tinsdale. Of course, I passed the other material you were carrying over to Dr. Leland before that request was made, so those items are out of my hands. Nor do I feel any obligation to turn over your personal property. So, I assume this is yours, and I would not violate your privacy by reading your personal journal. And if you are going to tell me that you copied the digital video from Petty Officer Parker's camera onto your smartphone, I don't want to know. In fact, we didn't have this conversation at all."

I stuffed the journal in one pocket and the smartphone in the other.

"So, what have we been talking about?"

"Your son. I understand that you have been emailing him daily. After what you've been through, I thought you might want to make a video call before you leave the *Nottawasaga*. You won't be able to give details, but he should know what a hero his mother is."

I think I blushed, and I know I had trouble meeting his gaze. "I didn't feel very heroic. In fact, I'm not sure I would have held it together if it wasn't for you and Chief Gravell."

He lifted my chin, forcing eye contact. "I think you would have managed. Speaking for myself at least, it was an honour to have been of service. But tell me, does this mean you've forgiven Chief Gravell?"

"I'm not sure I'd go that far."

I had forgiven him for lying. I imagine that was part of his job description. I hadn't forgiven him for making me like him.

Doc wasn't happy with my heightened colour when I returned. My flush wasn't solely due to embarrassment. I had a low-grade fever. Confined to bed for the rest of the day, I slept through the afternoon. Visitors were kept away. Even the ghost left me alone.

After dinner, Chief Gravell came to take my statement of events on the station. He confirmed that a security detail was on board the *Émil Gagnan* and that things were going smoothly now.

"Does that mean that they are trying to raise the station again?"

"No, not that."

"Are the Americans are going to sink the station."

"No. That's not going to happen immediately either."

"Have you come clean to the team—Dora at least?"

"More or less."

I tried to find out more. I don't think he would have given me the time of day unless it had been cleared first. Still, he must have said something, because I fell asleep listening to his voice.

"This is the most significant mission I have ever taken part in. This is my chance to show that I have the right stuff."

These are the opening sentences of the journal. They are followed by details about the long, slow trip, towing the station through the Arctic waters. I read them over the shoulder of Minton, who is sitting in the wardroom. The aroma of sweet, milky tea wafts on the steam from the mug by his left hand.

Two men enter. One gives him a warm welcome. The other teases him about burying his nose in work again. They are his friends: Mitch Shore and Margolo. The faint aroma of cigar smoke clings to them mixed

with the scent of damp salty air.
   Minton smiles.
   "I am a lucky man to have such friends," he writes.

A trickle of sweat hits the page. Minton is now sitting on his bunk on the station. Bitterness twists his features.
   He flips through the journal to the next blank page. Wiping the sweat from his brow with the sleeve of his uniform, he takes a deep breath and gags. He swallows a couple of times, then starts writing.
   "I am cursed to be here with a crew of mad men..."

Dora Leland visited as soon as she was allowed, which was while I was trying to force down breakfast the next morning. She was beside herself with indignation over the affaire and hardly noticed that I was in a cold sweat from the dreams I had suffered overnight.

"The team is being removed. The crew of the *Émil Gagnan* was told to recover their equipment."

She punctuated her sentences with broad arm gestures that reminded me, as usual, of John Cleese in his *Fawlty Tower* days.

"Franchot is stalling. Even Gravell is being helpful, though we all know he was sent to spy on us. I need to get some political clout behind us to back us up. US Navy divers are preparing to scuttle the base, which they say is too dangerous to salvage. Bullocks! Our crew thinks otherwise. I'll say this, however, Captain Campbell isn't as useless as I thought. He's managed to get the Americans to return our equipment and notes. Not the artifacts, though. Mary Lou is raising hell and Reuben is threatening legal action."

She sniffed and pulled a seat up to my bedside.

"You look terrible," she said, looking at me properly for the first time. "I had some work for you, but I think I'll ask Mary Lou instead. You rest. Try to get some sleep."

When she left, I hoped to take a walk on deck. Instead, I received a visit from Lieutenant Redding looking for information under cover of returning my laptop and finding out how I was.

We played a little game for the next half hour. He tried to grill me without seeming to do so and I did my best to wheedle information out of him. Neither party got any satisfaction. Eventually Dr. Stern came to my rescue and kicked Redding out. Exhausted, I decided I really wasn't up to a walk on deck after all. This time, I didn't need Gravell or Gravol to help me sleep.

I am back on the station. I'm not seeing through Minton's eyes, it more like I'm sitting on his shoulder. I'm the ghost here, watching him write in his journal.

"I am concerned. I don't know why Mitch picked these men out of all the men that applied. Golanger is earnest, if nothing else. He is clean-living and makes an honest effort to work up to my standards. I wish he didn't hang on Boreman's sleeve, but at least he doesn't copy the man's vices.

"Kant doesn't take our situation seriously enough. He thinks it's all one great adventure. On the job, he performs well. In his off time, he spends so much time reading fantasy novels, I fear he will lose grip on reality."

Minton reacts to a noise. He tucks his journal out of sight and picks up an engineering journal. Boreman enters, giving him a friendly nod on the way to his bunk. The man strips down to his skivvies. Minton's nose wrinkles in disgust. Boreman stretches like a gorilla, holding on to the bottom rail of his upper bunk with one hand, then dropping his body down and backwards until his joints crack. Then he repeats the move with his other hand. Dropping to the floor, he does thirty push-ups and thirty sit-ups. Finally, he grabs his towel and leaves his superior officer in peace.

"Boreman is the worst," Minton writes. "He's too smart for a non-com. I think there is more to him than meets the eye. He is trying to intimidate me into leaving him alone. It won't work."

Now Minton's hand is shaking. Sweat is seeping from every pore. Red rimmed eyes look up in my direction, unseeing. He starts writing, the words are barely scribbles.

When I woke, my duffle bag from the *Émil Gagnan* was sitting beside my bunk. Briseau poked her head in soon as I tried to sit up.

"Feeling better?"

"Much," I lied. I pointed at my luggage. "Does this mean I'm allowed to get dressed?"

"Allowed and encouraged. You've been invited to dine with the captain in the wardroom. I'll help you shower. Believe me, unless you've been on a naval vessel before, you'll need help with the shower your first time using it."

It was all more complicated and time consuming than I had anticipated. Eventually I was clean, and I looked forward to putting on real clothes. There was only one problem. I had been using my duffle as a laundry hamper. Someone grabbed that and didn't look for anything else. I opted for reasonably clean, but rumpled khaki pants and my new best friend, Sophie Briseau, brought me a pristine white t-shirt from ship's stores. I even managed to put on a little makeup because at least they picked up my toiletries. In the middle of my preparations, the doctor showed up in dress uniform. He checked my vitals and declared me fit for limited duty, including dinner. Then he took my arm and offered to be my escort.

If I had been thinking straight, I should have realized I was not in for an intimate soirée. But no, I was caught flat-footed.

Chapter Eighteen ~ *Reconstruction*

Dora greeted me, glass of wine in hand. She had more forethought than I. She'd brought a silk knit tunic, which made her the dressiest civilian in the room. The navy personnel were all in pristine, crisply pressed whites. The research team looked drab in comparison.

"Good news! Captain Campbell has arranged a stay of execution."

"Who won't be walking the plank?" I asked.

"Not who, what," said the doctor.

Dora shook her head. "Are you sure Jen should be up and around? She seems out of it."

"I'm standing here, Dora. I'm fine. I just needed a little context."

Dora huffed.

The doctor patted me on the shoulder. "She'll get better faster if she get up and around."

Now the doctor was talking about me as if I wasn't there. I was tempted to walk off, but I still felt a bit shaky.

A steward touched my elbow. I jumped, almost spilling his tray of appetizers. He made a great save.

"Sorry, ma'am. I just wondered if you wanted something."

The tray held mini quiches and tiny sausage rolls. I took a couple of the cherry tomatoes that garnished the platter.

"Can I get you a glass of wine, ma'am?"

The steward was actually a Leading Seaman. His kitchen whites had his rank and name attached.

"Thank you, Leading Seaman Ogilvie, but I'd prefer a coffee if possible."

Ogilvie looked past me. Was he checking with the doctor?

"I think that's been taken care of, ma'am."

I turned around. It was Chief Gravell, wearing his usual black except that a double-breasted jacket replaced his windbreaker. He kept his distance until I got over my surprise. He no doubt had seen what happened when I was startled and didn't want coffee all over him. As soon as he passed me the mug, I wrapped both hands around it, enjoying its warmth. It seemed like I couldn't get warm enough these days.

"Thank you."

"Well done on the rank recognition, Jen," said the doctor.

"Madame Kirby has a son in cadets and has, no doubt, helped him memorize the ranks. Am I correct?"

I gave Gravell a nod and a smile. "I also know the NATO phonetic alphabet. I have to admit, it helps that Seamus was recently promoted from Leading to Master Seaman."

"Very well done for an eleven-year-old."

Yup, I was definitely getting over being mad at Gravell. I'm not sure what won me over the most, that he brought me coffee, or that he praised my son. Probably the coffee.

Dora was a bit more cynical. "Don't get too warm and fuzzy with him. He's still a spook."

I shivered. It was like someone had opened the door and let in a cold draft. I didn't see anything, but it occurred to me that if a ghost was in the room, he might find Dora's statement amusing. The thought made me smile, but I also pulled my coffee closer to my chest, trying to spread the warmth.

"She's chilled," Dora said, directing herself to the doctor.

"Maybe it was too soon for her to be out of bed."

"I'm okay! I'll be even better if you two stop talking about me like I'm not here."

Dora turned to me, taking in my outfit. She could be a bit oblivious about such things. "No wonder you're cold. You only have a t-shirt on. Silly."

Before I could defend my wardrobe choices, a bell was rung and we were called to the table.

I was led to the seat at Captain Campbell's right. Dora was ushered to the seat on his left. Tim, who was the only member of the documentary crew present, pulled out the chair for Dr. Leland with uncharacteristic gallantry. He took the seat beside her.

The captain, doctor, and Gravell went for my seat at the same time. Tim gave me a knowing smirk. The captain won by virtue of rank. Dr.

Stern then took the seat beside me for medical reasons, he said.

Other officers guided the other researchers to their places. Left to their own devices, I think the team would have lined up along Dora's side of the table. The Us versus Them seating was avoided. Lieutenant Redding, the only dinner guest from the *Scranton*, was placed at the far end of the table, about as far away from me as possible, which was fine with me. I wondered if he had brought Marines with him this time. I looked around. No Marines. Maybe they weren't invited to the party.

Dr. Stern patted my hand. Someone had asked me a question. How was I?

I smiled apologetically at the speaker, a lieutenant sitting next to Tim. "I'm a bit tired, still a bit spacey. Mostly I'm thankful to be in the warmth and light."

Tim gave a knowing nod. "It was a near thing for a while. But all's well that ends well."

I looked over to Captain Campbell. His expression was bland. It was hard to tell what he was thinking.

Not so, Dora. "Well? You call that ending well? All our work and the Americans want to sink the station. If nothing else, you should be upset for the sake of the documentary."

Chastised, Tim shut up and Redding took up the gauntlet.

"The documentary isn't worth it if someone else dies, right Captain Campbell?"

The captain said nothing, one way or the other.

Dora replied, "The crew of the *Émil Gagnan* is willing to try."

"With all due respect ma'am…"

Captain Campbell cleared his throat noisily. Redding's mouth snapped shut. "For the benefit of our civilian guests, I should point out that controversial topics are barred at the table until after the meal."

On cue, the soup—crab bisque—was served. This was followed by a garden salad, before a roast of beef was brought the sideboard to be carved and distributed. I didn't think I was hungry until I was faced by a slice of tender, medium rare beef, roast vegetables, and Yorkshire pudding. If Doc had let me, I would have gone for seconds. He warned me to save room for the *crème brulée*.

Once the plates were removed and the coffee served, Dora immediately started arguing her case. Reuben and Mike added their mite, Reuben with the relentlessness of a courtroom lawyer and Mike with the pragmatism of a mechanic. In the opposite corner, Redding and a couple of the *Nottawasaga* officers pointed out the dangers of raising the station again.

Captain Campbell intervened. "Perhaps, we would better spend our time making the most of the information gathered so far."

It was plain that Redding was not pleased by this suggestion. I don't think any of our team was anxious to share information either. It was one of the *Nottawasaga* officers that broke the ice.

"We know the engine room had been shut down. The nuclear piles were properly damped. There is no evidence of residual radiation."

"Nothing we could detect," said Redding.

Mike made a derisive snort. "Interesting, that we almost got blown up, but everyone was clear of engineering when it exploded. No military casualties."

Reuben raised a hand. "You're forgetting Petty Officer Parker was killed. Also, there were some injuries in C&C when the controls shorted. Just because the Navy wants to scuttle the station now, a decision I plan to fight, doesn't mean that they rigged the explosions."

A Canadian officer spoke up. "I heard they found something and that's what triggered the bombs."

Captain Campbell held up a hand. "Let's not indulge in hearsay, Mr. Jones."

Mr. Jones, who was a woman, blushed and pursed her lips as if she wanted to defend herself, but knew better than to contradict the captain.

"I think CIA operatives planted the bombs," said Jamal.

Tim put the damper on this time. "Let's not go there without proof. That kind of thing happens in movies. We need to keep this real."

Jamal, who had been encouraged by Tim before, was surprised by the rebuke. So was I, but I thought better of Tim for not taking the flashy angle.

I let the conversation go on without me. I heard the discussion, only half-listening. The other half of my attention was elsewhere.

There is a theory that we take in far more information than we can process at the time, yet all that information is stored. Many psychic experiences can be explained away by this discrepancy between perception and processed information.

At that moment, I was back in the galley, moments before the explosion, seeing things I had perceived, but not noticed. It was neat and clean, just like the living quarters had been. In my vision, or hallucination, when I saw the crew sitting around arguing and then saw their quarters, there was the normal clutter that accumulates over time. Before the explosion, despite having sunk, nothing was out of place. It was almost as pristine as it had appeared in my dreams, before the blood started flowing. What little shifting of materiel there had been seemed to have happened when the base was pulled up or so the faint dust patterns suggested. Before being abandoned, the place had been cleaned up.

They were still talking about the explosions and what could have caused them. Redding was pushing the notion that it was a malfunction of the security systems. Jamal was still convinced it was sabotage, though he shifted to blaming a foreign agency. Dora leaned towards a single human agent, the result of sociopathic or psychopathic behaviour.

"There were three explosions," I said, cutting through the babble of conversation.

A murmur of confirmation travelled in a wave across the table.

"Three separate, but not equal, explosions," I said.

Mr. Jones spoke up. "According to the evidence we have, the explosion in engineering was comparable to the one in the galley. Without someone to halt the flow, it flooded a storage compartment."

"No flour and oatmeal there," said the swarthy officer beside Jones.

"Could it have been a malfunctioning scuttling charge, Mr. Hassan?" Jones asked him.

"Malfunctions aren't likely. One explosion might have been a malfunction, but two? Besides, a nuclear vessel is not scuttled like that. And what about the short in the command controls. It seems a bit of a stretch for three accidents to happen simultaneously."

Everything tidied away, I thought. *Too tidy.*

"Why rig explosives in the galley?"

Everyone looked at me.

"Why the galley?" I repeated

Captain Campbell shrugged. "Any ideas, Mr. Hassan? Mr. Jones?"

They looked at each other in silent consultation. Just guessing, but I think Hassan was a senior engineering officer and Jones his subordinate, possibly one with expertise in a relevant area. In any case, Hassan nodded to Jones and she answered the question.

"The galley was near the outer hull. This would be so if there was a fire and the automatic fire controls were not sufficient, the compartment could be flooded."

"Where did you get this information?" asked Redding.

"Safety systems are my specialty."

Bingo, I thought.

"It also fits the evidence we have of the explosion. The same thing would apply to the engineering compartments. Those are the two areas most vulnerable to fire. Of course, as safety measures go, flooding the compartment is last ditch. Even then the navy had reliable chemical suppression systems."

Mike leaned forward. "Does that mean that the galley and engineering could be flooded, sinking the base, without seriously damaging the rest of the station?"

"That's how I would scuttle the station."

Hassan gave Jones a solemn, but approving nod. "Commander Redding may be able to confirm this. Or he may not. I am just thankful no one was in engineering at the time. To die, trapped in a flooding compartment is every sailor's nightmare."

I gave a full-body shiver and felt a bit nauseous. I had come close to dying that way. My coffee was cold, and I wasn't sure I could stomach it anyway. I pushed it away and tried to concentrate on Redding's response.

"That makes my point, doesn't it? It was a security protocol. In case of emergency, sink the base without seriously damaging it, right?"

Jones shook her head. "An ad hoc measure, maybe. As a security measure, the galley isn't the logical choice for a second charge. weapons' control, which is at the opposite end to the flooded engineering compartment, would have made a better choice."

"Maybe that was rigged too, but it didn't go off," Mike said.

At that moment I felt a warm weight fall on my shoulders. Chief Gravell had given up his jacket to drape it around me. At that point, I realized that I hadn't seen him at the table. A moment later, he disappeared again.

I turned my attention back to the verbal skirmish between Mike and Redding.

"Whether you blame an ancient conspiracy or malfunctioning equipment, the vessel isn't safe."

"Or maybe, the scuttling charges were set by someone aboard the *Scranton*. They had access to the station before we were allowed aboard."

Hassan interjected, shaking his head. "If that was the case, it would be more likely that the charges would have been set to go off before you boarded. Apart from endangering human life, if there was something to hide, why risk the possibility that you might find it during your investigation?"

"Unless, we were meant to be blamed for triggering the explosions," said Jamal.

Tracy nodded her head so vigorously it made my neck hurt. "Maybe the explosions were timed for when we were supposed to leave. We did overstay our original allotted time."

Redding gave a brittle laugh. "I can see that you are determined to discover a conspiracy where none exists. I'm just surprised you are allowing this line of debate, Captain Campbell."

The captain was in the process of pouring me a cup of tea from the pot that had appeared when I wasn't paying attention. He waited until he was done before addressing Redding's remark.

"Just because I don't subscribe to the conspiracy theory myself, doesn't mean that Mr. Naire and Mr. Martouk haven't a right to express their opinions. Speculation is natural."

"Well, I think it's irresponsible to sink the station before we find out more," said Reuben, before more speculation could ensue. "What if there is an unexploded charge in weapons' control? It should be made safe. Furthermore, we still haven't discovered the disposition of the crew. To that end, I intend to take the case to the Solicitor General, the Naval Criminal Investigation Service, and their Canadian equivalents."

"That's ridiculous," said Redding.

I shook my head. "Not at all. Unless Captain Tinsdale comes forward and tells us that he ordered the setting of the charges as per his own orders to scuttle the station, the explosions have to be considered suspicious until proven otherwise."

I looked over at Dora. She gave me the nod to state what we had both concluded. "It is quite possible that this is a murder case, possibly multiple counts of murder, assuming the original crew was killed."

I looked over to the Captain to gauge his reaction. Our eyes met and my fickle mind forgot about the puzzle we were trying to solve and homed in on a much more personal revelation. Captain Campbell admired me. I felt a blush start.

Dora took the lead, sharing her pet theory that what happened was the work of a deranged mind. Someone objected that it was too organized, too tidy. Deranged, Dora pointed out, did not necessarily equally disorganized. Many serial killers were very organized.

"Serial killers don't tend to pass the rigorous psychiatric exams necessary before this kind of posting," said Redding.

"Wrong and simplistic. There have been many serial killers that have fooled their family, friends, and mental health professionals. Until their particular stressor overwhelms them, they might seem and be perfectly normal. Even now, with the strides we've made in forensic psychiatry, it is extremely difficult to spot a potential murderer before they've killed—or at least immediately intend to kill."

Dr. Stern nodded. "She's right. Psychopathic personalities still slip through the system, that's why I have to be trained in psychology as well as surgery and general medicine. Back then? The chances of a person with latent psychoses getting into a high risk position were far greater."

Eventually the party broke up. While good nights were exchanged, I discovered that Mr. Redding was staying aboard the *Nottawasaga*. That being the case, he was likely to develop an ulcer if he had to endure too many more dinners like tonight's. I might have been more sympathetic if he hadn't nabbed me when I was trying to make my escape.

"Intense, huh? I hope you don't take it all too seriously. You shouldn't let it upset you."

I made a noncommittal noise because I was too tired to argue. He didn't take the hint.

"Will you be leaving with the research group tomorrow? They are being airlifted out, aren't they?"

"I have no idea. I wasn't aware that anyone was going this soon, and I don't think I've been released from medical care yet."

He smiled broadly. "Then maybe we can chat tomorrow?"

Dr. Stern interrupted before I thought of an answer. He offered to escort me back to sick bay. The captain forestalled him, suggesting I might want to take a walk on deck. That was an invitation I couldn't refuse, though I did look around for Gravell. After all, I was still wearing his jacket.

The air was crisp and cold but, if anything, I felt less chilled than I had in the wardroom. Although the sun was still up, I could see some of the brighter stars in the pale sky. We stood looking out at the sea. On the opposite side, we could have seen the *Scranton* and *Émil Gagnan*. Here it was as if we were alone in the Arctic.

"Is the research team being evacuated tomorrow?" I asked, wanting to get that issue cleared up first.

"You aren't being sent anywhere. Doc has not released you from sick bay. Between you and me, he is not going to release you until Gravell and I think it appropriate."

"Oh." I wondered what appropriate meant?

"Dr. Leland and Mr. Dawes will be leaving tomorrow morning along with the film crew, excepting Mr. Neville. I'm almost positive that it will be a temporary absence."

I shook my head. "I don't get it."

"Even if I wanted to, I couldn't get your team airlifted out of here all at once. Not with your luggage, equipment, and the ship's mail."

"I get camera crew leaving. They can't do much the way things are. Why Dora and Reuben?"

"Think of it as a chess game. Sometimes the moves don't seem to make sense until you put your opponent in check."

"I was never very good at chess."

He chuckled. It was a pleasant change from the verbal parrying I had been listening to all evening. He turned to lean on a support sideways so he could watch me. I gazed back for a minute or so, wondering what would happen next. It wasn't what I expected.

"Doc likes you. He was there, in a professional capacity, most of the time I was talking to you. He will treat anything he heard as confidential, of course. I just thought you should know."

My gaze narrowed to a stare. "So, when he said I had all my marbles, he had a basis for making the judgement."

"Something like that."

I looked out over the water. "I suppose he was also there to make sure you said the right things."

"He didn't tell me what to say, if that's what you mean. He did warn me that I might feel a false sense of intimacy towards you."

"Because we were thrown together, so to speak, in an adverse situation."

"Adverse?"

I looked over my shoulder at him and shrugged. "Dire?"

"Try life and death."

I didn't like to think about that. I pulled Gravell's jacket about me. The captain leaned toward me, not close enough to touch, but close enough that I felt his body heat.

"I don't think you realize this, but you are a hero. Your grace and resourcefulness under adverse conditions captured the imagination of many of my crew. I doubt your colleagues appreciate what you went through, though they were worried enough. It takes a sailor to understand what you were up against, better still, a squid."

"A squid?"

"A submariner."

He took me by the shoulders and turned me around to face him. For a moment we just stood there. Then he backed away. Putting a little distance between us, he continued.

"I gave some thought to your suspicions regarding Captain Tinsdale. He will scuttle the station if he gets the chance. That doesn't mean he would have ever put you in the position of being trapped below decks. As a submarine commander, he knows that he might have to make the decision to leave someone trapped for the safety of his boat. That kind of decision is harder to make than sending men into battle. He wouldn't intentionally put himself in that position."

Unless Tinsdale was a sociopath, I didn't really believe he'd do that either.

"Wait a sec! What do you mean, if he gets the chance'?"

He grinned.

"I know that you and the research team think I should have done more to help you. I hope that you, at least, understand that my hands were tied by decisions made by my superiors."

I nodded. I was willing to admit that now. He gave a quick smile and continued.

"The situation has changed. We're off-script. Dr. Leland and Mr. Dawes will be making a case to continue the investigation, calling on resources that they might be kept from contacting out here. In the meantime, I see it as my duty to make sure nothing happens to the station while we wait for a new script to be written."

Yay Captain Campbell.

The doctor was waiting for me. I was in such a good mood, I gave him a hug. He responded with a troubled grimace.

I laughed.

"Before you give me your lecture on false intimacy, I should tell you that the captain already passed it along. Besides, I already know that my feelings are vulnerable right now. In half an hour, I might remember how close to death I came and start weeping, but right now, I'm feeling good about the fact that the station is safe for a little bit longer. That's all."

"Hmph, that lecture wasn't meant for you."

"No?"

"My prescription for you is rest, mild exercise, and not worrying so much."

He started the routine of gathering temperature, pulse, O2 levels, and blood pressure stats, filling in my chart as he went.

"I hear you're not releasing me," I said, watching to gauge his reaction.

"I'll release you when you're ready and not a moment before."

I grinned and nodded. He sighed and smiled back, a little more relaxed.

"I'm moving you to an isolation room. It'll give you some privacy. I want to keep an eye on you. With a history of lung disease in your family, I don't want to take chances. I'm sure that the captain has at least hinted at the other reasons we want to keep you here."

"Not in so many words."

Not in any words actually, but the doctor didn't need to know that I was uninformed.

"The main thing is you're safe here. Tonight, Briseau has stayed to help you settle into your room. Tomorrow, I'll introduce you to anyone else who has business being here. Right now, I'm going to give the captain a reminder not to share his prescription with other patients."

Chapter Nineteen ~ *Boxed In*

My new home was small, sterile, and uncomfortable. It was certainly private. I felt like I had been sent to solitary confinement. Sophie did her best to make me comfortable. She brought me extra pillows and blankets and a clamp light I could use for reading. When she left, I tucked up and started reading Minton's journal from the beginning.

This is the most significant mission I have ever taken part in. This is my chance to show that I have the right stuff. This is what I have been working towards my whole life. Best of all, I am surrounded by friends…

This time I didn't skip the journey north. Imbedded in the descriptions of the voyage were his impressions of his colleagues.

Mitch and I have often been called the "Odd Couple." While he isn't quite Oscar Madison and he looks nothing like Walter Matthau, there is some truth in this. I think that's why we work so well together. Mitch sees the big picture. I notice the details. Mitch is easygoing and inspires loyalty. I am disciplined and demand excellence. Now, Margolo is an Oscar. He's a great guy, but one day I'm going to strangle him, he's such a slob and his socks smell like rancid cheese…

While the station was being towed into place, Minton was full of excitement for the coming adventure and, according to his journal, the pleasant anticipation was shared.

Golanger is like a puppy. I know he's not as young as he looks, but it's hard to believe when he spots a whale or walrus. Boreman teases him, but I think the man actually delights in Golanger's enthusiasm. No doubt, Boreman misses his kids and Golanger makes a good substitute.

Poor Golanger.

If we are delayed much longer, Doc Dawes will have emptied the pockets of every sailor foolish enough to sit down to a game of poker with our slick gentleman. Mitch says I should relax my personal rules about gambling, but it isn't going to happen while Doc is dealing.

The adventure palled quickly, once the team was on its own. After exhaustive training, the station itself held no surprises and the dark, frigid waters offered little outside stimulation. Minton didn't mention anything about their work in his journal. He gave brief comments to whether it was a busy, slow, or difficult day without mentioning what would make them busy or what kind of difficulties they faced. He wrote about personal things.

The poker games are a mistake, but they have been sanctioned by the commander so I can't do anything but keep tabs on the men.

When we started out, we agreed that smoking would be curtailed. The break room in engineering is the officially designated area, but Mitch says that the men can smoke in the kitchen as well because of the fire controls and extra air filters. As a result, all the food tastes like tobacco. There's a grimy sheen on everything. It makes me nauseous to go in there, but I force myself.

Mitch shrugs it off, but I know they are drinking during games. They have coffee cups in front of them, but someone always has a flask to tip. We're sitting on tons of nuclear material and they are getting drunk. It's unconscionable.

"Well, I'm with you on that point," I said aloud to the ghost of Minton, who had appeared at the end of my bed. "Drinking and nuclear arms don't mix, though I have a hard time believing they got drunk on a few swigs of whisky. Or would it be rum?"

Minton gave me a wan smile. Even if he had answered, I wouldn't have heard him.

"And smoking in an enclosed system, yuk. Well, I think smoking is yucky anyway. It must have driven you crazy."

Minton nodded grimly.

I set tucked the journal under my pillow and closed my eyes.

Minton is red-faced. I can feel the heat exude off his skin as I hang over his shoulder. Commander Shore is listening calmly, but the colour is rising in his face too, and I know that Minton is crossing the line towards insubordination. Minton picks up on this too and he hesitates. Something Shore says makes him pale. Shore seems to loom over Minton. He seems to suck the air away from Minton away from me. My chest feels heavy. Then the blood flows.

I woke deeply disturbed, short of breath, and parched. I went to the head and washed my face, taking the edge off my thirst with a couple of handfuls of water. It wasn't very satisfying. Worse, it gave my stomach something to want to throw up.

I needed to get out on deck.

On board the *Émil Gagnan*, I would have been able to go to the galley for a juice or coffee then go stand on the foredeck. There, Gravell would eventually find me and we'd chat companionably until our duties took us elsewhere. I missed that camaraderie.

Here, I had no idea where to get a coffee and only a vague idea how to find the deck. Add to that, I couldn't find my clothes and suspected that if I wandered around in scrubs, I would be escorted back to sick bay.

I'd have to take that chance. I couldn't stay here. The walls were closing in on me, and I had broken out in a fine sweat from fighting down the nausea.

There was no one between me and the exit. Still, I moved cautiously and opened the hatch slowly, peaking around outside before exiting. Then I closed my eyes and tried to remember the route the captain had taken me. I felt a wave of cold and opened my eyes to Minton.

"You know the way out?" I whispered.

He nodded. I followed. He led me to the port side, the side overlooking the station. Soon I was breathing blessedly cold, fresh air. Okay, I should have brought a jacket. But it was worth the chill.

Why would anyone willingly serve aboard a submarine? I would have gone bananas on that station. I probably would have loaded myself into a torpedo tube and shot myself to the surface for the chance to breathe fresh air.

Maybe Doc would let me set up a hammock on deck. Maybe he'd let me return to the *Émil Gagnan* where I knew where to find coffee and I didn't have to sneak around.

I felt a wall of warmth behind me and half expected to be taken back to sickbay in irons. Instead it was Gravell proffering a steaming mug.

"Bonjour, Madame Kirby."

I sighed happily, forgetting I was ever angry at him.

"Bonjour, Chief Gravell."

It was tea, not coffee, but he also brought a windbreaker and helped me into it.

"I would prefer it if you didn't leave sick bay unescorted. You scared Briseau and worried me."

"I'm sorry. I didn't realize it would be such an issue."

He looked at me, scepticism apparent.

"Okay, I was so desperate to get fresh air I didn't care if it was an issue. I didn't want anyone telling me I couldn't go outside."

He nodded. "Still seasick? I can't hand out pills here, but I can talk to the doctor."

"Since being trapped, I find I'm feeling less seasick and more claustrophobic."

We both turned to look out.

I could see the *Scranton*'s tower casting a shadow over the location of the station. Nearby, the *Émil Gagnan* was stubbornly holding its place amongst the big dogs.

Halfway through my tea, my legs started to feel wobbly. I suppose it was time to go back to bed. I was as ready as I would ever be, but my feet were reluctant. They didn't want to move, possibly having inside information on how my stomach was going to handle this. I decided to give them five more minutes. Though I didn't look, I knew that Gravell stepped away. I heard the murmur of his voice giving someone instructions. Then, when he returned, I felt the radiant warmth of his body and wondered at him standing so close. When I turned, I was surprised to find him at least a foot away. On the other hand, Minton wasn't around and that might have explained the sudden sensation of warmth.

"Ready to go in, Madame Kirby?"

I nodded.

"I'm going to give you a radio-phone. Next time you want to go on deck, call me. I'll make sure you have an escort. Don't worry about the time of day. Someone will be available at all times."

I stopped and stared at him.

"Are you afraid I'll be attacked? Or that I'll jump ship?"

"You're a civilian aboard a military vessel."

"So this is just protocol?" I stared at him in frank disbelief.

Gravell chivied me on. "It is a combination of things. The bottom line is, you can either comply or find yourself under armed guard."

"You'd do that to me?"

"I wouldn't have to."

I sighed. "I'll be good."

An armed seaman was waiting in sick bay with a flask of tea and a second mug. Gravell dismissed him with a word of thanks. We sat in my room with our tea, and I found myself telling Gravell about my dream.

"Perhaps you shouldn't read the diary at bedtime," he suggested, though I had been careful not to mention Minton's journal.

Of course, I had told him about the book when I was trapped, but I thought that the captain and I were the only ones who knew I still had it. Maybe this was a test.

I feigned innocence.

"What diary? If I had such an item, I would have to turn it over to the Americans, wouldn't I?"

Gravell's mouth turned up at one corner and his eyes narrowed with an expression that conveyed a degree of ferocity completely absent from his calm voice. "Not on my watch, you wouldn't. Your discretion is admirable, Madame Kirby, but I am the one person you can and should talk to about this."

"Why?"

"Because you need an ally and I am it, always have been."

"I trust the captain, but I know there are certain things he can't officially know right now. I assumed the same held for you."

Again, that amused smile, like there was a joke I wasn't getting. "Do you trust me, Madame Kirby?"

My immediate reaction was that I shouldn't trust anyone who asks that question in that light tone of voice. I trusted the captain with my life. I trusted his word. He had given no reason to doubt him and had been clear regarding his limitations. Could I say the same of Gravell?

"I have a question for you, Chief Gravell. I know that you won't tell me everything that's going on, but would you lie to me because it was expedient to do so?"

His smile faded. "I avoid lying. Withholding or being selective with information is easier." His eyes met mine and his tone was solemn. "I can't promise to always tell you the whole truth, but to date I haven't lied to you. I won't lie to you unless I need to and I don't anticipate the need."

Fair enough, I thought. I had my rational opinion. Gravell was, as stated, my ally. Irrationally, based on the fact that I felt safe around him, and possibly because he knew the words to some of my favourite songs, I decided that he was also a friend.

I smiled, triggering a tentative smile from Gravell. Warm brown eyes gazed expectantly and, once again, I thought of chocolate.

"I trust you."

Chapter Twenty ~ *Sabre Rattling*

With Captain Campbell's compliments, I was invited to a breakfast the next morning. My clothes had appeared, clean and pressed, including my underwear. Sophie had them laundered overnight.

This time I wasn't caught off guard when I walked in on a meeting. The Doc had to take sick parade, so Gravell acted as my escort. He followed me through the door then faded into the background.

Dora and Reuben were at the table, which had been reduced in length since dinner. Tim was included and was currently sitting opposite Dora and Reuben, carrying on animated conversation over coffee. Standing nearby, Guy Franchot was chatting with Captain Campbell, holding a glass of orange juice as if it was wine. Both men greeted me with a smile, which I took as an invitation to join them.

Franchot set aside his juice, took my shoulders and drew me into a Gallic embrace. I half expected him to kiss both my cheeks. Then he held me at arm's length and gave me the once over.

"You're looking much better than I expected. From what I heard, you were at death's door."

"Ms. Kirby is making an excellent recovery. The doctor wants to keep her under observation. She has a history of lung disease in her family."

Franchot looked startled and slightly reproachful. All the members of the research team were supposed to be in excellent health.

I reassured him. "My mother died of emphysema after smoking for fifty years. As far as I know, I'm fine."

"Well, I'm trying to negotiate your release. So far, Captain Campbell has agreed to let the other members of the team return. Dora and Reuben will be leaving to take our case to higher authorities. I think the good captain is keeping you hostage."

I turned my head, waiting for the captain's response, not sure what I wanted to hear.

"In many cultures, hostages were exchanged as a gesture of alliance. That's why I'm giving you Mr. Hassan in exchange for Ms. Kirby. You can have Mr. Neville back too if you like, though you may have a hard time convincing him to go."

Franchot gave a loud bark of laughter, drawing everyone's attention towards us. At that moment, the captain leaned towards me and said softly, "I hope you're not in a hurry to leave."

Knowing that I was blushing, I decided it wiser not to try to reply and further embarrass myself. While I was gathering my wits, Gravell appeared beside me with a glass of orange juice. I started slightly, setting off a chain reaction. Gravell steadied me, only slopping a drop or two of juice on his uniform. Franchot stepped forward, shifting from boisterous to protective in nanoseconds. At the same time, the captain pulled my free hand through his arm.

For a moment I was surrounded by three very attractive men, apparently squaring off on my behalf. Almost overwhelmed by the desire to giggle, I managed to stifle the urge and just as well. The assembly wasn't complete. The hatch opened and Mr. Hassan appeared. He stepped back for a man who could only be Captain Tinsdale.

"Permission to join you, Captain?" he said, his voice deep and gravelly.

Captain Campbell released my hand with a squeeze and stepped forward to greet his guest. I could feel Gravell and Franchot take up position behind me. I sipped my juice, hoping it would steady my nerves. Then I drank it down quickly when I saw the two captains heading my way.

Gravell took the empty glass.

"More?"

I nodded.

I will never forget the comfort that Captain Campbell's calm voice brought me when I was trapped. Neither will I forget the irritation that Tinsdale's brusque questions and abrupt manner engendered. His face matched his voice: rough, lined and a bit bristly. He reminded me of Humphrey Bogart in the Caine Mutiny with a bit of John Wayne swagger.

Captain Tinsdale offered his hand. It was square and callused and not that much bigger than my own. I could look him in the eye, without standing back, which more than I could say of the two men behind me.

"We made a bad start, Mrs. Kirby. I hope we can get along better now."

"We were both under a lot of stress," I replied, trying to sound gracious, though I hated being called missus.

Captain Campbell gestured us towards the table.

Dora had taken the seat she had the night before, on the captain's left. Reuben was beside her and Tim was in the seat Doc had taken, leaving the seat on the captain's right open for me. He gave me a bright smile and stood to hold my chair.

I hesitated. As much as I would have liked to sit beside Captain Campbell, I knew that Tim would pick up on any hint of romantic interest and exploit it for the documentary. I didn't doubt that the captain would give anything away. I wasn't sure I could be trusted.

"Madame Kirby," Gravell said, directing me with a firm hand to my back. "If you will allow me."

Captain Tinsdale had been placed at the opposite end of the table to Captain Campbell. Gravell sat me on Tinsdale's left, across the table from Franchot who was waiting to sit. Tim found himself holding a chair for Mr. Hassan, who also waited to sit. Since there were four places on this side, Gravell could act as a buffer between me and the filmmaker.

I sat. Captain Campbell sat. Everyone else sat. Had it been this formal last night? I ran the scene back in my head, a talent I had honed from years of having to process too much information during interviews. Yes, the naval officers had observed the formality of seating the guests first, then waiting for the commanding officer to sit. Somehow it seemed less stilted last night. This morning there were three captains at the table with three different agendas. No doubt there would be some polite sabre rattling over the meal.

Dora caught my eye. Her grin told me she analysed the situation differently. Her gaze made the rounds from Captain Campbell, to Chief Gravell, and then to Captain Franchot, then they darted momentarily to Captain Tinsdale, who I noted, was offering me my napkin.

"Rather warm," she muttered, looking at me over the rim of her raised coffee cup.

"Your coffee must be cold by now," said Reuben deliberately misinterpreting her.

"So it is. We need more hot coffee here."

Coffee was served and the juice jug made the rounds. I was feeling a little lightheaded and sucked back my glass of juice quickly, so I could refill my glass.

"Still dehydrated, Mrs. Kirby?" asked Tinsdale.

"Low blood sugar," I explained. It was a better explanation than the truth.

"I should have asked Petty Officer Briseau for some juice or a piece of fruit this morning. I generally manage my hypoglycemia better."

"And when you forget, my first mate remembers. That is, or perhaps was, Mr. Gravell. He took good care of the research team, Jen especially."

"Ah, that explains it," said Reuben.

"Explains what?" asked Dora.

"Lil and I wondered why Gravell acted like a mother hen around you, Jen. I'll have to tell Lil about your hypoglycemia. She thought you were having an affair."

I tossed back another glass of juice, wishing it was something harder. Then I could blame my flushed cheeks on the alcohol. I shot Reuben a killing look and received a mischievous one in return.

I reached for the jug. A hand stopped me. I looked over and Gravell was shaking his head.

"You'll spike your blood-sugar if you drink too much juice. You need protein and complex carbohydrates now."

"He's right," said Dora. "Maybe you could get her a piece of cheese."

She was having way too much fun at my expense.

Mercifully, the topic was dropped once food was in front of everyone. French toast, doused in real maple syrup, peameal bacon and sausages, and wedges of melon demanded our full attention. When the coffee was making the rounds again, I waited expectantly for Dora to step onto her soap box. The topic was not broached by my friend. The silence was breached by our American guest.

"I hear you enjoyed a lively discussion last night. A regular brainstorm."

Dora nodded at Captain Tinsdale. "Brainstorming definitely took place. When we raise the station, it will be interesting to see whose hypotheses come closest to the truth."

"If you raise the station. There is no guarantee that you will get permission to make a second attempt and no guarantee you'll succeed if you do."

Reuben jumped in. "Oh, we'll get permission. Count on it."

"And we'll raise the station," said Franchot with confidence.

"Would you go back, Jen?" Tim asked, leaning around Gravell.

Would I? It wasn't as if my presence was strictly necessary, and I had a good reason to excuse myself.

"To get answers, I'd go back. To recover Matt Parker's body and put the ghosts to rest, yes, I'd go back."

I lifted my chin and fixed my gaze on Captain Tinsdale, silently daring him to say he didn't think the risk worth the rewards. He acknowledged my point with a nod that I took to denote respect, not agreement.

So, I thought, *Tinsdale may be my enemy, but he isn't a villain.*

"Are you going to see us off?" Dora was asking me.

"Of course."

Franchot made a flourishing wave. "The whole team will be there to wish you luck. Then I'll take them back to our ship. I'd like to take you back too, Jen."

I shrugged. I was torn. I would be more comfortable aboard the *Émil Gagnan* , but staying here might have its compensations. I looked from the captain to Gravell and back again. Would I be allowed the choice?

"Ms. Kirby will stay for the time being. I will speak to the doctor. When he releases her, we can reconsider the arrangement. Regardless, you're still getting Mr. Hassan, Captain Franchot."

Franchot gave Mr. Hassan a gracious bow of the head.

"He is welcome. Your security detail, on the other hand, is eating us out of house and home."

Captains Campbell and Tinsdale exchanged glances. The unspoken question was did the security detail need to be there? With a slight nod, Tinsdale conveyed that he wouldn't encroach on the *Émil Gagnan* directly.

"They can come back on the boat when you return to the *Émil Gagnan*. We can probably replace some of your supplies too. We have more incoming."

Supplies and mail arrived. Dora and Reuben left. Then Mr. Hassan left with Mike, Mary Lou, Lil, and some fresh food. I returned to sick bay for my daily checkup. Someone told on me to Doc, because he put me through a blood glucose test.

"So, will I live?" I asked.

"I'll tell you when I complete the tests. Your lungs are clear. Your blood pressure is good. You should have told me you had hypoglycemia," he chided.

"I put it on my medical form for the voyage. It's not my fault you didn't check it."

"I'd need your permission for it to be released to me, my dear."

"You didn't ask."

We stared at each other.

I always told Seamus to own up to his responsibilities. Could I do no less?

"Sorry. I should have mentioned it. I forgot. I often forget about it.

Dealing with it is almost automatic." I gave him a sheepish grin. "As my son will attest, I sometimes forget to take care of myself when I get preoccupied."

He granted me one of his charming smiles. "Understandable. From what I hear, you have someone looking out for you aboard the *Émil Gagnan.*"

"The first mate took care of all of us. I just gave him more to do. I was horribly seasick the first couple of days."

"And again last night? Briseau mentioned you went AWOL."

I groaned. "I've been told off for that already. I apologised to Sophie and agreed to get an escort from Gravell before going walkabout again. Maybe it would be easier if I returned to the *Émil Gagnan.*"

Doc stood back and crossed his arms. "Hmm. You're an honoured guest and everyone's sweetheart here. Are you sure you want to go?"

I wasn't sure.

"Why did you tell me not to take the captain's prescription? Doesn't it apply to me as much as him? Or you."

Doc blushed. I had caught him out. That'll teach him to tease me.

"Right now, you have enough to process without worrying about whether or not your feelings are appropriate. Let us hold the line. That's our job."

Now I felt like a heel. I sighed and hopped off the examination table. All the attention was nice. Weird, but nice. Nevertheless, it was going to get old fast if everyone kept walking on eggshells around me. What if I wanted a little false intimacy? It might be fun. It was all so frustrating. I wasn't sure if the captain would ever cross the line, but I was damned sure Doc wouldn't. I needed something else to think about besides my nightmares and my daydreams.

"I need to work. Do you have a table I could use?"

Doc set me up with an adjustable bedside table and a chair. I set up a mini-office beside my bed. A little later Gravell showed up with a thermos of tea.

"Are you going to be all right in here?"

I shrugged. "I'd prefer a room with a view, but I'm okay. Fortunately, I'm not so claustrophobic when I work."

"Well, Doc is taking you to lunch and the captain has invited you to tea. I will come for you at fifteen thirty hours. That way you'll get a chance to take a walk on deck first. It won't be a long walk, since there aren't many places to stroll, but fresh air will be involved. Is that acceptable?"

"Of course."

"Then I'll let you get to work. Call me if you get claustrophobic."

"Merci, Chief Gravell."

"Bienvenue, Madame Kirby."

I felt a bit like a bird in a gilded cage. After years of being a single mother, being taken care of was a pleasant novelty. However, I wished I could go to lunch with Sophie. I could use a little more female companionship.

I finished reading the early part of the journal and caught up with the section I read aboard the station. Minton was growing suspicious of his fellows. At this point he wasn't finding find fault with their work. It did seem as though the more he learned about his colleagues' private lives, the less he liked them.

Margolo seems to have only one thing on his mind. Sex. I've always known he was a player, but I never suspected the depth of his depravity. Yet, as bad as he is, Boreman is worse. He has a wife and two young children, yet he is as debauched as Margolo. The two are like-minded in their perversion and often share stories of their various triumphs with the opposite sex.

Dawes is too slick. He makes jokes at my expense, tells me to loosen up. He has convinced Mitch to only allow smoking in the wardroom after meals as if the odour miraculously disappears before the next time I have to sit down to eat. What can I expect? He smokes too.

Golanger looks innocent. He doesn't smoke or drink. He writes his mother every day. If he's so squeaky clean, why is he playing poker with the others? Why does he smile at Boreman's stories? He's playing a deep game.

Minton might have been disgusted by the stories, that didn't stop him from recording some of them. I gave the ghost a long look after reading a couple of them aloud. He looked embarrassed, and I think he would have blushed if it was possible. I was beginning to get the impression that the man who wrote this journal was quite different from the spirit that hovered before me every time I opened his book.

"These are the kind of stories I heard my father's cronies swap when they thought I wasn't around to hear. Sexist jokes and tales of sexual prowess that were grossly exaggerated for entertainment value, if not outright lies."

The ghost shrugged.

I read on. There were more character assassinations, more snooping around, more hyperbole. Then a turn for the worse.

Boreman is watching me. He knows I'm onto him. I found the letter from his lover and it's worse than I thought. He's got a wife and two children, yet he's been performing acts of bestiality and other perversions upon another man. The letter is explicit and detailed. I've

read it over and over. Boreman's lover is using him and it scares me to
think what Boreman might be willing to do for him.

Well, that explained the extreme stories and machismo of Boreman. He was covering up for a sexual preference that could have had him dishonourably discharged from the Navy and probably ruined his life at that time. I hoped to hell that Boreman was smart enough to get rid of the letter once he knew that Minton found out about it. If it was as explicit as Minton suggested, I didn't want Mary Lou reading it.

I shook my head. "Is this what got you killed, Mister Minton?"

Tim managed to stay on board. He said he wanted to interview the key players in my rescue. He joined us for lunch, and I discovered that Doc wasn't as good a buffer as Gravell. In fairness, Tim treated me like a buddy and I was too polite to repulse him. Then, when Doc's attention was diverted by another officer, he swooped in.

"Are you mad at me, Jen?"

"Why? Have you done something I should be angry about?"

"Dora's mad at me. I made the mistake of telling her not to worry if she didn't get the permissions she wanted. We already have the makings of a great doc. It might even be better if we could catch the Navy scuttling the ship. No matter what they say, it's going to scream conspiracy and conspiracy sells."

I paused. I counted to ten. I still had to say it.

"You're an idiot! Dora doesn't care if it sells. She cares about the truth. You're here because Dora and Ruben could raise more money for the expedition if there was a documentary."

"Does the truth matter if someone dies down there? You almost did!"

Good lord, I must give off some kind of damsel in distress pheromones. I was surrounded by heroes who wanted to rescue me. Time to show I wasn't in need of rescue any more.

"If you don't want to make anyone else mad, including me, I suggest you learn from Dora's response."

"You have a son, right?"

I glared at him.

"I was just going to ask if you'd heard from him."

"Seamus is at camp. He might remember to send me a postcard."

"You miss him, don't you?" Tim said with suspicious display of sensitivity.

"Yes."

"Then don't you think…"

I held up my hand. "Don't say it, Tim. Just don't."

I didn't feel like dealing with Minton after enduring Tim. Instead, I started writing a detailed description of everything I saw on the station. Then, because the lines were getting blurred between what was physically there and what I saw, I set up a table for comparison. In one column was a physical description, using the images I had saved on my smartphone as reference. In the second column, I put down my memories of what I saw, including the hallucinations or dreams or whatever they were.

I needed to check the artifacts against my lists. All the papers were put in Dora's hands. Did she still have them? Were they on the *Nottawasaga*? Or had she sent them back to the *Émil Gagnan*? I had to find out. Too bad I hadn't thought to ask Dora before she left.

At two, Sophie showed up with a glass of milk and some cheese and crackers. Doc's orders.

At three-twenty, I had started a third column for an artifact list. Once I had access to the list of recovered items, I could check it against what I remembered. In particular, I wanted to find the Boreman letter. Sophie poked her head in to remind me I was going to tea with the captain.

I looked through my clothes and picked out the most feminine items in the pile. I hadn't exactly packed with femininity in mind, but not everything was Palinesque. There was the sweater I wore the first time I met the captain. It was beige, of course, but it had a sweetheart neckline and was a bit clingy. I had one almost identical, in deep purple. I hadn't worn it since spilling coffee on it during the flight north. The *Nottawasaga* launderers managed to get the stain out, though now the top was faded to an amethyst mauve.

I like amethyst. I had an amethyst bead bracelet and matching earrings. They went everywhere with me because they were a gift from Seamus. I hadn't worn them so far because I was afraid I might lose an earring, something I was prone to do. I decided to take the chance, then laughed at myself. Here I was trying to dress to impress when the way things were going, I could show up in sackcloth and ashes and still get attention.

The earrings were still in my hand when Gravell arrived. I had opened my door in anticipation and for the air as soon as I was dressed.

"Wear them, Madame Kirby. I'll keep an eye on them for you."

I was beginning to think the man was a mind reader. He didn't say, "Wear them, they go with your outfit," which would have been a natural conclusion to draw from the way I was holding the earrings up. He knew what really concerned me. Then a simpler explanation came to mind. He was trained in behavioural analysis. He had the kind of observation skills I expected from Dora, when she wasn't wrapped in an academic haze.

I put the earrings on.

"They do go well with your outfit," he added.

I narrowed my eyes at him.

"Who are you, Chief Gravell?"

He gave me a half-smile. "Right now, I am the man who has the pleasure of your company for a walk on deck."

"Very prettily said, even though I know you're laughing at me. I'll accept your reply as a polite way of telling me to mind my own business. Someday I expect you to satisfy my curiosity."

"That would be impossible, Madame Kirby. You have, I imagine, a bottomless supply of curiosity."

The sky was overcast. The air was cool and damp. I smelled rain in the air and hoped that didn't mean a storm. Aside from the effect it would have on my stomach, I didn't want to think of the potential damage to the station.

"If there's a storm, the station will be safer undersea, won't it? Safer than being on the surface?"

"The greatest danger is to the ship tethering the station."

"Is that the *Émil Gagnan* or the *Scranton*?"

"The *Émil Gagnan*. The *Scranton* cut umbilicals after the explosions."

I felt Gravell's eyes on me and turned towards him. He was standing at parade rest. I suspected that as well as being chief aboard the *Émil Gagnan*, he was a chief petty officer in the Navy.

"How do you know a storm is coming?" he asked.

"How did you know I was afraid of losing my earrings?"

"Observation."

"Not many people are that observant or that confident in their observations. For instance, I observed signs of a storm coming. The sky, something in the way the air smells, a pain in my wrist that has been a fairly accurate barometer ever since I sprained it falling off a horse, but I didn't know a storm was coming until you confirmed it. I assume you have access to the National Weather Service or the like. I have a feeling you have access to a lot more information than I do."

An amused smile lit up his face. "I sincerely hope so!"

I rolled my eyes dramatically and he laughed.

"Okay, that was not one of my more brilliant observations," I said.

He removed and rolled his watch cap, tucking it in a pocket, leaned back against the top cable, just enough so the wind ruffed his dark brown hair.

"You have good instincts, Madame Kirby. Why don't you tell me who I am?"

I stepped back and considered him. I had edited and polished enough of Dora's work to pass an undergraduate exam in forensic psychology. Gravell could have picked up his skills in analysis the same way I did, on the job. It didn't necessarily mean he was more than a common and garden spook sent to keep an eye on the team. Yet, I knew he was. Did it matter? When my vision refocused, I found myself gazing into Gravell's chocolate brown eyes. Was it my imagination that they seemed darker?

I took a step towards him.

"You are Chief Gravell, and you have the dubious pleasure of taking me for a walk. Shall we go?"

Bittersweet melted into milk chocolate. Gravell drew himself up and offered me his arm.

"There is nothing dubious about the pleasure, Madame Kirby."

Half an hour later, Gravell was pouring tea. The captain was preparing scones with jam and cream. I split my attention between the two activities and wondered what I was going to about my attraction to the two men.

Maybe nothing. As long as they stuck to the doctor's prescription, I could enjoy the attention without worrying about the consequences. After all, what were the chances either one of them would be part of my life once I went home? They were ships that passed in the night, two big, heavily armed ships.

"Something has amused you," said the captain, passing me a plate.

Bite-sized pieces of scone were arranged artfully on the dessert plate. Each piece had a layer of deep red jam and a dollop of fresh whipped cream on top.

"Looks wonderful," I commented. I wasn't about to share my cruise romance analogy.

"Your tea, Madame Kirby," said Gravell.

I balanced the plate on my lap and took the cup and saucer. This was looking like an accident ready to happen. I wasn't one of those ladies who could balance dishes, eat, and drink safely at the same time.

"Why don't we sit on the couch," the captain suggested.

He looked to Gravell who had stuck around after delivering me.

"Please help Ms. Kirby over, Chief, and then you can go."

One ship was pulling out the big guns.

"Aye, sir." Gravell took my cup and plate and set them on the table. He then brought the pot and placed it near my cup. Once I was settled, he turned to the captain. "Anything else, sir?"

"No, Chief."

The men exchanged stiff nods. Then Gravell turned on his heel and headed for the hatch.

At the last moment he turned back. "Call me when you need me,

Madame Kirby."

He didn't wait for a reply.

"The man is a bulldog," the captain muttered.

"More like a Rottweiler."

"Does he scare you?"

I looked sharply at the captain. He was serious. True, Rottweilers could be pretty scary. I was thinking of *Good Dog Carl*, the creation of artist Alexandra Day. Carl was big, strong, gentle, and protective of his young charge. Seamus loved the books when he was little. I still did.

"No, he doesn't scare me. He's welcome to scare Commander Redding off, if he likes."

He relaxed. "That's Gravell's job, to look out for you and your team and to scare off other people especially those under Captain Tinsdale's orders."

"Captain Tinsdale and I were starting to get along."

"He respects you, Ms. Kirby. He likes you. Everyone likes you. But Tinsdale also has his orders."

I sighed. "Why pick on me? Dora and Reuben lead the team. Guy Franchot skippers the salvage ship. Except for having the bad luck to be trapped in the station for half a day, I'm nothing special."

"You are something very special," Captain Campbell said with a mixture of admiration and something I couldn't identify, but it raised a red flag.

I waited for more.

"Apart from your courage and grace, you are recording history. It's your perception of events that will find themselves in print and your story that will dominate any documentary made. Once Dr. Leland and Mr. Dawes get the word out, you are going to be a celebrity."

It took a moment for this to sink in.

"Oh, shit."

He laughed.

"It's not funny" I said, draining my tea and pouring another cup. Now my befuddled brain was working on overdrive. "I need to get hold of my son. I don't want him reading about his mother's near-death experience without hearing about it from me first. Will is going to go spare."

"Will?"

"My ex. So far he just thinks I'm a bit flaky. I've got damage control to take care of." I could feel the blood drain out of my face. "My dad. I've got to contact my father."

"Anyone else?" the captain asked, bemused.

I thought about this seriously, though Captain Campbell seemed to be taking my concern lightly. "No. That should do it."

"I don't suppose you can wait until after tea?"

He was still on his first cup and had only taken a few bites of his scone. I popped the last bite of scone into my mouth and washed it down with my second cup of tea.

He sighed. "I suppose not."

Although I had been carrying around my smartphone, I had not set it up for roaming in the Arctic. I'm not sure I could. On the *Èmil Gagnan*, I was connected to the outside world via WiFi and the ship's satellite link. On the *Nottawasaga*, I had to go to Communications. There I was introduced to Petty Officer Marian Sloan. She greeted me warmly, telling me that it was a pleasure to meet me after talking to me over the radio. I supposed she was the com officer I fell asleep on.

"Don't you worry, Ms. Kirby, I'll contact as many of your family members as you need." She then shot a look at the captain, wondering if he'd refute her. He just nodded.

I suggested that we should try Will first, since he'd have the number where I could reach Seamus. When I mentioned that Seamus would be at CFB Kingston, Sloan laughed, and I felt silly for thinking that she wouldn't be able to reach a Canadian military base from a Canadian military vessel.

"We'll call Kingston first. We can get the Duty Officer to fetch him and call back at a pre-appointed time. Meanwhile, we can try your ex-husband's and father's phone numbers."

"My dad always has a cell phone on him. It's a carryover from being a cop and always having his radio handy."

Sloan set up the call to Seamus and reached my dad shortly afterwards. From the sound of it, he was enjoying happy hour at his favourite pub.

"Hey, Dad! *Ca va bien?*"

"Just peachy, *bébé*. Can I call you back? It's a bit noisy here."

"I don't think so, Dad. I'm calling ship-to-shore. It kinda important I talk to you now."

"Hold on, *bébé*."

Everyone in the room heard him bellow, "Shut up!"

Sloan and the captain grinned.

"Okay. Go ahead."

I had worked out my approach while I waited for the connection. As I started, Gravell walked in looking rather stern. It threw me off. He exchanged a few words with the captain. I forced myself to ignore them.

"There was an accident, and I was trapped under the sea for a while. It's going to hit the papers sometime soon. They may make a big deal out of it, or it might be a paragraph on page three. Either way, I'm fine.

Okay?"

While my dad asked who, what, where, when, and why, I watched Captain Campbell remind Gravell who was commanding this vessel. Gravell stepped back and turned to scrutinize me. I looked from one to the other. The captain mouthed, 'Don't worry about it.'

"I can't go into details, Dad. I still have to call Seamus and Will so they won't worry. I didn't realize the press was going to get hold of the story so soon and, like I said, I don't know what they're going to do with it."

"Don't worry about me, *bébé*. I know how the press can twist things. I'll wait for your report. Be safe, okay?"

"*Bien sur.*"

The conversation with Will was even shorter. I cheated and told him to call Dad. The main thing was he knew I was safe.

I thought I did pretty well. I conveyed a lot less information than Dora would at the press conference Reuben had probably already organized. Yet, there was Gravell, hard as stone and looking like he was just waiting for an excuse to shut me down. Captain Campbell wasn't looking too happy either. I had put him on the spot. There was no doubt in my mind now that Gravell held more power than his position implied.

"I would prefer to talk to my son in private."

Gravell shook his head.

Captain Campbell shrugged apologetically.

All day I had been hearing the metaphorical sound of sabres rattling, and I was ready to rattle my own. I started with the big dog.

I walked up to Gravell and poked him in the chest.

"You're looking for trust? Try giving me a little."

I turned to Campbell.

"Captain, if you cannot give me privacy, can you at least listen somewhere else. Then, maybe I can pretend I'm not as angry as I really am."

He nodded and ushered Gravell out before him.

Sloan didn't move. "I have to stay, Ms. Kirby. Sorry."

"I know. I understand. I'm probably being unreasonable."

The woman stuck her chin out defiantly. "I think you're holding up pretty well, under the circumstances."

I gave her a grateful smile, took a few deep breaths, and managed to settle down by the time I heard my son's voice asking "What's up, Mum? Something happen?"

"Yeah, something happened, but it's okay. I'm okay. The only reason I'm calling about it is 'cause the papers might make a big deal and I wanted you to know that everything is okay now. Besides, it gives me a chance to talk to you. How's it going, Shay?"

"I'm glad you called. I sent you a letter. I was a bit strung out at the time. Things are better now, so don't worry about anything you read okay…Hey! We both have the same problem."

"That's right. Neither of us will believe everything we read. Of course, if you say you miss me, I'll believe that because I want to."

"Yeah. I miss you, Mum."

"Miss you too, Shay. I love you."

There was a pause and then a whispered, "I love you too, Mum."

I gave the handset back to Sloan.

Sloan dug into a pocket and handed me a tissue. "Don't worry, it's clean."

Chapter Twenty-One ~ *Descent*

I didn't feel like being social at dinner, so when the captain sent his compliments, I sent my regrets. Instead, Briseau brought me soup and toast. She sat with me while I ate, fussed over me a little, then let me rest.

I pulled out Minton's journal. His downward spiral made my problems seem tame.

I'm afraid for my life. Boreman has tried threatening, cajoling, even bribing me. I stand firm, but he scares me. I wish I could hide my feelings like Mitch does. He took my report and Boreman's letter very calmly. He agreed that there was no place for Boreman's kind in the Navy, then reminded me that our mission was secret and we would have to live with Boreman until our relief arrives. I find myself counting down the days.

"Did Boreman kill you?"

Minton's ghost shook his head.

"Did he attack you?"

He shook his head again.

"Someone else was the killer."

He nodded.

Boreman avoids me. That is fine with me. I am worried for Golanger's sake. The young man seems to look at Boreman with something like hero-worship. I know that it is the womanizing, stock-car driving image that Golanger admires, but what if Boreman is seducing him? I must be vigilant.

Okay, so Boreman was gay. Golanger probably would have had a fit if he'd known his macho hero preferred men over women or maybe he knew and was good with it. In either case, Minton must have worried them both with his spying.

I have been watching them play poker. It gives me a sick headache to be around the smell of smoke and alcohol. I think that is when Boreman is most likely to try his tricks on Golanger. They always sit together. Though I cannot see, I believe their knees touch.

"Geez, Minton, you were turning into a class-A pervert. Didn't you see that your behaviour must have seemed threatening?"

The ghost's eyes narrowed and he floated purposefully towards me. He oriented himself to my body and drifted into me, like a cold fog in the early morning.

The room shifted. Everything was out of focus. There was a foul stench in the air. It was me. My own body odour was making me nauseous. The metallic smell of the bulkheads made my meagre soup dinner rise up in my throat. I felt the room close in around me. No voice to cry out. Knees folded.

Blindly, I reached for the phone Gravell gave me. I fumbled and caught it on the way down. My thumb found a button. I hoped it was the right one.

The first thing I noticed was the smell. It was me. My sweat. My vomit. I retched.

Someone held my head and a cool cloth wiped my face. I was in the recovery position. It felt like I was still on the deck, but I was still too out of it to be sure.

"I've got most of the vomit collected. That should help." That was Briseau's voice.

If she was collecting it, not just cleaning it up, she must suspect food poisoning. Little did she know I had just been assaulted by a ghost. If I had my way, she'd never know.

The cool cloth stroked my forehead, paused over my temple, and smoothed away the sticky heat on my cheeks. There was a pause then, refreshed, the cloth returned to cool the back of my neck.

"The doctor is here, Chief."

I opened my eyes.

"Bonjour, Chief Gravell," I whispered.

"Bonjour, Madame Kirby. Do you think you can get up?"

I heard the now familiar sound of Doc grumping. "I'll tell her when she can get up." He knelt beside me. "Can you get up?"

With help from Gravell and Doc I sat. When it was clear I could handle that position, they helped me stand.

"I really need a shower," I said. "I don't think I can stand to smell myself any longer."

"You're no bed of roses, that's for sure. First I'm going to check your blood pressure and temperature."

He checked blood pressure, O2 saturation, temperature, blood glucose level, and he took a vial of blood to check who knows what else. Finally he let Briseau take me to the shower. When I got out, Gravell was gone and Doc was all for sending me to bed.

"I'd really like to go out on deck. I know the way. I won't wander. Besides, I think it was claustrophobia, not food poisoning that got to me."

Doc hesitated, then nodded. "Go ahead. Gravell said you'd want to go. He's probably waiting for you." He nodded towards the hooks on the wall. "Put a jacket on."

I did as I was told. I tucked Minton's journal into a pocket and gave my thanks to Doc and Briseau on the way out.

Gravell wasn't waiting outside sick bay. I had mixed feelings about that. For what I had to do next, it was probably just as well. I was still angry about the phone calls, but I also felt safer knowing he was there. Besides, I was still feeling a bit weak. A strong arm to lean on would have helped. Maybe the gangway wouldn't seem so long, the steps so steep.

The bulkheads were closing in on me again. The metallic smell was assaulting my nostrils. Reaching the stairs was a great relief. I had something to hold onto, and I had a goal. No step was too steep, no wall too close, to keep me from my destination.

Finally I reached the side. The air around me was cold and still as the grave. It smelled stale, damp, and metallic, like the galley. I could taste salt and blood in the air. Holding tightly to a post with one hand, I reached into my pocket with the other and pulled out the journal. I held it over the sea, poised.

"Back off, or I drop it."

The cold receded. A cool, fresh breeze blew away the cloying feeling, the nausea and the claustrophobia. It almost blew the book out of my hand. I pulled it back and pocketed it. Minton appeared before me, frantically beckoning me away from the rail.

"I get your point. If that's how you were perceiving reality, no wonder you were paranoid. Regardless, if you ever pull a stunt like that again, I'll destroy the journal. You need my help more than I need yours."

Gravell stepped out of the shadows. "Please tell me you are not speaking to me."

"Oh shit," I sighed.

I leaned back and the top cable gave way. I lost my balance and started to fall. The middle cable seemed to snap.

Time slowed.

I still had a hand on the post. I just had to hold on. This was easier said than done. My palms were slick from fear and my grasp was awkward. I tried to dig my heels into the deck. I tested the strength of the third cable with one ankle. It held. I tried to pull myself to safety.

Cold suffused my body. Dread? No, Minton. This time there was no nausea, just a tugging sensation at my ankles, a pulling at my knees. My feet were flat against the deck, and I had enough leverage to halt my outward momentum, but not enough strength, even with Minton's help, to pull myself back from the brink.

Gravell grabbed me by the shirt front and pulled me to safety. Instinctively I grabbed him. A moment later, his arm was around my waist. My cheek was pressed against his chest. I could hear his heart beat gradually slow as his rush of adrenaline receded. Minton receded. Time resumed its normal course. I started to shake.

"What happened?"

"Something caused the cables to slip their anchors."

"Accident?"

I looked up. Gravell shook his head. "Can you stand on your own now?" he asked.

I probably could. Did I want to? No way!

Suck it up, Kirby, I told myself. What would your son say if he knew you practically fainted against an NCO? He'd be aghast.

I straightened up, steadying myself with a hand on Gravell's chest. He arm loosened its hold and dropped as I pushed myself away.

"So," I said, my voice steadier than my knees, which still threatened to buckle, "if it isn't an accident, is it attempted murder?"

"There are other possibilities. That one is the most likely. Would you like a cup of tea, Madame Kirby?"

His voice was calm, as if this sort of thing happened every day. It didn't happen to me every day. To the best of my knowledge, no one had ever tried killing me before. "No. I want a coffee and a stiff drink."

He didn't argue. He checked the sabotaged hardware and made a call. Soon a couple of petty officers joined us. One had a rifle and flak vest. The other brought a couple tool boxes. The first one he opened was an evidence kit.

"Ma'am, we'll need to take your prints, for elimination purposes."

I nodded.

He had a fingerprint scanner, a gadget my father would have killed for when he was a cop. As soon as he was done, Gravell led me to the captain's wardroom. The table was already laid for breakfast. He cleared one end of the table. A seaman showed up with a carafe of coffee and three mugs.

"Three?" I asked.

"The captain will be joining us shortly. He's bringing the stiff drink. Before he gets here, do you want to tell me who you were talking to, Madame Kirby?"

I wrapped my hands around an empty mug. He took the hint and poured the coffee. I sipped it, burning my tongue. I caught him wincing in sympathy.

"You saved my life. I owe you."

"You owe me nothing. You can trust me."

"You don't trust me," I countered, anger rising again.

He sighed and shook his head. "What happened in Communications had nothing to do with me not trusting you."

The fatigue in his voice softened my anger a little.

"That was between Captain Campbell and me. This ship is under his command, but I have been assigned to the mission as an intelligence officer. I need to be kept in the loop. Besides, if I had known, I could have simplified things immensely."

My eyes narrowed. "How?"

He reached into a pocket and pulled out the phone he had given me. The last time I was aware of it, I was clutching it as I collapsed retching.

"I cleaned it up while you were showering. You can call your father back now, if you like. Or check in with Dr. Leland. I would rather you didn't tell them that someone might be trying to kill you. Not until we solve that mystery."

I stared at him. "You gave me a phone that I could use to call off-ship?"

"It's a phone," he said shrugging. "I thought you'd know what it was for."

I started to laugh and I must admit, there was a manic edge to my laughter. I almost died under the sea. I almost died falling into the sea. I was walking around in the Twilight Zone with a ghost of questionable sanity. Then this great looking spy-guy gives me a phone and trusts me to use it without compromising national security.

"Madame Kirby?"

"I'm sorry. This has been a very strange day. A very strange week."

Gravell's eyes narrowed. "Now, we're on borrowed time. Who were you talking to?"

Damn. I hoped he had forgotten that question. "It's a long story." The door opened. "Which I'll save for later."

Chapter Twenty-Two ~ *Calm Before the Storm*

I let Gravell bring the captain up to speed. I poured a shot of brandy into my coffee and sipped on it. As the hot beverage and alcohol suffused me with warmth, I noticed that I finally stopped shaking.

I learned a couple of things as I listened to the debriefing. Doc had reported my collapse to the captain. No big surprise. Doc was testing the collected vomit for toxins. I didn't have a fever, so infection was unlikely, but he wanted to continue to monitor my condition. Gravell had someone tracing my dinner back to its source to see who, if anyone, might have tampered with it.

When there was a break in the dialogue, I made use of it.

"I'd like to return to the *Émil Gagnan*. I think my collapse in sick bay was the result of a panic attack. I had a flashback to being trapped. Doc has done his best to make me comfortable and you've all been great, but the ship feels a like the station to me especially when I'm in that small room. Besides, if I'm on the *Émil Gagnan*, I won't have as far to fall if I get thrown overboard."

Captain Campbell looked pained. I gave him an apologetic shrug.

"I think we could make it workable for Madame Kirby to return to her ship," Gravell said.

The captain nodded. "Very well. I'll miss you, Ms. Kirby."

I smiled. "I hope you'll invite me back for tea now and then."

Twelve hours later, I returned to the *Émil Gagnan*.

The captain and I had a private breakfast before I left. He assured me that I could call on him if ever I had the need or the desire. Because he knew Tim was getting on my nerves, Captain Campbell found pretext for keeping him a couple more days. Since this involved a re-enactment of my rescue, as witnessed on the *Nottawasaga*, he was happy enough.

Gravell accompanied me. That was his workable solution to my return. I strongly suspected he wanted to return to keep tabs on the rest of the team, not just me. It was also possible that Franchot wanted his first mate back.

Before we left, Tim took me aside.

"You want to keep an eye on Gravell," he said.

"You don't trust him?"

"He's a spook, of course I don't trust him. You shouldn't either. The only other prints around the accident were his. They could have been there before."

I shook my head.

"If he wanted me dead, I'd be dead."

"Maybe he only wants you scared."

I smiled. A really wicked part of me was glad that this was going to happen to someone other than me.

"I do want her scared," Gravell said, at Tim's shoulder.

Tim gave a satisfactory yelp of surprise.

"I want her scared enough to be careful. Don't worry, Neville, I also want you to be scared for her and I don't require your trust."

As soon as we boarded, we were summoned to a briefing with Franchot. Gravell gave an expurgated account of my activities and a brief report on Captain Campbell's expectations. He was relatively up front. He needed Franchot's cooperation, and I hoped he wanted to maintain my trust.

"So you think Dora and Reuben will be successful," Franchot said, topping up coffee mugs as we sat around his desk.

"Captain Campbell has been given a heads-up to that effect. The Canadian government is as interested as you are in learning the truth. That's the primary reason I'm back to make sure no one interferes with your work."

He turned and gave me a small bow.

"And to keep you safe, Madame Kirby. I think the two are entwined, either because of something you are suspected to have learned while trapped on the station, or because you are documenting the mission."

Franchot frowned. "Anybody could have leaned against that cable. It's a haphazard way of killing someone specific. The simplest explanation is that someone wanted to scare people. A current investigation into attempted murder would take precedence over a cold case mystery."

Gravell nodded. "Which is why we're keeping quiet about it. The trouble is, it isn't a credible accident and while it is a risky way to commit murder, Madame Kirby is known for spending time at that particular spot."

"Did you get any prints?"

"No. Nothing. No prints were on the adjoining posts other than Madame Kirby's and mine, where I braced myself. That in itself is suspicious. There is no doubt that it was deliberate, and there is no doubt in my mind that Madame Kirby was the target."

Franchot shrugged. "Your instincts are usually pretty good. You were right about Jen. I guess I'll have to cough up that bottle of rum."

"The good stuff, Skipper. Now if you'll excuse me, I'm going to grab some sack time. Madame Kirby, if you need me, you know how to reach me."

I nodded.

Franchot stood and held out his hand. "You may need some rest too, but first there some people waiting to see you."

It was a relief to immerse myself in my work, even if it meant having Minton hovering nearby. Dora had turned the documents and photographs over to Mary Lou for forensic examination. As a first step, everything had been photographed and converted to digital files. Tracy brought me a copy. The first thing I looked for was Boreman's letter.

The nice thing about an electronic archive is that it's so easy to search. I called up everything that involved Boreman and started with those items in his effects. This included a series of letters to his daughter, catalogued chronologically; a few letters to his son and wife; a large pile of photographs; no sign of the offending letter. I was both disappointed and relieved. I would have liked to judge the contents myself, but I was relieved that Boreman had been wise enough to destroy anything that would have such a negative impact on his family.

Since I had them handy, I read the letters.

Dear Mary Lou,

Gosh, I miss you sweetie. Been days—feels like forever. Didn't think it would be so hard. Keep expecting you to wake me up in the morning to walk the dog. Love that time of day with you, when your mom and brother're still asleep and it's just you and me and Puddles. When I get home, that's the first thing I want to do. You and me, we'll take Puddles to the park. After, we'll all go to the diner for bacon and eggs. You can have pancakes. When I get tired of living in this sardine can, that's what

keeps me going.
  Love, Daddy
  PS: Give my love to Mommy.

There were more like that. Short letters, written every couple of days, talking about projected outings and things they'd do when he got home. Then they stopped.

I skimmed the few letters to Boreman's son, Ray. They were written in block letters, using short words and simple concepts. They were typical of the kind of letter you write to a child who is learning to read. The letters to his wife weren't much different.

Hey sweetheart,
  Miss you guys so much. I know you didn't want me to go. You've given up a lot for me. I'll make it up to you when I get home. Promise.
  Lou

I looked through the photos. Most of them were of Mary Lou with or without her mother. A couple were of Lou Boreman posing with cars. In one, his arm was draped across the shoulders of a young man who was leaning into him, just a hair's-breadth. There were cars and a trophy in the shot as well my eye was drawn to the young man and the proprietary way that Boreman looked down at him. I remembered when Will looked at me like that.

"I don't care what was in that letter. Boreman wasn't a degenerate. He was a man in love. And more than anything, he loved his daughter." I held up the photos of Lou and lover, and Lou and daughter. "He might not have been a good husband, but this is not a bad man."

Minton mouthed, 'I know.'

Lil came to fetch me for dinner. "Don't tell me you're not eating because that won't do. You've been cooped up here all afternoon. Besides, we're starting a new euchre tournament tonight."

It was so calm, I had forgotten I was at sea. Food sounded good. Company sounded good too, especially the company of the living. I tidied away my work and, because I was learning to be cautious, I locked Minton's journal in the cabin safe.

Gravell was at dinner. It was interesting watching him win over the team again. He wasn't as cheery as he had been before they knew he was a government agent, but not as serious as he acted aboard the *Nottawasaga*. Being a spy seemed to add to his allure. In any case, he suddenly had the admiring attention of Tracy and Lil.

I grabbed a plate and loaded it up with Spanish rice, salmon kebabs, and fresh tomato slices that came, no doubt, from the *Nottawasaga*'s shipment of fresh food. There was a space between Mike and Jamal, directly across from Gravell, who was bracketed by Lil and Tracy. I took it. Without dropping the thread of his conversation with the women, Gravell acknowledged my presence with a nod and a moment of eye contact that conveyed welcome, and an invitation to share his enjoyment of the situation.

Later, he manoeuvred things so that I was partnered with him for euchre. There was no ulterior motive I could discern for him doing this, so I chose to be flattered by the attention. In fact, I received a lot of flattering and solicitous attention throughout the evening. I suppose it was my brush with death, but suddenly I had been pushed into the limelight, out of my comfort zone.

In all, it was one of the most pleasant evenings I had enjoyed since leaving home. Naturally, it was the calm before the storm.

Gravell and I were four points away from winning our latest game, and I had a strong hand. Right and left bowers, two off-suit aces, and a nine of trumps sat in my hand. The ace was turned up and it was my partner's deal. If Gravell picked up the ace, we could potentially get all the tricks. Or I could order him up and try for four points.

Minton showed up, looking worried. At first I thought it was disapproval at me playing cards, then I got the message.

"Pick it up," I told my partner. "I'm going alone."

As chance would have it, the remaining ace was led, which I trumped. I swept up my trick and plopped down the two bowers. I got the last two tricks just before the storm hit.

Chapter Twenty-Three ~ *The Storm*

The warning bell sounded. The speakers gave a squawk of feedback. Then we heard Captain Franchot's voice. "All hands on deck."

Gravell stood. "I need to go. Stay here. Make sure everyone else stays put and listens to Cookie."

I nodded.

"I'll come too," said Mike. "Once a swabby, always a swabby."

As soon as they left I looked around and took in the varying degrees of fear evident on the team's faces.

"Let's clear everything up. Everything loose should be secured. Tracy and Jamal, you take care of that. Mary Lou, you and I will batten the hatches."

Two weeks at sea and I was picking up the jargon. I wasn't sure if we were actually battening hatches, but we were making sure the portholes were latched.

We had everything done by the time Cookie poked his head in to tell us to do the very same thing.

"Need any help in the kitchen?" asked Mary Lou.

"Si, señora. I could use one or two helpers."

Mary Lou looked around. Lil shrugged and the two women followed Cookie to the galley, leaving me with the most nervous members of our party.

"Let's make sure everything in here is secure. There's a checklist on the wall. We can run through it."

There wasn't much on the checklist that we could do that we hadn't already done. Still, going over it and double checking things passed the time and took our minds off the pitch and roll of the ship.

Cookie, Lil, and Mary Lou joined us.

"The Skipper wants you to make sure everything is stowed safely in your cabins," Cookie told us in his perfect, heavily accented English.

"Return here with your PFDs. There is nothing to worry about. This is just protocol, *si*?"

I plastered a bright smile on my face.

"Hey, if we're not needed, we can play cards when we get back."

I taught them Blackout Bridge. The six of us could play it together and it was an easy game to pick up if you already played bridge or euchre. One of the adaptations we had to make was to find creative places to stash our tricks. The ship's movement made it unwise to leave things on the table. Lil used her lace bra. Mary Lou had her tricks poking out of her hair, which was pulled back in a ponytail. Jamal used his left shirt pocket and Tracy his right. Cookie stuck his tricks in his hat. I used my bra strap as a holder then switched to my cup when I lost a trick down my sleeve.

I desperately wanted to know what was going on and would have loved the excuse to go on deck for fresh air. Only willpower kept me from bringing up dinner. I was damned if I was going to be the weak link. I had a new-found reputation to live up to. While I made my bids and kibitzed over play, I sought a reason for me to check on things.

"All hands to emergency stations. All hands to emergency stations."

"Be careful what you wish for," I muttered.

Cookie directed us to put on our PFDs and checked each of us before leading us to the divers' ready room. There we were directed to put on our thermal gear, as we had when we went to the station. Staying afloat was only part of the task. We also had to keep warm.

Mike and a couple of the divers were present. They assured us collectively and individually that we would probably not need to leave the ship and if, by some chance we did evacuate, we'd be on enclosed life rafts. This was just a precaution.

I wasn't buying it. I remembered what Gravell had said about the danger the wreck presented to the ship tethering it. As soon as I could, I took Mike aside and asked him the million-dollar question.

"What's happening with the station?"

Mike gave me a funny look.

"Why do you ask, Jen? What do you know?"

"I know that it's less likely to sink as it is to sink us right now. I have faith in the crew's ability to handle the situation. I just want an update. Inquiring minds want to know, y' know?"

"Skipper's playing the station like a marlin, but he might have to cut it loose."

I nodded. No doubt I'd get a more technical answer later, which I would duly record and understand less than Mike's simple analogy.

"How's Gravell doing?"

I asked, realizing that it was a dumb question as soon as I asked it.

"Funny, he wanted to know the same thing about you."

Chapter Twenty-Four ~ *The Rain*

For well over an hour, we waited for the worst to happen. Lil started a game of Fact or Fiction. We took turns coming up with three bizarre statements, only one of which was true. The others tried to guess the fact. When that palled, I suggested my stand-by for long car trips with my son and nieces: the Alphabet Game. We took turns picking a topic and went round finding items in alphabetical order. Food and animals were easy. I'm aces at geography. When Mary Lou suggested legal terms I wavered.

"Affidavit," said Mary Lou

"Ballistic report," said Lil.

"Cadaver?" I suggested.

They let that one go. I had to drop out at 'I.'

We'd moved onto sea animals. The divers were cleaning up. The rest of us floundered. We got to 'Q,' with no one dropping out, when Mike reappeared. He looked exhausted and elated.

"We've still got rough water and rain to contend with, but the storm is receding. Franchot says we can stand down and go to bed. He wants us to keep our gear handy so we can suit up if there's a second front."

He reached out for his wife.

"I've been relieved so I can get a few hours in the sack, so if you'll excuse us."

Mike and Mary Lou left with Tracy and Jamal close behind them.

Cookie rubbed his hands. "The Skipper will want coffee and breakfast is only a few hours away."

I shook my head. "I'll make coffee. You get some rest. You've been up longer than any of us."

"I'll help," said Lil.

Cookie thanked us, then rattled on with instructions all the way to the galley. I had done enough early morning KP to know how things worked, so as well as brewing coffee, we assembled sandwiches.

"Do you mind if I take the bridge and you take engineering?" I asked Lil. "I really need an excuse to get some fresh air."

We secured the galley and headed out, each armed with a couple of thermal carafes and a large plastic container of sandwiches. Lil wished me good night. As soon as her delivery was complete, she intended to hit the sack.

I zipped up my suit and secured my PFD. From neck to toes, my gear kept me warm and dry. However, I hadn't secured the hood tightly enough. Within seconds of stepping on deck my hair was soaked and rivulets of water poured down my face.

The deck was slick and the wind steady. With one hand holding the carafes and the sandwich container tucked under that arm, I was able to hold onto rails. When I got to the exposed steps up to the bridge, I almost had a failure of nerve. Wind whipping tendrils of hair in and out of my eyes, I hesitated. The rail was on the opposite side. I had to shift everything over to my other hand and for a moment I felt like I was going to fall.

I wasn't even close to the edge. I would have had to fly to go overboard, but for a moment, that's what I felt was about to happen.

The ghost of Lieutenant Minton entered me and a different sort of panic rose. I grabbed hold of the rail. Clutching, white knuckled, I dragged myself up the steps. The cold receded, leaving the slightest pressure on my back, like a chilled hand pushing me upward. He wasn't trying to scare me, he was trying to help me.

Franchot almost bowled me over when I reached the top. He was coming out as I was about to go in. He stopped, steadied me and pulled me inside.

"What the hell are you doing?"

"B-bringing c-coffee and s-sandwiches." I took a deep breath and brought my diction under control, despite the chattering of my teeth. "Lil's taking some below. We wanted to let Cookie rest before he had to get up and start breakfast."

He stepped forward and relieved me of my burden. "With that kind of thinking, I should invite you to join the crew. I take it you didn't know there is an inside way up to the bridge."

"Oh."

I had only ever entered via the forward deck.

He pushed my hair out of my eyes. "I'll have to remember to include that information next time we conduct tours."

"Why were you going out then?"

"I went to look for you. Gravell just informed us that you were missing."

"I was in the galley. Then I came here." I narrowed my eyes at him. "You didn't really think I'd gone to the foredeck, did you?"

Franchot blushed. "It was Gravell's suggestion. I'll let him know the lost is found."

"Tell him I'm on my way to my cabin. Maybe you could show me the inside way out of here. I think I've had enough fresh air for tonight."

Gravell was sitting on Dora's bunk when I entered the cabin. He had dark circles under his eyes, a frown on his face and the phone he gave me in his hand.

I winced at my stupidity. "Oops."

He stood, towering over me. "Never, ever, leave this behind again. Do you understand, Madame Kirby?"

"Yes, Chief Gravell."

He took my hand, wrapped it around the phone. "It has a clip. It can be worn on your belt. You can put it in a pocket. Or you can tie a string around it and wear it around your neck, but never, ever leave it behind."

"Yes, Chief Gravell."

He nodded and started to leave.

I grabbed his shirt front with my free hand, clipped the phone on my waist band, as suggested, then put my arms around him. He responded cautiously.

"Lil wanted me to give you a hug from her," I explained, with a forced chuckle.

Nothing.

My fists balled up around handfuls of sweat-damped cloth. My knuckles were pressed into his back. My forehead was pressed against his chest. My voice was shaking again.

"I j-just n-need to hold onto something s-solid and real."

His palm flattened against my back and he pulled me closer. His other hand held my head against his chest, and I heard the quickened beat of his heart. Gradually both of us calmed.

"I was worried about you too. And I didn't mean to forget the phone. I completely forgot about it and almost everything else in the heat of the moment. I should have taken the journal out of the safe and kept that on my person too. Though, in fairness, I hardly need it anymore."

He held me at arms' length, forcing me to look up or seem like a wimp. His brow was furrowed, eyes narrowed, lips held tightly. It must be disturbing to an intelligence officer to have lines like that just dropped out of the blue. Then his eyes widened and I could tell he had only just noticed that I was dripping wet, even though I had transferred a fair portion of the damp to his sleeves and shirt front.

"Get dry first. Then explain."

Chapter Twenty-Five ~ *Admissions*

"I'm being haunted."

I was warm, dry, and comfortably dressed in a flannel nightshirt. I sat on Dora's bunk with my comforter tucked around me and a hot mug of tea wrapped in my hands.

While I showered and changed, Gravell had acquired tea for two. Now, all our outerwear, including his boots and socks, were drying in the shower stall. His damp shirt was draped over one of the cabin chairs. His t-shirt was stretched taut over tense muscles. He was sitting, elbows on knees, hands wrapped around his tea mug.

"Haunted?"

"Haunted," I repeated. Though I had only just got comfortable, I started to get up.

"What do you need, Madame Kirby?" Gravell asked, holding up a hand.

"I want to get the journal out of the safe."

"I'll get it," he said, going to the small safe hiding in a cupboard over the desk. "Tell me the code."

I hesitated.

"You can set a different code when you use the safe again."

I blushed. "It's not that. I used a word, and I had to work out the numbers."

The safe had an alpha-numeric pad like a telephone. When you locked it, you keyed in a code and it would only open again with that code.

"Eight. Seven. Six, six. Five."

He keyed the coded and the door opened. Inside were the diary and a little white bean-filled cat. Gravell solemnly passed both objects to me after closing the door.

"Spook," I said, holding up the cat. I had to smile at his expression. He'd been hearing that name bandied about quite a bit lately.

He went back to the key pad and confirmed that spook was my code word.

"When Seamus went away to camp the first time. I sent a black dog named Boris with him. He was a leftover Halloween toy that I got on sale. I charged him up with kisses, a week's worth for the week my son would be away from home. Boris still goes away with him, it's a tradition. I guess Shay thought this was like going to camp for me because he gave me Spook before I left."

"Charged up with kisses?"

I looked to see if he was laughing at me. Nope. That melting look wasn't amusement.

"I have been assured that Spook has been charged with enough kisses to last to September." I tucked the little cat under my comforter. "Getting back to what I was saying, I was about to introduce you to Lieutenant Minton."

Minton, who had appeared at the end of the bed, gave me a 'you must be crazy' look.

"Are you telling me there's a ghost here?" Gravell's eyes narrowed in disbelief.

"There is for me. I see him. Ghost or projection of my imagination, he's been haunting me since I discovered the journal."

"You talk to the ghost? The ghost talks to you?"

"Sometimes I find myself talking to him when we're alone. Presumably he can hear me."

Minton rolled his eyes.

"I can't hear him. I can only see him...and sometimes I see his memories."

Gravell sipped his tea and said nothing.

"Minton gave me the heads up about the storm coming. Right now he's gesturing me to shut up before you have me carted away."

Gravell smiled. "Where would I cart you?"

I returned a shadow of that smile. I was taking a big risk telling him about this. I hoped he appreciated the level of trust involved.

"Between the journal and the memories of Lieutenant Minton, I've been building a picture of what happened on the station before the murders."

"We don't know it was murder," Gravell reminded me.

I looked over at Minton who was rolling his eyes again. I'm pretty sure he'd picked up that mannerism from me.

"I know it was murder. If the samples weren't compromised, I think we already have some physical evidence. I doubt we'll ever have conclusive proof I'm right. I'll settle for being sure in my own mind what happened."

"If I remember correctly, you told me that there was nothing in the journal that definitively explained what happened."

I sighed and, it seemed to me, Minton heaved a sigh as well. "It's a journal, Chief Gravell, not an affidavit. It expresses Minton's observations of what was going on. By itself, the view is pretty skewed. When you found me in sick bay…" I hesitated. That was only a day ago, a little over twenty-four hours ago. Only two days since I had been trapped.

I shivered. "It wasn't food poisoning. Minton decided to give me a more visceral example of what he experienced on the station. I saw the world through his eyes, coloured by claustrophobia and altered perception of reality. It made me nauseous and dizzy and," I paused, shuddering from the memory, "you saw the results."

Gravell looked troubled. "He would have been rigorously tested before being assigned to that mission. How would he have passed the tests if he was that affected?"

"I think he learned to cope with it, to a certain extent."

I looked for confirmation from Minton and he nodded.

"I was hit as hard as I was because it was all thrown at me at once the smells, the disorientation, vision tunnelling." I took a deep breath. "Also, I think his behaviour was triggered by smell. I bet tests don't look for reactions in small spaces that stink. In his journals and the visions he's shared, smell is…" I sought out the right term and gave up. "Here, listen."

I pulled out the book.

"He's talking about Margolo. He still likes Margolo at this point. 'He's a great guy, but one day I'm going to strangle him, he's such a slob and his socks smell like rancid cheese.' Bodily smells are bad enough, but smoke…" I found the place and read, "'It gives me a sick headache to be around the smell of smoke and alcohol.'" I flipped back a couple of pages. "'Mitch says that the men can smoke in the kitchen because of the fire controls and extra air filters. As a result, all the food tastes like tobacco.' It was driving him crazy."

"It was common for people to smoke just about anywhere, back then," Gravell pointed out. "They didn't understand the dangers of smoking and second-hand smoke."

"They knew," I snapped, suddenly angry. "They've known since the fifties that smoking was linked to lung disease and cancer. The dangers of second-hand smoke have been known for decades. I am sure they knew it wouldn't be healthy have people smoking in a closed system. It was unconscionable."

Tears welled up in my eyes. This wasn't just about Shore allowing the crew to smoke in the kitchen. This was about my mother who wouldn't give up smoking, even when it was killing her, whose second-hand smoke affected my father's health and probably mine too. It was about the smell that got everywhere, necessitating a shower and the immediate laundering of my clothes after every familial visit. Having had a taste of how aware Minton was of smells, and how that awareness bent his perceptions, I could see how that would make him crazy.

I hugged my knees, letting the journal and my empty mug fall.

"You killed them, didn't you?" I asked Minton.

He nodded.

Gravell picked up the journal and turned the pages. He was scanning, looking for something I knew he wouldn't find, something I already told him wasn't there.

"This is nonsense," he said, holding the book open so I could see.

He was correct. A few entries after the one about Boreman's letter, the journal became unreadable. There were squiggles, little more than wavy lines and loops. It didn't even look comprehensive enough to be a code.

He flipped a few more pages and held up another series of squiggles and loops, then tossed the book back to me.

"How can you know he killed the crew? It's not here. Has he shown you?"

"No. Not yet." I wasn't looking forward to that part. "I think I need to go back to the station first."

He rubbed his forehead, as if smoothing the lines across his brow could make what I was saying more comprehensible. Not that I blamed him. I knew what it sounded like.

"I know it seems crazy, but I'm not making this up."

"I know." He gave me a sad half-smile. "I wish you were making it up." He rubbed his eyes tiredly. "Minton made you sick?"

"Yes. He wanted me to understand. I do. And he understands he can't do that to me again."

"That's who you were talking to just before. Could he have been responsible for the railing?"

I shook my head. I wasn't sure it was possible. I was sure he wouldn't do it. He really did need me. Minton had confessed, but that was just the start. There had to be reparation. That meant finding enough proof to be able to support Minton's story, enough evidence to be able to tell his story and give the families of the men he killed some peace.

Then there was the issue of someone trying to stop me. I shivered. Not everyone who had a stake in this was dead.

Gravell stood and stretched, then crouched down to my eye level.

"We need to sleep, Madame Kirby. I don't intend to leave you alone with a ghost that can make you pass out even if you do insist he won't do it again. So, you tuck up where you are. I'll use your bunk."

I started to disentangle myself from my comforter.

"I won't need it," he said, tucking it back around me. "The sheet will be sufficient."

He straightened and peered into my bunk.

"I wouldn't say no to one of those pillows."

I handed him one from the pile I had propped myself up on while we talked, then rearranged the rest so I could cuddle down on the bed comfortably.

Gravell climbed up on my bunk without using the ladder, the show off. The mattress creaked alarmingly until he settled. Only then did his earlier words sink in.

"If you won't leave me alone with the ghost, you must believe in the ghost."

The mattress creaked and Gravell's head and shoulders appeared. "I believe that you believe, Madame Kirby. Now go to sleep."

"I can't sleep with the lights on. No!" I said as he started to get up. "Let me. I have to get up anyway."

Several minutes later, in the almost perfect darkness, Gravell said, "Better?"

"Yes."

"Now you'll go to sleep?"

"Maybe. Don't let me stop you from sleeping."

"I could tell you about my day, the boring bits before the storm."

"I'd rather hear about the storm."

"That might keep you up. I could sing."

"Tempting. I'd want to sing along and we're supposed to be going to sleep. I know, tell me what you were doing when you were thirteen years old."

"That's easy. I was a Sea Cadet."

"My son is a Navy League Cadet."

"I know. You told me."

"Did I?"

"Uh-huh."

"So tell me about being a Sea Cadet, Chief Gravell."

I made it as far as his first weekend training before falling asleep.

Chapter Twenty-Six ~ *Reports*

I woke up at five, thanks to an internal alarm clock that I had mentally set right after being given early morning KP duty. It was a trick I learned in my teens as a way of waking ahead of the dreaded alarm clock.

Gravell was still fast asleep, and I did my best not to disturb him as I dressed as quietly, and with as little light as possible. I thought I would make a clean getaway. I went back to the bed to get Minton's journal and a hand grabbed my shoulder.

"Phone," he mumbled, his voice muffled by the pillow half covering his mouth.

"Clipped on my waistband."

"Good."

The hand fell off my shoulder. I tucked it back into bed. Judging by the soft snores, Gravell was already back to sleep.

The sea was still choppy, the sky was grey, and the rain had stopped for now. I enjoyed a few moments of fresh air and peace before heading to the galley and work. I hadn't slept long, no more than three or four hours, but I slept well. For the first time in a week, I didn't dream about the station. Was it because Minton had confessed? Or was it the knowledge that if I had a nightmare, Gravell would be there to take care of me?

The sea didn't have any answers so I went to the galley. Cookie set me to work laying out cold cereal and fruit. There was another storm warning, though it would probably pass south of us. To be on the safe side, he wasn't going to fire up the stove and oven. Instead, he hauled out an electric waffle iron. As soon as the cold food was laid out, he taught me how to use it, letting me eat my first successful waffle (and the edible portions of the previous two). When I was done, I took over waffle production while he sat with his coffee and planned lunch.

The crew members were the first to eat. They came in pairs, first the ones who had been relieved at the end of the storm, then the ones finally coming off watch. All looked tired. All managed smiles when I offered them fresh-made waffles. Later, when I got a chance to look in the mirror, I realized that the smiles might have been because of the sprinkling of flour in my hair and the batter smears on forearms and eyebrows.

No, I don't know how I got batter in my eyebrows. It's a talent. All I can say is that it's worse when I make cookies, and it's worse still when I paint.

Mike and Mary Lou were the first of the researchers to make an appearance. They looked refreshed, and I suspected that the excitement of last night had carried over into the bedroom. I was envious. They each ate three waffles with fruit, syrup, and cream. I gave myself a mental slap for trying to imagine what they had done to work up such appetites.

"You're looking wistful," said Franchot, suddenly appearing. He nodded towards Mike and Mary Lou.

"Only a little. Waffle?"

"Actually, I'm wondering if you know where Gravell is. I seem to have lost him."

Cookie appeared touching my elbow to get my attention. "Take a break, señora. The rush is over. You sit too, Skipper. I'll bring you something."

Franchot poured us coffee and we found a seat apart from Mary Lou and Mike, who had been joined by a bleary-eyed Lil.

"He spent the night with you, didn't he?"

"Only because he was too tired to move. He was waiting for me, to tell me off. Then he fell asleep on the other bunk. He was bone tired as I am sure you were last night."

He nodded.

"He earned his sleep. Now I need him on the bridge so I can sleep. I'm running out of rested crew."

"While you're still awake, can you tell me about fighting the storm? My part isn't going to make very dramatic reading."

He sat back in his chair and grinned.

"If you want drama, you need me to get some rest and tot or two of rum. I'll give you the Cliff Notes version."

As Franchot talked, the divers showed up for breakfast and hovered within earshot. Mary Lou, Mike, and Lil moved closer.

He started the tale from the storm warnings.

"We knew it was coming, but we didn't expect it to hit so hard and fast. That's why we let the crew have some down time and you guys enjoy your evening. The storm wasn't due until the wee hours of the morning and even then, it might have bypassed us like it did earlier in the week."

"That was bypassing us?" I asked.

"We only got the edge of the storm. The brunt hit the coast south of us. It hit you harder because you were still getting seasick. You're a better sailor now."

I didn't know about being a better sailor. I was a better passenger.

"Señora Jen was great," said Cookie, bringing a fresh carafe of coffee to the table. I blushed as he gave a flattering account of my activities the night before.

"Well done. Your group is pretty good. Sometimes the researchers we carry have no common sense at all. We spend all our time keeping them from doing something stupid."

"Instead, I only had to be reminded to eat, sleep, and get out of the rain."

That got a few chuckles.

"What I want to know is how you kept the station from dragging us down," Mike said you played it like a marlin."

Franchot liked the analogy and ran with it. He really was a good storyteller, though I detected a few touches of Hemingway and Melville in there. Lil found me a pad and paper so I could take notes. It was a score-pad from the games cupboard. It was long and narrow and printed with columns. I hoped I'd be able to read my cramped writing when I was done.

Peripherally, I noticed that others joined us, including Tracy and Jamal. Gravell came up behind me. I didn't pause to look around, but I felt someone there and knew who it was by the expression on Franchot's face. That's why I didn't react when my phone was unclipped and placed on the table between me and Franchot.

"It can record. You don't mind, do you Skipper? I think Madame Kirby's hand is getting tired."

Franchot gave a nonchalant wave.

"I don't mind, but I need you on the bridge. Andre isn't ready to be left in charge, even if we aren't going anywhere."

"I sent Hassan to the bridge. He can direct damage control from there and maybe get what we need from the *Nottawasaga* for repairs."

"Okay. Then sit down and have some breakfast."

Cookie left the table and returned a little later with a stack of waffles and a jug of juice. Gravell, and the few others who had not yet eaten, made short work of the stack. Another appeared in time for Franchot's conclusion which was that as soon as the second storm front passed, he'd be sending the robots down to check out the station.

"And now I want to eat," he said, pulling the plate of waffles towards him. Then he looked around at the members of his crew that had stopped to listen.

"I am almost positive some of you are supposed to be working right now."

The wardroom emptied, leaving Franchot, Gravell, and me. Even Tracy and Jamal left, perhaps remembering they had jobs to do too.

I flexed my hands and stretched my arms.

"I suppose, I had better get to work too. I need to translate my notes before I forget what they mean."

"Where will you be working, Madame Kirby?" Gravell asked.

"That depends. Can I occupy a corner of ops again, Skipper?"

"Don't see why not. It might get a bit busy in there later, but you'll want to be in the thick of that too, won't you?"

"That's my job."

"Perhaps I can help, Madame Kirby. You could dictate from your notes, and I could type."

I gave him an odd look.

"Not that I want to disparage your offer of help, Chief Gravell, but I'm getting the impression that your offer is just an excuse to watch me."

"I wondered that too," Franchot remarked, pouring a second glass of juice.

Gravell leaned back in his chair with such an expression of genuine and obvious amusement on his face that I found myself smiling back automatically.

"I don't need an excuse to watch you, Madame Kirby. It's my job. Speaking of which, Skipper, you better let Mercuros know he's back to being First Mate."

"He never stopped."

Gravell nodded and turned back to me.

"Since I'm going to be watching you, Madame Kirby. I might as well make myself useful."

"I need to go get my briefcase," I said, figuring I could use the privacy of my cabin to get some answers out of Gravell, answers I didn't think he'd give in public.

"I'll meet you in ops."

Damn him. He knew.

"Fine, bring coffee."

"Don't forget the phone, Madame Kirby."

Chapter Twenty-Seven ~ *Answers and Questions*

The research team had a cramped, but well-equipped lab. On the way to ops, I stopped by to see if Mary Lou had processed the samples from the station's galley. In this setting, it was clear that Mary Lou wasn't just a good ol' country girl, she was every inch the professional. As I noted aboard the station, in this mode, she took the lead and Mike stepped down from his role as alpha male and protective husband. He, Tracy, and Jamal were serving as her assistants.

"Can I come in?" I asked.

"Sure thing, hon. Just put on a white coat, hair net and a pair of gloves. We don't want to contaminate anything with stray organics."

At least I wasn't going to be shedding waffle batter. I cleaned up when I went for my stuff. I left my brief case with my windbreaker by the door and picked out a lab coat that looked like it was about the right size. There were a few spares besides the one with Dora's name sewn on it. The disposable hairnets and gloves were on a shelf above the coat hooks.

"I just dropped by to find out if you had started on swabs you took. Now I'm suited up, maybe I can get a closer look at what you're doing. If that's okay."

"As a matter of fact, we're working backwards through the evidence collected 'cause I wanted to start with the swabs. Mind now, we can only do so much here. I can tell you we found blood from at least two people, because we have two blood types. One is almost certainly from Reuben's daddy. He was the only one with type B negative. The other samples could be from Papa, Mike's uncle, Golanger, or some combination of them. They were all type O positive. If I had the chance, I could have sent the samples with Dora so she could get them to a lab for DNA mapping. As it is, it'll take a couple of weeks from whenever we do get the samples out."

"It looks like murder to me," Jamal remarked.

"Suspicious deaths," Tracy corrected.

"We have no proof that anyone died. If they died, we don't know that the deaths weren't accidental. We don't even know if the blood has anything to do with the deaths. There isn't enough of it to make a judgement call. Someone cleaned up. Jamal is currently processing cleanser residue while Tracy processes finger prints with help from Mike."

I turned to Tracy.

"And?"

"We didn't get anything in the galley. All the surfaces we got to, before the explosion, were clean. I'm working on the material we took out of the living quarters. There's a lot to go through. They must have passed stuff around a lot. Most items have the owner's plus at least a couple of other people's prints on them."

"Did anyone touch everything?" I asked.

"We haven't processed everything," Tracy reminded me, "but Lieutenant Minton's prints show up a lot."

I nodded. If he went through Boreman's personal belongings, he probably went through the others.

"In contrast, Petty Officer Naire's prints have only shown up on his own belongings so far."

Mike snorted. "Token black man. The others probably didn't want him touching their stuff."

"Black cooties," Mary Lou said, shaking her head.

"Huh?" I asked, taken aback.

"Still see it sometimes. Not as much and not so much blacks as other visible minorities now. People are treated like their colour or culture might be contagious if you touch 'em."

"Unclean!" said Jamal, waving his hands dramatically.

I decided to go back through Minton's journal to find references to Naire. This reminded me that I was withholding a vital piece of evidence albeit with the tacit consent of anyone who would charge me with a crime. That didn't make me feel better about not being upfront with the team.

"Is that your phone?" Tracy asked.

I listened. There was a low buzz I had assumed had to do with something in the lab. Since no one had called me on the phone Gravell gave me, I didn't recognize its ring tone.

"Hello?"

"I thought we were meeting in ops, Madame Kirby."

"Yeah. Sorry. I got sidetracked. I'll be right there."

I hung up and gave a sheepish shrug.

"Gravell?" asked Mike.

"Yep. For some reason, he needs to keep an eye on me."

Mike grinned. "I could think of a couple of reasons. Only one of them is job related."

Mary Lou rolled her eyes.

"He's with CSIS, isn't he?" Jamal half asked, half stated.

Mike shrugged. "Not necessarily. He could be Naval Intelligence or whatever you Canadians call it."

I knew, but didn't think it was for me to tell. More lies. "Whatever he is, he's going to come looking for me if I don't get going. See you guys at lunch."

I didn't have to go outside, but I did. It had started raining. It wasn't a drenching downpour and it was worth the damp to clear my head of the lab smells. It felt so good I called Gravell to postpone work a little longer.

"Madame Kirby?"

"Want to meet me on the foredeck? My visit to the lab made me feel a bit icky. I don't think I can handle being inside yet."

"It's raining, Madame Kirby."

"There's the overhang. Please."

I waited for his answer, wondering why I didn't just hang up and go. I had told him where I would be. Keeping an eye on me was part of his agenda, not mine.

"I'll meet you there."

I hung up and sighed. I was relieved. Why?

"Minton?"

Nothing.

Maybe he was embarrassed. I realized that his prolonged absence was worrying me at some level. It might be why I wanted Gravell's company. Should I? He wasn't just a nice looking man who felt the need to take care of me. When push came to shove, Gravell might end up my enemy.

I shook my head. Even if it was naive, I didn't really believe that.

"You look troubled, Madame Kirby. Did something come up in the lab?"

"Nothing unexpected. Mary Lou found blood from at least two sources. Tracy corroborated my belief that Minton went through his crew mates' belongings. Then there's the whole issue of the journal. It was catalogued when it was first recovered. No one's asked about it. I suppose they assume that it was kept by Captain Tinsdale. Dora is going to go ballistic when she finds out I've had it all along, but if I tell anyone right now..." I finished my sentence with a sigh.

"If you're worried about getting in trouble."

"It's not that. It's Dora's trust and the trust of the others. I think I can make Dora understand once she sees that it was either keep it or lose it to Tinsdale. I'm not so sure about Mary Lou. The whole situation feels out of control, yet, it seemed like the only safe plan at the time."

Was I trying to convince Gravell or myself?

He laid a hand on shoulder.

"You did what you thought was right at the time. When Dr. Leland returns, you can do what you think is right for now."

I nodded. I can't have been very convincing.

"There's something else troubling you, what is?"

"I have a bad feeling. Geez, that sounds so *Star Wars*."

"Someone is trying to kill you. You should have a bad feeling about that."

"You're sure it wasn't an accident or me just being in the wrong place at the wrong time?"

He gave me a sorrowful grimace. "I'm sure. That's why I'm here. I think you're sure too."

I nodded. "Someone aboard the *Nottawasaga*?"

"It isn't likely to be a member of the *Nottawasaga* crew, though I haven't ruled out the possibility completely. It could be someone here or one of the visitors from the *Scranton*. The Boremans and Lilian Dawes were aboard a few hours before the incident. For that matter, Reuben Dawes and Dora Leland could have done it before they left. Tim Neville is a possible suspect, as he stayed onboard. Captain Tinsdale didn't have the opportunity, but that doesn't mean he didn't give the order. There has been a US security contingent onboard since you were trapped. One of the reasons I agreed to you returning here was because it would narrow down the number of people I would have to watch."

Anything was possible. For that matter, it could be Gravell.

I pushed myself away from the bulkhead and went to the rail. The rain was a cold, gentle spray. It washed away the sudden nausea and rising paranoia. Holding onto the rail, I leaned back, unsurprised to find Gravell behind me.

No, I decided. Gravell couldn't be the saboteur, or he could, but I wasn't going to go there. That was Minton's route, not mine. Everyone was innocent until proven guilty and Gravell had given me more reason to trust him than not.

"I refuse to be paranoid," I said aloud.

"Paranoia is bad. Careful is good. Dry is good too, Madame Kirby. Do you think we could get out of the rain now?"

I chuckled and thought, poor man. What a trial I could be.

"Okay. Let's get to work. Hope the coffee is still hot."

"It's tea, and it's in a thermos."

Chapter Twenty-Eight ~ *Voices from the Past*

By lunch time, the rain had stopped and the sun was starting to break through the clouds, giving the sky a cathedral-like beauty. No one was going to get me inside.

"Let's have a picnic on the deck. We can fetch sandwiches and refill the thermos. By the way, do you have some objection to me having coffee after breakfast?"

"It's harder to mask poison in tea."

"Seriously?"

He smiled and shrugged, making me wonder if he was messing with me.

I wasn't the only one feeling cooped up. The rest of the research team joined us on the aft deck. Naturally, we started talking about the station.

Mary Lou shared the information about the blood. Tracy told us that Minton had his fingers over everything, but Dawes had his hands on Minton's few personal items. I wondered about the journal and had a sudden pang of guilt because, no matter what I said about being careful, I had badly compromised that piece of evidence. I should have been handling it with gloved hands if at all. Gravell gave me a grimace that said the same thought had occurred to him.

"Did you read the letters from your father?" I asked Mary Lou.

She shook her head.

"Dora wanted you to go through the material first. She hasn't given us access to it yet. To be honest, I'm a bit nervous about it. The letters could be very personal or disturbing. That's why I'm letting Tracy process the written material. She doesn't have the same stake in the contents as us."

I pulled out my smartphone. Everything I was working on was backed up on it and, unlike the phone, I never forgot to keep it with me. I called up Lou Boreman's letters and read a couple of them aloud. Mary Lou teared-up with emotion.

"I remember Puddles. I don't remember walking with my daddy. I suspect I was in a pram at the time."

"I'll send you copies of the other letters for you to read at your leisure. There's one that involves your mother that I'd like to hold back until I speak to her, if that's okay with you."

"Course, honey. I trust you."

I hoped that she would still trust me later, when she learned about the journal. On the whole, I decided I was comfortable with my decision. I had no illusions that anyone else would share my perspective.

"Did you come across anything from my uncle?" asked Mike.

I consulted my archive list.

"There's one letter to his brother."

"My father was dead."

I nodded. "I know. Sometimes that doesn't stop you. I haven't had a chance to read it yet. I can call it up now, if you like."

He nodded, so I began to read.

Dear Johnny,

Lord, I wish I could put a stamp on this letter and know it'll reach you. I've never felt so alone. I thought I was used to this shit, but sometimes I feel like I'm invisible. I always thought you were crazy to settle for the infantry when you were the brightest one of us, but at least you had friends. I've got what I always wanted, and now I wish I settled for being a cook.

Boreman's not bad, the red-neck son of a bitch, and Golanger is okay except he looks at me like I'm from another planet. The officers deal with me only as much as they need to. I was forced on Shore and he resents it. His friends resent me on his behalf. Of the lot, Minton's the only one who seems colour blind. He only cares that the job is done well and he doesn't socialize much with anyone, so I can hardly take offense if he doesn't pay much attention to me.

"It goes for several pages," I said. "From the looks of it, each paragraph is written at a different time. The whole thing is treated like one big letter."

This could provide some perspective on what was going on a counterpoint to Minton's journal. Since I wanted read further on my own, I searched for a reference to Naire in other documents.

"Here's something about your uncle written by Margolo."
Weapon's Tech Joey Naire
Has skills that make the ladies stare
I stopped, red-faced.

"On second thought, I won't read that one. In fact, maybe I'll get back to work."

Of course, Mary Lou and Lil had to look over my shoulder. Despite the fact that neither was a giggler by nature, both giggled. Out of a sense of fair play, I showed it to Mike.

He read it, smiled and said, "Probably true."

After lunch, Gravell asked for permission to look at Minton's journal. He had gloves on and an evidence kit. When I wasn't reading it, I kept it in a sealed bag. When I was reading it, I tried not to touch it any more than necessary. Even so, I couldn't imagine what he would find that wouldn't have been compromised either directly by me or by exposure to salt and damp in the atmosphere.

While he worked, I continued reading the Naire letter.

To think I was complaining that I was being ignored. I'm thankful now.

...

Johnny, some of these people are stark raving. The Commander won't back down on the smoking issue, even though Lt. Minton has made a formal protest. Personally, if I thought I had to give up smoking, I'd never pushed to be a submariner. Still, I do see Minton's point. With common living quarters and the galley and wardroom being connected, there's nowhere for him to get away.

...

Worried about Minton, bro. I don't blame him for standing up for what he thinks is right, but he's taking this way too personally. Looks like the Dawes and Margolo tried to intervene and it has gone from bad to worse.

...

Counting down the days.

...

When I get home, little bro, I am never leaving. This is my last tour of duty. The only thing holding me together these last few days is the thought of getting home to Nora and Mike. Maybe it's time Nora and I gave Mike...

That was the last entry. Whatever Joe Naire wanted to give Mike, young cousins, time, possibly a real family, he never got to write about it, let alone do it.

Chapter Twenty-Nine ~ *Hitting the Deck*

The limerick about Naire had already made the rounds. Lil suggested that I read the rest of Margolo's poetry as after-dinner entertainment. When the time came, Lil introduced me, and I stood.

"Lieutenant Margolo had a wicked sense of humour. He composed rhymes for each member of the crew, mostly on scraps of paper, which he collected in his shaving kit. Other scraps included a list of books to read and how much money was owed him in the weekly poker game and how much he owed Doc Dawes. I've compiled the poetry, such as it is, and will NOT be reading it aloud."

This got a laugh.

"You'll have to read it yourself."

I had a copy for each table in the wardroom. I handed them out and went up for seconds of dessert. Before long, there were snorts and guffaws and a few shocked oh my's as the limericks and other doggerel were shared.

After dinner, Gravell excused himself to make a report to the *Nottawasaga*. Jamal and Tracy had disappeared, no doubt to their shared cabin to work off the meal. Mary Lou, Mike, and Lil were looking for a fourth for Bridge. I begged off and one of the crew joined them. Making sure I had my radio-phone, I went to the foredeck and let the Arctic breeze blow away the emotional detritus of the day. No longer suffering from seasickness, I realized I needed to come out here for my mental health as much as my physical well-being. Minton's journal, the personal letters, even the research team, left me clogged with residual emotions, weighed down with loss that wasn't my own.

The cold, salty wind wasn't a perfect cure, but it did help. *Of course, it would have been nice if I had remembered to wear a jacket*, I thought. On cue, a windbreaker was placed across my shoulders.

Gravell?

I felt a rough tickle on my neck and knew it wasn't him. Eyes open, I turned, startled. There was no one there. There was no windbreaker. A shiver of fear went through me.

"Minton?" I whispered.

Not Minton. Margolo. He had a ghostly five o'clock shadow, a rakish grin, and he held out a ghostly jacket. An invitation.

I shook my head.

The jacket disappeared.

Margolo stepped forward. I flattened myself against the rail. He wasn't touching me, but I could feel his presence exactly like I could feel Gravell except Margolo exuded cold, not warmth. Behind him, fanned out on either side, were Dawes, Boreman, Golanger, Naire, and Kant. I looked around for Commander Shore. He appeared right next to me.

I fainted, hitting wood and metal on the way down.

I woke up on a stretcher. I was moving. Someone was shouting. I tried to lift my head to see who was yelling and who was carrying me.

"Keep still, Madame Kirby. You are safe."

I tried to nod, but it seemed I was wearing a neck-brace. The movement of the stretcher made my head swim, so I closed my eyes until it stopped.

"Where am I?"

"We've brought you into ops, Jen."

"Sorry to be a bother, Skipper." I giggled. It was the first time I had called him that and it sounded funny. "Now I just have to meet Gilligan."

He patted my shoulder then went on to order one person to contact the *Nottawasaga*, another to fetch an icepack and the rest to get lost.

"I'll stay, if you don't mind," said Gravell.

"Naturally."

"Me too," said Lil.

"Good idea."

As my head cleared, I took stock.

"Why is my neck in a brace?"

Franchot reassured me. "It's only a precaution. Let's see you wiggle your fingers."

I wiggled my fingers. That was easy.

"Good job. Now, Gravell is going to make himself useful and take your shoes off so you can wiggle your toes for me. While he does that,

I'm going to bug you with a penlight."

I knew the routine. He'd check my pupils, then make sure I had feeling and movement in my legs and feet. I'd had to go through the process a couple of times once when my son ran his bike into a parked ice cream truck (in a hurry for a slushie) and once when I tripped on my son's skateboard and was knocked out.

Shay had to call 911. This was around the time my mother was in and out of hospital, shortly before she died. I was on a first-name basis with most of the EMT crews. After a brief chat with Riley, a fire fighter and paramedic, Shay never left his toys under foot ever again.

I smiled at the memory. Riley was cute.

"Stay with us, Jen," Franchot said, summoning me back to reality.

A sharp point scraped my foot.

"Hey!"

Gravell was a little gentler on the other foot.

I was released from the board and Franchot reached under me to manipulate my spine. He executed the task with professional indifference. Next he tested my ability to move arms and legs. Finally the brace came off. I was allowed to sit up and ice arrived for the lump on my head. Feeling slightly nauseous, I looked around the room carefully. The ghosts were still hanging around. Great.

A crewman came in and spoke to Franchot in heavily accented French. I only caught a few words. "X-ray" and "*Nottawasaga*" stood out.

"I fainted," I said, just in case anyone was interested.

"And hit your head on the rail," said Gravell.

"How long was I out?"

"We're not sure. Lil was looking for you. I suggested the foredeck and accompanied her. There you were." His tone was tight, controlled, all business. "Why did you faint?"

"Good question."

Gravell wanted better answers. I looked at him, then beyond him to the ghostly crew. Margolo grinned sheepishly. Dawes and Naire appeared apologetic. The others were impassive. I focussed my gaze back on Gravell.

"I want to go to bed. I know I can't go to sleep for a while, but I want to tuck up in bed. I'm cold and shaky."

Gravell nodded to me. He understood. He explained to Franchot. I got the tail end as he walked back to me.

"Dr. Stern wants her in sick bay for x-rays. He's agreed it can wait until the morning, but he wants her under observation."

"I'll stay with her tonight." It was a statement that did not invite opposition.

"Works for me," I said, swinging my legs to the side and sliding toward the floor.

Three men and seven ghosts started towards me.

"Hold it!" I yelped, pulling myself upright with the help of the stretcher. "I'm okay. Skipper, let Doc know I'll see him as soon as possible tomorrow. I'll need help to my cabin and my shoes back. Chief Gravell, can you meet me there with coffee? I'm serious. Coffee, not tea. And maybe something plain to eat, like croissants."

Then I forgot myself momentarily.

"The rest of you, give me some peace, okay?"

Chapter Thirty ~ *Revelations*

Lil helped me to the cabin and offered to stay with me. I declined. As I pointed out, Gravell would insist in staying anyway. No point in two people being tied up.

"I could use some help before he gets here."

I really wanted a shower. Just a quick one to warm me up. Although I felt less shaky, I knew I'd catch all kinds of grief if I showered alone. After, Lil helped me get into my nightshirt and tucked up comfortably, all while keeping up a steady stream of tales when she had been injured in embarrassing ways. She was telling me about rear-ending a cheating husband she had been following when Gravell arrived.

"I felt so bad, but there was nothing I could do. I hit a patch of black ice and just slid until I hit his car. Awkward. Worse, he was so nice about it. I felt like a real heel when I turned over photos of him and his lover to his wife."

"Did he ever know it was you?"

"Never saw him again, thank heaven. Now, I better go so Gravell can have his way with you. Let me know if you want me to pick up the pieces later."

Gravell was not a happy camper. He rounded on me the moment the door closed behind Lil. "Never, ever, go off by yourself again. If I'm not unavailable stay with the group."

"No one attacked me. I fainted, for heaven's sake."

"Why? Did the ghost possess you again?"

He said it like he really meant, 'Did you have a delusional episode again?'

I stared at him. Thoughts were buzzing around my head like angry bees. They made my brain ache. Why did I trust Gravell with my secret? What if he was right about me being delusional? How dare he get mad at me when I hadn't done anything wrong?

Finally there was acknowledgement that Gravell had a point. I shouldn't be by myself. Whether it was ghosts or delusions doing it, I had passed out twice and almost been killed two other times.

"Fine, however, unless I'm working or in a group, it will have to be you watching my back. I don't want anyone else thinking I'm a nut-bar."

"I don't think you're a nut-bar, Madame Kirby," he said, his tone gentle and suddenly tired. He sat at Dora's desk and poured tea for himself and coffee for me. He brought to mugs over and gave me one, then sat at the edge of the bed.

"Was it Minton?"

I shook my head.

"It was the rest of them. They were rather overwhelming. With the exception of animals, I've only ever seen one ghost at a time and even then, excepting Minton, not since I was a teen. This evening I had seven closing in on me."

"Why?"

"I don't know." *Yes I did*, I thought. "They want something from me."

I narrowed my eyes at Gravell, weighing what to say and what to keep to myself. It was disturbing the way I mistook Margolo's spirit for someone living and how real ghostly whiskers had felt when they tickled my neck. One moment I was alone, the next, I was surrounded. I shivered with the memory.

"Madame Kirby?"

I reached out and grasped Gravell's free hand. This was solid. This was real. This was alive.

'In for a penny, in for a pound,' as my mother would say. I would rather face the ghosts with Gravell beside me than be surprised by them on my own. "Minton?"

Nothing.

"Margolo?"

The temperature dipped noticeably. Even Gravell shivered. "He's here?" he asked, holding my hand a little tighter.

"They are all here, except Minton. They seem to be a package deal."

Margolo threw his head back in silent laughter. He was in the forefront, large as life and handsome in a chilling way. Behind him, set apart from the others, Shore shook his head. The others gave shrugs and nods. Golanger also pressed his hands together, as if praying.

"This would be so much easier if I could actually talk to ghosts."

Margolo, a twisted grin on his face, stepped forward. He went down on one knee, as if about to propose. His hand reached out to me. I shivered as his hand cupped my cheek and an irresistible pressure pulled me towards him even as he leaned forward.

'Set us free,' he mouthed.

"Madame Kirby?"

"What happened?"

"That was my question. You blacked out."

I took in my surroundings. I had spilt almost a full cup of coffee on the covers. I was still holding Gravell's hand, and I was shaking like a leaf.

"Lieutenant Minton was a lot easier to handle. I don't know if it's Margolo or being visited by seven ghosts at once, but this passing out is starting to get old."

"Worrisome."

I studied Gravell's face. I saw concern, and I think a touch of fear. Although he didn't see them, I think it would be fair to say that he believed in ghosts now.

It was a long night. Gravell wouldn't let me sleep until the swelling had gone down, then he woke me every couple of hours. He pulled down the bedding from the upper bunk to replace the wet covers. He grabbed a pillow and a spare blanket from the closet and camped out on the floor beside me.

To pass the time, I told him about the ghosts in the forest where I used to camp as a Girl Guide and shared my embarrassing ghost story tale as told to Captain Campbell earlier in the week.

"What I didn't tell the captain was that I got the material for my stories from real ghosts. They would show me things and my imagination would fill in the gaps."

"Did you see a lot of ghosts?"

"Grandma Allard, when she died and later Nana, my mother's mother. I saw things about their lives that I was able to confirm later. I was really good at seeing the ghosts of dogs. They hang around quite a while and are usually friendly. The ghost in the forest was the only stranger up until now. She gave me nightmares still does sometimes. I'm not sure if that is because of the ghost or my guilty feelings at scaring those girls."

"Nothing since then?"

"I stopped looking."

"Not even your mother?"

"She said her good byes before she died."

He nodded. "I've lost friends, and I never knew my grandfathers, but my parents and grandmothers are still alive. They can be a bit overwhelming in life. I hope I never have to face their ghosts."

"Tell me about them. Your family is from Quebec?"

"Yes, my mother is English, my father French, like your parents. I was brought up bilingual and mostly bi-cultural. My mother's mother only speaks English. My father's mother only speaks French. Yet, they manage to share an apartment built into the family house."

"Both in-laws in the same house? Your parents are brave."

Gravell laughed. "Brave and foolish, like you. My grandmothers occupy a two-bedroom basement walkout that my parents used to rent when they needed the extra income to pay the mortgage. When Grandma Gravell had to sell her home because she couldn't do stairs, she moved in. Grandma Verity is a retired nurse. She decided to move in to take care of, that is keep an eye on, Grandma Gravell."

I listened to him talk about his family, warmed by his obvious affection for them, relaxed by his deep, rich voice.

"Madame Kirby, you're not allowed to go to sleep."

"My name is Jen Kirby, maiden name Allard. Father Merle. Brother Lance short for Lancelot. Mother Win short for Gwyneth, deceased, and, as you can guess a fan of Arthurian romance. I am currently aboard the *Émil Gagnan*. Can I go to sleep now?"

He checked my lump.

"Very well. You can sleep for now."

"Tell me more about Grandma Verity."

I woke to find my arm draped over the side of the bed, resting on Gravell's shoulder. His hand was holding it in place. Except for one thing, I would have happily stayed and enjoyed the moment. The one thing was my bladder. All that coffee and tea I had been drinking when I wasn't allowed to sleep wanted out.

Now I had a problem. I didn't want to wake Gravell, but he presented a substantial obstacle in my path. First, I gently disengaged my hand. Then I stretched a leg over the mass of man and rucked-up blanket. I was doing fine until I shifted my weight.

He turned over.

I fell on top of him, my foot trapped between him and the bunk.

"Huh?"

"Sorry!"

I looked down at Gravell.

Sleepily amused, he looked back at me. "Are you going to move?"

"I'm thinking about it. Right now I've got a feeling anything I do is going to make the situation worse."

I shifted slightly. I couldn't get the leverage to go straight up. I tried going sideways. My foot was caught under the lip of the bunk.

"Madame Kirby, do you have any idea what you are doing?"

I didn't take the hard mass under my pelvis personally. I knew that men can just wake up like that. I also knew I wasn't helping matters. What was I supposed to do?

"Yes, Chief Gravell," I said, using asperity to cover my embarrassment. "My foot is trapped. This position is equally awkward for me and probably more painful."

I took a deep breath.

"Maybe you should roll away from bunk. That might free my foot."

He rolled, and I yelped with pain as my foot was dragged against the rough underside of the lip. Now he was almost on top of me. He was almost fully dressed. All I was wearing was a nightshirt. I can't abide wearing underwear overnight. If he decided to look, he'd find that out since my nightshirt was no longer covering everything.

"Are you going to move?" I asked, trying to sound as sanguine as he had a moment ago.

"I'm thinking about it."

"Think fast. I really do need the toilet."

He leaned over me, bringing his lips tantalisingly close to mine, chocolate brown eyes, warm and sweet. I considered pulling him down, but opted for pulling down my nightshirt instead. Then he pushed himself up and stood, hands reaching down to pull me to my feet.

"You're bleeding," he said, pointing at my ankle.

I darted to the head, closed the door and sank gratefully onto the toilet, relieved in so many more ways than I could say.

Despite having hair from hell, I asked Gravell if he needed the head before I showered. He took me up on my offer. Then he checked out my ankle. It wasn't a bad scrape. He suggested that he shower and change elsewhere and return to bandage my foot and take me to breakfast. About a half hour later, Lil called on the intra-ship phone system.

"Gravell says you could use an escort to breakfast."

"I suppose so."

"Are you ready to go?'

"I can be in five minutes."

Actually, when the phone rang, I was still sitting in my towel and robe, wondering what might have happened if I hadn't been so desperate to pee.

Chapter Thirty-One ~ *Be Prepared*

Be prepared: the motto of Boy Scouts, Girl Guides, and mothers everywhere. That's why I went to breakfast with my briefcase, packed with laptop, notes, and a change of underwear. In the pockets of my cargo pants I carried my smartphone and Minton's journal. Clipped on my waistband was the radio-phone. I wasn't going to assume Doc would let me return to the *Émil Gagnan.*

I was late for breakfast. Almost everyone else was done but, unusually for the morning, the team was lingering over coffee. They were here to see me off. This gave the perfect, unwanted opportunity to do what needed to be done.

Lil nudged me toward the group.

"Go sit. I'll get our food."

"Keep it light for me. The boat trip can be a bit rough."

"Gotcha."

I made a beeline for Mary Lou. She stood to give me a big hug.

"We heard about your accident, hon. You're going to see someone about the fainting, right?"

"Right after breakfast. It's already arranged."

I took a deep breath, pulled out Minton's journal and passed it to her. I had got as much as I could out of it and Gravell had scanned the pages for me. I didn't think the ghosts needed the journal to reach me, and if they did, that was okay too. I got the message. I didn't need them making me pass out anymore.

"I don't understand," Mary Lou said, turning the baggied book over in her hands.

"When I was trapped in the galley I pulled this out and started reading it. At the time, I wasn't sure if either the journal or I would get out of there, and I thought it might have some answers. I've had it ever since."

"Jen."

"I know. I should have given it to you earlier, but I had good reason to hold on to it."

I faltered. Of all people, Mike came to my rescue.

"This is the kind of thing that Tinsdale would have held onto if he got it. If it weren't for you, he would have got the letters and photos."

"Of course," Mary Lou said.

I knew from her tone it would take time for her to forgive me for tampering with an artifact.

"I'm going to take this to the lab now."

Mary Lou left me with an obviously shocked Tracy at her heels. Jamal gave an apologetic shrug and followed.

Lil placed large plate in front of me. The piece of toast and poached egg looked forlorn on it, especially compared to Lil's loaded plate.

"I think I'm ready to forgive Chief Gravell," Mike said, as if nothing had happened.

"Oh?" Maybe forgiveness would be catching.

"Yep. Although we haven't got official sanction to raise the station, he got us permission to examine the wreck and fix any damage done during the storm. We've already sent the bots down to look."

"Sounds great. How are the Americans reacting?"

He laughed.

"What?" asked Lil.

"You haven't been on deck today, have you?"

He wouldn't say any more so I rushed my food and took my coffee to go. He took me up to the far side of the deck for maximum impact when we reached the foredeck.

The first thing I noticed was a diving platform tethered to one of the lines between the *Émil Gagnan* and the station. Divers were already in the water.

Mike explained.

"Early this morning we found out that we had permission to go back to work. Reuben and Dora pulled it off."

Other than clucking over me like a mother hen for not taking proper care, Doc Stern didn't make a big fuss over my injuries. Once he checked my x-rays to make sure nothing was cracked, he was pretty stoic. My blood pressure was on the low end of normal. There were no other indicators of trouble. Since I had passed out and then fallen down and hit my head, not the reverse, concussion wasn't a given. Regardless, he wanted to keep me aboard the *Nottawasaga* so he could observe me. He also told me to stay away from electronic devices for the next twenty-four hours. I was assigned a guest stateroom with a portal. If I didn't pass out again, I would be allowed to return to the *Émil Gagnan* the next day. Since Dora was en route, by then I'd have her to keep an eye on me.

Too tired to do much else, I let Briseau take me to my quarters. She would be checking in on me periodically during the day. When she left, I called my dad for a dose of normalcy, which was fudging Doc's prescription, but too bad. Dad reminded me that Shay would be at his father's in a couple of days. I would be able to call him there soon. I hung up feeling better. Who needed romance when I already had two great men in my life?

Well, maybe I did, but it wasn't absolutely essential.

I must have been tired because I lay down for a rest and woke up several hours later when Briseau returned to check my vitals. She brought a couple of sandwiches and glass of milk, since I had missed lunch. Gravell showed up just as she was packing up the blood pressure cuff. He brought my luggage.

"Am I moving in?"

"I brought your clothes over and mine because I thought we could make use of the ship's laundry services."

I grinned. "Good plan."

"Planning is one of my fortes." He produced a thermos and two mugs from the top of my bag. From a pocket he pulled out a ziploc bag of Cookie's brownies.

"Tea?"

I might as well resign myself to it. He was going to make a tea drinker out of me. "Want to split my lunch?"

He accepted the offer and we set up on the table that would double as my desk. Compared to my cabin on the *Émil Gagnan,* the stateroom was comparatively roomy and well appointed. If I had to, I could get used to the accommodations.

"So, what were you up to while I was being poked and prodded? "

"Sitting in on the conference of the captains."

"How is Captain Tinsdale taking the news?"

"I can only guess."

Casting my mind back on the man I met briefly and my impressions of him, my guess was that he would be taking it one of two ways. "If his first interest is in controlling the situation, he'll be pissed-off. If his first interest is the truth, he might be relieved that the Canadian government is determined to find out what his government is trying to cover up."

Gravell shook his head and swallowed his last bite of sandwich. "There are plenty of people who want the truth on both sides of the border, and only a few well-placed people who are afraid of what will be discovered. In any case, the meeting was about logistics. Captain Tinsdale still has some negotiating leverage there."

I finished my sandwich and drank my milk in thoughtful silence.

After a while, Gravell spoke. "There's something else you want to ask me, Madame Kirby. What is it?"

I looked across the table. His face held a mildly troubled expression, as well it should.

"There are a lot of things I want to ask you," I said, trying to return his gaze without getting lost in it. "Some of them are quite personal and have nothing to do with Arctic Station Alpha. Right now, I'm thinking of what I need to tell you."

"Which is?"

"I need to go back on board. Raised, sunken, in a wetsuit if need be, I need to go there."

He rubbed the bridge of his nose, breaking eye contact. "I know," he said with a sigh.

"I don't particularly want to, mind you," I said, reaching for the thermos. I poured us each a cup, closed the thermos and pushed a cup towards him. "I just need to do this. I won't get any peace until I do."

Chapter Thirty-Two ~ *Mess Dress*

Next time I go to sea, I must remember to bring formal attire. My amethyst purple sweater was ruined, thanks to Minton. This left me with an assortment of t-shirts and sweaters chosen for warmth and washability, not style. Even my dressier khaki pants were in the laundry. That is why Marian Sloan found me in bra, underwear, and amethyst beads and a robe.

"I've got shorts, cargo pants...or shorts or cargo pants."

"Or a wrap skirt," said Sloan, holding up a length of colourful woven material. "Sophie mentioned that you might need something to wear tonight. I picked this up to make a skirt eventually. But wait, there's more."

She held up a pink t-shirt.

"I have a buddy whose daughter put her red sweater in with Daddy's whites. He has matching pink boxers, but I didn't think we should accept those."

I laughed and shook my head.

The t-shirt was a couple of sizes too big for me. It fell off one shoulder. I adjusted it and it fell off the other.

"It looks cute that way. I got just the thing to make the outfit work too."

"What?"

"Scissors!"

She slit the shirt up one of the side seams so she could tie it at my hip. She fluffed my hair, applied some eyeliner and lipstick, then stood back and grinned.

"Not bad. Not bad at all."

"Thank you—" I hesitated.

"Call me Marian."

"Jen. Good. I'm getting tired of being addressed as Ms. Kirby or worse, Mrs. Kirby."

"Sometimes I feel the same way about being called Sloan. Although, I don't think I'll mind being called Chief Sloan, when the time comes."

"How about Mister Sloan?"

She laughed. "No way! It would take me forever to get over the pay cut of becoming a junior officer. Plus, eventually I'd be expected to purchase mess dress."

I wracked my memory. In Navy League, the cadets only had one uniform. Did Seamus have to learn about more?

"Mess dress is military formal wear," Marian explained.

"For ceremonies."

"No. That's ceremonial dress. And in the navy, it gets worse."

She didn't get to tell me what was worse. Someone was knocking on the door, no hatch. Whatever.

Gravell walked through the hatch in a high-necked white uniform with naval insignia.

Marian leaned toward me.

"Ceremonial whites. For winter we have ceremonial blues. Only commissioned officers wear mess dress."

She straightened and addressed herself to Gravell. "I was answering Ms. Kirby's questions about uniforms, Chief."

He smiled. "I see you also found something for Madame Kirby to wear."

"Yes, sir."

Gravell turned his attention to me. "Are you ready to go to dinner?"

"Hm?"

"I'm sorry I didn't warn you I was also in the navy."

I rolled my eyes. "You didn't have to. I guessed."

"So, are you ready to go for dinner?"

I shrugged and turned around slowly. "You tell me, Chief Gravell."

He looked me over and there was attraction as well amusement in his eyes.

"Perfect. The amethysts add a touch of class."

He offered me his arm. I took it and for a moment he covered my hand with his, then he opened the hatch and helped me over the coaming. It was then he noticed that I was wearing flip-flops. I had packed them in lieu of slippers and wore them tonight because they went with the outfit better than running shoes or hiking boots.

"You're going to laugh at me, aren't you?"

"Not at all. I was just going to say, nice shoes."

As I feared, all the Canadian naval officers wore mess dress which, to my civilian eye, looked like a hybrid of what Gravell was wearing and a tuxedo. Captain Tinsdale and Lieutenant Redding were present from the *Scranton,* wearing dress whites. Captain Franchot was present in dress blues. Gold embroidered epaulettes indicated that he was a merchant captain. One of the divers was present, similarly dressed, but with the rank of commander. Franchot reminded me his name was Alexis Mercuros. He was a wiry fellow, not particularly young, but with a boyish face. When he smiled, he reminded me of George Clooney. The thought occurred that this was the Skipper's Gilligan.

The *Nottawasaga*'s First Officer, Commander Belinda Harvey, introduced herself and told me she was happy to finally meet me and complimented me on my resourcefulness in finding dinner attire.

I looked at her, tall, elegant and professional, then down at myself. As I took her offered hand, I leaned in towards her.

"It isn't too much, is it? I feel a bit like mutton dressed as lamb."

She chuckled and shook her head.

I could see that the situation amused her, but since she seemed inclined to laugh with me rather than at me, I decided to go with the flow. It wasn't like I had much choice.

She introduced me to the five other *Nottawasaga* officers present, of whom I had only met Jones and Dr. Stern.

Doc looked me over with eye wide and brows raised.

"You better not go on deck without a jacket. You're likely to catch more than a cold."

"Not on my ship," said Captain Campbell. He welcomed me with a hand clasp and then pulled my hand through his arm.

"Shall we sit?" he asked, addressing the assembly.

He led me to the seat on his right. Gravell took the seat to my right and everyone found their places. The numbers were odd, so the far end of the table was clear. It might have led to an international incident deciding who would sit there.

"Thirteen for dinner," Redding remarked.

He didn't add that superstition held that this was very unlucky, but it was clear what was he thinking. I wondered if he was aware of the belief that when thirteen sat down to dinner, one would die. I wasn't particularly worried. I'm not free of superstition, but I knew there was a fourteenth guest. Lieutenant Minton was back. I gave him a discrete nod of acknowledgement. He responded with a worried smile and sat at the head of the table in a non-existent chair.

"Are you all right, Madame Kirby?" Gravell asked, using the serving of the soup as cover to his inquiry.

"I'll let you know later."

He nodded and responded to a comment made by Commander Harvey. From then on, outwardly, he only paid polite attention to me. Under the table, his knee was pressed lightly against mine.

"It's good to have you back," Captain Campbell said, pulling my attention away from its wanderings.

"Thank you, Captain."

"I've missed our chats. I imagine you have been quite busy."

"Yes. I'm hoping you'll let me interview you again. A lot has happened since I last got you on record. It would be nice to interview Commander Harvey too."

"What do you think, Belinda? Will you consent to be interviewed by Ms. Kirby for the documentary?"

Harvey turned her attention away from Gravell and flashed me a smile.

"Sounds like fun. Where would you like to conduct the interview? How about the bridge? We could start with a tour. It might be nice for you to see something other than sick bay, the captain's office, and here."

"Can I video tape the interview?"

"The interview, yes, but the tour only as directed."

"The camera crew left, but I think I can set up a video recorder."

"I can be your cameraman," Gravell offered. "I'll also know what parts of the tour can be recorded."

This would be convenient, as he was likely to want to be there anyway. Seeing an opportunity, I turned to Tinsdale and gave him a speculative stare until I knew I had his attention. It didn't take long.

"How about you, Captain Tinsdale? Will you relax your policy to be interviewed? I'd hate you to be the only captain left out."

The smile he returned said volumes. It was appreciative of my use of tactics and warned me not to push the issue and it also managed to seem amused in a patronizing way.

"We can't have that, can we, Mrs. Kirby."

I was ready to tie him down to a time and a place when the food arrived.

Between the salad and the entrée, I asked Captain Campbell about Dora and Reuben.

"As a matter of fact, Ms. Kirby, Dr. Leland and Mr. Dawes are en route. They should be here well before the station is ready to be boarded. Now that the *Émil Gagnan* has officially been given permission to recover Arctic Station Alpha, I imagine Captain Franchot is poised to start work at first light."

"I might eat breakfast first."

"However, the station is still the property of the US Navy," said Redding.

Franchot rocked his hand.

"Sort of. Salvage rules don't generally apply to military vessels, but the protocols governing military vessels only apply in international waters."

I suspect there might have been some argument about this if naval tradition allowed the discussion of politics during dinner. I had wondered why Captain Campbell always had these meetings over a meal. Now I knew. I bet he kept them formal so that no one forgot those traditions.

While I ruminated, Captain Tinsdale asked Franchot how long it would take to raise the station.

"We're not going to raise the station. We've determined that it is more stable submerged. Instead, we'll patch the hull and pump her out. How much time that will take will depend on how much flooding occurred after Jen was rescued. Normally, this would only be a minor inconvenience. We have a diving bell that we could use to take the researchers down to the station."

He turned to me, the landlubber. "It's a bit like a submersible elevator."

"I read about those. They're used in submarine rescues, right?"

"Amongst other things. Unfortunately, we can't use it here."

"Why not?"

"The simple answer is that I'm not convinced that it's safe. After some discussion, we've decided that the most prudent thing to do is to enter via the breach in engineering and set up an internal airlock." He gave me an apologetic smile. "That means that most of the researchers will only have remote access to the station. There are only three trained divers on the team."

"Mike, Tim and?"

"Mrs. Mary Lou Naire," said Mercuros.

That figured. Mike probably trained her.

"And Madame Kirby," said Gravell.

I tried not to look surprised.

Franchot narrowed his eyes and gave me a questioning look.

"I didn't know you were certified, Jen."

"Well."

The gentle pressure of Gravell's knee against mine increased slightly. I decided to say nothing and gave Franchot a noncommittal shrug.

Captain Campbell raised his hand.

"Let's table this discussion until after dinner. I can smell the roast lamb and I, for one, prefer my dinner hot."

Two hours later, I felt like a prisoner at a parole hearing. Still in the wardroom, I was on one side of the table with Captains Campbell and Franchot, and Commanders Harvey and Mercuros on the other. I didn't have Gravell to back me up. He hadn't been invited to the party. Even Minton had left.

"I've snorkelled," I said. An admittedly lame answer to Captain Campbell's opening question regarding my diving skills.

"Did you tell Chief Gravell you could scuba dive?"

"No. I just told him I needed to get aboard the station."

Franchot shook his head. "Why? Setting aside a natural desire to be part of the adventure, why would you? You'll see everything via video cameras. All artifacts collected will be brought back and you'll probably be the first to go over them. You won't really be missing anything."

My head was hurting. I wished that Gravell was here to sort this out for me, and I felt like a coward as a result.

"Jen, diving in arctic waters to a potentially unstable vessel isn't the best place to learn the ropes. It's not safe for you or the other divers."

Mercuros nodded. Commander Harvey kept her face a perfect blank. I wondered about that while I tried to think of something to say. I fell back on the truth.

"I have to go. I saw something when I was trapped. I'm the only one who can follow up on it."

"It's too dangerous," said Captain Campbell.

There was a knock. Gravell entered without waiting for an invitation. He was followed by woman in uniform who was vaguely familiar. They stood at the end of the table. I made a quarter turn in my chair to watch them.

"Captain, you are familiar with Lieutenant Welland? She was one of the divers that rescued Madame Kirby."

My eyes widened.

So did Campbell's. He addressed the Lieutenant. "Of course. You and your partner did an exemplary job under difficult circumstances."

"Thank you, Captain. We wouldn't have been able to do it if Ms. Kirby had not followed directions as well as she did. That's why I'm willing to teach her the necessary skills and to dive with her when she goes to the station."

The devil, I thought. He did have my back.

Franchot was another matter. "My insurance only covers certified divers."

"I'll waive liability," I said.

"What if I also worked with them?" said Mercuros.

Franchot opened his mouth to object.

"*C'est fait, mon ami.* At least this way I'll know that Ms. Kirby can do the dive."

Franchot looked like he was wavering, but Captain Campbell was not happy.

"It is not done unless I give permission, Mr. Mercuros. I don't. Even an accelerated diving course would take weeks, and I wouldn't be satisfied with less."

Mercuros shook his head. "Certification can't be done in less than a couple of weeks, but the course work preliminary to the first open water dive can be completed in a couple of days. It will require a lot of homework, Ms. Kirby."

"Okay."

"I've run civilian courses before and can administer the written exam. There's no rule that the first practice dive can't be on the job. In fact, there are underwater research teams that offer diving certification to volunteers as they work."

Franchot looked up, apparently for heavenly guidance. "In tropical waters! We don't do that up here."

"There's always a first time, Skipper."

Franchot looked from Mercuros to Gravell and back again. Mercuros gave an infinitesimal nod which I took as evidence of Gravell getting his support ahead of time.

"Okay," said Franchot.

Campbell sighed heavily and nodded. With the air of one who was greatly put upon, he gave conditional consent. "Go ahead with the training. If I'm not satisfied it's safe, I'll veto Ms. Kirby's involvement, even if it means scuttling the station myself. Now, if you'll excuse me, it's been a long evening."

Welland shot me a smile and made a quick getaway. I tried to do the same while the officers exchanged handshakes and polite farewells.

"Not you, Ms. Kirby," Captain Campbell said over his shoulder.

I sat back down. Soon there was only the captain, Gravell, and myself left.

"Gravell, I am mystified why you have thrown yourself behind this harebrained scheme."

"Sir?"

"Don't play with me. Is Ms. Kirby one of yours? I know Franchot and Mercuros are."

That was startling. The implications made my head hurt even more. I rubbed my eyes and tried to smooth the tension lines from my forehead.

"Madame Kirby is exactly what she has presented herself as, a civilian writer working with Dr. Leland. What she has gone through has put her into a position of having special knowledge that I am not at liberty to discuss at this time. I might add, sir, Madame Kirby's life has been threatened. It is in everyone's interest to resolve the issues presented by the station, but it could be a matter of life and death to her."

Life, death, and my sanity, I thought.

The captain rubbed his chin. His expression was grim, but resigned. "Very well. You're dismissed Chief."

"Aye, sir."

Gravell left and once again I felt very alone.

"I thought you trusted me, Jen."

His face was so sad I wanted to hit him. I didn't need a degree in psychology to know when I was being emotionally manipulated.

"I do trust you, but I also understand that there are limitations to what you can do to help me. You have certain responsibilities. Now, it turns out, so do I."

Chapter Thirty-Three ~ *Confrontations*

I headed for the deck, desperate for fresh air even if it wasn't allowed. Like the old saying goes, sometimes it's easier to seek forgiveness than permission.

Unsurprisingly, Gravell was waiting for me.

"The captain is really pissed off at us."

He shrugged. "He'll forgive you. As long as nothing happens to you, he might even forgive me."

I tested the security of the rail, a habit now, and then leaned against it, looking out onto the late setting sun. It would barely finish setting before it rose again.

I wanted to cry.

"Are you all right, Madame Kirby?"

"Nope."

"Anything I can do?"

"Can do? Maybe. Will do? Nope."

He looked down at me, eyes soft like milk chocolate. "You want to be held."

"I want to be made love to," I said, voice remarkably steady, all things considered. "I could use a good dose of endorphins right now."

There was a long pause.

"The captain..." Gravell started

"He won't. You won't. Nobody else appeals right now."

"You want both of us?"

"Not at the same time."

I turned and saw that he was staring at me with a startled expression. I chuckled. Nice to know I could surprise him.

"I'm not a slut or anything. I'm a mature woman, unattached, with excess hormones, and a natural desire to feel something besides fear and stress."

He turned around and stared out over the water. I did the same.

"There are other ways of producing endorphins," he said eventually.

"If you are going to suggest running, forget it. I'm a walker, not a runner."

"I was thinking of chocolate."

I turned back to him and pulled at his shoulder until he was facing me. "Are you serious? You have chocolate?"

He laughed. "It's not a controlled substance, Madame Kirby."

"Let me rephrase. Do you have good chocolate?"

He had really good chocolate.

Early morning I was summoned to sick bay to undergo a thorough checkup. Doc had heard about the diving lessons and wanted to make sure I was in reasonable physical shape.

"Good enough. Remarkably good considering what you've been through. It seems you have a very hard head. I'll check again before you actually dive."

Next I reported to Lieutenant Welland for my first class. I was introduced to Lieutenant (Junior Grade) Cross, the other diver who rescued me. He introduced me to the equipment, and I was walked through a maintenance check. Welland gave me the diving safety lesson. Then I was given a textbook to read. I would be tested on my homework in the afternoon. It wasn't exactly scintillating. In fact, I dozed off.

Before my afternoon class, Gravell took me for a fitness walk on a circuit I would never have been allowed to take alone. He walked, I half-jogged to keep up. I put up with it because he promised me more chocolate in the evening if I went for two walks during the day. I suggested we do morning and evening. After lunch, what I most wanted was a nap.

The next morning, while trotting alongside Gravell, I saw a cargo helicopter arrive. It was a good excuse to pause, since I was short of breath. As a result, I was amongst the first to welcome Dora and Reuben.

I threw my arms around Dora in what was, for us, an uncharacteristic display of emotion. "I'm so glad you're back."

Then the deck officer took over, taking Dora and Reuben to meet with the captain.

After three hours of intensive classroom instruction, I was glad to retreat to the *Émil Gagnan* for a couple of hours off. I entered the wardroom in time to catch the beginning of Reuben and Dora's tale of political intrigue. Reuben was used to spinning information for effect and Dora had a dry wit, so it was an entertaining story. Then I was prompted to tell them about my misadventures, including passing out and almost falling overboard. I also confirmed the rumour that I was taking a crash course in diving so I could go back to the station.

Lil looked wistful, but Reuben stated that putting on a scuba mask was too much like being prepped for surgery and Dora shrugged saying, "Better you than me."

After lunch, I had a little time before returning to the *Nottawasaga* so I followed Dora to our cabin and watched her unpack while she grilled me.

"Who is doing this to you and why, for heaven's sake?"

"I really don't know. It's like I said, someone seems to think I know more than I do that's why I need to go back to the station. I need to find out what I'm supposed to know already. I could also use your professional skills. I'm hoping you'll be able to narrow down the suspects."

"Maybe. If it's a secret agent, he or she would be good at dissimilation. For instance, I didn't catch that Gravell was a spy."

"I think he's more an investigator than spy. Besides, you hardly had anything to do with him. You left before he started guarding me."

"Uh-huh. Whatever he is, he has more than a professional interest in you."

"You think so?"

Dora laughed. "It doesn't take a trained observer to work it out, though I am a trained observer. He's careful, but not that careful and you are practically transparent."

I blushed. No one likes to hear that they are transparent.

"I thought you were interested in Captain Campbell," Dora continued, ignoring my discomfort.

I blushed hotter. She shook her head.

"Don't take it so seriously. It's just hormones. You're at that time of life when your body is trying to get you to produce a few more children while you still can. Couple that with the heightened sense of danger you've experienced, it's a wonder you haven't jumped one of them by now, or vice versa. After all, men are even greater slaves to their hormones and you seem to trigger the instinct to protect. I noticed it with Franchot."

Oh brother, I thought. Just what I needed. Now that she was on a roll, Dora would be hard to stop. I knew my libido was in overdrive, I even guessed the reason. I didn't need to discuss it.

"You need a safe romantic fling to keep you busy. I'm not sure

Campbell would go for it and I'm pretty sure Gravell isn't safe."

She tilted her head to one side and eyed me appraisingly.

"How about Franchot? He strikes me as a perennial bachelor and I'll bet he's a considerate lover. He looks the type. If I was wired that way, I'd take him."

At that point I beat a hasty retreat.

Mercuros claimed me for the afternoon. He wanted me learn about the *Émil Gagnan* facilities and equipment, since I already had gear on board. I would be wearing the thermal gear already fitted to me with a wetsuit instead of the bright orange flotation wear.

Alex, as he insisted I call him, stripped down well. He was a nice looking man in uniform, but in a skin tight suit, he was hot. Why hadn't I noticed earlier? Because my libido hadn't kicked into overdrive. I reigned in my hormones and concentrated on applying everything I had learned so far to the pre-dive maintenance checks, refilling tanks and gearing up for the dive.

Strictly speaking, my practice dives should have been in a pool, or at the very least a sheltered area. On the other hand, I doubt any diving student was as well backed-up as me.

One of the *Nottawasaga* boats, crewed by a couple of shepherd-hook-wielding sailors, was a few metres off the *Émil Gagnan's* diving platform. Welland, Cross, and a couple of our divers were in the water before me, and Alex was right behind me. Franchot and Mike were on the platform, which was equipped with rescue gear, and I noted that I had audiences on the *Èmil Gagnan, Nottawasaga,* and *Scranton.*

I was less afraid of the dive as I was of doing something embarrassing.

The part I had the least trouble with was breathing naturally in the mask. It was something that gave a lot of students problems, and I anticipated feeling anxious because, like Reuben, I associate masks with medical procedures. I had seen my mother with nasal cannulas, masks, bipap, and intubated. Those memories intruded when I practised breathing with the scuba mask out of the water. In the water, I remembered the fresh-tasting air that filled my lungs and cleared my head after escaping the fetid galley.

Below the surface, it was a whole other world. I thought about space and how astronauts used diving experience for training. Despite the heavy gear, I felt almost weightless. The view wasn't great, but the sensation was amazing.

Although we were hooked up for radio transmission, Alex wanted us to use hand signals only just for practice. Responding to his signals, I went up, down, and side to side. I tried to find the right stroke to glide through the water efficiently. I checked his gauge and, using hand signals, told him his levels. Then he did the same. I then signalled back a confirmation query, because he just told me that I had a lot less air than I should. He corrected himself, letting me know he just wanted to make sure I was paying attention.

All too soon, he signalled me that it was time to go up.

That's when I embarrassed myself. I was fine getting into the water, but getting out I didn't have the upper body strength to get myself back onto the platform.

I had to climb something that looked more like an upside-down antenna than a ladder. The vertical support was in the middle with rungs going out either side. Like an iceberg, most of it was under water. Theoretically, it should have been easy to climb and it was until I broke the surface.

With great effort, I tried to haul myself up. The tank pulled me backwards and my limbs felt like sandbags, heavy and clumsy. I lost my grip, flailed gracelessly and fell. My flipper caught in a rung, and I hung upside down, hitting Alex as I dropped. Welland had to help me get free, then I had to try again.

The second time around, Mike and Franchot grabbed my arms and while Alex pushed up from behind, his hand on my bottom. I flopped on the deck like an overturned turtle for a few seconds, until Franchot helped me up. Alex managed to climb aboard without assistance.

"You okay?" I asked. I had fallen on him, after all.

"I'm fine. You did great. I should have warned you about the feeling of dead weight when you got out. My bad."

For someone who had only spoken Greek accented French for most the voyage, his English was excellent and idiomatic.

"You should be finished your classroom work tomorrow morning. We can do another practice dive tomorrow afternoon."

He waved me in the direction of the divers' ready room.

"Let's go. Class isn't over yet."

We had to strip down the gear and stow it for next time. By then, I was getting a bit chilled. Alex, wearing boxer briefs and a singlet, seemed impervious to the cool air.

"We should celebrate your first dive. I can't take you to a bar for a beer, so how about the wardroom for a coffee?"

"Sounds good to me. First I want a hot shower and to get some warm clothes. Then maybe you can explain why you were pretending to not speak English before. Are all the divers bilingual?"

"Some are trilingual, but not all of them are comfortable in English and some of us are limited in what we can share with your team. Besides, it's fitting. You know who Émil Gagnan was, right?"

I nodded. I'd looked it up. "He was Jacques Cousteau's partner in the invention of scuba gear."

"*Apropos, n'est pas?*"

He gave me a thoughtful look, head cocked to one side.

"Why don't I walk you to your cabin? You can get comfortable and I'll go do the same. Later we can go for that coffee."

Automatically, I agreed. It took a couple of minutes for suspicion to strike.

"It's your watch until Gravell returns, right?"

He started. "How did you know he was on the *Nottawasaga*?"

"He's not here."

His bark of laughter echoed in the passageway. "Yes. You're on my watch right now. Although I don't think he'd be too happy if I watched you too closely."

That was an interesting thought to dwell on. I decided to set it aside until I had more time to enjoy it.

I returned to the *Nottawasaga* after dinner. Dora complained, but all my clothes were over there, and I had diving class with Welland and Cross in the morning.

"Ready for your walk?" Gravell asked, once we had reported to the Deck Officer.

I sighed.

"Do you still have chocolate?"

He nodded.

"Okay. I'm ready."

He started off at a brisk walk and then started to run. Running and I don't get along well, but I made the effort to keep up. When we running the inside gangways and ladders, rivulets of sweat ran down my back and between my breasts. When we had a stretch outside, the cold breeze turned the sweat to ice water. Face flushed, calves aching, I started falling behind. Gravell slowed and we fell back into a brisk walk, which we maintained until we reached my cabin.

"I'll be back with tea and chocolate. You'll need something to keep you going while you study."

I nodded, not having enough breath to comment. Once I was inside, I leaned on the closed hatch thinking that I should have asked for coffee. I closed my eyes and heaved a sigh. Even if I had found my voice in time to make the request, Gravell would probably have ignored it. He didn't seem to approve of coffee after noon.

A shiver passed through me. Opening my eyes, I found that the gang had returned. Margolo was in the forefront, hands on hips, giving me a charming smile that didn't reach his eyes. His eyes were troubled. All of them looked troubled.

The pages of the diving manual ruffled. I could feel the deck vibrate and my knees buckle. Shore stepped forward, reaching out for me. Perhaps he meant to steady me, but he only succeeded in sending a deathly chill through me.

"Give me a break. I'm working on it."

I took a couple of deep breaths and straightened my knees.

"Remember, if you make me pass out again, I won't be able to help you."

They faded away.

Shakily, I found the bed and sat on the edge, head between my knees. When the nausea passed, I took stock.

I had plenty of studying to do, but my tablet beckoned. I still had letters to read, photographs to examine, gaps to fill. I started by calling up anything related to Margolo. There wasn't a lot. He didn't keep a journal or write letters he couldn't mail. All the references were in other people's documents.

In what seemed like a few minutes after I started reading, Gravell announced himself with a knock on the door. I looked up as he entered and received a scowl.

"What happened?" he asked.

"What do you mean?"

"You are still in the clothes you were running in and you are, if that's possible, even sweatier than when I left you."

I pulled at my t-shirt and made a eww face. Closing my tablet, I pushed it to one side and invited Gravell to put his burden down. He had arrived with a thermos and a couple of cups. Unlike me, he was showered and in fresh clothes. In his case, a hooded sweat shirt and matching shorts. I hoped that the pocket of his hoody held chocolate.

"I had another visitation from the crew. It threw me a bit."

I grabbed my nightshirt from under my pillow and headed to the shower.

"I'll be quick."

He stood back as I passed him, lending credence to the adage that you could smell fear. In my case it stank.

I took a little longer than I intended. The hot water felt wonderful, and I was determined to be thoroughly clean and smelling only of my vanilla shower gel. Once out of the water, I towel-dried, dressed, and was finger combing my hair as I emerged.

Gravell stopped mid-pace when I entered the room. His stern expression had evolved to grim.

"You should have called me."

"You were coming back. And I wasn't in danger. It's just that they are a bit overwhelming. It's a physiological response. I break out into a sweat and feel light-headed."

"And can pass out and hit your head on the way down."

"But I didn't. I was okay."

He grabbed me by the shoulders hard and for a moment I thought he might shake me. If not shake me, he might kiss me. Then he regained control, released his grip, and let one hand slide down my arm as if smoothing my sleeve. The other hand glided down my back then applied pressure, guiding me to the chair I had recently vacated.

"What were you reading?" he asked, pouring the tea.

I had to take a couple of deep breaths because what just happened freaked me out almost as much as the ghosts. Chief Gravell was afraid for me and he was scary when he was afraid.

"Are you all right, Madame Kirby?" He was back to being cool and courteous.

I flexed my shoulders and nodded.

"Did I hurt you?" This time there was concern in his voice.

Again I nodded.

"I'm sorry."

I fought for control of my emotions. At this point, I was fighting the urge to grab and shake him. Instead, I tried to lighten things up.

"Why can't you be more like James Bond?"

"Excuse me?"

"If you were James Bond, and assuming I qualified as one of the Bond girls, we could be working off some of this tension in bed."

He stared at me for a minute or so then started to laugh.

"Well, that's a start," I said, grinning.

I picked up my mug and took a sip of tea.

I had never been a big tea drinker. My mother was a tea drinker. Tea, for my mother, meant a dark, bitter brew leavened with lots of milk and sugar. I never developed a taste for it. Gravell's tea I could get used to. When he wasn't having 'tea, Earl Grey, hot,' he drank green tea, which had a light taste and needed nothing to enhance it.

At least that's what he brought me.

I still preferred coffee, but I was beginning to appreciate tea's relaxing effects.

Laughter and green tea seemed to have a beneficial effect on Gravell too. He settled in the chair opposite and pulled out two mini chocolate bars out of his pocket. They were the size you give out as Halloween treats, but no sane adult would give this craft chocolate to tick-or-treaters. I wondered if they came from ship's stores or whether he had a private stash, but I didn't want to ask. Some things should remain a mystery.

"I noticed something a bit odd," I said, getting back to business.

"When the crew visits, Lieutenant Margolo is always in the forefront. Not Commander Shore. The first time, I thought it was because Margolo was being flirtatious. Before he made contact, I sensed someone coming up behind me, and I thought it was you. I only felt the chill when he reached out and touched me. It was almost like he was trying to seduce me."

Gravell's face screwed up into an expression of distaste. He gave his head a shake.

"Is that's what made you black out?"

"No. He wasn't threatening, just playful. Then he got serious and they all closed in on me. That's what made me pass out. It's almost like they suck the air away from me. The point is, I thought Margolo was flirting and that's why he took the lead, but he was the first to appear when I summoned them in my cabin and tonight..." I shivered and took a sip of tea to steady myself. "Tonight they came to remind me to get the job done. Margolo was still the leader. So, I thought I'd try to find out why."

"That's what you were doing when I arrived."

"Yes. I looked up Margolo's effects, but he didn't keep a journal or write letters home. So I looked up references to Margolo."

I opened the file on my laptop. Damn. I was forgetting Doc's instructions again.

Gravell rearranged our mugs and the flask so there was room and shifted his chair around so he was sitting beside me. His knee brushed mine. Experimentally, I shifted so our legs touched. He didn't move away.

"In Minton's journal, Margolo goes from being a mildly respected, but fondly regarded friend, to being a dilettante and degenerate. In Shore's letters to his wife, he describes Margolo in similar, but less inflammatory terms. He likes the man and appreciates the talent of the engineer, but he doesn't seem to respect Margolo as an officer."

"Yet, Shore selected him for his crew."

"I think Shore selected his friends. Yet, he underestimated Margolo, was disparaging of Dawes' gambling, and laughed at Minton's foibles. Doesn't say much for the man's command ability."

Gravell grunted. "That sounds like twenty-twenty hindsight."

I turned my laptop slightly so that Gravell could get a better view.

"I might have the benefit of hindsight, but someone else showed foresight. She just wasn't in the position to do anything about it. Look. This is a letter to Golanger from his mother. It looks like she packed it with his things just before he left. Shore and his family hosted a backyard barbeque for the crew and their families. Mrs. Golanger attended."

My dear son,

I know you don't want your mother raining on your parade, but when you have children of your own, God willing, you'll understand the need to protect your young. Not that you aren't a man now, but to a mother, your son is always your little boy.

You're going on a dangerous mission. I know that, even though I don't know where you are going or what you'll be doing. Just as I know that your life will depend on those men I met at that shindig your captain threw. Because of that, I want to make sure your eyes are open to a few things.

Boreman's full of talk, and Dawes acts foolish, but I don't see any real harm in them. Even though he's a coloured man, I think you'll find that Petty Officer Naire holds the same values you were brought up with. You look to him when you need advice. If you got real trouble, go to Lieutenant Magoo. I wasn't sure of him at first, but I think he has a good head on his shoulders.

Your captain, bless him, is too much like your Pa. He wants everyone to be happy and doesn't always know when to put his foot down. Mr. Minton reminds me of your Aunt Ida, too ready to put a foot down. Maybe they'll balance each other out or maybe not. Either way, you look to Mr. Magoo.

"Mr. Magoo?"

"That's what Dawes and Shore called him. Mrs. Golanger probably thought it was his real name. There's more. Later, Golanger writes back to his mother."

I've been thinking about what you told me, Ma, how people aren't always what they seem. I'm beginning to see what you mean. I suppose Boreman is mostly talk, but at least he's interesting. He says he'll take me rally racing when our mission is over. Even if he doesn't, I like listening to his stories about racing and I'm learning a lot about cars and mechanical engineering from him. Naire is a good guy, but he has a bit of a chip on his shoulder. I don't know that we'll ever be close, but I'm taking your advice and looking to him for an example on how to work and cope with things.

You are scarily right about the captain and Mr. Minton. They are exactly like Pa and Aunt Ida, except that Aunt Ida is louder. Sometimes I have to bite my tongue because I want to laugh, but it isn't really very funny.

I haven't gone to Lt. Margolo (NOT Magoo, Ma), but only because I don't need to. One thing I learned from Naire is to keep quiet and do your job.

I scrolled down the page. "Later he writes…"

Since we started, the captain, Mr. Minton, and Mr. Margolo have been friends. Sometimes they rub against each other, but eventually they sort it out. Now, I don't know.

Seems to me thing are falling apart between them. They act polite, but I know that the Doc and Mr. Margolo are concerned about Mr. Minton and the captain isn't taking them seriously. He's not taking Mr. Minton seriously either, even though he has some serious concerns. I can't quite see how the Captain can have it both ways.

Then there was this argument between the four of them. Mostly, I think it was between the captain and Mr. Minton. I think Mr. Margolo and Doc Dawes were trying to calm things down. Anyway, now they are all being brittle and polite. It's like that Christmas when Pa and Aunt Ida had that big fight then tried to pretend it was nothing. Doc Dawes is like Uncle Nels, trying to smooth things over by also pretending. Mr. Margolo reminds me of you, trying to fix things and hold the family together. I hope it blows over soon.

"That's the last thing he writes. Given the timing, compared to the journal, I think Golanger found out that Minton was starting to spy on them."

Gravell shrugged. "It doesn't prove Minton was the killer, but I suppose we are building a circumstantial case realizing that no court is going to accept the confession of a ghost."

"I'm less interested in proof than understanding what happened." I grabbed my tea and leaned back. I stretched my legs out and Gravell shifted his leg so we still maintained some contact. I gave him a covert glance. His expression seemed determined not to give anything away, but his eyes had softened to milk chocolate. I forced myself to focus on work.

"There are several theories about what ghosts are and why they haunt. Of course, one of the most reputable theories is that they don't really exist at all. What we think are ghosts are projections of our imagination. We imagine ghosts because we don't want to let go of a loved one, or we need to manifest our fears or feeling of guilt. Maybe that's true most of the time, but I'm not inclined to hold to that theory in this case, for obvious reasons."

Gravell acknowledged my point with a nod.

"The most popular theory is that ghosts hang around because they have unfinished business. They are attached to a place or thing or, sometimes, a person. Sometimes the spirit isn't aware that they are dead. Often the circumstances surrounding their death tie the spirit to this world. Regardless of whether the apparition is manifested by the living or the dead, it's all about resolving issues and letting go. Someone has to see the light."

Gravell picked up one of the mini bars, unwrapped it, and offered it to me. I took a bite and leaned forward to put the other half beside my cup. Now our legs were intertwined. There was a pause, then he disentangled, still keeping contact.

"Chief Gravell."

He forestalled me with a raised hand. "Madame Kirby, our position is rather awkward. Your safety is my responsibility. My job is to uphold Canadian interests in this investigation. I need you to do my job, and I think you need me to do yours. I am sure you don't want to broadcast your talent, so I can't delegate my duties much. If it were otherwise, I could have Sloan or Briseau guard you over night. So, whatever attraction I may feel towards you, I need to keep a professional distance."

"I see."

He sighed. "I bet you don't. I have had to address the question of why I am keeping an eye on you twenty-four seven without actually answering directly. So, I've fostered the belief that I am under the captain's orders to keep his girlfriend safe and," he shook his head, "I am pretty sure half the crew thinks I was chosen because I'm gay."

I stared. "But you're not are you?"

"No, but even if anyone asked, which they won't, I wouldn't say one way or another because it is a convenient assumption. It means that people perceive you being perfectly safe with me, which you are in any case."

It was my turn to shake my head. "The captain doesn't think you're gay. He thinks you're competition."

"I'm not." Those chocolate eyes gripped me with their bitter-sweet expression. "Circumstances have thrown us together, Madame Kirby. All too soon, they will pull us apart."

I gave an impatient shake of my head and pushed away from the table. "The same can be said of Captain Campbell, and everyone else I've met this summer."

"Yes, but you'll always know where to find Captain Campbell. The same cannot be said of me."

I took a couple of turns about the room. I was feeling agitated, irritated, and confused. Sure, I was attracted to Captain Campbell, but I didn't like having my choices made for me.

"Dora said I needed to have a safe fling. Maybe she's right. She suggested Franchot, but I'm thinking Alex Mercuros."

Gravell's eyes hardened.

"Not funny, Madame Kirby."

"Not a joke, Chief Gravell. I can handle the loss of privacy. I am getting used to the ghosts. But I will not be railroaded into a relationship because it's expedient."

"I thought you cared about Captain Campbell."

"I do. And I care about you. But both of you have decided that a relationship is not in your best interest at this time. Okay. Fine. That's your prerogative. Just don't get your knickers in a knot if I look elsewhere for less complicated companionship. As Dora so indelicately put it, I'm packed with raging hormones."

I sighed and sat down to close up my tablet. Again our knees touched and my anger deflated. Gravell started to move, and I laid a hand on his sleeve. He covered it with his hand. The dark scowl had disappeared. We seemed to have a problem. We couldn't go forward and we didn't want to back away.

"Mercuros will enjoy the flirtation," he said eventually. "I'm sure Franchot will too. Neither will complicate your life and neither will change our relationship." He gave me an odd smile. "Whatever it happens to be."

I nodded. I gave his arm a squeeze and pushed myself up again.

"I have lots of studying to do tonight. Do you include diving among your many talents?"

He shook his head.

"Then go. If you stick around, you'll distract me. I have to be able to pass the exam tomorrow."

He left, reminding me to call if the crew descended on me again, or I felt the need to take a walk on deck. Once he was gone, I addressed the room.

"So, is there any one of you who can help me cram for my test?"

Chapter Thirty-Four ~ *Examinations*

Franchot was impressed at how much I had managed to absorb in such a short time. I gave credit to my teachers. Welland and Cross smiled. Alex gave a valedictory nod. Behind him, Naire gave me a broad wink. He had managed to detach himself from the group and, with hand signals, tested my memory mostly by telling me when I was wrong. He also hung around in the morning during my final training session with Welland and Alex. He complicated their hands-on instruction with a bit of poltergeist-like activity. He made everything I did just a little bit harder. It was good preparation for Franchot's test.

Now we were crowded into Franchot's office. Welland, Gravell, and I took the available extra chairs. Naire perched on an invisible seat about halfway up the wall.

Alex stood, but didn't look as if he was going to stick around anyway. "I want Jen to take another practice dive after lunch. If that goes well, and if you're okay with it Skipper, I have no objection to Jen joining the dive tomorrow."

Franchot nodded.

"Cross and I would like to join the dive," said Welland.

"Cross is the other diver who rescued me," I said, for the benefit of those who didn't have a clue.

"After all, we promised to look out for Ms. Kirby for insurance purposes."

Franchot rolled his eyes. "I expected as much. Tinsdale wants to send a couple of divers too. It's going to get rather crowded. How about this, I'll allow one observer per ship to join our team, of which Jen is now a part."

Welland and Cross looked at each other for a minute then shook a fist each. Welland's rock beat Cross's scissors. I tried not to look as if it mattered, but I was glad to have another woman along. I didn't bother hiding my pleasure in Franchot's assumption that I'd satisfy his requirements during this afternoon's dive. Now we just had to convince Captain Campbell.

Gravell escorted me to the captain's office and tactfully withdrew. I brought some of Cookie's Tollhouse cookies. Gravell made sure that fresh coffee was supplied for the meeting. I poured and waited for the captain to put aside some paper work.

"Bribe?" he asked, looking at the container of still warm cookies.

"Social lubricant. I thought cookies were more appropriate than liquor before lunch."

He allowed me a half smile.

"Have you talked to Franchot?" I asked, knowing he had.

"Oh, yes," he sighed.

He shuffled the pages in front of him. "This pile contains a certificate of completion for the written portion of the diving test. Captain Franchot has also included a note attesting that he is willing to oversee your open water dives pursuant to you completing your qualifications for a diving certificate."

He held up a handwritten note. "This is a less formal, but similar offer from two of my own crewmembers. Then we have this."

He held up a page with a US Navy logo. "This is Captain Tinsdale's official objection to civilians entering the station. He doesn't want you or anyone from the *Émil Gagnan* on the dive. This note is a personal request that you not be included in deference to your health and safety. The rest of this pile represents the paper trail of negotiations concerning who will, and will not be on the dive tomorrow."

"Captain Franchot suggested that each military ship send one observer."

"I have that documented. Captain Franchot forgets that it is not entirely up to him."

"I need to go aboard. I'm not trying to dictate terms, I just need you to realize how important this is."

"Why, Jenny? For the love of God, why?"

I blushed. Not only was this the first time that the captain had relaxed his formal address with me, but no one had called me Jenny outside my family. Not sure how exactly to handle the situation, I went over to the couch and hoped he'd come and sit with me. After a minute or so, he did. I rewarded his effort with a playful smile.

"If you're going to call me Jenny, do I have to call you Captain?"

"In public. At least for now. My name is Sean."

I knew that, but I sighed anyway.

"Sean is such a nice name. Well, you can guess I like the Celtic names since I called my son Seamus."

"Is that why you were named Genevieve?"

"Sort of. My mother was a great romantic. She called me Genevieve, after Queen Guinevere's patron saint. My brother got saddled with Lancelot. If she had got her first choice, he would have been name Galahad."

His smile broadened. "I think I would have liked your mother. Do you mind me calling you Jenny?"

I shook my head.

"You're not going to answer my question, are you Jenny?"

I shook my head.

He shrugged stoically. "I'll want to see for myself that you know what you are doing sufficiently to do the dive. If I'm satisfied, I will sign off on your participation. If I'm not, I'll put you in the brig so you can't go behind my back."

"Can't ask for fairer than that."

I was almost the hatch before it hit me. "Who wrote the personal request?"

"Your video director."

My second practice dive drew an even bigger crowd than the first. In addition to Welland, Cross, and Mercuros, Franchot and Tim joined the dive.

Though I was tempted, I didn't say anything to Tim. I decided my best recourse was to show him I was capable enough not to endanger myself or anyone else.

Observing on deck, there were the *Émil Gagnan* divers, ready to jump in if needed. Captains Campbell and Tinsdale were there, and Gravell, of course. Was I intimidated? Just a bit.

Alex and Franchot watched while I suited up. The others diving with me were standing by. Knowing I was being tested, I went over all the equipment carefully. It looked okay, but I got a head shake from Naire. I went over it again.

"This hose is leaking. Pretty tricky test, guys."

Franchot examined the line and scowled. He looked to Alex who shook his head. They looked at Welland and Cross who also shook their heads. I cast a glance at Naire. He shrugged.

"Not a test, Jen. I want the maintenance records checked, Alex.

Meanwhile, let's switch out that line for another."

Franchot let me check everything again. Then rechecked everything. I didn't take it personally. I was happy to have the back up. Naire's expression was grim and that worried me. It wasn't his handiwork, and I could tell he didn't think it wasn't an accident either.

On deck, Tinsdale was impatient. Tim explained that my gear was faulty. Alex added that I caught the problem myself and chalked up two imaginary points for me in the air.

"Madame Kirby?" Gravell's voice was soft in my ear. I hadn't even noticed him come up behind me.

"Maybe nothing," I whispered. But I doubted it.

"Be careful."

I nodded.

"Ready Jen?" asked Franchot.

Welland and Cross went into the water first. I was next. Franchot, Tim, and Alex followed. Once again, I followed Mercuros's hand signals and was put through my paces. Then we went over radio protocols and camera operation. We were equipped with the same shoulder mounted video cameras we would use while exploring the station. We swam under the ship and dove down to the anchor.

I was surprised how interesting it was down there. Somehow I got the impression that Arctic waters wouldn't be exactly teaming with life, but I was wrong. I would have loved to explore longer, but I wasn't given the chance. Alex took a picture of me holding the anchor. After, we practised safe ascension, gradually climbing up the chain. This was considerably deeper than the station.

When we breached the surface, I was greeted by applause. Alex gave me a push from behind as I mounted the ladder. Gravell was in place to give me a helping hand. Captain Campbell gave me the thumbs up and even Tinsdale wore a grin.

"Well, I'm satisfied," said Franchot, once he was on board. "How about you, Alex?"

"As far as I'm concerned, Jen is four dives away from certification."

"Captain Campbell?"

The captain nodded. "I have no objections. Do you want to raise any, Captain Tinsdale?"

"I made my official objection to civilians being involved. Unofficially, I can't see any reason why Mrs. Kirby shouldn't be one of the team."

Once we were in the ready room, I was treated to back slaps and handshakes on my performance from Mike and the *Émil Gagnan* divers, all of whom had been watching my dive on video. Mike gave me a hug and his uncle appeared behind him, smiling wistfully.

"Mike, can I have a private word with you when I'm done here?"

He nodded. He helped me clean and stow my gear. No one objected. I had already proven I could do it.

"Where do you want to go?"

"Do you think the wardroom will be busy? I could go for a hot chocolate right now. I better let Gravell know first."

"Still playing bodyguard?"

I tried to think of a snappy answer to that, but couldn't. I let it go, contenting myself with an eye roll that only Naire Senior caught.

The wardroom was busy, mostly because people followed me there. Dora, Reuben, and Lil were there to congratulate me. Mary Lou, Tracy, and Jamal were conspicuously absent. The command staff went to Franchot's office to discuss matters, but several off-duty crew members passed through to pat my back, figuratively if not literally.

Mike shrugged.

"Not a quiet place to talk. Is it urgent?"

"No. It can wait."

Gravell, who was sticking to me like something too uncomplimentary to mention, leaned in to me and spoke sotto voce.

"You could interview the team going to the station one by one. I'll see if you can use ops."

"Good idea."

"I'd like to talk to you first," he added.

I nodded. The feeling was mutual. I had a bad feeling about that leaky hose, and I wanted to share it with someone who was at least as paranoid as I was becoming.

Gravell helped me set things up, or vice versa. Tomorrow morning the documentary crew would return in time for the expedition. They wouldn't be making the dive, but they'd be able to tape what was going on topside while Tim and a couple of the *Émil Gagnan* divers, would be our onsite videographers. Today, Gravell was going to be my cameraman. Tim was kept out of the loop with the help of Alex, who insisted on a pre-dive meeting with the documentary crew.

"Why do I get the impression that you want to talk about ghosts?" Gravell asked, while we were waiting for Mike.

"Why do I get the impression you are a mind reader?"

"Not minds. Just body language, tone of voice, the way you were looking just beyond Mike Naire when you were talking to him."

"His uncle helped me study last night."

Gravell looked up as if much needed patience might shower down upon him.

"I thought you were going to call me if the crew returned."

"They didn't. Just Naire. I can handle one ghost at a time."

The deck was consulted this time. I gave him a light punch on the arm.

"Don't dis Naire. He's the one that warned me about the hose."

I didn't mention that he was also the one who had fiddled with the equipment to test my knowledge and make sure I was paying attention.

"Tell me about that."

I outlined the situation as best I could. The bottom line was the divers would have checked the equipment earlier. Franchot's reaction made it clear that my checking the equipment was just part of the test. In any case, if he wanted to test my knowledge, he wouldn't have damaged the hose.

"It was less than a pin prick almost invisible. But, under pressure, it would have cut short the dive or worse."

"Killed you?"

"Not likely. Stop me from diving tomorrow, maybe. But why?"

Gravell watched me fuss with papers. I was nervous and he knew it, and I knew he knew it which made me more nervous. I set aside the papers and folded my hands in my lap.

A smile twitched on Gravell's face.

I smiled in response. It was always best to keep a sense of humour about things. After all, if someone did manage to kill me, I could come back and haunt Gravell…or maybe the captain…or both.

"Jen?"

It was Mike Naire.

"Showtime," muttered Gravell, going behind the camera.

"Come and sit down, Mike. This is just a follow-up interview. I want to talk to you about your impressions when we were on the station and anything you feel you've learned about your uncle, Joe Naire."

His uncle appeared when I spoke his name. I smiled in spite of myself.

"Ready, Chief Gravell?"

"Ready, Madame Kirby."

I took a deep breath and put on my game face.

"Okay, let's start with your impressions of the station."

"Spooky. Except for the smell, it was like the crew might return any minute."

"What about the smell?" I asked.

His nose wrinkled with distaste. "Dank, metallic, like an iron grave which I guess is apt. Sometimes I thought I could smell blood, but it was probably my imagination."

"Tell me about your Uncle Joe's berth."

"He had photos of me and my aunt, and one of my mother holding me as a baby. I never knew that one existed. He didn't have them up like some of the others. He kept them in a little album under his pillow. I've printed off copies from the scans. I'll carry them with me tomorrow and put them under his pillow."

Joe Naire stood behind his nephew and placed ghostly hands on the man's shoulders. Mike was almost ten years older than his uncle had been when he died, but I saw the boy reflected in his uncle's eyes. Mike gave a shiver and Joe backed off a step.

"I don't think I realized how much my uncle loved us. When I see those photos, I know that this was just a job for him. We were what was important." He sighed heavily and rubbed his arms as if cold.

"You okay? We can take a break."

He shook his head.

"Your uncle was the weapons' tech, right? But he was also a diver?"

"They were all divers, but diving was one of my uncle's pleasures as well as a necessary skill for the posting. And he wasn't just a weapons' technician, he was a marksman and an engineer. He was interested in martial arts and ancient weapons, but also poetry and music."

Joe Naire shrugged modestly.

"If he hadn't been black, he would have been an officer."

Naire shook his head vehemently.

"Maybe," I said. "Or maybe he refused officers training. My grandfather turned down promotion because he made more money as a sergeant than a second lieutenant."

Naire grinned sheepishly and nodded. Mike shrugged.

"I guess I'll never know. I do know he was a renaissance man and a warrior. I can't believe he went quietly into the night."

I let it go at that. Tempted as I was to tell Mike that his uncle was proud of him, I realized it wasn't prudent or necessary.

When the interview was over, Mike wondered what I'd wanted to talk to him about.

"Just this," I said, lying.

In fact, I wanted to ask him about the hose and what might have happened if I hadn't caught the leak. The problem was, he could be the culprit. Someone tried to sabotage my dive. I was betting it was one of the living.

Mary Lou was up next. I asked Gravell to hold her for a moment, made sure the camera was off, and called on Lou Boreman.

"Just Lou Boreman," I added.

I didn't see anything at first, but when Mary Lou entered the room he appeared. Gravell made a few adjustments to the camera angle and we started.

"What were your impressions on the station?" I asked.

"Creepy and exciting. I can understand why you forgot protocol when we arrived. It was surreal how intact the site was. I saw the pin-up calendar and knew that was my father's bunk. He was always being sent stuff like that by gas stations and oil companies and tool suppliers. He gave most of them away, but always picked out one to hang up because it was expected."

"Was there a particular smell?"

"Not that I remember. Nothing unexpected anyway. Actually, the place smelled cleaner than I expected. I mean, there was a salty-metallic scent, but underneath that, the place smelled well-scrubbed."

"What are you hoping to find when you go on board tomorrow?"

"Answers, of course. I have no specific expectations." She frowned. "While we're talking about answers, I'd like a couple from you. You might not want to record this, however."

I took a deep breath. "You think it shouldn't be recorded?"

"No, I think it should. You just might not want it to be."

"Go ahead," I said, signalling Gravell to keep rolling.

He held up a hand and adjusted the position of the camera, and me, so that we were both in the shot. I grimaced. Gravell gave me a thumbs up, and I forced a calm, neutral expression onto my face.

With her country-girl prettiness, ponytail, and youthful appearance, it was easy to forget that Mary Lou was a forensic professional. I had no doubt that she traded on the fact that she was often underestimated, but this wasn't one of those times.

"You stated that you took out Lieutenant Minton's journal, compromising the integrity of the evidence, and started reading it because you felt compelled. Compelled by what?"

I hesitated. I didn't want to lie to her, but I wasn't about to tell her about the ghosts. I was tempted with Mike, not with his wife.

"I was trapped, alone, and injured. I hit my head when I was thrown off my feet during the explosion and again when I passed out due to fatigue and poor air. Both times I had dreams of the crew and I saw the journal in those dreams. I felt compelled to read the journal as a result."

It was the truth, just not all of it.

She wasn't convinced. "You knew rescue was just a matter of time. Why didn't you wait to look at the scans? What if you had dropped the journal in the water? Didn't you understand the responsibility you had?"

Over her shoulder, Boreman smiled apologetically.

"Were you told my rescue was just a matter of time?" I countered. "I wasn't."

She looked startled. Gravell gave me the slightest of nods. I continued.

"As reassuring as Captain Campbell was, he didn't make false promises. He said he'd get me out. Neither of us knew if I'd be alive."

Okay, that was a bit of a stretch. I am assuming that the captain wasn't sure he'd succeed. He never voiced those doubts.

"Have you read the journal?" I asked.

Mary Lou nodded. "Parts of it."

Naire reappeared next to Boreman. Both looked at me expectantly.

"Then you know that Minton suffered from claustrophobia and was probably had an obsessive-compulsive personality. He abhorred disorder, dirt, and strong smells especially tobacco smoke."

Boreman rolled his eyes. I tried to keep my eyes focussed on Mary Lou. It wasn't easy.

"On a ship, he would have seemed a bit fussy. On a submarine, he obviously found ways to cope. Trapped on the underwater station, he was in hell. The men he was with transformed from friends to monsters and that transformation is recorded in his journal. Your father, the antithesis of Minton, was the first to be warped. Minton saw him as a threat to himself and Golanger."

Golanger appeared, looked to the other two ghosts then to me. Golanger and Boreman both shook their heads, not in refutation of my interpretation, but with sadness.

"Margolo, one of Minton's best friends, was next."

Margolo's ghost showed up. His demeanor was grim, but he nodded, acknowledging I was on the right track.

I continued, a fine sweat breaking out on my upper lip and forehead.

"Ironically, I think Margolo understood Minton best and was trying to intervene with Commander Shore to take Minton's complaints more seriously."

Even as I said the name, Mitchell Shore appeared. I could tell I had summoned him because, unlike the others, he really didn't want to be here. His expression was pinched. No doubt he didn't appreciate the implied criticism. I could feel the air grow heavy and cold.

I took a ragged breath.

"Getting back to your question, yes, I did understand the responsibility I had...that I have."

Margolo signalled his crew to back away. The hatch flew open. Fresh air ruffled my papers and dried the cold sweat on my face. I could breathe again.

Startled, Mary Lou looked around. Her father broke formation and stepped forward to stroke her hair. She shivered.

I forced myself to be matter-of-fact amidst the rampant spookiness. "Mary Lou, you and I have different ways of approaching the truth, but we're on the same quest. Now I think you should go."

Under my breath I added.

"All of you."

After a break with tea and chocolate, I was able to complete the interviews. I was careful to refer to the crew generically and didn't invoke any more spirits. The *Émil Gagnan* divers were succinct. Alex Mercuros was charming. Welland and Cross were modest, but excited.

I thought of interviewing the members of AFFA that weren't diving and decided to defer. I thought Ben's presence might summon Dawes, and I wasn't up to that. Dora would just take too long. Tim would ask why I did this without him. If I didn't interview them, I couldn't very well interview Lil, Tracy, and Jamal, so Gravell and I packed up.

"You okay?" Gravell asked.

"I'm not sure." My hands were shaking as I tried to manipulate the camera. "Here, you better do this. I'm trying to put Humpty Dumpty together again and not having much luck."

"Why did you take it apart?"

I shook my head and concentrated on warming my fingers. They felt like ice. Another weird side effect of ghosts.

"I'm not scared," I said aloud, as much for my own benefit as Gravell's.

"I never said you were. Although I wouldn't blame you."

He took my hands put them under his arms. I closed the distance between us so that I could lean my cheek on his chest. He picked up my jacket, draped it across my shoulders and held it in place.

"You need more tea and chocolate," he stated.

I smiled and he must have felt it because his arms tightened a little, then he let me go. At least, that's how I interpreted what happened.

My hands were warm. The chills had passed. The anxious feeling that remained wasn't part of the ghostly aftershock. It was a nagging feeling that finally allowing itself to be identified.

"I need to get the journal back. I'll need it with me tomorrow." I gave Gravell an apologetic grimace. "I think you'll have to get it for me. I'm not sure Mary Lou will be inclined to acquiesce to my request."

Chapter Thirty-Five ~ *Mending Fences*

It was rather crowded in the wardroom that evening. It didn't make sense for people to go back and forth between ships unnecessarily, so Welland and Cross were staying on board. So was Captain Campbell. He had asked permission oversee the operation from the *Émil Gagnan*. In fact, it was probably a politely worded order.

"I think I'll eat later," said Gravell, stopping at the entrance.

I was ready to back out too.

"You go ahead, Madame Kirby. I'll take care of a little business while you dine."

People came and went. Stopping to eat. Stopping by to give a word of encouragement. In turn, I ate dinner with Captain Campbell and Tim, then dessert with Alex and Franchot. Welland, Cross, and the other divers joined us at various intervals so that I had constant company. Yet, I felt left out.

At the other large table, Dora held court with rest of the research team. One look from Dora told me that she knew about the journal and probably the interview with Mary Lou. Jamal and Tracy were obviously taking Mary Lou's side. Both gave me the evil eye. Reuben didn't go that far, but he was cool. Only Mike and Lil were friendly. Each made a point of coming to congratulate me on qualifying for the dive. Neither stayed to chat.

When Dora left the wardroom, I excused myself from the table. If Mary Lou was angry at me, so be it. If every member of AFFA decided to give me the cold shoulder, I could deal. I wasn't going to let a long-time friendship get flushed over one lousy journal. I had to make peace with Dora.

Dora was at her desk, working at her laptop. She shot me a blank look when I came in, but said nothing. I decided to cut to the chase.

"So, are you pissed off at me too?"

Once upon a time I would have hated to confront anyone like that. Working with Dora had taught me it was the best approach with her.

"Mary Lou is pissed off. I'm disappointed. Jamal thinks you've been planted by CSIS and you're working with Gravell."

"I'm not working with Gravell. He's working with me."

That got her attention. Now she was more curious than angry. I pulled up a stool and closed the physical gap between us.

"It started while I was trapped. You know I rescued the document satchel, well I also copied the digital memory from the cameras, ours and Parker's."

She whistled.

"I knew Tinsdale would have the memory chips confiscated so I copied them to my smartphone. I am so glad I beefed up my memory before I left home. Anyway, I had lots of time, so I viewed the video on the camera and imagined what the place was like when the crew was still alive. I got the notion that the journal might have some answers. When I took the memory chips out, I used the blue screen to read the journal."

It wasn't a great explanation. I hoped Dora would be more excited about having the video than angry about me reading the journal before it was processed.

"And you have the video here?" she asked.

Bingo, I thought and suppressed a sigh of relief.

"I'll upload a copy to your laptop."

"Excellent," she said, changing seats with me. "While you do that, you can explain that comment about Gravell and tell me why you held on to the journal for so long."

I didn't bother suppressing the next sigh. How far was I willing to go? Did I mention ghosts? Dora would think I was nuts.

"It's complicated," I started.

"No it isn't. Don't lie to me Jen, I'll know and be offended."

Maybe it wasn't complicated. I took a deep breath and told the truth, uncluttered by inconvenient facts.

"Someone is trying to kill me, Dora. Gravell is trying to protect me. We're both trying to find out what happened thirty years ago and why it matters so much to someone now. The journal is a key piece of evidence."

I clicked and dragged the file with the journal scans.

"I couldn't let the journal be confiscated by the Americans so I held onto it. Gravell dusted, swabbed, and scanned it. If he hasn't already, I'll ask him to turn over any forensic results."

She nodded.

My smartphone made a tingle-ling sound, telling me it was finished its assigned task. I packed it away and let Dora sit at her laptop again.

"Still disappointed in me?"

She shrugged. "I'll forgive all if you go fetch coffee."

She handed me her mug and shooed me out the door.

Outside, I took a deep breath and smiled. I did it. I survived the wrath of Dora. Now I had to call Gravell or be subjected to his wrath.

"Bonjour, Madame Kirby."

"Bonjour, Chief Gravell. Did you get the message that I went to my cabin to confront Dora."

"I was told you went to your cabin. Are you there now?"

"No. I'm fetching coffee for the boss."

He sighed. "Didn't you mention someone is trying to kill you?"

"She knows. I know too, which is why I'm calling."

"I'll bring a carafe of coffee."

"Can't we just meet in the wardroom?"

He heaved another sigh. "Yes, but take the inside route."

My first thought was the man's paranoid. My second thought told me to walk briskly until I was in the wardroom where there would be safety in numbers. A third, cowardly thought wanted to call Gravell back and tell him I'd let him fetch coffee. I'd go hide in bed with the covers over my head.

"Minton?"

Nothing.

"I could use a little help here."

I felt a chill creep up my spine. When it reached the nape of my neck I had the sensation of whiskers tickling my skin.

"Margolo? If you're trying to freak me out, you're doing a good job. If you're trying to flirt, you need to warm up. I'm going to catch a chill."

I backed against the bulkhead and Margolo appeared before me. He spread his hands out in a mute query.

"Do you want me to find the truth about what happened to you?"

His expression was impatient. His nod was curt.

"Well somebody doesn't. So I need you to watch my back. Okay?"

His expression shifted to concern and he nodded again. A pleasantly cool hand was placed on my shoulder. With his other hand he pointed two fingers at his eyes then at me. He would be watching me.

Other than a card game being played by a few of the off-duty crew, the wardroom quiet. Gravell waited by the coffee brewing machine. He greeted me with nothing but a stern expression.

"I know I'm being a bug, but I just made peace with Dora, and I didn't want to blow it by refusing to get coffee."

"At this point she could hardly fire you."

"Maybe not, but we're friends, and I value her respect."

His expression softened. "I understand, and I don't mind being on call. What worries me is how long it took you to get here."

I suppressed a grin…or maybe a grimace.

"I recruited a backup bodyguard," I said, turning my back on Gravell and filling Dora's cup with coffee at the machine.

He came up behind me, close enough for me to feel his radiant warmth. Head bent, his breath tickled the back of my neck, just as Margolo's whiskers had a little while ago.

"A ghostly backup?"

I nodded. "Lieutenant Margolo volunteered. Don't worry, I can handle them one at a time."

"And if something happened to you?"

"He'd warn me first."

"And if you couldn't get away?"

That was an excellent question. I looked to Margolo for an answer. He shrugged, then a wicked grin spread across his face. He walked through Gravell, who gave an involuntary shiver.

"Did you feel that?" I asked.

"What was it?"

I smiled, "My ghostly backup warning you."

"Is he still here?"

Margolo gave me a salute and faded away.

"Not anymore. I guess it's your watch again."

After preparing Dora's coffee, I made tea and invited Gravell to join me.

"I'd like to get some fresh air, but if you're tired, I can just go back to my cabin."

"If we're going out, you better pick up a jacket or sweater. It's chilly tonight."

Dora was immersed in the journal scans. She accepted her coffee, and my announcement that I was going on deck, with a grunt. I changed into a warmer sweater and grabbed my *Nottawasaga* windbreaker. At least, I hoped it was mine now.

Gravell was waiting in the gangway. He held the jacket for me.

I murmured thanks.

"Am I supposed to give this back?"

"I would consider it a gift," he said, smiling.

"I'm glad. I've grown rather fond of it."

"Because the captain gave it to you?"

"That too. It's comfortable and it repels the water better than my windbreaker." I grinned. "And my son is going to be so impressed when he sees it."

"Speaking of which."

He handed me an envelope.

"I'm sorry you didn't get it sooner. The captain arranged to have the mail for the *Émil Gagnan* picked up with the ship's bag. Your letter got misdirected. I've had it since this morning, but I didn't want you to be distracted during your test."

"Uh huh?"

"And then I forgot about it. I've been carrying it around with me all day."

I looked at him. He was blushing. He really did forget. He wasn't perfect after all.

I opened the letter and skimmed it. This must be the letter he told me to disregard. It involved a girl who was following him around and the girl's older brother, who was also a cadet. I decided to save the letter for later. I had a feeling it was going to be too entertaining to rush.

"Everything okay?"

"Oh yeah. I'll call Seamus tonight, after I read the letter, but he's already told me that it's old news."

"He'll be home now, right?"

"He'll be with his father," I corrected. Home was with me.

I led the way to the foredeck. Gravell followed, holding our mugs in one hand.

"Have I offended you, Madame Kirby?"

I stopped suddenly and he bumped into my back.

"No. Why do you ask?"

"You seem a little stiff. Is it because you and your ex-husband don't get along?"

"We get along fine."

As soon as I reached the foredeck I turned and accepted my mug of tea.

"Missing your son?" he asked.

"Yes. This is the longest stretch we've been apart since he was born."

"You're close."

"Very."

"Is that why you haven't remarried?"

I gave that some thought.

"I don't know. Maybe. Dating, when you're a single mother, isn't easy."

"Is dating ever easy?"

I looked at him. I couldn't imagine him having trouble getting a date yet, he was serious.

"Maybe not," I said, turning back to the sea, which was a lot less complicated. "When I'm at home, I'm usually too busy to date. So I tend to take advantage of the times I'm away on business trips to…"

I felt myself blushing and decided to leave the sentence unfinished.

"I understand, Madame Kirby."

Then, after a minute or so he added, "No wonder you're so frustrated."

I laughed. "Oh yeah."

He turned to half sit on the rail then drew to attention.

Captain on the deck, I thought. I looked over my shoulder and my suspicion was confirmed.

"Good evening, Ms. Kirby, Chief Gravell."

"Good evening, Captain," we said in unison.

"Nice night," I added.

"More tea, Madame Kirby?" Gravell asked, holding his hand out for my mug.

I had hardly started my tea, but I said yes and let him take it away. It was a gracious way to depart and it made clear he would return. *Very well played*, I thought. The captain seemed less impressed by the manoeuvre.

"How are you, Jenny?" he asked, once we were alone.

"Okay. I'm a bit nervous about tomorrow, but mostly I'm fine."

"Good," he said nodding. "I've been discussing the dive with Captain Franchot. I want both Welland and Cross with you. He's agreed. Tinsdale wants his own team on board. We've whittled him down to two Marines and an engineer."

"That's seven."

"Franchot, Mercuros, and two of their divers will also board the station with you, along with Mr.and Mrs. Naire, and Mr. Neville."

"That's thirteen people in total."

"Yes. Mr. Hassan tried to talk us into leaving someone behind. He suggested Mr. Neville."

I gave a huff of laughter. Poor Tim was getting on everyone's nerves. Not just mine.

"I bet Captain Tinsdale seconded that motion. One less civilian, and a media type to boot."

I expected a chuckle, or at least a smile.

Nothing.

"I will guide operations from here. Tinsdale will be monitoring from the *Scranton*. I still wish you weren't part of it. I'd rather keep you safe."

"I'd rather be safe, but I won't be until this is taken care of."

He leaned on the rail and looked out at the lights on his ship. I stood beside him. One of us inched closer. Maybe both of us did. Our shoulders touched. He took my hand.

"When this is all over…" he started and stopped.

"When this is all over I'll be going home."

Chapter Thirty-Six ~ *Into the Depths*

The day didn't start well.

Dora kept me up late. She was too engrossed in her work to talk, but I'd got used to complete dark when I went to sleep and she wasn't giving it to me. Not that I asked, mind you. I was too happy she had forgiven me to push my luck.

In fairness, it wasn't all Dora's fault. After talking to Seamus for half an hour, I felt desperately homesick and sorry for myself. I found it hard to settle and impossible to concentrate on reading, an activity that usually relaxed me.

Then there was Margolo. As soon as Gravell left, he appeared. He watched me get ready for bed, but accepted my veto of his following me into the head. Then he stood at the foot of my bed, looking over Dora's shoulder. After a few minutes, Dora went to put a sweater on, otherwise she was oblivious to his presence. I pulled the covers up over my head and tried to will myself to sleep. Eventually it worked.

On the upside, for the first time in ages, I didn't dream.

Although I had been relieved of kitchen duty for the day, I woke up at my usual time. Dora was fast asleep, but she left me a note.

"Read Kant's story."

Grumpy and in desperate need of caffeine, I considered my options. I could call Gravell. He wouldn't appreciate it if he was asleep. I could call Alex. He might be sleeping too. I decided to make use of Margolo instead. He wasn't visible, but I figured he hadn't gone far.

Too right. I had a quick shower and found him waiting for me when

I reached for a towel.

"Bored?"

He shrugged.

What the hell, I thought. I continued as if he wasn't there. He beat a hasty retreat.

"So you are a gentleman as well an officer. Good for you, Margolo."

As it turned out, I didn't need Margolo's escort. Someone had posted a guard outside my door. It was one of Franchot's crew, a fellow I hadn't traded more than a couple of words with so far.

"Bonjour, Madame."

"Bonjour."

He followed me to the wardroom then left me. I poked my head in to ask Cookie if he wanted me. Mary Lou was taking my place, so I didn't press when the offer was politely rebuffed. I put the juice out on the buffet, helped myself to a glass and made a cup of coffee. Then I pulled out my tablet and called up Kant's story. He had no letters, no diary. Instead, he had been writing a story in a series of thin notebooks. The handwriting was difficult to read and the spelling creative, but mostly I hadn't spent any time on them because they were clearly fiction. Obviously Dora saw something I didn't.

These are the adventures of Kirkland Bane, a newly minted officer of the Earth's Space Patrol.

I skimmed over Kirkland Bane's origins. He was bridge officer on the United Earth Space Ship Intrepid. His best friend was an alien named Pox. His commander was the heroic Captain James. His nemesis the stern first officer, known as Number One. The country-doctor-like Bones McGee was a confidant to all and Chief Engineer Frenchie LeBeau provided comic relief. Golanger was there as the ingénue Cadet Penn. Boreman was the athletic bully, Chief Gabore. It took a while to discover that Naire was an idiosyncratic robot named MO. The writing was a cross between bad fan fiction and a half-decent send-up of his fellow crew members.

It started to get interesting in his second notebook in a chapter he called Feet of Clay.

Bane didn't think he had any innocence to lose until he lost the last scrap at Terra Nueva. That's when he learned that even superstars make mistakes and sometimes the real hero is the guy you never thought much of.

"I'm in command, damn it. You'll do as I say," Captain James growled menacingly.

"You're putting ze crew in unnecessary danger," Le Beau argued. "It is crazy! Fou fou! There has to be a better way, Capitaine."

"Against my ardent desires, I am forced to agree," said the coldly logical Number One.

"Earth command doesn't tell you everything, gentlemen," the captain sputtered.

Bane listened to the argument with growing concern. He was beginning to think Pox might be right. Maybe the Remans had brainwashed James when they held him in captivity last month.

Reading between the lines, Shore was acting out of character. Margolo and Minton were questioning his behaviour. Also, despite his ravings in his journal, Minton's outward behaviour wasn't that remarkable at least, not to Kant.

"You should have called me, Madame Kirby."

"Good morning, Chief," I said, setting aside Kant's prose for the time being.

"I had an escort to the wardroom. I assumed you knew."

He made himself a cup of coffee and sat beside me.

"Someone broke into ops. They smashed the video camera and took the memory chip."

He looked at me.

"And you don't seem upset."

"Compared to almost falling overboard and passing out on deck, this doesn't rate getting too upset. Besides, I copied the chip onto my smartphone. Nothing has been lost."

With a surprised look he asked,

"How much memory does that thing hold?"

"Lots. What troubles me is why someone would do it. There wasn't anything earth-shattering said in the interviews. The loss of one camera won't stop the dive. The documentary crew is due this morning. It just doesn't make a hell of a lot of sense."

"Unless someone is trying to scare you. That's why I asked Franchot to assign a guard to your cabin."

I nodded. We sipped our coffee. The first hit of caffeine produced a shiver of distaste from Gravell. I grinned and nudged him with my knee.

"You must be exhausted to drink coffee instead of tea."

"I didn't sleep well."

"Then go back to bed. I'll be fine. I'll stay here. Or maybe I'll go back to bed for a couple of hours too. I didn't sleep that well either."

"Breakfast first, then maybe we'll both sleep."

That sounded enough like an invitation to cheer me up, even though I didn't expect anything to come of it.

We should have escaped while the going was good. Before I finished my granola and yogurt, Franchot joined us. He wanted to discuss the vandalism. Then Mercuros appeared. He wanted to go over instructions for the dive. When Captain Campbell joined us, Gravell reminded me that I needed to rest.

"Dora kept me awake," I explained.

"Dr. Leland is having breakfast now, so perhaps this is a good opportunity to get another couple of hours sleep," said Gravell.

"Good idea," I said, gathering up my things.

Campbell started to get up. Franchot also rose.

"Sean, we have some business to discuss with Tinsdale. This might be a good time."

I left before Campbell could reply. Gravell was right behind me. Neither of us said anything until we reached my cabin and the door was locked behind us.

I laughed.

"I don't think I can have an affair with Franchot. He's too loyal to you."

Gravell smiled, but his eyes were solemn. "You need to rest, and I need to leave."

"Some bodyguard you are," I said, but I saw his point. Especially since Franchot ran interference for him, Gravell had to been seen elsewhere.

"Go. I'll lock up behind you. Get some rest. I won't leave the cabin without calling you first. I promise."

"Thank you, Madame Kirby."

Once I was alone, I considered going back to Kant's files. I dismissed the notion. I really did need to rest. The trouble was, this was easier said than done. Just lying down didn't work, so I stripped down to my underwear and a t-shirt. That was better, but my mind was still buzzing with dive instructions, Kant's prose, Minton's journal, Gravell's knee pressed up against mine.

My phone warbled.

"Hello?"

"Bonjour, Madame Kirby."

"Bonjour, Chief Gravell."

Funny how that simple exchange of greetings had a calming effect on me.

"Are you in bed yet?" he asked

"Yes. You?"

"Yes. I thought you might have some trouble getting to sleep."

"You thought right. There's too much to think about."

"Since my voice seems to have a soporific effect on you, I thought I could tell you more about my Grandma Verity. She was a war bride, you know?"

"Really? I'd like to hear about that."

And I did. But not for long.

A cool hand on my shoulder woke me first. Then I heard the warble of my phone. I looked up to see Margolo and reached blindly for the phone. His hand guided me.

"You're warming up," I said, flipping the phone open. He winked in response.

"Bonjour, Madame Kirby."

"Bonjour, Chief Gravell."

Margolo backed away from me, fading from view.

"The documentary crew has arrived and the director is hoping to talk to you before the dive."

"How long have I been sleeping?"

"Four hours. I made sure no one disturbed you until absolutely necessary. Dr. Leland is not happy with me."

"Oh dear."

At least she wasn't mad at me.

"I'll get dressed. I'll be ready in…" I considered what I had to do. "Fifteen minutes."

"I will let all interested parties know and meet you in the gangway. Wait for me."

"Merci, Chief Gravell."

"Bienvenue, Madame Kirby.

I was starting to appreciate how political leaders must feel, constantly being followed around by armed guards. Gravell didn't wear the ubiquitous black suit, or the Ray Ban shades, but now he wore an earwig and an expression of stolid immovability. He was standing at parade rest when I left my cabin.

"What? You look like someone over-starched your shorts."

The mere hint of a smile flickered on his face and was extinguished.

"The captains are waiting for you as well as the director."

"Am I in trouble?"

"No, Madame Kirby."

"Are you in trouble?"

No answer.

I folded my arms.

"Are you in trouble, Chief Gravell?"

"People are waiting for you."

"They can wait."

He shifted from parade rest to standing easy. I'd sat through enough cadet parades to know the difference.

"I am not in trouble, but I have been reminded of the extent of my duties."

My eyes narrowed in anger. "Captain Campbell reminded you?"

"He is my superior officer."

"I thought Franchot was officially your commander."

His next words sounded like they were pushed through clenched teeth. "Not anymore. He thinks I should have assigned a same-gender guard for you. He mentioned Petty Officer Briseau in particular."

I thumped the bulkhead with my fist. "Sophie's a nurse, not a bodyguard."

"The captain has a legitimate concern, given his knowledge of the case. My apparently single-minded attention to you doesn't follow protocol."

I nodded. I hadn't told Campbell about the ghosts and I wasn't sure I ever would.

"We should go, Madame Kirby."

Again, I nodded. I squared my shoulders and set off, pretending that I was the leader of a small, but important, nation state. Gravell followed two steps behind.

As summits go, this one was pretty tame. I took Dora aside and gave her copies of all video material, discretely suggesting that she not go over the material until she could do so in private.

Via video phone, Tinsdale made it clear that the United States Navy had not relinquished its claim to the station and let me gather what I would from that statement. Captain Campbell made a similar politically motivated declaration.

Franchot reminded everyone that it was his crew and AFFA that made this operation possible.

Zoe, back behind the camera, recorded all this then went off to confer with the *Émil Gagnan* divers who would be acting as videographers on the station. Once the cameras were off, everyone relaxed.

"Excited?" Alex asked me.

"Nervous. Anxious. Maybe a little scared about the dive. Maybe a lot scared about going back on the station. And yeah, excited."

"You won't be alone this time," said Franchot.

"I wasn't completely alone last time. I had Captain Campbell and Chief Gravell."

I looked from one man to the other. It was time to make my official statement.

"I don't think I can ever fully express how grateful I was for your company then, nor how much I appreciate your friendship since. I also want to thank you for facilitating my inclusion on this expedition."

A short, embarrassed silence followed. Then Franchot outlined the goals of the expedition.

"We're splitting into three teams to cover as much ground in as short a time as possible. Each team will have one person in charge of forensic collection, one videographer, and two military observers. One American. One Canadian.

I did the math and said, "That leaves one extra."

"That would be you and Petty Officer Welland," said Captain Campbell.

The math still didn't work, but that wasn't my problem.

"Chief Gravell says that you will be able to point out places for the teams to concentrate their search, based on your research of the personal effects of the crew. So, instead of being tied to one team, you'll help each in turn."

"Yes, sir."

"That's 'aye, sir,'" said Alex, giving me a wink.

"Aye-aye, Captain."

"Actually," Campbell said, giving Franchot a respectful nod, "there's only one captain on a ship and here that's Captain Franchot."

I almost apologised for my unintended slight when I realized they were all laughing at me, even Gravell.

After a light lunch, we geared up. Franchot had two of his divers go over all the equipment and a guard was posted. Naire was also on guard. He drew my attention to an item added to my radio.

"A bug?" I whispered.

He shrugged. Technology had come a long way in thirty years, he probably wasn't sure.

"Do you know who?"

He nodded. He drifted over to hover behind Tim.

I stepped over to Gravell who was hugging a wall to stay out of the way. He confirmed my suspicion. He gave my radio a once over and, using his broad back to mask his activities, switched out my batteries. Batteries and bug went into a plastic baggy he just happened to have with him.

Franchot, now suited-up, joined us.

"Is there a problem?"

"A little extra technology found its way into Madame Kirby's communication set." Gravell held up something that looked like a hearing aid battery. "I'm tempted to leave it. Since we share all information gathered, it seems a bit redundant."

"Spooks. Beaubien! *Vas y. Aide Jen, si t'plait.*"

Beaubien was one of the *Émil Gagnan* divers. He would be acting as videographer for one of the teams. Evidently he'd been added when they decided to go with three teams. I knew Beaubien from the euchre games. Nice guy. Terrible player.

I wasn't quite the last one ready, but I was the last on deck. Gravell blocked my exit and indicated that Welland and Beaubien should go ahead.

"Be careful," he said, tucking Minton's journal into a waterproof pouch on my utility belt.

I nodded.

"About what you say as well as what you do," he added, putting my radio-phone into another pouch.

I gave him an eye roll. Then, because it seemed as though he were reluctant to let me go, I patted him on the chest.

"You should have thought ahead and taken up diving. Just be handy when I get back, okay?

He nodded and stood aside.

The *Émil Gagnan* was close enough to the station to dive straight from her deck. A RHIB from the *Nottawasaga* picked up the divers from the *Scranton*. There were a lot of familiar faces. The Marines, Madison and Dippel, were back. USN engineer, Sinclair, was new to me. Sophie Briseau there as a medic and, with a couple of rescue divers, would stay on the RHIB in case of an emergency. Sophie waved when she saw me. I gave her a thumbs up.

We arranged ourselves in our teams.

Franchot was leading the team that would investigate engineering. He would be in charge of collecting evidence. Hassan had been designated the RCN observer and was doubling as videographer because Tim wanted to follow me with a camera. Lucky me. Sinclair was the official observer for the USN, but his real job was investigating the cause of the explosion.

Mary Lou was examining Command and Control, which, on the station, served as control, communications, and briefing room. Time permitting she intended to return to the galley. Jorge, one of the *Émil Gagnan* divers, was her videographer. Petty Officer Cross had been pulled from watching me to being the RCN observer and Gunnery Sergeant Dippel completed the team.

Mike led the third team by virtue of his position on the research team, and was assigned weapons control and the sonar room. He had Beaubien as videographer; Madison and Alex Mercuros as observers. It turned out that Alex, like Gravell, was in the Naval Reserve as well as Merchant Marine.

Me and my shadows, Welland and Tim, were attached to Mike's team to start. We went in first since we had the furthest to go once on the station.

We came up under the station to enter via a pool created by a flooded lower section of the propulsion compartment. The emergency lights were working again. They cast an eerie red glow over everything. All of us had shoulder mounted cameras with built-in lights. They cut through gloom in slices. In comparison, the hand-held lights supplied by the film company shone with spotlight brilliance, but only on demand.

"Smile," said Beaubien, as I pulled off my mask and shut off my air.

As water had been pumped out, air had been pumped in, restoring the station's attitude and buoyancy. We would keep our tanks with us, but all going well, we shouldn't need them until we left the station. The quality of the air was a bit suspect, in my opinion, but it tested fine, so it might have been my imagination that I was slowly suffocating.

"Deep breaths," Welland said, as she helped me remove my flippers. "You'll be okay."

"You can always go back," said Tim. "It's not too late."

"She'll be fine," said Alex.

Mike led the way forward. As we headed out, the first members of the next team appeared.

It was weird being back. We were retracing the route I had taken when Welland and Cross led me out. I was glad to get past the crew areas and into new territory. Just outside weapons control, I called a halt.

"This is your show, Mike, but can I go in first?"

He frowned. I gave him a wry grin.

"This is the only place I'll be able to do this. I won't touch anything, I just want to get a sense of the place. It'll help me recall points from the journal."

"What journal?" asked Tim.

"Jen rescued a journal from the station when she was trapped," said Mike, which I thought was very nice of him. His wife would have put it quite differently.

"Whose is it? What's in it?"

"Now is not the time, Mr. Neville," said Alex, sounding more formal than I'd ever heard him. It immediately made me shift from thinking of him as Alex to thinking of him as Mercuros.

Tim backed off and Mike almost pushed me into the room.

"Go ahead, Jen. Do your thing."

I went to the centre of the room and looked around me. Banks of electronic equipment lay dormant. Access to the torpedo room was marked with warning signs on the hatch. I closed my eyes, silently summoned the ghost crew, and opened them again.

The room is bright. Lights blink or glow on the consoles. Video screens display schematic and text information in a green monotone. Naire is scrolling down information on a terminal, his face screwed into an expression of vague worry.

He pulls out a thick manual and flips through pages. Without having a clue what he is doing, I get the impression something isn't right.

I follow him into the torpedo room. He pulls out a screwdriver and opens a plate, exposing a tangle of wires. Scanning them, he quickly tugs at one. He reaches in and pulls a hand-held radio out from behind the bulkhead. It has two wires connected to it.

Smiling grimly, Naire disconnects the radio and follows the second wire behind the bulkhead with a flashlight.

Further along, there is a gauge to indicate the status of one of the torpedo tubes. Naire unscrews it and in behind the mechanism is a box, wrapped in electrician's tape, with the wire going into it.

Naire rocks back and forth on his heels and purses his mouth as if whistling. His head cocked to one side, he listens. He pushes the box back. He jams the disconnected radio in with it. The gauge mechanism is replaced. No time to tighten the screws. No time for anything.

He is prepared to lie. He is prepared to fight. He is not prepared for a knife to come out of nowhere and pierce his throat.

I staggered. Welland and Mercuros caught me by an elbow each. We were in the torpedo room. Naire's ghost hovered before the scene of the murder.

"I think it's behind that gauge. Or it might be one of the others. Try there first and look for blood evidence wherever you find the bomb. Someone found the bomb and disarmed it. They might have died here."

I hoped that sounded plausible and backed away from the activity.

They found the radio and the bomb. Mike bagged and tagged the items and started dusting the area for prints. I stood and tried to get my heart to settle down. It didn't help that a ghostly montage was playing over the activity across the room.

Minton was dragging bodies in on a makeshift sled and laying them out in a neat row. When they were all present, he stuffed them into the torpedo tubes. Then he swabbed the deck, once...twice...three times until he was satisfied. I saw fragments of a job that must have taken him hours to complete. Cleaned up and neatly dressed, he bowed his head in prayer. Finally, he fired the tubes, then collapsed on the deck, face in hands.

"You should check inside the torpedo tubes if possible," I said, feeling a bit like collapsing myself. "That would be the logical way of disposing of the bodies, right?"

Tim was incredulous. "That's in the journal? All of that is in the journal?" He looked as though he wanted to shake me.

Mercuros and Welland saw it too. Welland took up a defensive posture and Mercuros lay a hand on Tim's shoulder.

"Not just the journal," I assured him, trying to keep things friendly. "It's a combination of sources."

I shifted my gaze to Mercuros.

"I'm going to check out the other teams now."

I hope he understood that it would be best to keep Tim from following me.

Mary Lou was in Command and Control.

Mary Lou still wasn't very happy with me.

After dealing with Tim, I knew I wasn't up to dealing with her. On the other hand, I wasn't sure I was up to the galley either.

"Are you okay?" Welland's professional tone was modulated with concern.

She covered the microphone on her head set and waited for me to do the same.

"Chief Gravell warned me that you might feel faint. He didn't say why, but it seems to me you have some psychic ability to read the history of places."

"It's complicated…"

I was spared the necessity of trying to explain by Captain Campbell who asked if there was something wrong, because he had lost our audio signal.

Welland tapped her mike noisily.

"Can you hear that, sir?"

I had to bite my lip not to laugh.

"Yes, Welland. Please don't do that again."

Welland made a face at me and mouthed 'oops.'

"We're going to the galley," I announced, to Welland and whoever else was listening. No one objected.

I hesitated at the entry. Most of the water had been pumped out of the room, but there was still a few centimetres covering the floor. That and the red glow reminded me too much of the night I was trapped.

"You okay?" Welland asked.

I nodded and forced myself to walk down the stairs.

In my dreams and in the visions I had experienced in the galley, I saw the crew sitting around the table. They played poker. They apparently talked about Minton behind his back. I saw his point of view and with it his anger and isolation. Then I saw blood. I suspected now that Minton blanked out the rest.

I needed to see another point of view.

Margolo? I thought the question and closed my eyes. I opened them as a cool finger flicked my cheek.

Naire is alone at the table, a half-eaten sandwich and empty mug in front of him. Margolo comes to the table with a carafe and second mug. He pours coffee and signals Naire to continue what he was saying. Naire talks. He pulls out a folded sheet of paper which Margolo examines. With a shrug, he hands it back. He says little, but his expression in thoughtful. Naire is watching him. Margolo nods, and I see him mouth the words, 'Check it out.'

Naire must have shared his suspicions with Margolo. This must have happened just before Naire was killed. What happened after? I cast my mind back to the vision I had when I was trapped.

Four men sit around the table. Lou Boreman is on a rant, punctuating his statements with table thumps. Kant is fiddling with a cigarette pack, Dawes is listening calmly, but his face is troubled. Golanger keeps looking around and gesturing Boreman to keep it down.

Commander Shore enters the room, points to Boreman and Golanger, says a few words and they leave. Kant gets up and clears the table of the dishes. Dawes takes the commander aside. Shore nods towards the storage area. Dawes sees Minton and shakes his head.

Shore leaves and Dawes heads towards the storage area, but Minton is gone.

"Ms. Kirby?"

I blinked a couple of times and focussed on Welland.

"Do we need to be this formal, or can you call me Jen?"

She smiled. "We don't need to be that formal. I'm Barb. Can you tell me what you're seeing, Jen?"

I shook my head. "I'm not sure. According to his journal, Minton was convinced that the other crew members were conspiring against him. He spied on them, read their personal letters and notebooks, exaggerated their flaws in his own journal. I'm beginning to think it wasn't all in his head. Something odd was going on. I'm just not sure what."

"Did he plant the bombs?"

"He doesn't say."

"Who else would?"

I thought about Kant's story. I wished I had read more of it. I shrugged by way of an answer and closed my eyes again. This time I thought about Kant and his alter-ego, Kirkland Banes.

Kant was washing dishes, but his mind kept wandering. Through his eyes, the backsplash was a panel of futuristic displays, with a future vision consistent with old Star Trek episodes or the original Battlestar Galactica. He turned to Dawes, reading at the table, and saw Bone's McGee bent over a tricorder. When Dawes spoke, Kant snapped back to reality.

He brought over a couple of mugs of coffee and sat down. Dawes was reading one of Kant's notebooks. He was smiling and his comments seemed encouraging to Kant. Then Minton entered, white as a sheet. Dawes helped him sit down and signalled Kant to fetch more coffee.

Kant went to the percolator and scooped a couple of spoonfuls of sugar into a cup, then filled it up. When he returned to the table, Dawes was talking, an earnest expression on his face. Kant pushed the cup towards Minton who immediately wrapped shaking, blood-stained hands around it.

Kant recoiled. Dawes stared, mouth dropping open.

Boreman and Golanger entered, armed and weapons drawn on Minton. Boreman seemed to be doing the 'stop, you're under arrest' line. He kept talking as he approached Minton.

Minton stood, apparently at Boreman's command. He held onto his mug. He was still pale, but he seemed calm. He started talking.

Golanger paled. Boreman's mouth formed the words 'Shut up,' over and over again.

Kant watched the scene and tried to back away from it without anyone noticing. He looked from Boreman to Minton to Dawes, then back to Minton as the lieutenant threw his hot coffee at Golanger and grabbed his weapon. Boreman shot and missed Minton, but Kant fell back.

Kirkland Bane felt the blaster fire rip through him. The cool Number One was berserk. The behemoth Gabore fell like a ton of bricks. Poor young Penn died bravely. Bones McGee was caught in the crossfire. Then when the smoke cleared, Captain James walked through the door. Fade to black.

"Jen. Jen!"

"Ms. Kirby...Ms. Kirby? Jenny?"

"I don't know what happened, Captain," I heard Welland say. "She just blacked out. I tried to catch her but...Wait. She's opening her eyes."

I was? I blinked. I suppose I was.

Over my headset I heard Captain Campbell's voice, "What happened Jenny? Talk to us."

"I had a vision." I shook my head. I hadn't meant to say that. "Is

Dora there?" I asked.

There was a pause, and I heard Dora's voice. "What is it, Jen? What happened?"

"What was the last thing Kant wrote in his story?"

"I don't have it here," she said, "but it was something about mind controlling aliens and not knowing who to trust anymore."

I nodded. Close enough.

"I've been looking at things in light of the material I've been reading, and I sort of envisioned a scene from Kant's story. You were trying to tell me that his story might contain his observations of what was really happening, right?"

"Right," she said, but her tone was doubtful.

I looked around from where I sat on the deck. Then I felt around on the deck and found a dent behind me. A chill went through me. That dent wasn't from when Kant was first shot. That was the result of a bullet shot through him when he was on the deck.

"I need something to mark this spot," I told Welland. She handed me a patch, and I pressed it onto the deck beside the dent. "I'm pretty sure that was caused by a bullet. Mary Lou should examine the surfaces for other evidence of a gun fight."

"I'm sending her," said Dora. "Maybe you should come in now, Jen. Passing out isn't good. Captain Campbell agrees."

"Got to visit engineering first. Then I'll be happy to get out of here."

Franchot had Sinclair and Hassan working, scanning surfaces with their flashlights, looking for anything that was out of place or suspiciously discoloured. Jorge was methodically recording everything. Their tanks were off but kept close. Engineering, which included the nuclear power plant, was a large area with many sections that weren't easy to access with a tank on your back. It was going to take them a long time to cover everything.

Franchot came over as soon as he saw me. Evidently, he was in the loop regarding my fainting episode in the galley. He gave me the once over, decided I was okay and asked what I wanted to look at.

"I'm not sure yet."

I gazed about, compared what I saw to the diagrams I had studied and waited. Nothing.

I tried another area. Closed my eyes. Opened them. Nothing.

"Margolo?" I whispered, covering my mike. "Help me out here."

I felt a slight pressure at my back and let it guide me towards the ladder that led to the lower area of engineering. The part that was underwater.

"Shit."

"Jen?" Welland sounded nervous.

"What I need to see is down there," I told her. I took a deep breath and retrieved my flippers.

"Uh, Jen?" Franchot noticed what I was up to.

"I need to check something out. I'm not leaving the station, I just need to go down there."

"Down where, Ms. Kirby?" asked Captain Campbell via my headset.

Franchot answered the question.

"I would rather you didn't go down there until you're ready to leave."

I looked at Franchot.

He nodded. "I'll accompany Jen as a backup to Lieutenant Welland. If there is something down there to find, I should be there."

A heavy sigh whooshed in my ear. "Be careful."

Franchot fetched his gear. We donned flippers and masks. Welland went ahead. I backed into the water like a pro. Franchot followed. As soon as I was on level with the deck below, I saw it.

It was peculiar because I was aware I was floating, but what I saw was a dry and well-lit compartment. Margolo's guiding hand faded as I saw him appear next to me, feet firmly on the deck, sleeves rolled up.

Margolo is looking over Boreman's shoulder as he unscrews an access plate. One screw loose. Two.

Margolo looks up. Golanger is leaning over the rail from the upper deck. With a hand to his shoulder, Margolo halts Boreman's work. A moment passes and Commander Shore appears. He slides down the rails of the ladder, Golanger following him.

Margolo starts to talk then notices that Shore is wearing a sidearm.

I follow bits of the conversation by lip-reading, a skill I should augment if I continue to see ghosts.

Minton killed Naire. Shore wants Boreman and Golanger to go with him to arrest Minton. Margolo sends the men ahead and tries to tell Shore about what was he has discovered. Shore nods and Margolo turns away to continue unscrewing the plate. Shore draws his gun and shoots Margolo in the back.

"Holy shit!"

"What is it, Ms. Kirby?" asked Campbell.

"Nothing," I said, remembering Gravell's warning. "Nothing I can do anything about, in any case."

I signalled Franchot and Welland that I was ready to go up.

"Well?" Franchot asked, when we were sitting on dry deck.

"It's all gone with the explosion. Our only chance of confirming what I found out is if the Americans took photos when they first came on board. If they did, I'd like to see them."

He nodded. "You okay? You're looking rather pale, Jen, like you've seen a ghost."

I decided it was best not to respond to that comment. Instead, I asked him if he'd heard about the disconnected bomb found in the torpedo room.

"I think the radio trigger was hooked up to the station's power grid. That's how it was discovered."

"It wouldn't pull much power," said Welland.

"True, but if you had a bunch of engineering guys trapped in a place without much to do, they might follow-up small discrepancies, don't you think?"

"Possibly."

"Plausible," said Franchot.

"It was found and disconnected, so something must have drawn attention to it."

I remembered Naire's sheet of paper. "There would be data collected, wouldn't there?"

Franchot nodded. "If it was a power fluctuation, there should be a record of it in engineering." He stood and looked around. "Sinclair! Can you get the computers running on the power available?"

He met the man halfway and they conferred. I waited long enough to see Sinclair crack his knuckles and grin.

I turned to Welland. "Let's go, I think I need to see the living quarters again."

"Captain Campbell wants you out of here."

"Barb."

She shrugged.

"Fine. We'll check out the living quarters. I thought you guys went over everything there."

"True, but that was before we had evidence of violent deaths. I have a theory that in the end there was one man left alive and I'm curious who it was and what happened to him, aren't you?"

She nodded.

Over the head set I heard a sigh, then Campbell's voice. "Go ahead. We're all curious about that."

Chapter Thirty-Seven ~ *Back to the Beginning*

I walked through the living area trying to remember what it looked like before it was stripped of artifacts and flooded with water.

"Talk to us, Jenny. Tell us what you see."

"Easier said than done, Sean."

There was a pause. I heard a tiny gasp and looked to Welland, but she was holding her breath.

"Do your best, Ms. Kirby."

That's right, I thought. *I'm not Jenny unless you're Sean, mate.* Welland started breathing again. I covered my mike.

"Reciprocity and respect. In the same circumstances that you would call me Ms. Kirby, I wouldn't dream of calling you Barb."

"Doesn't work like that in the military."

"I'm not in the military."

I went to the centre of the room and did a three-sixty slow turn. Nothing and no one came to me.

"Everything was left as if the crew might walk in any minute. Beds were made, personal effects arranged neatly."

Now I could see Minton, smoothing covers trying to tidy up after the depredations of the last week. His ghostly form fussed. I closed my eyes and when I opened them Minton was still fussing in the intact room.

He makes Boreman's bed, arranging the little quilt on top when he is done. Naire's rack requires little work. He fluffs Golanger's pillow and strips Margolo's rack to start from scratch. When he is done, he sweeps the deck. Finally he goes to his locker and pulls out his journal. Sitting at the edge of his mattress, he starts writing. The words are little more than wavy lines and loops on the page.

"What are you doing?"

I snapped back into the here and now like a stretched elastic band. Mary Lou was yelling at me from the entrance to the galley

"I'm remembering. I need a little quiet, please."

She marched toward me, nostrils flaring.

"Hon, I don't know who or what the hell you think you are, but this is a scientific investigation not…"

Welland stepped between us.

"Back off, Ms. Naire."

Cross appeared at the hatch. Welland addressed him while still keeping an eye on Mary Lou.

"Please keep your team out of here until Ms. Kirby is finished."

Mary Lou looked as if she was about to belt Welland. Cross stepped forward and put a hand to her elbow. She shook it off irritably.

"Captain Campbell respectfully requests—"

"I don't care what the hell he requests. Damned military! Messed up my scene in the control room, wiped computer memory, just happened to fry circuits where there were records so the fire and fire retardant would ruin evidence. Then he has the nerve to tell me where to go next."

Mike and his team arrived from the forward section. He crossed the room and laid a hand on his wife's arm. She almost rounded on him before she recognized him. He leaned into her and spoke softly.

"The hell she did," Mary Lou replied.

He nodded.

She turned to me.

"You found a bomb? Using that damned journal?"

"Among other things," I said.

I stepped around Welland and met Mary Lou's gaze. "I've taken in a lot of information the past few weeks. Every report you've made, Dora's notes, the logs, journals, and letters of the crew, I've been over it all at least once. I'm probably the only person who has. Now I'm remembering it not in bits and pieces, but as a whole picture. But I need to concentrate so, please, be quiet."

It was a good lie. It was made up of one hundred percent true parts.

Mary Lou backed off, but she didn't leave the room. None of them did. I hoped I could recapture the scene knowing I had an audience.

I closed my eyes. *Come on, Minton*, I thought, *let's finish this.*

At first I thought nothing had happened. I opened my eyes, and I was still in the wrecked living area. Then I saw Minton's ghost. He gave me a troubled smile and turned around. Stepping backward, he superimposed himself on me. Again. The salty, metallic smell of the air overwhelmed me again. I was dizzy and nauseous again. I closed my eyes and almost retched. All I could smell was blood and cleanser.

We go to his locker and pull out his journal. Sitting at the edge of his mattress, we start writing. Tears blind us, but I can feel the shape of the words as we write.

"Everyone gone now and I am to blame. I didn't see. I refused to see. I wanted it to be anyone else. Boreman and Golanger dead at my hands. Dawes and Kant hit in the crossfire. I might have saved Kant. I might have saved them all."

We write "saved them all" over and over again, then find a fresh page.

"They died because of me. He knew how I would be. He told me I would be fine, but I was always meant to be the killer. I might as well have been the killer."

We write "killed them all" over and over again, filling pages.

Finally, we shut the book and put it back in his locker. We smooth the covers where we had been sitting, take a last look around, and leave.

We walk to the torpedo room. A wet suit is waiting.

Minton pushes me out of him. I watch him strip down and suit up. All his clothes go in a torpedo tube and are ejected like the dead bodies of the crew. Perhaps if he could have managed it, he would have done the same to himself. Instead, he has to find another exit. I start to follow him.

Hands tugged at me. Different voices were calling my name. I blinked a couple of times and looked from side to side. Welland had one of my arms, Mercuros the other. I was in the torpedo room. Mike, Mary Lou, Dippel, and Tim stood nearby with identical expressions of troubled concentration.

"What?" I asked, irritated at being interrupted.

Mercuros leaned in towards me.

"You were sleepwalking. Then you started to undress and we couldn't wake you."

The front of my wetsuit was unzipped to the waist, and I was showing some bare shoulder.

"Oh," I mumbled. "I was a little warm."

Now that was a rotten lie. The place was like a fridge. I gave Mercuros a weak grin and covered up.

"Did you find evidence of blood in the tubes?" I asked Mike, trying to sound like nothing weird had just happened.

"Not inside, but at the outside rim. Did William Minton kill them all?"

"No. Not all. He was the one who cleaned up."

My phone warbled. Awkwardly, hands shaking a little from the aftereffects of what I saw, I pulled it out and answered it.

"Hello?"

"Hi, Mum."

"Hi, Shay." I turned to the others and said, "It's my son." Then to Seamus I said, "What's up sweetie?"

"I'm back from camp. Dad says hi. Oh, and a Chief Petty Officer Gravell wants me to tell you that now is not the time. What does that mean?"

"I'll let you know when I find out. Talk to you later, okay?"

"Sure, Mum. I love you."

"I love you too."

I hung up, put the phone back in its pouch on my belt, and took a deep breath. Eight pairs of eyes stared at me in frank amazement. Tim recovered first.

"You were saying, Jen?"

"Minton cleaned up."

"That's it?"

I ignored Tim's question and turned to Welland.

"Do you think we could go back to the ship now, Barb. I'm feeling a bit nauseous. I should go while I still can make it on my own."

"Of course, Jen. We can pick up Draco on the way through engineering."

Mercuros closed in again. "Or I can accompany you. Mike and Mary Lou's teams are going to search the galley together. I'm not really needed there."

Tim added his mite. "If you're not needed, neither am I, right? I'll come with you, okay? When you're feeling a bit better, I can interview you."

If I could have, I would have said no. Tim was obviously curious about what I had been doing. I suppose everyone was, but he had a documentary to make. We had a documentary to make.

"Draco?" I asked, addressing Welland and walking ahead with her. "I thought Cross's first name was George."

She grinned.

"George Cross. Saint George's Cross. Saint George and the Dragon. Dragon—Draco. See? Anyway, he's never liked the name George. He says you can't pick up chicks with a name like George."

Behind us Tim snorted. "He should try Tim."

Chapter Thirty-Eight ~ *Out of the Dark*

Guy Franchot saw us coming and stopped what he was doing. I could tell by the look on his face that he knew about my 'sleepwalking.' He didn't ask how I was directly. Instead he looked to Mercuros, who gave a small shrug.

"I'm fine. This place is just getting to me a little."

"I understand, Jen," Franchot said. His tone was kind and only a little condescending. "You have to understand we are worried about you. Will you be all right diving?"

"Actually, I'm looking forward to it. I know the air is fine, but the smell reminds me of when I was trapped. I'm looking forward to breathing the air I've been lugging around in this tank all afternoon."

He grinned. "You could have taken it off."

"Not on your life!"

He chuckled, but held up our progress long enough to send Dippel with us. He said it was for my benefit, but I had the feeling the Marine was getting underfoot. Unlike Sinclair, who was digging into the consoles like a terrier after a rat, Dippel was just standing there, watching. He must have been bored because he took Franchot's suggestion to leave with us without argument.

Once in the sunken section of engineering, I thought of one more thing I wanted to settle. I stopped at the site of Margolo's death.

"Wait a sec," I said over the radio.

Silently I addressed Mitchell Shore, "Why?"

The section is dry. Shore is giving orders about Minton. Margolo
sends Boreman and Golanger ahead and tries to tell Shore about what
he has discovered. Shore nods and Margolo turns away to continue
unscrewing the plate. Shore draws his gun and shoots Margolo.

He doesn't hesitate, but his mouth is pulled down and his brows are
puckered in a pained expression. He bends, presses the barrel of his
pistol into his friend's skull and shoots again. Then he stands, turns and
looks directly at me.

'Necessary evil,' he mouths clearly, knowing I have to read lips.
Then he points his gun at me and fires.

I didn't die, but I started to choke. Mercuros and Welland grabbed
me and hauled me to the surface. Franchot helped pull me out of the
water where he and Welland got my mask off. Once I could get a good
breath in via my nose, I was able to cough and clear my airway. Nothing
came out, so the best we could guess was I choked on my own saliva.

Tim and Mercuros checked my gear. They couldn't find anything in
the scuba equipment to account for me choking, but they determined that
my radio had become disconnected when I put my mask on. No one
heard me when I asked them to wait. From their point of view, I just
froze.

I was frozen now. I didn't want to stay, but I was too scared to go.

"I'll have the rescue sled brought down," said Franchot.

He patted me on the shoulder.

"We just have to get you out of the station. It will take you the rest
of the way."

"Captain Campbell concurs. He wants Ms. Kirby to be taken to the
Nottawasaga so she can be checked out by Dr. Stern."

Mercuros took my hands in his and spoke gently, as if to a child.
"Can you do this?"

I returned the clasp of his fingers. "Alex," I croaked. I cleared my
throat and tried again. "Alex, if you can help me get out of this damned
station, I can swim to Churchill Falls if necessary."

He grinned, and I knew he wanted to say "good girl" but he was
smart enough to bite his tongue. Tim wasn't so smart, and I shot him a
venomous glare.

We tried again, Tim leading the way, Mercuros sticking close to me,
and Welland and Dippel bringing up the rear. Once the station was
behind us, I felt like I could swim back to the *Émil Gagnan*, but
Mercuros insisted that we go to the *Nottawasaga*'s boat instead. Sophie
Briseau was waiting for me with a warm blanket and a blood-pressure
cuff.

It was wonderful to breath fresh, un-canned air, and I didn't realize how cold I was until the blanket went around my shoulders, but I still wasn't crazy about going to the *Nottawasaga.*

"There's nothing wrong with me that Doc can fix. It's just situational anxiety and I'm out of the situation now."

Sophie shook her head. "Sorry, Captain's orders. He guessed you'd balk. He told me to tell you that dinner's in the captain's wardroom tonight. I imagine it's going to be quite a party."

"Not dress uniform again," said Alex.

"You'll have to ask the captain, sir."

I huffed before asking, "Forget about what you're going to wear to dinner. What are we going to wear when we get out of our wetsuits? Our clothes are on the *Émil Gagnan.*"

Tim and Alex exchanged shrugs. Dippel looked stoic.

"Welland and I will work something out," Sophie said, grinning.

Barb concurred. "I'm sure I have something Jen can wear and we won't let you gentlemen run around half naked for long. Of course, you can go to the *Scranton,* Corporal Dippel. The boat can drop you off on its way back to the dive site. And you gentlemen could return to the *Èmil Gagnan.*"

"Not on your life," said Tim.

Alex's only answer was a shrug.

We reached the *Nottawasaga.* A cargo hatch was open, just above the waterline. Welland threw a line to the seaman handiest and practically threw herself after it. We passed our tanks to her. Alex helped me to board, offered Briseau a hand up, and her replacement a hand down. Then he lithely jumped onto the deck and threw the line to the coxswain.

"I'll see you later, gentlemen."

"That was neatly done," I said as we watched the hatch close.

"I got the impression that Tim wasn't your favourite person right now."

"He just gets on my nerves sometimes."

We continued to an equipment room where we removed shoulder cameras, radios, and stripped down to our thermal underwear. I buckled my utility belt back on since I didn't have any pockets for my phone and Minton's journal. Then everything had to be safely stowed. It was almost as lengthy a process as gearing up. It gave me a chance to think.

"I got along with Tim fine at the start. He was a bit pretentious. I chalked it up to his artistic temperament. He didn't start annoying me until just after the Americans showed up. It seemed he was more on their side than ours. I also have a feeling he hung up on me when I was trapped in the galley."

Barb stopped and stared at me.

"It was probably an accident. I kinda freaked him out."

"Like you've been freaking everyone else out today?" she said, giving me a wry grimace.

"Maybe."

"Wimp."

"I better get you to Doc Stern now," said Sophie.

I looked at my gear and then at my current bodyguard.

Barb nodded.

"Go ahead. I'll finish up."

"Thanks, Barb—for everything."

I turned to Alex.

"Your watch now?"

He offered me his arm.

"Yes, until Gravell shows up."

I reached for my phone. "I should…"

"Already taken care of," he said, tapping the side of his head where his radio used to be.

"He'll be here as soon as he can, in the meantime, I have the pleasure of your company. I have it all planned out. While you're being checked out by the doctor, I'll shower and change. Then, when you're showering and changing, I'll get someone to procure a flask of hot cocoa and three cups."

He threaded my hand through the crook of his proffered arm.

"With any luck, Gravell will join us by the time it arrives."

"Sounds like a good plan."

With any luck, he'd find some rum too.

Chapter Thirty-Nine ~ *Respite*

Try as he might, Doc couldn't find anything wrong with me. When Alex returned, clean and dressed in *Nottawasaga* sweats, I was released into his custody, although no one quite put it that way. I was taken to what I was now thinking of as my cabin, and I finally got a moment to alone by locking myself in the head.

I stripped down and threw my thermal-wear and undergarments into a laundry bag and out of the door. They were pretty whiff and my nose was a bit sensitive ever since Minton took me over. Then I winced. All I had with me now were a few undersized towels and my utility belt. Not well thought out, I told myself.

I pulled out my phone and called Gravell.

"Bonjour, Madame Kirby."

"Bonjour, Chief Gravell."

"Can I help you?"

"I think I have some clothes in the laundry here. How would I get them?"

"If they're clean, they are probably already in your cabin. Check the drawers. Is that why you called?"

"No."

I hesitated. Why did I call? Was it just to hear his voice? If it was, I could hardly admit it.

"Is this a bad time to ask a personal question?"

"It is, Madame Kirby."

"Okay. Well, if anyone asks, this was all about laundry."

I hung up feeling like an idiot. I started the hot water running and discovered that, last time I was here, I had left my vanilla cleansing gel in the shower. At least I'd be a nice smelling idiot. When I was done, I had to admit to Alex that I had no clothes and asked him to find me some. Fortunately, clean laundry was in the drawers. He passed them through to me hardly trying to peek at all.

A little later we sipped hot cocoa and, to my delight, it was spiked with rum. The amount was a fraction of what Franchot had served me, way back when.

"You, Franchot, and Gravell are good friends, right?"

He nodded.

"How long have you known each other?"

"Luc and I have known each other since we were teens. We were in the Sea Cadets together."

"You're from Montreal too?"

"West Island, Beaconsfield to be exact. Luc's from Pointe Claire. That practically makes us neighbours."

"Did you go to the same high school?"

He laughed. "No way! Our schools were rivals. But after we tried beating the shit out of each other a couple of times, we got to be fast friends. Sometimes our lives have gone in different directions, but we remained pretty close."

"Both in the Navy."

He nodded.

"Both in INSET?"

He gave me a broad grin. "Cute."

I shrugged. "Guilty of investigative journalism in the first degree."

"That's all?"

I smiled and lifted my brows. "Now you're fishing. How about Franchot?"

"We're partners in the *Èmil Gagnan*."

"That's all?"

He laughed. "That's all I'll admit to."

I sipped my cocoa to buy myself enough time to talk myself out of the next gambit. I didn't succeed.

"Gravell told me you'd be a safe person to have a romantic fling with," I said, carefully casual.

He had just taken a sip of cocoa and now choked on it.

"You okay?" I asked, poised to get up and give him the Heimlich if necessary.

He held a hand up and nodded. A second sip cleared his throat. "He said you should have a fling with me?"

I nodded. "You or Guy Franchot. I said it wasn't likely to happen. I couldn't see you going for it."

He shook his head, eyes wide with wonder.

"I can't see you going for it, Jen. Campbell maybe, but you don't look at him, let alone me or Guy, the way you look at Luc."

"How's that?" I asked, blushing.

There was a knock on the door. There was only one person I was expecting, and I must have reacted accordingly.

"Like that," Alex said, smiling.

I was disappointed. Instead of Gravell, it was Marian Sloan with tea and a message from Captain Campbell. He respectfully requested the company of Mr. Mercuros in his office.

"I can stay with Ms. Kirby."

Alex hesitated. I reassured him.

"If the captain is back, Gravell will be too. I'll be fine."

He nodded and started to leave. Then he stopped and bent to give me a light kiss on the cheek. "If Luc wasn't such a good friend."

Sloan sighed and leaned against the hatch when it closed behind him. "If it was me, I'd pick him. He's hot."

"Maybe, but like every man I've met this trip, he's determined I'm meant for someone else."

Chapter Forty ~ *Out of the Frying Pan*

Marian and I had tea and played a couple of hands of gin. At this point, I was almost falling over from fatigue. We still had an hour before dinner, so she suggested I lie down for a nap and she'd round up something interesting for me to wear. As long as I locked up behind her, there was no reason I couldn't have a few minutes to myself, right?

As I suspected, I wasn't totally alone in any case. Margolo made an appearance as soon as Marian left to let me know he was still watching out for me.

It had been a hell of a day, with more information than I could begin to digest. Understanding might come with rest. Mostly, I just wanted sleep and understanding could wait a few hours.

I slipped out of my shoes and shorts and between the covers of my bed. Sleep came quickly and with it, a dream.

It is a typical suburban backyard. The back deck takes up half the yard. The other half has a well-manicured lawn, except under the kid's swing set, where it is patchy and brown. A girl is swinging, reaching out with her toes on the upswing, trying to hit a low branch. An older girl is holding a toddler and swinging sedately. Nearby, a couple of boys are digging up the narrow flower bed along the fence line.

On the deck, the men sit around smoking and drinking beer. Two sit apart slightly. Naire's attention is on the boys in the garden, the younger one being his nephew. Minton watches the other men, smiling slightly, satisfied to be with them even if he does feel apart.

Shore excuses himself from the group and goes into the kitchen. He kisses his wife at the nape of the neck as she washes dishes. Boreman's wife and Margolo's date dry as Lorraine Dawes puts things away. Naire's wife sits out the chores sipping tea. She isn't showing much, but she is obviously pregnant.

Shore continues through the house to a small den done up in a decorator's idea of a nautical theme. All the knickknacks and photos are sports related except for a photo of Shore, Dawes, Minton, and Margolo in uniform. He picks the photo off the desk and stares at it, blindly reaching for his swivel chair arm and pulling it around so he can sit.

The phone must have rung, because he answers it. As he listens, he stares at the photo. At one point, he slams it, face down on the desk. When he hangs up he is calm again. He picks up the photo and puts it back where it belongs.

"Necessary evil."

I woke to the sound of knocking.

Feeling more tired than when I lay down, I dragged my shorts on and padded across the cool deck on bare feet. I hoped it was Gravell with tea. I expected it was Sloan with another fashion-challenged outfit. I was disappointed and irked to find Tim Neville.

"Did I disturb you?" he asked, pushing his way into the room regardless.

"I was having a nap," I grumbled.

I sighed and tried to shift into professional mode.

"I have to get up anyway. Sloan will be back soon to help me get ready for dinner."

"Yes, I'll have to be quick."

I woke up a bit at this remark. His tone was urgent and direct. Curiosity at what he wanted now pulled ahead of the immediate irritation Tim tended to trigger.

There was another knock. He turned to answer it.

"That'll be Dippel, I bet. He's been following me around most of the afternoon. Might as well let him in."

I shrugged. Irritation was now neck and neck with concern. Curiosity was still ahead by a nose.

Tim let the Marine in. While his back was turned, I mouthed to Margolo, 'Get Gravell.' Curiosity might be ahead, but it was following caution.

Margolo nodded and disappeared.

Meanwhile, Dippel was straddling the coaming at the entrance.

"In or out, Dippel. You'll give Jen a chill if you keep standing there."

"Perhaps we should both leave, sir, let Ms. Kirby get properly dressed."

"In or out."

Dippel chose in. Tim closed and dogged the hatch. Dippel turn to unlock it and Tim pulled the marine's sidearm and used it to cosh him on the back of the head. The man staggered and fell to his knees. He struck again and Dippel fell.

I wanted to go to Dippel or call for help, or even do something stupidly heroic like attack. I froze.

Tim turned and pointed the gun at me.

"Now we can chat, Jen."

I thought madly. Where the hell had I put the radio phone? I staggered backwards, keeping my eyes on Tim, and sat heavily on the edge of the bed.

"What do you want?"

"The journal for a start. Then I want to know what you know and how you know it."

Okay. This wasn't entirely unexpected. He got pretty intense when he first heard about the journal. I tried to act like he wasn't holding a gun, hoping to put him off guard.

"The journal is in the top drawer of the dresser. Be careful with it. I'm already in trouble with Mary Lou for holding on to it."

In the moment his back was turned, I found the phone under my pillow, where I had left it when I lay down. From now on, I wasn't going to go to a door without a phone in hand. I swear.

"Don't get any funny ideas about calling for help with that phone of yours."

He turned and levelled the pistol at my chest.

I held up my hands to show they were empty. I managed to push a couple of buttons and hoped they were enough.

"Let's sit at the table where I can keep an eye on your hands."

I stumbled to the free chair. Fear made me clumsy.

"Hands on the table."

I complied, sitting in silence while he thumbed through the journal. Minton appeared, and I finally noticed the family resemblance.

"You are related to William Minton."

Tim looked up, startled.

"How did you know?"

"A hunch. Was he your uncle?"

"Father."

"But you would be too young."

Then I had the answer to what had been puzzling me. Where did Minton go after he tidied up? "Minton escaped and took a new identity.

But how?"

"It doesn't matter."

He wasn't the one I was asking. Behind him, Minton nodded. He gave me the diving hand signal for surface.

"Tied to the journal after death, even though it was miles and years away."

Minton nodded.

"What the hell are you talking about?"

Tim's voice betrayed his frustration. He was obviously not finding what he was looking for in the journal.

"Tell me what you know about your father, Tim."

He looked up from the scribbled pages he was trying to decipher.

"Why?"

Why? Because I wanted to buy time, that's why. Also because I wanted to know what happened.

"Because you want to." I might not have the voice of command, but I had the firmness of a mother used to getting confessions out of misbehaving boys. Besides, drawing on my mother tone helped me sound braver than I felt.

It worked. Tim closed the journal and sat back. He still held the gun, but his eyes were no longer focussed on me.

"My father was a hero. He saved the station from falling into enemy hands. He escaped death, against the odds, and got a new life, a new name, a new family." He gave a harsh laugh. "Except he couldn't let go of the old life. He was haunted by it."

I kept my eyes on Tim, but what I said next was more for his father's benefit. "I think he was a basically good person, but he suffered from hypersensitivity which sometimes triggered paranoid delusions."

"In other words, he was crazy?" Tim snorted. "You know he just about made me crazy? I tried to love him. I tried to cover up his episodes."

He flung the journal to the floor.

"What does he do? He commits suicide, by taking slow poison, so he has time to tell his teenage son his whole sordid past, then begs him, with his dying breath, to make it right. What kind of father is that?"

"A mentally ill father." *And the acorn didn't fall far from the tree,* I thought.

"He was mental, all right, but not at the end. At the end he was quite sane, I think. He wanted me to make everything right, so no one else would know. No one else can know what he did."

Behind him, the ghost of his father shook his head emphatically.

"That's not what he meant. He wanted to make amends. He wanted the families of the men that were killed to know what happened. He covered up the truth, but he can't rest until people know what really happened."

Tim shook the pistol at me. Someone, not me, might have been able to take advantage of that. "How do you know what he wanted?"

I took a deep breath. Odds were he'd think I was loony, but the truth was worth a try. "I know because he let me know. I can see him now and he wants you to end this. He wants to find peace."

Minton nodded. His son shook his head. "You think I'll believe that shit? Hah! Let me guess, you talk to spirits like a ghost whisperer."

"I wish. If I could talk to ghosts, maybe your father would tell me something that would make you believe me. I see spirits, Tim. I see your father now and he wants you to help him make peace with his ghosts."

As I spoke, Margolo appeared. He gave me an encouraging nod. He must have warned Gravell. Behind him, the shades of Boreman, Golanger, and Dawes appeared. The temperature in the room dropped considerably as a result, but Tim didn't seem to notice.

"You're crazy or you think I am. Either way, you can make peace with my father." He stood. "You can join him as a ghost."

He leaned in and swung at me with the butt of Dippel's pistol, and I suddenly realized that he didn't want to shoot me. I should have taken advantage of that when I could, instead I blocked his blow tried to get away. His second swing connected with my jaw and threw me back onto the bed. Margolo and crew closed in on him, but Tim was oblivious.

He pressed me down, pinning my arms under me. Snatching my pillow, he stuffed it over my face, sending my phone bouncing across the deck. With surreal acuity, I heard the phone skitter and slide to a stop while, in the distance, someone was hammering on the hatch.

Tim hesitated a second, and I managed to get a hand free. Shoving hard, I got a little air and tried to scream, but was cut off. He threw himself across my body, compressing my chest with his knee and catching my arm.

I dug my nails into his hand and managed to steal another mouthful of air when he shifted his weight. Then the pillow was pressed hard against my face.

I tried to kick, but couldn't connect. I tried to rock him off me, and felt ghostly hands trying to help, but I didn't have the strength and neither did they. While I struggled desperately, a calm part of me was thinking, *this sucks*.

Then I could hear Minton in my head I was sure it was his voice.

"Keep fighting."

"Hang in there, beautiful." That was Margolo. "I'd rather haunt you than be haunted by you,"

Fine words, but hang in for what? Gravell was on the wrong side of a locked door, and I was already close enough to becoming a ghost that I could hear them.

"Don't give up now, sugah."

"We need you, ma'am."

"Live long and prosper."

Suddenly, the weight lifted, and I sucked air, able to breathe, but finding it difficult to fill my lungs. I wanted to get off my back and rolled onto the floor, only to be struck by a falling body, knocking the wind out of me again.

"Pardon, Madame Kirby," Gravell said, pulling the unconscious Tim Neville off me. "I got your message, but had a little trouble with the door."

Behind him, Naire gave a little wave.

"Good timing," I gasped, getting my breath back.

"Nick of time, I think."

He cuffed Tim's hands behind his back, then reached down and pulled me to my feet. I clung to his shirt front for balance. He put a steadying arm around my waist. I would have collapsed against him and sobbed, but he had brought a security detail with him and he was busy giving orders.

Tim was taken away.

Briseau showed up with a stretcher and more help.

Dippel was taken away. He was alive, but still unconscious.

Briseau checked me out: O2 saturation, blood pressure, temperature. Nothing was perfect, but nothing was terrible either. On Gravell's orders, she took scrapings from under my finger nails and photographed my face and torso. Since the doctor was going to be busy with Dippel for a while, she agreed I could report to the captain before reporting to sick bay. Before leaving, she gave me a cold-pack and a warm blanket.

Throughout, I maintained outward calm except for the death grip I had on Gravell's shirt. I managed to keep hold of it even when Briseau had eased me around so she could lift my t-shirt and see the pattern of contusions across my ribs. As soon as she left I returned to the supportive embrace of Gravell's arm and leaned my head on his chest, more out of exhaustion than anything else.

"Sloan will be here next," I said, voice barely audible.

Gravell put a thumb and forefinger almost, but not quite together. "Sloan is that close to being charged with dereliction of duty. She will stay out of my way if she knows what is good for her."

I shook my head. Bad move. It hurt like hell. "I shouldn't have let her go."

"No you shouldn't have."

I looked up at him, wondering if he was going to pick now, of all times, to chastise me. I didn't think I could handle it. His lips were pressed into a thin line, eyes pinched as if in pain. That's when I noticed how tightly he was holding me.

Our eyes met and he made an effort to relax his facial features into their usual stoic expression. He gently pried my fingers from his shirt and eased me into a chair, making sure the blanket stayed around my shoulders. Then he activated the cold pack and handed it to me. It did feel good on my chin, just not as good as Gravell's arm around me.

He saw my phone on the floor and retrieved it.

"You set it to record," he said, turning it off.

"I tried to, yes. If it worked, there might be some stuff on there about ghosts."

"I'll take care of it," he said, pocketing the device. "I shouldn't have trusted Sloan with your safety. She wasn't aware of the stakes. I was."

"Why did you trust her?"

"Captain's orders."

"Then you didn't have a choice," I said, giving a little shrug. A big shrug would have hurt too much. Every muscle in my body ached. I was on the edge of tears, but still managed to keep my voice relatively calm. "You can't refuse an order from the captain of the ship, can you?"

"I can if I think it's wrong."

"Did you know it was Tim trying to kill me?"

"I suspected he might be trying to scare you. I had no proof, and I knew he was being watched."

Gravell met my gaze. It was difficult. I could tell that he felt he had somehow failed me. "I never expected such a direct attempt on your life, and I still don't understand what prompted it."

I gave him a grim smile. "I do. I think we should visit Captain Campbell now. I don't think I have the energy to tell this story twice."

Captains Campbell, Tinsdale, and Franchot presented a picture worthy of a Norman Rockwell illustration: "Privileges of Command." Tinsdale was in the chair I sat in during my visits, back straight, but shoulders hunched as if he carried the weight of the world there. Franchot was slouched in the second chair, legs outstretched, ankles crossed, eyes half-closed. The captain was pouring whisky over three glasses of ice. He looked over his shoulder as we entered.

"Ah, Ms. Kirby, can I offer you a drink?"

Then he turned and got a better look. His face drained of colour.

"What the hell happened?"

Franchot went from slouch to stand so fast he knocked over his chair. Tinsdale threw his shoulders back and scowled. Having checked myself in the mirror while I dressed, I could understand their shock. My face was blotchy, eyes red. My lips and eyelids had been a scary shade of blue. For all I knew, they might still be. A puffy purple bruise was developing on my jaw. I was wearing a long-sleeved sweater over my cargo pants, otherwise they would have seen the contusions on my arms.

The captain put down the bottle of Canadian Club he was holding and in a couple of steps was tilting my chin to look at the damage.

Then he turned to Gravell. "Report."

Voice cold and controlled Gravell testified to what he had witnessed more or less. Margolo's ghost was left out and there was no mention of the fact that the door was locked when Gravell arrived and it mysteriously unlocked.

Evidently, only seconds passed from the time Tim Neville compressed my chest with his knee and Gravell entered. It just seemed longer. Gravell also neglected to mention that my phone was set to record. Any mention of ghosts would be edited from the memory before that piece of evidence was turned over.

"While being subdued, Neville's nose was broken and jaw dislocated. There were also deep scratches on his hand, defensive wounds inflicted by Madame Kirby. Neville is in the brig where he is receiving medical attention. Gunnery Sergeant Dippel is in sick bay. We checked on him on the way here. He has regained limited consciousness, but the extent of his injury is yet to be determined."

Tinsdale nodded at me and sighed. "I'm sorry, Mrs. Kirby. I didn't see that coming."

Despite the pain and a muzzy feeling that my brain wasn't working properly yet, I managed to make a small intuitive leap. "But you suspected Tim. You had Sergeant Dippel following him."

"Yes, Mrs. Kirby. Neville was placed on your team to report on, and possibly hinder, your progress. I suspected he had other orders, but it took a while for me to confirm that he was working from his own agenda."

One of my hands had gone back to holding the cold pack on my jaw. The other held the first arm up by the elbow. I tried to convey the idea that I would wait forever for a complete explanation. In fact, I was ready to keel over any time now.

"I think Jen deserves to hear what you just finished telling us," said Franchot to Tinsdale. "I also think we should invite her to sit. Chief, if you could pick up that chair, you can help her to my seat."

Gravell picked up the fallen chair and held it for me. As I sat back, I felt his knuckles graze my shoulder blades, and I pressed against them for reassurance. His thumb gave me the tiniest stroke before he straightened no doubt to stand at parade rest.

"I'd like to check on the gunny, with your permission, Captain. I'll leave you fill in the details."

The captain nodded, first to Tinsdale, then to Gravell.

"I anticipated your request, sir," said Gravell, not moving from his self-appointed post behind me. "I have a man standing by to escort you to sick bay."

Franchot took the seat Tinsdale left. He gave me the shadow of a smile and shot a concerned look over my shoulder at Gravell.

Campbell passed Franchot his drink and offered one to me. I shook my head. I was already feeling weak and achy. Alcohol would not help.

Finally the captain sat and addressed himself to me. "Tim Neville is with US Naval intelligence. As Captain Tinsdale mentioned, he was placed with your documentary crew to keep them informed."

I caught Franchot's eye.

He gave me a sheepish grimace. "It was a surprise to me too, Jen. Tinsdale only told me about Neville because it was the only way to keep him with the team. Reuben and Dora were all for laying him off with the rest of the documentary crew. I couldn't tell anyone though. Sorry."

Campbell swished the ice around in his glass, a summons for our attention.

"In addition to Neville, Captain Tinsdale had two investigators from the Judge Advocate General's office reporting to him. One of them was injured in the control room when the explosions went off."

"That charge was new," I said.

Campbell looked surprised.

Francot nodded. "That's what made Tinsdale suspicious. The only people who could have laid the charge were the divers who did the precheck. He couldn't see one of my divers doing it. That left Neville."

"As you no doubt remember, Ms. Kirby, he was talking to you when you were cut off," Campbell said. "He was on board when the barrier was tampered with, and on the *Émil Gagnan* when your diving gear was sabotaged, then again, on the station. By that time, he was being watched by Dippel."

"But he gave Dippel the slip by attaching himself to me."

Campbell gave me an apologetic grimace. "We didn't know he was trying to kill you, only that he wanted to scuttle the station. The two most likely places to accomplish that were in engineering or the torpedo room."

"So, you were kept in the loop?" I asked Franchot.

"Alex and I knew that Neville was a suspect."

"And you, Chief Gravell?"

I stood, shaky on my feet, but determined to watch him when he answered. He was, as I had guessed, standing at parade rest, hands behind his back, eyes forward. Without otherwise breaking his pose, his eyes lowered to meet mine.

"I was the one who alerted the others to the possible danger to you. Neville was, as I told you, a suspect. I had no knowledge of the plan to use you as bait."

"But you did," I said, turning to Captain Campbell.

"The plan was worked out between Captain Tinsdale, Sergeant Dippel, and me." He set down his whisky, still untouched. "Neville was to be given the opportunity to create another accident. To do that, it was necessary to keep Chief Gravell out of the way, make you seem more vulnerable. No one expected him to attack you directly in your quarters. I have no idea why he would expose himself that way."

"I do."

I wobbled and steadied myself on the chair. A warm hand on my lower back steadied me. I resisted the urge to turn and thank Gravell and kept my gaze fixed on Captain Campbell.

"Must be almost dinner time. Think I'll wait until we're at the table."

Campbell shook his head. "You can't be serious, and I can't believe Doc would allow it. In any case, I can't allow it."

Though my voice was level, it was getting a bit slurred from the swelling on my jaw. I made the effort to speak clearly, though it hurt to do so. "With all due respect, Captain, if you want to know what I know, you'll have to allow it."

I was angry, and I felt betrayed, but years of dealing with temperamental clients made me back-peddle a little, for diplomacy's sake. "If the skipper and chief would give us a moment alone. I think I can make a case you will accept."

Campbell nodded.

Franchot nodded and gave my shoulder a pat on the way out.

Gravell hesitated, then he too complied, leaving me alone with a man with whom, a few days ago, I was thoroughly infatuated. I sat, only because standing was no longer a viable option.

"Well, Jenny?"

I gently pressed the ice pack to my jaw. I needed x-rays and pain-killers and rest, but this had to come first. I had to strike while the guilt was fresh.

"You need to let me do this, Sean. It isn't grandstanding. Everyone needs to know what this is about. It's why we're here and it's the only chance I have at being safe again."

He rubbed his eyes tiredly. "Just give me the gist of what you're going to say. That's all I ask."

"No." I heaved a sigh and pushed myself out of the chair. "I'm not angry. Well, not much. You made it clear from the start that I couldn't confide in you. I respect that. I also know that whatever constraints you have to work under, you want the truth too. So, will you give me your arm? Or shall I call Chief Gravell?"

Chapter Forty-One ~ *Into the Light*

My colouring must have improved, because the only stares I got were directed at the developing bruise on my jaw.

"What the bloody hell happened to you?" Dora demanded, swooping down on me. Then she answered her own question. "Blunt force trauma."

"Pistol butt," I said.

She nodded. "You should get it x-rayed. Some facial oedema with evidence of petechial haemorrhaging about the cheeks and nose."

"Pillow over the face."

"No cyanosis."

"Been there, got over that."

"Muscular fatigue?"

"Oh yeah. But not as bad as it was."

"I look forward to hearing all about it."

It was a tossup what shocked people more, my state or Dora's reaction to it.

I felt a hand on my back. It was Alex. He had a tall glass of juice for me and stayed close. Franchot joined us. His expression told me that he felt bad enough. I forgave him. I forestalled apologies and let him take up position with his first mate. My bodyguards.

Looking around, I counted heads. All the research team was present. Tracy, Reuben, and Lil were watching me with a mixture of curiosity and concern. Mary Lou and Jamal were regarding me with suspicion. Mike's expression was unreadable. It matched the look on Marine Corporal

Madison. Barb Welland and Draco Cross were also present. If I had a third shoulder, I think Barb would have been at it.

An awkward moment of silence stretched into a minute or so. Then Tinsdale appeared with Gravell behind him and the dance began.

Campbell greeted Tinsdale. Tinsdale gave me a slight bow.

Franchot gave up his spot to Gravell and offered Dora his arm. They exchanged words with the captains and we all went to the table. Captain Campbell sat me at the end of the table opposite him. Gravell sat next to me on one side. Alex invited Welland to sit with him, and he took the other side. Dora was on Campbell's right, with Franchot beside her. Lil was on Campbell's left with Tinsdale next and so on until the naval officers and the researchers were thoroughly mixed.

I caught the captain's eye and smiled. I wonder if remembered his comment about diplomacy being a dance. In any case, he smiled back.

Soup was served. Normal table chatter commenced. Pass the salt. Pass the rolls. I had agreed to let the captain give me my cue, and wondered if he was going to wait until the end of the meal.

The soup was taken away. The main course arrived and immediately I understood Captain Campbell's timing. As soon as it was offered, I waved away the plate of roast beef au jeu, string beans, and roast potatoes. My jaw wasn't up to that kind of chewing.

"Perhaps you'd like to start, Ms. Kirby," Campbell said, once everyone was served.

I nodded. Then I closed my eyes and thought about the crew of the station. When I opened them, they were there. Naire, Boreman, and Dawson stood behind their children. Shore took up a position behind Tinsdale. Kant and Golanger bracketed him. I could feel Margolo behind me. Last, but not least, Minton appeared next to me.

Gravell's knee pressed against mine. He knew they were there. From their faces, I thought Barb Welland and Mike Naire could sense something too. The rest waited expectantly. I began.

"An hour or so ago, Tim Neville tried to asphyxiate me. He didn't want me to tell anyone what I had pieced together using your work, my research, and William Minton's journal. Ironically, Tim filled in a few important gaps between assaulting Sergeant Dippel and almost killing me."

Tinsdale spoke up. "I left the gunny in surgery. Neville hit him with sufficient force to cause a subdural haematoma. Dr. Stern is guardedly confident that the damage is reversible."

I sighed and blinked back tears of relief.

Dora rapped on the table. "Get on with it, Jen. You can fall apart later."

This seemed to produce equal amounts of angry grunts and nervous laughter. The important thing was it worked. I was able to continue.

"The point is, although I have recently found out that he was under suspicion of sabotaging the station, Neville's actions don't make a lot of sense until you know, as I do now, that he is William Minton's son."

The reaction was dramatic, and I took the opportunity to ice my jaw while everyone settled down.

"Minton escaped the station. He started a new life, but eventually the old one caught up with him. He confided in his teenage son who, mistakenly I think, assumed that his father wanted him to keep the truth from being known."

Jamal punched the air. "I knew it! I knew there was a conspiracy."

At the other end of the table, Captains Campbell and Tinsdale heaved sighs. I could sense an argument coming and nipped it in the bud.

"It was either government conspiracy or treason. That remains to be discovered."

Now the Tinsdale and Campbell looked uncomfortable. They knew something.

Then I remembered Shore repeating "necessary evil" and something clicked.

"If was going take a shot in the dark, I'd say that Commander Shore was not treasonous. Not from his point of view."

Shore acknowledged the hit with a tip of his ghostly cap.

Tinsdale frowned.

Gravell hit my knee so hard it hurt.

I'd said too much. Fortunately, Dora came to my rescue.

"You're not becoming an armchair forensic psychologist are you?"

I laughed, partly from relief. "Not that. This is not an expert opinion, just an informed guess. This is what I do know..."

I couldn't tell them about the barbeque and Shore's phone call. I'd tell Gravell later. Instead I started with Minton's growing paranoia and Kant's fictionalized observations. Neither, by themselves, was a reliable account of events, but together they showed that something wasn't quite right.

"I don't know why he did it, but Mitchell Shore planted the bombs in the torpedo room, galley, and engineering. He tried to set the rest of the crew against Minton. He probably found ways of exacerbating Minton's paranoia. He had known and worked with him long enough to know what buttons to push."

Shore flashed me a bitter smile.

"I would like to think, that Commander Shore's intent was to set Minton up as the fall guy, but that he never intended to kill his friends. Naire ruined this plan when he noticed something wrong in weapons control, probably an unexplained power drain. He alerted Margolo who noticed a similar problem in engineering."

"Hold it, what evidence do you have for this?" Reuben asked.

"I'm not saying my story is admissible in court. I don't know if a court would accept Minton's journal or Kant's story, and some of it is based on hearsay from Tim. There is evidence to back up some of this and we're not done investigating yet."

I waited for further interruptions before continuing.

"Shore's plan went south when someone, Naire, I think, found and defused the bomb in the torpedo room."

"The blood sample is consistent with Naire," Mary Lou said.

"Shore discovered Naire in the act and stabbed him. The he went to engineering to send Boreman and Golanger to arrest Minton, who going to be the fall guy. They left and Margolo probably confronted Shore and was killed."

"How could you know if Minton wasn't there?" asked Mary Lou.

"That's where the bomb was," said Alex.

"And that's where Minton found Margolo's body. Meanwhile, Minton decided he could trust Kant and Dawson and was sharing his concerns with them in the galley. Given his state of mind, who knows whether they believed him."

I glanced over and saw Kant nod and Dawson shrug.

"That's where Boreman and Golanger tried to arrest him. Minton defended himself. He knew he killed Boreman and Golanger. He wasn't sure whether it was his or Boreman's bullet that accidentally killed Dawson and wounded Kant."

A pot of tea had appeared beside me. Gravell poured. It was too hot, but I took a sip anyway. Then I wrapped my hands around the cup to absorb its warmth. I was feeling chilled and shaky. I had to wrap this up as soon as possible.

"Someone shot Kant when he was down," said Tracy. "That is, someone was shot while lying on the deck."

I nodded. "Shore shot Kant. Minton wouldn't have. I'm sure of it."

I gazed beyond the living.

"Shore selected Minton to be his First Mate in order to set him up. I think he picked his friends, Dawes and Margolo, because he underestimated their abilities. The one thing he didn't underestimate was their loyalty. None of them believed he was the culprit until it was too late. Minton knew something was going on, almost from the start. The last person he wanted to suspect was Mitchell Shore. Shore was his best friend and probably his hero."

The ghostly Shore was not a happy camper. He broke free of Kant and Golanger, walked through Tinsdale and the table, his finger pointing, leading him to me. My hands shook, slopping scalding tea over them, and my chest felt tight. Yet, I forced myself to breath slowly and deeply.

Naire and Boreman floated into place between him and me. Dawes came up behind Shore. I could feel Margolo's hands cover mine, cooling the burn, lending me strength.

"Something wrong, Jen?" asked Franchot.

Gravell took a napkin and mopped up the spilled tea. Though I know he sensed Margolo's presence, he patted dry my hands with barely a shiver when he and the ghost intersected.

I took a cleansing breath and the weight across my chest lifted. Tim hadn't been affected by ghosts. Maybe I didn't need to be either.

With a reassuring smile to Franchot, I continued. "Shore killed Kant. Minton killed Shore. Minton cleaned up, including giving his shipmates a proper burial at sea. In his journal, he scribbled that he should have seen it, that he was to blame. I think he preferred to think he killed them all, rather than face the fact that his hero was the enemy."

Minton's ghost faced up to it now.

There was a tremor as Minton walked through the table to Shore. Liquids vibrated in their vessels, though I doubt many of the living noticed. Minton reached out for Shore in almost the same way that Shore had reached out for me. Both disappeared.

The ghosts retreated, to my great relief. They didn't feel suffocating anymore. I think that was Shore's doing. I could even get used to the cold. But it was hard maintaining my eye contact with the living when I had to look through semitransparent figures.

"Minton left the station. I doubt he intended to survive, but he did. There might be someone left who remembers him coming to shore. Tracking him down under the surname Neville should be easier."

"I'm more interested in corroborating your information about Mitchell Shore," said Tinsdale.

"Did you suspect him?" asked Campbell.

Tinsdale shook his head. "The best guess of Naval Intelligence at the time was that there was a Soviet agent aboard the station. Based on Soviet movement at the time, they could have been waiting for a signal from their operative to steal the disabled vessel. Of course, you didn't hear that from me."

That struck me as a bit pat, but I wasn't about to summon Shore's ghost to find out.

I turned to Dora. "Maybe you can get Tim Neville to repeat what his father told him on his death bed. I'm sure there's more to learn."

She nodded. "It won't all come out at once. He was more open with you because he thought he was going to kill you. It will be an interesting challenge."

Tinsdale grunted. "You are assuming I will allow you to interview a federal agent."

Campbell chimed in on cue. "Mr. Neville attacked a Canadian citizen and is currently in my custody, where he will stay for now. Besides, Dr. Leland is one of the foremost forensic psychologists in the world. Why not use her expertise?"

Dora, of course, had to add her two cents. I turned my attention to Mary Lou who was explaining to Tracy how I felt the shape of Minton's words by tracing my finger over his scribbles. They were discussing how to repeat the experiment.

"Tired, Madame Kirby?"

"Exhausted! Also hungry. Chief Gravell, do you happen to know what's for dessert?"

He signalled a server over, listened, smiled and sent him away.

"Crème Caramel, Madame Kirby. I asked him to bring you one now and one to sick bay after you see the doctor."

I smiled and nudged his knee with mine.

I spent the night in sick bay. Once pain killers were administered, it didn't matter that the bed wasn't very comfortable. It was better than sleeping in the bed I almost died on. To make sure I got to sleep, Gravell stayed with me and told me another story about his grandmother. I drifted off with my hand in his, his hypnotic voice sending me into dreams of soft brown eyes, strong arms, and really good chocolate.

After breakfast, Captain Campbell dropped by to invite me for a walk on deck. We started by looking out on the other vessels. We didn't bother with idle speculation about what would happen next. He probably knew and I, for the moment, didn't really care. We maintained a companionable silence while we walked around to the other side before stopping in my favourite place. Then the captain leaned sideways against a post and waited until I returned his gaze.

"I missed the boat, didn't I?"

I hesitated, not wanting to risk misunderstanding. He clarified.

"Somewhere between throwing your arms around me and now, you lost interest."

I blushed. He was right. The moment I found out that I had been set up as bait for Tim, I lost interest. But, it had been fading before that.

"You should have told me about Tim," I said, opting for honesty.

"Does Gravell tell you everything?"

I shot him an incredulous stare. "As if! He's a spook for heaven's sake."

That made him smile in spite of himself.

I continued in the same light vein. "He wouldn't tell me the time of day if he didn't think I had good cause to know. I'm sure he would have gone along with setting me up as bait, if you had included him in your plans. The difference is he would have let me know I was bait. I wouldn't have been blind to the risk. And I would've accepted that risk to get answers."

It was his turn to blush, but he also took the high road. "I'm sorry. You're right. You should have been told."

I smiled, then chuckled as a song came to mind.

"What?" he asked.

"Gershwin," I said. "Let's kiss and make up. No need to break up. For I need you and you need me."

He laughed and held out his hand. "Friends?"

"Friends."

Chapter Forty-Two ~ *The End?*

We raised Arctic Station Alpha. The research team was given almost free access to every part of the ship...right after NCIS was through with it. Dora and I started outlining the book while we waited. With Tim Neville arrested, I was allowed to rejoin the *Émil Gagnan*.

The ghosts came with me all except Mitchell Shore. I never saw him after he tried to scare me to death. I suppose he moved on. Whether or not light was involved, I can't say.

I didn't see Golanger and Boreman much, but Minton, Margolo, and Naire stayed close, and Kant and Dawes always showed up when I was writing. It was like having a committee looking over my shoulder while I worked. I had a feeling I wasn't going to get shut of them until the book was complete. By then, I'd probably miss them.

The *Scranton* left shortly after NCIS were done. Sinclair stayed as a consultant, a guest of the *Nottawasaga*. Sovereignty and jurisdiction issues were, at least for the moment, established amicably.

Barb and Draco were granted permission to join our divers and temporarily moved over to the *Émil Gagnan*. Chief Gravell also came along. After all, he was originally a member of Franchot's crew.

Mid-August, Gravell and I were summoned to appear before a military court for Tim Neville's pretrial hearing. It was a joint US-Canadian tribunal, held at CFB Esquimalt. The Canadian venue was chosen because the crime occurred in Canadian territory and the primary witness (me) had been advised by Canadian intelligence (Gravell) not to step onto American soil.

The hearing wasn't as interesting as they make it look on TV. There were no courtroom dramatics. Thank heavens, there were also no ghosts. I managed to leave them behind on the ship.

The case against Tim Neville was straight forward. He tried to kill me and was caught in the act. Gravell was a witness to the attack, but I think he would have come anyway. He coached me on what to expect so I wouldn't get flustered and start babbling about ghosts and visions. Despite Gravell's assurances, I went in feeling anxious, but mostly the process was tedious…and long…very long.

Although my involvement with AFFA was brought up, there were no trick questions. Neville's counsel was obviously leaning towards an insanity plea. Mostly she wanted me to confirm that instability ran in the family, which really was a question for Dora, not me.

Unless I was recalled, I was done. Gravell was done. In celebration, we were spending the afternoon on the patio of a local pub, eating nachos and drinking Coronas with wedges of lime.

"You know, my life used to be so mundane before this summer."

"I don't believe it," Gravell said, giving me a half-smile.

"Well, maybe not totally mundane. I have worked for some interesting people and the life of the self-employed always has its own level of risk, financial if nothing else. But this is the first time anyone tried to kill me. And I have never almost died so often in such a short period of time."

"You handled it very well." He raised his bottle of beer in a toast.

"I tried," I said, answering the toast by raising my bottle. "When I fell apart, it wasn't until after the action. When I was rescued from the galley, I literally threw myself at Captain Campbell."

"I don't think he minded."

"Then I threw myself at you."

He didn't say anything, but his half smile said he didn't mind either.

"And you had to pry my fingers off your shirt after Neville's attack," I reminded him.

I'll admit, I was fishing for an acknowledgement that he was as interested in me as I him. I caught a different kind of compliment instead.

"You have nothing to feel ashamed of. You were, and are, one of the bravest people I know."

I blushed. To cover my embarrassment, I chugged the rest of my beer. He signalled the server for another round.

"I tried to live up to your example of cool detachment," I said, as lightly as possible.

"Professional veneer, Madame Kirby, that's all. Inside, I was scared

I was too late to save you. I think you saw that."

I nodded.

Okay, I told myself, stop fishing. Be direct.

"Y'know, you're not on duty right now. You could call me Jen, and maybe give me permission to use your given name?"

"I'm always on duty. Besides, I don't want to call you Jen, and I won't call you Jenny."

I am sure my colour deepened because I felt like my face was on fire. Captain Campbell called me Jenny. Even though we were only friends, it started off as a term of endearment.

"You know my given name," I pointed out, forcing myself to look him in the eye.

"You know mine."

The beer arrived. Gravell paid for them, waving aside my offer to contribute. He then turned the conversation to my son. Seamus was begging me to come home early because his father and stepmother were driving him around the bend. Dora wanted me to stay to the end of September to keep an eye on things since she had to leave. She had classes to teach.

I was in the middle of a tug of war. No matter who won I'd end up in the mud.

"So, have you decided yet? I noticed you've brought everything with you."

"Only because I don't have that much." I sighed. "I need to shop. I am so tired of wearing the same things day in, day out."

A silent chuckle shook him.

"It's different for you. You either wear a uniform or what passes for a uniform on the *Èmil Gagnan*."

"I take it you haven't made a decision yet."

"No. You'll stay until the *Émil Gagnan* has to leave, right?"

"That's my primary job, yes."

His eyes widened, and I think he finally understood what I needed to know.

"Since keeping you safe is also my job, it would be easier for me if you stayed."

I grinned. "I wouldn't want to make your job too hard."

I loved my son, and I missed him too, but I had a feeling that when I went home, I wouldn't see Gravell again. The thought was sad and a bit scary. I addressed the scary part.

"What will happen when I do go home?"

"You will be under surveillance for your protection. I will check in with you from time to time and you will have a contact number in case something comes up."

He leaned over the table and our knees touched. "Even if I can't be there, you won't be alone."

I felt tears well up and blinked them back. "I'll tell Dora I'll see the expedition through to the end. Seamus won't be happy but…"

He interrupted. "He could join you. He can take Dr. Leland's place. There's no real danger now and I'm sure the educational opportunity would outweigh missing a couple of weeks of school. We just have to run it by the skipper."

Not giving a damn if I embarrassed myself, I jumped up and threw my arms around Gravell's neck and fell into his lap. He hugged back and his breath tickled my ear.

"Genevieve, I have spent more than a month resisting temptation so that I won't be reassigned. Let's not blow it now."

"Resisting temptation?"

"It hasn't been easy," he whispered.

Gravell stood, lifting me to my feet at the same time. He offered me his arm. "Let's walk, Madame Kirby."

It was as well I took his arm. It was the only thing that kept me from floating away with happiness. I was alive. I had a great job. Soon my son would be with me. Gravell admitted he was resisting temptation.

"How long before you can give in to temptation?"

I felt his silent laughter. "You are incorrigible, Madame Kirby."

"Absolutely. Lucky for you, Chief Gravell, I'm also patient."

~ * ~

Message from the Author

I've only actually seen one ghost, my grandmother, when I was six. You might argue that I was dreaming, but she let me know she'd died and her death was sudden, not anticipated.

I have sensed the spirits of the nearly, and not so nearly departed. My friend Allan was with me at his funeral, making sure it went off as planned. He knew he was dying and planned everything down to the canapes. I don't think he hung around after. He had places to go, other lives to live.

There is a sceptical part of me that questions my perceptions. The writer in me says, "Who cares! It makes a good story."

If you enjoyed this book, please consider writing a short review and posting it on your favorite review site. Reviews are very helpful to other readers and are greatly appreciated by authors, especially me. When you post a review, drop me an email and let me know and I may feature part of it on my blog/site.

Thank you.

~Alison
writer@alisonbruce.ca

About the Author

Alison Bruce writes History, Mystery, Romantic and Paranormal Suspense. Her books combine clever mysteries, well-researched backgrounds and a touch of romance. Her protagonists are marked by their strength of character, sense of humor and the ability to adapt (sooner or later) to new situations.

Three of her novels have been finalists for genre awards, including the Arthur Ellis Award for excellence in Canadian crime writing.

Email: writer@alisonbruce.ca
Website: http://www.alisonbruce.ca
Twitter: @alisonebruce
Facebook: https://www.facebook.com/alisonbruce.books
Pinterest: https://pinterest.com/alisonebruce

www.deadlypress.com